Dear Reader,

Anne Stuart. Chelsea Quinn Yarbro. Maggie Shayne. Masters of the genre, their very names invoke images of fog-shrouded streets. Together for the first time in this original collection of short fiction, these three bestselling authors have written haunting love stories that are as scary as they are sensual.

Lock all the doors, turn on all the lights and prepare to sit on the edge of your seat as you discover who the mysterious stranger is in Anne Stuart's *Dark Journey,* why a dream lover turns dangerous in Chelsea Quinn Yarbro's *Catching Dreams,* and how a forbidden love finds fulfillment in Maggie Shayne's *Beyond Twilight.*

But don't worry—where there's a shiver crawling up your spine, there's a sigh of relief to follow...at least for a little while.

Happy Hauntings!

Leslie Wainger
Senior Editor and Editorial Coordinator

ANNE STUART has been writing about love and death since she was a teenager. She's been published for more than twenty years, writing Gothics, Regencies, romantic suspense, historicals, mainstream suspense and series romance, and during that time she has won almost every major award in the romance genre. She lives in a tiny town in northern Vermont with her husband and two children, and when she's not working she can be found talking on various computer bulletin boards.

In her twenty-seven years as a professional writer, **CHELSEA QUINN YARBRO** has sold more than fifty books, over sixty short stories, a baker's dozen of essays and a handful of reviews; her work has been translated into more than two dozen languages, including Russian and Thai. Her work covers many genres: horror, science fiction, fantasy, thriller, mystery, historical, romantic suspense, young adult and Westerns. Her best-known series are the historical horror Saint-Germain cycle and the accompanying Olivia novels. She has received the Fine Foundation Award for literary excellence and versatility. When she runs out of words, she writes serious music. She loves opera, horses, the antics of cats, good company and conviviality, and occult studies. She dislikes boredom in all forms. Her only domestic accomplishments are needlepoint and cooking. She has served as both president and chair of trustees of the Horror Writers Association, and regional vice-president of Mystery Writers of America.

Bestselling author **MAGGIE SHAYNE** has written eight novels for Silhouette. *Beyond Twilight* is a spin-off of her *Wings in the Night* miniseries for Shadows. Her books have earned her numerous awards, including a Golden Leaf award from New Jersey Romance Writers; two WISH awards from *Romantic Times;* and Best First Book and Best Supernatural Romance awards from *Talisman*. Recently she was a finalist for the Romance Writers of America's prestigious RITA Award. Maggie lives in a rural town in central New York with her husband and five daughters.

GET ALL THIS FREE
WITH JUST ONE PROOF OF PURCHASE:

$50 VALUE

◆ **Hotel Discounts**
up to 60%
at home
and abroad
◆ **Travel Service -**
Guaranteed lowest published
airfares plus 5% cash back on
tickets ◆ **$25 Travel Voucher**
◆ **Sensuous Petite Parfumerie**
collection ◆ **Insider**
Tips Letter with
sneak previews of
upcoming books

You'll get a FREE personal card, too.
It's your passport to all these benefits– and to
even more great gifts & benefits to come!

There's no club to join. No purchase commitment. No obligation.

SPT-PP6A

Enrollment Form

☐ *Yes!* I WANT TO BE A *PRIVILEGED WOMAN.*
Enclosed is one *PAGES & PRIVILEGES*™ Proof of
Purchase from any Harlequin or Silhouette book currently for
sale in stores (Proofs of Purchase are found on the back pages
of books) and the store cash register receipt. Please enroll me
in *PAGES & PRIVILEGES*™. Send my Welcome Kit and FREE
Gifts -- and activate my FREE benefits -- immediately.
More great gifts and benefits to come.

NAME (please print)

ADDRESS _____ APT. NO

CITY _____ STATE _____ ZIP/POSTAL CODE

**NO CLUB!
NO COMMITMENT!**
*Just one purchase brings
you great Free Gifts and
Benefits!*

Please allow 6-8 weeks for delivery. Quantities are limited. We reserve the right to
substitute items. Enroll before October 31, 1995 and receive one full year of benefits.

Name of store where this book was purchased_____

Date of purchase_____

Type of store:

☐ Bookstore   ☐ Supermarket   ☐ Drugstore
☐ Dept. or discount store (e.g. K-Mart or Walmart)
☐ Other (specify)_____

Which Harlequin or Silhouette series do you usually read?

_____

Complete and mail with one Proof of Purchase and store receipt to:
U.S.: *PAGES & PRIVILEGES*™, P.O. Box 1960, Danbury, CT 06813-1960
Canada: *PAGES & PRIVILEGES*™, 49-6A The Donway West, P.O. 813,
North York, ON M3C 2E8

SPT-PP6B

▼ DETACH HERE AND MAIL TODAY! ▼

Strangers in the Night

Anne Stuart

Chelsea Quinn Yarbro

Maggie Shayne

Silhouette Books

Published by Silhouette Books
America's Publisher of Contemporary Romance

SILHOUETTE BOOKS

STRANGERS IN THE NIGHT

ISBN 0-373-48312-0

The publisher acknowledges the copyright holders of the individual works as follows:

DARK JOURNEY
Copyright © 1995 by Anne Kristine Stuart Ohlrogge

CATCHING DREAMS
Copyright © 1995 by Chelsea Quinn Yarbro

BEYOND TWILIGHT
Copyright © 1995 by Margaret Benson

Printed in U.S.A.

CONTENTS

CONTENTS

Dark Journey
Anne Stuart

PROLOGUE

He could control it all. The power of the elements, the storms and the night, the wind and the bright sunlight. He could make people do his bidding, draw them to him with no more than a faint beckoning of his hand and that seductive brilliant white light that promised everything.

He could give them the answers they were seeking to all the questions that plagued them. He held the keys to the future for each and every soul.

But he couldn't answer his own questions. Couldn't give himself the peace and finality he offered others. He was doomed, as nothing else was, to exist in a black-velvet ether of comfort and emptiness. Alone.

It was little wonder he looked out over all he surveyed and felt the need of centuries building up inside him. Little wonder that he rebelled against his destiny. Was it better to rule in hell than to serve in heaven? He wanted to find out.

In the end, it all came down to one of the frail souls he was called to take. One woman, who'd been his since childhood, one small, sweet soul who should have gone on to her destiny years ago.

He'd refused to take her. Because he'd known he wouldn't want to let her go.

He no longer had any choice. This time the voice calling to him was so loud that he had to answer.

But this time he would answer in his way.

"Two days," he said, his sepulchral voice echoing through the heavens. "Just allow me two days."

There was no answer, only the power of the wind that he'd started, that he'd called forth. All his thoughts were centered on a tiny spot in the middle of a vast country, on a tiny soul, and all the other shrieking spirits calling to him were ignored.

"Two days," he said again, and he didn't bother to hide the desperation in his voice. "You owe me that much."

Again nothing from the one power greater than he. Her voice was louder now, louder than all the others, crying for him, and he knew this time he couldn't leave her. This time he had no choice. He closed his eyes, drawing all his power around him like a black-winged cape, and a moment later he was on the side of a mountain in Colorado, looking at her as she lay in the pine needles, eyes closed, dying.

It was a sight he knew well.

Because he was Death. Come to take her.

CHAPTER ONE

Wednesday afternoon—late summer

Laura Fitzpatrick was running. Panic welled up inside her, a deep, nerve-shattering panic as she raced across the thickly wooded hillside, the branches of the evergreens slapping at her face. Her heart was pounding unmercifully, her breath was rasping in her chest, and she could feel the cold sweat prickling her body. She should slow down. She should walk, calmly, safely, back to the house. Someone else could find Justine.

But she couldn't stop. The fear that swept over her was all-encompassing. She couldn't rid herself of the notion that death was all around, just waiting to pounce. Back at the house, her father lay in his massive bedroom, drifting in and out of a coma. Her older sister, Justine, had taken off into the woods, tears blinding her eyes, her voice taut with anguish as she said, "I just can't sit and watch him die."

Justine was the sensitive one; Laura knew and accepted that. She was somewhere deep in the piney forests that surrounded the family compound high up in Taylor, Colorado, no doubt close to hysterics. And if Laura had any sense, she would let her be.

But only a few moments after Justine ran out, William Fitzpatrick had taken a turn for the worse. He would be dead by nightfall—they all knew it—and there was no way that Justine would forgive herself if she wasn't there to help his passing. Even if she was bound to accompany it with noisy sobs.

The others didn't know that Laura had gone after her. They had all huddled closer around the frail, dying figure of their father, and Laura had slipped out the back, certain she could find Justine before she got too far.

But she must have lost her way. Night was closing in around her, the wind had picked up, and in the distance she thought she could hear Justine's heartfelt sobs.

She should have sent Ricky after his wife, but Ricky was half-drunk already, and he would doubtless just have shrugged and poured himself a double. She should have sent their stepbrother, Jeremy, after her, but he was glued to William's bedside, and Cynthia, his wife, had never been known to exert herself for her in-laws.

There were servants. There were people who watched her like a hawk, to make certain she didn't overexert herself. She didn't care. Justine needed her, and for once Laura had the chance to take care of her family, not just sit around and let them take care of her.

The first pain hit her like a hammer blow, directly between her breasts. She went down on her knees, landing on the springy, pine-scented earth, rigid with agony. This couldn't be a heart attack, she told herself. This couldn't be the end, so abruptly. Not when her father was dying, as well.

But the gathering dusk grew inky-black. Far above the towering evergreens she could see the faint glitter of stars, and the scent of pine danced in her nostrils as she collapsed on the forest floor. She could no longer hear Justine's cries. She could hear nothing but the noisy, painful beating of her own heart, slamming against her chest as she struggled for breath.

And then she heard it stop. Silence reigned in the night forest. No sound, no heartbeat, no gasping breath. Nothing at all. There was a bright white light ahead of her, like the outline of a door, and she could see a man silhouetted there. She wanted to reach out and touch him, but she couldn't move.

All she could do was close her eyes with a faint, inaudible sigh and let go.

He looked down at her for a moment, not moving. She lay utterly still, her tawny hair spread out around her pale face. Her eyes were closed, and he wanted her to open them again. He remembered the color—an exquisite warm brown that had seduced him when she was a mere five years old.

He squatted down next to her, careful not to touch her. It had been ten years since he'd last seen her. She'd been seventeen then, chafing against the restrictions her health placed on her. It had been her last act of defiance, and it had nearly cost her her life.

She'd run away from home. Her overprotective family had concluded that she was too frail to handle college, that she should continue her schooling at home. And Laura had rebelled, taking off in the middle of the night with nothing more than a heavy backpack that only put added strain on her already weak heart.

She'd hitchhiked, taking the first ride that was offered, and it had been sheer luck that she made it as far as she did. She'd ended up in the tiny town of Austinburg, Nevada, with no money and no prospects, accepting a ride from a very dangerous man.

Billy Joe Nelson had already killed five young women. Laura would have been his sixth, and they never would have found her body.

But Billy Joe had been the one to die, and Laura had never known how close she'd come. She'd never known he was there, watching over her. And that he got to Billy Joe before the killer could put his hands on her.

He should have taken her then. He'd already let her go too many times. When she was five years old, choking to death, and she'd looked up at him, quite fearlessly, something had made him hesitate.

Or when she was twelve, and she'd fallen off that horse she was forbidden to ride. She was always being protected by her family—the doctors hadn't expected her to live past her tenth birthday. If he hadn't been suddenly, inexplicably capricious, she wouldn't have.

But she'd climbed on a horse that was too big and too strong for her, and taken off. The horse had thrown her, her weak heart had erupted, and she'd lain as she lay now, turning a delicate shade of blue, dying.

He'd reached out a hand to take her. And then drawn it back when she looked at him again. The same eyes. The same calm, unquestioning curiosity. And no fear.

Time meant nothing to him. There had been no need to take her then. Once he put his hand on her, she would be gone. Out of his reach forever. And for some strange reason, he hadn't wanted that to happen.

He hadn't expected to be called for her this time. He'd assumed her father would be next, the old man who'd cheated death too many times as it was. But fate had a nasty habit of playing tricks on him. Now Laura Fitzpatrick lay dying in the forest, and he would have to take her, as well.

He leaned over her. Her heart had stopped, time had stopped. The trees were motionless, as the breeze was frozen at twilight. He looked down at her, and a great rebellion rose inside him.

Not this time. Not this one. Not now.

He tilted his head back to glare at the darkening sky, waiting for the answer he'd sought. This time it came, silently. Two days.

He closed his eyes, summoning all the massive power that lay quiet within him, making it hum and grow. When he opened his eyes, the leaves were rustling in the breeze. An owl hooted.

And Laura Fitzpatrick opened her eyes.

She knew him. It seemed as if she'd known him all her life, and yet she couldn't place him. For long moments she stared up at him, disoriented, confused, trying to look past the mirrored dark glasses and remember where she'd seen him.

"Are you all right?" he asked.

His voice gave her no clue. It was husky, ageless, oddly sensual, with the faintest trace of an accent that might have been French and, then again, might not. His face was narrow, tanned beneath the mirrored glasses, and his dark hair was long.

She struggled to sit up. He didn't help her, didn't touch her, simply sat back on his heels and watched her. "Fine, I think," she said, amazed that her own voice sounded so shaky. "I must have passed out."

"You shouldn't be out here alone."

"I was looking for my sister."

"She's gone back to the house."

She stared at him. "Who are you?" she said, then flushed, realizing how rude she sounded. "I mean..."

"Alex," he said. "Alex Montmort. I'm afraid I must be trespassing. I was hiking when I thought I heard someone cry for help."

"My father owns this mountain."

A small, devastating smile curved his mouth. "Not so much of a mountain, is it? I'm used to the Alps."

"I've never seen the Alps."

"Ah, but you have the Rocky Mountains. They are as spectacular in their own way, even if this one seems a small specimen. Do you ski?"

The simple question shouldn't have bothered her. She had learned to live with her infirmity. With the restrictions her life and health had placed on her. With the restrictions her family had placed on her. "No," she said. "Do you?"

"That's why I'm here."

"It's a little early."

"So it is. I can wait for the snow. I am infinitely patient."

She believed him. He seemed possessed of almost unnatural calm, willing to wait for anything. The entire conversation seemed bizarre, as she sat on the ground in the twilight, conversing with a stranger, the sudden, erupting pain in her chest long vanished.

"You could probably find work in town," she said, striving for a tone of normalcy as she pulled herself upright. He didn't touch her, didn't offer her a steadying hand, and despite the weakness in her legs, she was oddly glad of that. She wasn't ready to have this stranger touch her. "That's what most ski bums do while they're waiting for the first snow."

His smile broadened. "I am not certain I qualify as a ski bum." He rose, standing patiently as he looked down at her. He towered over her, but then, she wasn't a particularly tall woman. He really wasn't that massive, and yet he seemed to loom, like a creature of darkness.

An owl hooted in the night wind, and a streak of unexpected lightning flashed in the sky. "We're going to have a storm," she said, surprised.

"Perhaps," he murmured. "Let me see you safely back to the house, Miss—"

She had the oddest feeling that he knew what her name was, but she obediently supplied it anyway. "Laura," she said. "And I wouldn't want to put you to any trouble. I can find my way home, and you should get back to wherever you came from before the storm hits."

"I have endless time," he said. "Come." He held out his hand, making no effort to touch her, letting her make the first move. There was a curiously expectant air about him, as if he were curious to see what would happen.

She stared at his outstretched hand. It was an elegant one, long-fingered, well shaped. All she had to do was take it, and life would be very simple.

She tucked her hands in her pockets, smiling up at him with unfeigned cheerfulness. "As a matter of fact, maybe you'd better come with me. This place is crawling with armed guards and attack dogs. Daddy—" Her voice caught for a moment, then strengthened again. "Daddy always worried about our safety."

"Why?" It was a simple question, one that was oddly soothing. She started down the path, and he fell into step beside her.

"Daddy is William Fitzpatrick."

"And?"

"That name doesn't mean anything to you? Oh, I forgot, you're not . . . that is, you aren't from around here, are you?" she asked naively.

"No."

"My father is a very powerful man. And when people have wealth and influence, they have enemies. Over the years there have been threats, extortion attempts. Someone once tried to kidnap my older sister, Justine."

"Did they succeed?"

"No. But she's always been a little high-strung since then. We all look after her." She wondered why she was telling this dark stranger such intimate details of her life, but it seemed so logical, so natural.

"Your family look after each other," he observed in a neutral voice.

"A little too much at times." She couldn't disguise her own bitterness. "My stepbrother Jeremy is the worst, always hovering." She shook her head. "You'd be better off with me. I can't imagine how you got so far onto the land without running into some of the security precautions, but even so, I doubt your luck would hold. The dogs can be particularly savage."

"I'm very good with animals."

"Not these," she said. "They've been bred to kill."

She sensed rather than saw his smile. "You are good to be so concerned," he said. "They won't hurt me."

The sheer, calm arrogance of his words should have bothered her, but instead she found it oddly soothing. She'd seen what her father's dogs could do to a rabbit that strayed into their path, and she had been assured they could wreak just that much havoc on an unwanted human. But somehow she believed that they wouldn't hurt this man.

Lightning crackled overhead, illuminating the dark, storm-ridden sky. "I've been away from the house too long," she said again. "My father's dying. He's probably gone by now." She was proud of the unemotional calm of her voice. She'd lived with the knowledge of death all her life—she refused to let the sudden, unpalatable fact of it destroy her.

Alex looked around him, considering. "I don't think anyone will die this night," he observed.

She bit back her instinctive answer. She believed him on this one, too, but it was probably just a case of wishful thinking. "I'd better get back," she said. "Are you coming with me?"

"Yes," he said. "I'm coming with you."

* * *

The Fitzpatrick compound at the top of Taylor Butte was fortified, determinedly rustic, and as comfortable and elegant as money could make it. And there was a very great deal of money—Laura had grown up with that knowledge, as well as the knowledge of her uncertain health. The compound consisted of the main house—a great, sprawling log structure with half a dozen porches and wings, a marvel of rambling charm. There was a spacious guest house, as well, a stable, a building for the servants, a security outbuilding, and a five-car garage. All made of the same golden-hued pine logs that blended so beautifully with the towering evergreens.

Laura hadn't realized how chilly the night was until she stepped inside the big house, with Alex just behind her. A huge fire was blazing in the fieldstone fireplace, sending waves of heat out into the room where her family was gathered.

"Is he gone?" she asked flatly.

Justine sat huddled in a chair, a glass of whiskey clutched in one shaking hand, a defiant expression on her tear-streaked face. "Where were you?" she demanded.

He was directly behind her. She wasn't sure how she knew—she had no sense of his body heat, and he didn't touch her. But he was there, and she found herself grateful. "Looking for you, Justine," she replied, mildly enough. "Is he dead?"

"Morbid, aren't you?" Ricky said, his voice faintly slurred. "But as a matter of fact, my esteemed father-in-law is not dead. We thought he was about to bite the bullet, with both his precious daughters off communing with nature or whatever the hell the two of you were doing, but he suddenly seemed to take a turn for the better." Ricky rose, ignoring his wife, and swaggered toward Laura. "Though I guess I can see what you were doing. Who would have thought it of sweet Saint Laura?"

"Please, Ricky..." Justine begged.

"Listen, guys, could we stop arguing?" Jeremy said from his stance by the fireplace. "Father's not dead yet, but he's living on borrowed time, and we certainly don't want his last memories to be of us squabbling with each other."

"Laura doesn't squabble," Cynthia murmured. Jeremy's pampered, undeniably gorgeous wife was curled up in the most comfortable chair. She, too, had noticed the shadowy figure behind Laura, and her expression had altered from one of sullen boredom to faint interest. "Who's your friend?"

"Alex Montmort," Laura answered politely, then dutifully made the introductions. "This is my family, Alex. My stepbrother, Jeremy, and his wife, Cynthia. And my younger sister, Justine, and her husband, Ricky."

"Montmort?" Ricky said with a snort. "Mountain of death? That's a hell of a name, buddy. What do you do for a living, with a name like that?"

"I ski." The response was cool, faintly tinged with that odd, seductive accent.

"Extreme skiing, I suppose," Jeremy said, with an attempt at normalcy. "The kind of stuff where you ski over cliffs and hope you don't die?"

"Most people who ski over cliffs are fully prepared to die," he replied, closing the door behind him and moving deeper into the room. Once more Laura had the sense that he wanted to touch her, wanted to cup her arm. But he didn't.

"Gloomy subject," Ricky said carelessly. "We've got too much death around here as it is. Lemme get you a drink, Al. What are you having?"

"Alex," the stranger said calmly. "Cognac would be . . . pleasant."

"Cognac it is," Ricky said, taking his own empty glass over to the bar tray. "Ginger ale for you, Laura."

"She will have cognac, as well," Alex said.

They all turned to look at him with a mixture of shock and speculation. "Laura doesn't drink," Jeremy said flatly. "It's not good for her health."

"It won't hurt her tonight," Alex said calmly.

"It could kill her!" Justine cried.

"Not tonight."

Laura broke into the argument, feeling oddly unsettled. "Alex has decreed that no one will die tonight, including Father," she said with a faint smile. "Personally, I can't imagine fate daring to disagree with him. I think I'll risk a small glass of cognac, Ricky."

"Most unwise, my dear," Jeremy murmured, clutching his own tall glass of whiskey.

A few moments later the cognac burned quite nicely as she sipped it. Alcohol was just one of the many normal pleasures in life that were denied her, and having seen its inroads on her family life, she'd never regretted that. But there was something undeniably soothing about sitting on the overstuffed sofa with the dark stranger beside her, watching as he cradled a Waterford brandy snifter in his long, elegant hands.

"So tell me," Jeremy said, with a heavy-handed attempt at affability, "how did you happen to find your way up here? This is private property, and we do our best to keep it that way."

"Alex is an old friend." Laura didn't know where the words came from—they were instinctive.

"Where did you meet? Laura hasn't left this mountain since she was a teenager."

Alex glanced at her. She didn't know how she was certain, since he still wore those mirrored sunglasses that shielded his narrow, handsome face, but she felt as if she could read the expression in the eyes she'd never seen. "I've known her for years," he said easily.

For a bald-faced lie, it had the curious ring of truth. She didn't deny it, simply sat back, sipping at her brandy, oddly comfortable among her battling siblings.

"Odd that she never mentioned you," Jeremy said, and the undercurrent of suspicion was obvious. "Excuse me for being rude, but why are you wearing sunglasses? It's nighttime, and the house is far from brightly lit."

"My eyes are very sensitive," he said. "I'm sorry if it bothers you."

"Ignore my husband, Alex," Cynthia said, in her most charming voice. "He has the manners of a lout, and he's very possessive of his little sister. You'll be staying, won't you?"

For a moment, the world seemed to stop. Laura sat there, bathed in the heat of the fire, her family surrounding her, and yet she felt distant, apart, watching. Waiting for what Alex would say.

It mattered. She wasn't sure why, but it mattered terribly that he should stay. A matter of life and death, she thought oddly.

Please, she begged silently.

The moment passed, the voices returned, and Laura's damaged heart started beating again. "I will stay," Alex said.

And suddenly Laura knew that life had just changed, shifted, irrevocably. There would be no going back, and she wasn't certain whether she was frightened or glad.

Perhaps a little bit of both.

She stole a glance at the man sitting next to her. He was like no one she had ever seen, and yet he was so oddly familiar. A part of her, in some way she couldn't define.

It no longer mattered. The die was cast. He would stay. And life would change, forever.

CHAPTER TWO

He was afraid to touch her, he who wasn't afraid of anything. She sat close enough to him on that over-stuffed sofa that he could smell the trace of her per-fume, the scent of brandy on her mouth. It had been so long since he'd tasted brandy, tasted another mouth. He wanted to so badly he thought he might die of it.

He kept his sour amusement to himself. He knew better than anyone that one didn't die of lust, of longing, of loneliness. The acknowledged causes of death were far more pragmatic. But the real cause of death was that he chose to take someone.

Lightning crackled outside the thick pine walls of the house, and everyone jumped. Everyone but Alex. They were uneasy, this group of assorted siblings, and his presence wasn't making things any more comfort-able. He considered leaving. But then, if he was to go, he would take Laura with him. The old man, as well. And the assembled Fitzpatricks would be a great deal unhappier.

"Did you see the news tonight?" Jeremy said, try-ing to inject a note of normalcy into the evening. He was a pleasant-looking, undistinguished middle-aged man who probably had a long life ahead of him. There was nothing the slightest bit remarkable about him, and Alex was far more interested in his half sister. "Someone jumped off the Empire State Building."

"Why is that so remarkable?" Cynthia demanded in a captious voice. "People have been committing suicide since the dawn of mankind."

"But that's what makes it so interesting. The man who jumped didn't die. He fell God knows how many flights, and he didn't die." Jeremy took another swallow of his whiskey.

"Don't tell me he got up, brushed himself off and walked away?" Ricky demanded, his voice both belligerent and slurred.

"No. He broke every bone in his body. His internal organs were smashed to pieces. But he's not dead."

Silence reigned for a moment. "You choose the most morbid topics of conversation, Jeremy," Cynthia finally remarked. "Could we perhaps talk about something other than death? Considering your father is lying in bed, dying? Why don't we talk about the weather?"

"The weather's just as strange. There have been electrical storms almost everywhere. Apparently three people were struck by lightning near Monarch Pass."

"They must be toast," Ricky said unpleasantly.

"They're not dead, either."

"Would you stop with the gruesome stories!" Laura said, shuddering. "I don't want to hear any more."

"I don't think you'll have to worry about that," Jeremy said. "According to Mrs. Hawkins, the power's gone. We're making do on generators until it comes back on. The phones, the television, even the radio stations, are out. That news report I heard a while ago will probably be our last until the problem's solved."

"That's ridiculous. We can pick up radio stations from Mexico and Canada up here on the mountain," Cynthia protested. "Don't tell me none of them are coming in!"

"All right, I won't tell you," Jeremy said agreeably, his eyes unreadable. "But it's true. Beats me what could be causing it, though."

"The storms," Alex suggested. "Electrical storms do very strange things in Europe. I imagine once it calms down outside, things will be back to normal."

It should have amused him, how easily they swallowed his explanation. It fascinated him, instead—he'd always known how very gullible people were, how desperate to find comfortable explanations for the inexplicable. The Fitzpatricks, for all their wealth and power, were no different. Except, perhaps, for the woman sitting next to him.

"You're probably right," Jeremy said, albeit a bit grudgingly. "In the meantime, it's probably just as well you showed up when you did. We were worried when Justine returned and Laura didn't. We were afraid she might have gotten into trouble out there in the woods."

"What kind of trouble could I get into?" Alex recognized the faint note of defiance in Laura's voice. Life with her family was a battle she had long ago conceded, yet she still managed to rise to a skirmish or two.

"You ran into someone unexpected, didn't you?" Jeremy countered.

"It's a good thing I did," she snapped back.

Suddenly they were all attention. Cynthia moved closer, perching on the edge of the sofa, next to him. Her black silk dress was cut low, and her scent was musky, sexual. "Did you come to the aid of my little sister-in-law?" she cooed.

He glanced up at her. She would be an easier one to experiment with. She called to him; her ripe, abundant flesh luring him, even as her soul seemed strangely absent. He could content himself with learning what he needed to learn from her and leave Laura alone until he no longer had a choice but to take her. He had no inexplicable feelings for Cynthia, no strange, haunting desires. He could use her and feel nothing.

He didn't smile at Cynthia—there was no need. Her eyes were deep and blue and knowing. "She'd fallen," he said in an offhand voice. "She'd tripped over a root and knocked the breath out of herself. She was more frightened than anything else."

"Laura doesn't usually get frightened. She lets the rest of us get terrified for her," Justine said from her spot in the corner.

"There's no reason for anyone to worry about me," Laura said firmly. "Alex is right. I tripped, I couldn't breathe, and I panicked. Fortunately, Alex was there."

"Fortunate is right," Jeremy said. "We're doubly grateful to you, then. We're at the point of losing our father. I don't think this family could stand it if anything happened to Laura at the same time. She's the baby of the family."

Alex turned to look at her, saw the flush of annoyance on her pale face. He'd had time to watch them all: Jeremy, with his shallow, friendly pomposity;

Justine, with her fragile nerves and haunted eyes; drunken, bullying Ricky; and the voracious Cynthia. Not one of them had Laura's fine, tensile strength of character. She was clearly the grown-up of the family, despite the measurement of years.

He smiled faintly, wishing he could reach out and touch her clenched fist, which lay on the couch between them. He didn't dare. He knew too well just what his touch could do if he reached for her. She had to touch him first, and Laura wasn't a woman for casual touching.

Another crash of thunder shook the house; the lights dimmed and then brightened again. An elderly woman, clearly some kind of servant, appeared in the doorway. "I've sent the girls home, Miss Laura. If they don't leave now, there's no telling whether they'll be able to get down the mountain in this weather."

"Thank you, Mrs. Hawkins. Shouldn't you leave, as well? We're more than capable of seeing to our own needs. . . ." Laura said in her soft voice.

"Speak for yourself, Laura," Cynthia said rudely, interrupting her. "Justine's too much of an emotional basket case, and I *don't* cook."

"I can take care of things," Laura said.

"Not fragile little Laura." Cynthia's mocking voice was unpleasant, deliberately husky.

"Make m'wife do something," Ricky said, his voice getting even more slurred. "She might as well be good at something. She's lousy in bed, a lousy housekeeper, a lousy cook. She can't even get pregnant."

"Be quiet, Ricky," Laura said.

"If Justine's a lousy cook, that's hardly a recommendation," Cynthia added.

"Enough of this squabbling!" Mrs. Hawkins said. "I'm not going anywhere tonight. Not with Mr. Fitzpatrick in such rough shape. I don't know if the night nurse will make it up here, but Maria and I will take turns sitting with him."

"We'll all take turns," Laura said, pushing herself up from the sofa. "Me first." She glanced back at Alex. "Do you want to come with me? You don't need to—some people are uncomfortable in the face of death."

His smile was so faint that most people wouldn't have noticed it. Laura did. "If you think your father wouldn't mind," he said as he rose.

Cynthia piped up, still perched on the sofa. "He's been in a coma for almost a week now. I doubt he'd notice."

"You'd be surprised what people notice, even at the moment of death," Alex said.

Cynthia reached up and put her slender, manicured hand on his arm. He felt it like an electric shock, and she felt it, too, pulling her hand back in surprise.

"Static," she muttered.

She wasn't dead. She'd touched him, reached out to him, and she hadn't died. Interesting. But then, no one was dying. Not while he was otherwise occupied.

William Fitzpatrick lay motionless in the hospital bed that had obviously been brought in as his condition worsened. It looked odd in the midst of the huge southwestern-style master bedroom, amid the hand-carved furniture and rich Indian throws. William Fitzpatrick was beyond noticing, though.

"You can take a break now, Maria," Laura said in her soft voice.

The woman in the uniform lifted her head sharply, taking in the two of them before she concentrated on Laura. "You look like hell," she said frankly, setting down her paperback novel and moving toward them. "Did you run into a tree or something?"

"I'm fine."

Maria ignored the faint protest. "I think I should take a listen to your heart. I don't like your color. What have you been doing, racing around when you know you shouldn't?"

"Don't you pick on me, Maria!" Laura cried, but there was friendly exasperation in her voice. "It's bad enough that the rest of them hover over me, expecting me to keel over at any minute."

"And who's to say you won't?" Maria said darkly.

"Listen, if people can plummet from the Empire State Building and survive, then I think my heart will make it through the next few days. It's brought me this far, hasn't it?"

"Amazingly enough. No thanks to the care you take of yourself."

"No, you can thank my overprotective family," Laura said, more in resignation than anger.

Maria rose, a sturdy, comforting soul, and put a reassuring hand on Laura's shoulder. "Sit with him awhile. I don't think he'll notice." She glanced past Laura, directly at Alex, and for a moment her placid expression clouded with concern. "Have we met?"

"I don't think so. My name is Alex."

"I'm sorry. I should have introduced you. He's a friend of mine," Laura said, sinking down into Maria's vacated chair with an almost imperceptible sigh. "He just arrived."

Maria looked him up and down, her dark brown eyes measuring. "I could swear I'd seen you before," she said, half to herself. "But then, I wouldn't forget that voice. Besides, I specialize in hospice work. I'm afraid most of the people I work with die."

Alex said nothing, merely smiled faintly. She knew him, all right, but her brain couldn't assimilate how or why. It was just as well. He had no intention of telling anyone, until he was ready to leave. He'd asked for two days. He wondered if he would really get them.

"Get some dinner, Maria," Laura said, reaching out and taking her father's motionless hand. "I'll keep him company."

The room was utterly silent after the nurse left, the stillness marred only by the distant sound of thunder and the faint hiss and pop of the breathing device. Alex watched the old man with silent interest. He could sense his spirit, floating, waiting, frustrated by the delay in the inevitable.

"He's been like this for more than a week," Laura said in a hushed voice, her slender, strong hands wrapped around the old man's. "I was certain he was going to die this afternoon. That's what made Justine run off—she couldn't deal with it. But he's still here. At least in body, if not in spirit."

Alex said nothing, waiting. As if on cue, the old man's crepey eyes opened, blinking at the bright light. The sound he made was indiscernible—barely more than a croak—but they both understood. "Laura," he whispered.

"Oh, my God!" she breathed. "You're awake! Let me go and tell the others. . . ."

His hands were too feeble to stop her, and she ran from the room before either man could move. William Fitzpatrick, patriarch, millionaire, political kingmaker, raised his gaze to Alex's shaded stare.

"Take off your sunglasses." The words were barely spoken, but Alex heard them nonetheless. "Come here."

He didn't hesitate. He stepped up to the bedside, shoving the sunglasses up on his forehead, and met the old man's inimical gaze.

"Damn you," William Fitzpatrick wheezed. "You've come for me, haven't you?"

"Among other things," he replied, pitching his voice so low that most mortals couldn't hear him. Only those he chose.

Real fear crossed the old man's face for the first time. Not fear for himself, though. Another interesting facet of human behavior, Alex thought. They feared more for their loved ones than they feared for themselves. The number of people who had come to him, thrusting their children, their beloveds, out of his reach and making him take them instead, had been baffling and innumerable. Another question he needed the answer to.

"No," the old man gasped. But before he could say any more, his grown-up, contentious children pushed their way into the room, and Alex quickly slid the sunglasses down on the bridge of his nose and stepped back from the bedside.

All their fuss would have killed the old man if nothing else did. But for the time being, no one was dying. Not even a man so riddled with cancer that most of his organs had shut down. Not some poor smashed, mangled soul who'd tried to kill himself by jumping off a tall building. Not the three people in the car hit by lightning, not the three hundred people from the capsized ferry in Cambodia. Not the sniper's victims in Northern Ireland, not any of the poor souls ready to meet him. They would all have to wait.

Jeremy had pushed Laura aside, planting his sturdy frame at his stepfather's bedside. "We thought you'd left us for good, sir." His booming voice was loud enough to make the old man wince.

"Just a minor delay," he wheezed.

Laura slid next to Alex, a rueful expression on her face. "I might as well show you to your room," she murmured. "They're not going to let me anywhere near him for the time being."

Alex nodded, following her out of the room. But not before his ears caught the old man's fretful question. "Where did that fellow come from? Where's he going with Laura?"

He didn't wait for the answer, merely followed Laura's slight frame through the wide pine hallways of the rambling log house. "I'm sorry I can't put you in the guest house," she was saying, her voice light and slightly breathless as she started up the stairs. Too quickly for her damaged heart. "But Jeremy and Cynthia took up residence there a couple of weeks ago, when it looked as if Father was about to die, and Justine and Ricky joined them a couple of days ago. But there are plenty of empty rooms here in the big house, so you should be comfortable."

I want to be near you, he thought. He didn't say the words out loud. He knew perfectly well he didn't need to.

They reached the top of the stairs, and she started to turn to the left. She stopped and abruptly turned the other way. "I'll put you next to my room, if you don't mind," she said easily. "There's a wide balcony overlooking the mountains, and it's the prettiest view in the place. Unless you'd rather..."

"I'd like the view," he said, pitching his voice low and soothing. She was growing more agitated around him, and he wasn't sure why. He'd been careful not to frighten her, not to make her suspect a thing. The old man had known him, recognized him. He'd been hovering near him for too long not to be recognized.

And the nurse had known him, as well, even though she didn't realize it. They'd shared the same vigil countless times, but Maria's attention had mostly been on the patient, not on whatever else was waiting with her.

As far as he knew, Laura was straightforward, pragmatic and not the slightest bit fey. She would never imagine who and what he might be. And if she did, she wouldn't believe it.

She led him to a door on the left, cut deep in the middle of the pine logs that made up the interior, as well as the exterior, walls of the house. There was a second door beside it, left closed, and he knew it was her room. She pushed his door open and flicked on the light, and from behind the sunglasses he winced. He was so used to living in darkness.

There was a bed, and a set of glass doors overlooking the night forest. There was an antique mirror set on one wall, and he glanced at it, the reflection drawing him.

Laura stood beside him. Frail, with her honey-streaked hair and warm brown eyes, her pale face and soft mouth, she looked curiously vulnerable and childlike. Until he looked past, to see the determination in her jaw, the calm of her high forehead, the strength in her hands. He stood behind her, a tall, shadowy figure, dressed entirely in black, the dark glasses shading his eyes. His hair was long, tied back from his narrow face, and his mouth was thin, almost harsh. He was lean-looking, and strong. He looked as he'd imagined he would.

She moved away from him, bustling about the room, turning on more lights, plumping up the pillows on the bed. It was a high bed, hand-carved of rough-hewn pine and covered with a beautiful flowered quilt atop the wide mattress. He looked at her, leaning over the bed, and a wave of longing washed over him, a wave so fierce he shuddered.

He wanted her lying on the bed. He wanted to taste every part of her. He wanted to know what drew him to her, what made her different from every soul he had ever come for.

Why did she make him come alive? He who was the very epitome of death.

If he solved that riddle, he would be at peace again. He would fade once more into a velvet nothingness, where order and calm and destiny prevailed.

But for the next two days there would be no such thing as order or destiny. The world might as well stop spinning. In the next two days no one would die. In the next two days he would find the answers to all the questions that had plagued his soul for years past counting.

And in the next two days he would take Laura Fitzpatrick. He would take her innocence, her virginity, her body—and her soul.

He would take her love, because he knew he could have it. She was ready to offer it to him, and nothing would make him turn down that precious gift.

And in the end, when he was ready to leave, he would take her life, as well.

He made her nervous. Laura hated to admit that fact, but she'd never been one to shy away from the truth, and there was no denying that his presence unnerved her in ways that weren't entirely unpleasant.

She couldn't see his eyes behind the mirrored sunglasses, but she suspected she was better off that way. She hadn't touched him, hadn't even come close enough to feel his body heat. And yet she felt alert, alive, aware of him in every cell of her body, and that knowledge made her restless and uneasy.

She forced a friendly smile to her face. She was imagining things, imagining the strange, taut feelings that seemed to stretch between them. He was a ski bum, someone who'd happened upon her at an opportune time, a pleasant, charming, attractive man.

A man with a strong, elegant body, a narrow, clever face, and a mouth that was sensuous and cruel at the same time.

She laughed, half to herself, and went to draw the curtains against the stormy night.

"What amuses you?" he murmured.

"I'm becoming fanciful in my old age," she admitted, hoping to defuse the strange feelings that were assaulting her. "I don't usually indulge myself."

"What kind of fantasies were you indulging in?" he asked, his voice carefully neutral.

In another man she might have thought it was a come-on, leading up to some smarmy sexual innuendo that she would have to parry. But not with Alex. For some reason, she knew he wasn't some hormone-laden male, looking to score. He was simply curious.

She looked up at him, and suddenly she wanted to touch him. She wasn't certain why—something told her it would be very dangerous indeed if she put her hands on him. And that very warning made her all the more determined to follow through.

"About you," she said flatly. "You're very mysterious, you know."

He seemed to freeze. It was an amazing feat for a man who always seemed unnaturally still. "Do you like that?"

It was a reasonable question. She shook her head, crossing the room, oddly aware of the big bed behind her, oddly aware of the big man in front of her. "Not particularly." She lifted her hand, and he didn't move, watching her, watching her outstretched hand, like a snake coiled and ready to strike. "Would you like me to see about dinner for you?"

"No."

"No, you're not hungry?"

"No, I don't want you to see about anything for me."

She managed a faint smile. "Trust me, I enjoy being allowed to do things for other people. It's not often that I get the chance."

"No," he said again. "Are you going to touch me?"

It was a simple question, oddly phrased. She dropped her hand, embarrassed. "I wasn't planning to. I think I'll go downstairs and make sure my father's all right. That might have been his last lucid moment before he..."

"He won't die tonight."

She felt her mouth curve in a faint smile. "Is that a promise?"

"It is."

"I believe you." And before he knew what she was planning, she'd reached up and enveloped him in a brief, sexless hug. And then she left, without a backward glance.

CHAPTER THREE

He felt her embrace in every cell of his body. It shook him, more than he'd thought he could be shaken. She'd smiled, backed away, looking neither shocked nor dead. She'd simply kept that calm, tranquil expression on her face, and a moment later she was gone.

She'd left the door open behind her, and he could hear her footsteps as she moved quickly back down the hallway. She'd put her arms around him and nothing had happened.

He moved to the French doors, opening the curtains she'd pulled against the violence of the night. Lightning flashed through the sky, illuminating the mountains. The distant rumble of thunder was an angry counterpoint. But it wouldn't rain, he knew that. As surely as he knew that no one would die. Everything was on hold for the next two days. The weather would threaten, the wind would blow, but nothing would happen. The narrow road up the canyon would be blocked by fallen trees, and no one would risk coming out in such a storm to clear the way. No one would even know about it, with all outside communication severed. He had two days at his command, and no one would interfere.

He heard the sound of her breathing, smelled the heavy scent of her perfume. By the time he turned around, Cynthia was already in the room. She was carrying a down comforter, and there was a predatory expression in her shallow blue eyes.

She was scheduled to die in four years, in a drunk-driving accident with a married lover, though now that future seemed a bit uncertain, cloudy. Nothing was ever carved in stone; life had a habit of changing, and her fate was by no means definite. If he took her earlier, it would surely do the world no great disservice. He watched her through the mirrored sunglasses, curious.

"You must have caught a chill," she said in her deliberately husky voice. "I've never felt anyone so cold in my entire life. I brought you the heaviest down comforter we have, and later I'll see if I can find you some sweaters. What do you sleep in?"

"I beg your pardon?" He kept his voice perfectly polite, simply because he knew it irritated her.

She dumped the cover on the bed, then moved closer, attempting a sexy glide. She came up close to him, so close he could almost taste the whiskey on her breath. "I said, what do you sleep in? You seem the silk-pajama type. Or maybe you wear nothing at all."

She put her hand on his chest, and for a second he felt her flesh jerk beneath the touch of his. But she didn't break contact. "You're *sooo* cold," she purred. "I've never met a man as cold as you. I think I need to warm you up."

He didn't move. She stood too close to him, and the musky scent of her skin, the gleam in her eyes, the life that flowed in her veins, were all strong and stimulating. Take what she offers, he told himself. Maybe that will be enough.

She swayed against him, and her large, soft breasts pressed up against his chest. Her nipples were pebble-hard, but he had no illusions that the cause might be sexual excitement. He knew just how cold he could be.

But Cynthia was determined to persevere, even in the face of his lack of cooperation. She slid her arms around his waist determinedly, tilting her face up to his, a smile playing around her full, pink mouth. "Do you want me to warm you up, Alex? I think you do."

Her lush hips were tilted up against his, and he felt himself grow hard against her. So this was what it was like to be human, he thought absently. Mortal. The flesh could respond, even when the spirit was bored. Just how far could the flesh take him?

He had bent down to put his mouth over her open, smiling one when he glanced toward the doorway. Cynthia hadn't bothered to close the door when she began her little visit, and now they had a witness. Laura stood there, her pale face paler still as she watched them.

Cynthia must have felt the sudden stillness in his body. She slid her arms away from him, turning with a faint, mocking smile. "Hullo, Laura," she said smoothly, smugly, sauntering toward her. "Are you going to try your luck, as well?"

"I think you've had too much to drink," Laura said in a quiet voice.

"I usually do, darling. What else is there to do in this wretched place except sit around and wait for the old man to die? Don't look at me like that!" Her voice rose in a little shriek, even though Laura's face seemed entirely blank. "Don't you judge me. Jeremy and I have an understanding, and it's not up to you to come in and—"

"Go away." Alex spoke for the first time, his voice low and cool.

Cynthia cast an amused glance over her shoulder. "Yes, go away, dear Laura, and shut the door behind you. Alex and I—"

"No." His voice was implacable. "*You* go away. Laura stays."

Both women looked startled. Cynthia summoned up an airy smile. "Well," she said, "I suppose I can take a hint. Don't let me interrupt you." She moved toward the door in a sexy glide that left Alex totally unmoved. She put her hand on Laura's shoulder as she stood there, and a faint shadow crossed Laura's face.

"I'd be careful if I were you, my girl," Cynthia warned her in a cool, mocking voice. "He's a bit too much for someone like you to handle." And she walked past, her lush hips swaying.

The blank expression on Laura's face began to fade, and she looked embarrassed, uncomfortable, disturbed. "I didn't mean to interrupt anything. I just..."

"Close the door," he said.

Confusion joined the myriad of emotions that played over her face, and she started to step back. "Of course. I didn't mean to bother you...."

"With you inside."

He wondered whether she would do it. He could see the flash of defiance in her warm eyes. "I don't like to be told what to do," she said in a calm voice. "Too many people try to run my life for me. I don't like it. And I'm not sure if I like you."

He didn't smile, even though he was tempted. "Close the door," he said. "And come here."

She did, of course. He almost told her to lock it, but he knew there was no need. He wasn't ready yet. Even though his body was still responding to Cynthia's blatant sexuality, Alex had no intention of slaking his temporary lust with Laura. He would take her when he chose to. Now was too soon.

She was carrying a pile of white towels, and she set them on the bed beside the down comforter Cynthia had brought him. She glanced at it with a startled expression.

"It's not really that cold out," she murmured. "I don't know why Cynthia thought you might want that."

"Cynthia was looking for an excuse."

She smiled then, a faint, honest grin. "Well, I suppose I should have warned you about Cynthia. She's a bit...overwhelming. She and Jeremy are in the midst of a divorce, but they decided not to tell Father about it. He wouldn't approve, and he'll be dead soon enough. There's no need to make his last few weeks even more difficult."

"And you agree with that?"

She looked up, as if startled at his perception. "No," she said. "I don't like lies."

"And you don't like your sister-in-law?"

"I feel sorry for her. She's a very unhappy woman, and she and Jeremy were never well suited."

"Then why did they marry?"

Laura shrugged, wandering past him, moving over to stare out at the windy night. "Family pressure. Father thought they'd be a good match. Jeremy was the son of his first wife, not a blood relation, and Father didn't like that. Cynthia is a second cousin—he wanted that connection. The Fitzpatricks put family ahead of everything."

"Do you?"

She turned to glance at him. "To some extent, I suppose I do. I'm lucky, though. No one could develop any great dynasty-founding plans with me. I was pretty much left on my own. As long as I behaved, I could spend my time as I pleased."

"Why is that?"

Her smile was bright, calm and totally devoid of self-pity. "Because I'm going to die. I've been living on borrowed time since I was about five years old. I have a bad heart and an unfortunate allergy to most drugs. There was never any question of a transplant, even though I'm sure my father could have bought me a hundred hearts. I wasn't supposed to make it past my twelfth birthday, but here I am."

"Here you are," he echoed softly.

"I was frightened in the woods, you know," she continued, in a deliberately casual voice that didn't fool him for a minute. "When you found me, I'd passed out. Too much stress, I suppose. Too much worry. But right before I lost consciousness, I was afraid I was dying. It seemed to me that my heart stopped. And it scared me."

"Most people are afraid of death," he said.

"I'm not most people. I've known death would come for me, sooner rather than later, and I thought I'd made peace with my fate. But when I was alone in the woods, I was suddenly terrified." She seemed embarrassed by her sudden confession. "I don't know why I'm telling you this."

"Because I'm a stranger?" he said.

She looked up, startled. "I suppose so. And yet, I know what Maria meant when she thought she knew you. You must remind me of someone, but I can't figure out who."

He smiled faintly. "It will come to you."

She looked uncertain. "I suppose so." She gave herself a brisk little shake. "I still can't get over my father's recovery. He's been in a coma for weeks, and now he's talking, making sense. It's a miracle."

"I don't expect it will last," he said.

"No, I suppose it won't. If people can jump off the Empire State Building and survive, then my father's perfectly capable of cheating death for a few more days."

"No one cheats death. They only think they do."

He moved past her to push open the doors to the balcony. The wind was very strong, gusting into the room, and he felt it riffle through his hair, tug at his dark clothes. He loved the wind, the damp scent of rain on the air. He half hoped she would go away. He wanted her so badly he was afraid of scaring her again. She'd been afraid this afternoon, she'd said. He didn't want her frightened. Too many people were terrified of him.

But she moved past him, out onto the balcony, and the wind picked up her hair and tossed it away from the delicate, clean lines of her face as she tilted it upward, drinking in the wild night. "What do you think death is like?" she murmured, half to herself.

He heard the words with a kind of shock—and the knowledge that he couldn't avoid answering her. He leaned back against the glass doorway, folding his hands across his chest to keep from touching her.

"I don't know," he said deliberately. "I suppose death comes with a cloud of angels and harps and all. Heavenly choruses, songs of praise."

"I don't think so," she said in a meditative voice. "Do you believe in hell?"

"No," he said flatly, truthfully.

A faint smile crossed her face. "Neither do I. But I'm not too sure about heaven. What do you think?"

"I try not to think about such things at all. Life is to be lived. The present is what matters, not some obscure afterlife."

She glanced at him over her shoulder, and her smile was rueful. "I suppose I'm a little morbid. It comes from living with death for most of my life."

"It sounds most unpleasant," he murmured.

She turned and moved closer to him, and the wind caught her hair and blew it against him. It smelled of rain and wind and flowers, and he wanted to put his mouth against it. Against her.

"It hasn't been. It's actually been rather comforting." She managed a shaky laugh. "My family thinks I'm crazy. Death isn't supposed to be a friend."

"What about a lover?" He spoke the words so quietly that she could have missed them. But she didn't. She looked up into his dark, hidden face, and his eyes were clear and honest. And startled, as if she were considering the notion for the very first time.

"Laura?" Jeremy stood in the doorway, his solid bulk radiating disapproval. "We wondered where you'd gotten to."

"We were just having a philosophical discussion about the nature of life and death," she said with a faint laugh. But Alex could see the guilty stain on her pale cheeks, and he wondered where the guilt came from. And he wondered how he would stop himself from striking Jeremy Fitzpatrick dead the first chance he had.

"You haven't seen Cynthia, have you?" her step-brother asked in a casual voice, but his eyes swept the room, dark with suspicion.

"I think she might have gone back to the guest house."

"Great," Jeremy said. "Ricky's passed out cold, Justine's having a weeping fit, and you're up here... that is, you're here..." Words failed him.

"Yes," she said, in a deliberately tranquil voice that held just an edge of warning. "I'm up here making our guest welcome."

"Go on downstairs," he said, with an uneasy attempt at amiability. "Mrs. Hawkins has set out a buffet. You know you don't eat enough." He glanced at Alex, and his face was dark with dislike. "We'll be down in a minute."

"Jeremy." The warning in her voice was sharper now.

"Go along now."

She didn't move for a moment, her soft mouth set in stubborn lines, and Alex wondered with vague amusement what she was trying to protect him from. Whatever it was clearly caused her more pain than it could ever cause him, so he simply nodded at her. "Don't fuss, Laura. Your stepbrother just wishes to lay out the rules of the house."

"Damn straight," Jeremy said.

"Ignore him," Laura said firmly. "I always do."

The two men waited until she was gone. And then Alex turned to Jeremy, keeping the faint smile on his face.

"Could you take off those damned sunglasses?" Jeremy demanded in a well-bred whine. "I like to see who I'm talking to."

Not in this case you wouldn't, Alex thought cynically. "I told you before, my eyes are sensitive to light," he said in a deceptively civil tone.

Jeremy wasn't the type of man to make a stand. "Suit yourself," he said. "I just wanted to make a few things clear about our household."

"Certainly."

"You're to keep away from Laura."

It was just as well the mirrored sunglasses covered half his face. He kept it impassive. "And why is that?"

"We look out for her. My stepsister isn't…isn't like other women."

"And why not?"

"She's ill. Dying, as a matter of fact. Any stress could kill her."

"She told me about her heart."

Jeremy looked shocked. "You're lying. She never talks about it with strangers."

"I'm not a stranger."

"I don't care who the hell you are. You're to keep away from her. There are trees down all over the place, blocking the driveway, and the phones are out so there's nothing we can do about it now, but by tomorrow this freak storm should have passed, and I'm going to want you out of here."

"I'll leave as soon as the storm is over," he said in a tranquil voice, knowing he was conceding nothing.

Jeremy nodded. "As long as we understand each other. You're not to touch her, you understand?"

"I understand," he said, agreeing to nothing. "I would have thought you'd be more concerned about your wife than your unmarried stepsister."

"Cynthia knows what she's getting herself into," he said with a faint sneer. "Laura doesn't. She's a complete innocent when it comes to men. Do you understand what I'm telling you? A complete innocent."

He managed a bored yawn, pleased with the effect. "If you're trying to tell me she's still a virgin at her advanced age, then let me assure you, I understand. My command of the English language is actually quite good."

"And she's going to stay that way."

"Why?" It was a simple enough question, but Jeremy looked taken aback.

"Because . . . because . . ." he blustered.

"Never mind," Alex said gently. "I've never been all that interested in innocents."

"And Laura is uninterested in men."

It was a patent lie, one that sat between them like a coiled snake. "Of course," Alex murmured politely. And he followed his reluctant host out into the hallway, the darkness all around them.

* * *

Jeremy looked disgustingly smug when he walked into the dining room, Laura thought, squashing down her unexpected anger. But the man behind him didn't look the slightest bit embarrassed or chastened.

Oh, she knew perfectly well what Jeremy had told him. That she was a poor, dying virgin. That to touch her was to kill her, and he surely didn't want that on his conscience.

She'd seen it happen time and time again, as her father and then her brothers warned men away from her, and her embarrassment had faded to mild annoyance over the years as she told herself she didn't care.

Tonight was different, and she wasn't certain why. Tonight she was shaking with anger and a strange kind of despair, and she didn't want to examine the reasons too closely for fear of what she might see.

But she'd been nothing but truthful when she told him that she hated lies. And most of all, she hated lying to herself.

She accepted her future—and lack thereof—stoically enough. Accepted her family's overprotectiveness, knowing there was no escape.

She looked at the tall, dark figure in the shadows behind Jeremy. He was watching her from behind his enveloping sunglasses, and she wondered what he saw. A pale, sad creature, doomed to a foreshortened life?

He wouldn't have needed to be warned away from her. He would have no reason to have any interest, not with Cynthia throwing her voluptuous curves at him. He'd been about to kiss her, and Laura had stood in the doorway watching, transfixed.

She hadn't wanted him to kiss Cynthia. To put his cool, wide mouth against Cynthia's. But even so, she'd wanted to watch. To see how he kissed.

So she could imagine what it would be like if he kissed her.

"Your face is flushed," he said, his voice husky. Jeremy turned and sent a warning glare at him, but Alex seemed unmoved by the threat.

Laura put a hand to her cheeks. "I'm hot," she admitted. "Too much rushing around."

"You know it's not good for you," Jeremy snapped in a petulant voice. "You shouldn't be waiting on our guest. I think you should come down to the guest house and stay with us. You know I've been trying to get you down there for days. I think Justine and Cynthia could do with your company."

"That's enough!" Laura snapped, fury overcoming her embarrassment. "You don't have to be so transparent. Alex is not going to come creeping into my room in the middle of the night, so you can stop doing the protective-big-brother protective thing, all right?"

Jeremy looked back at Alex's expressionless face, then at Laura's angry one. He managed a rueful laugh, one that didn't quite work. "I suppose I'm being ridiculous, aren't I?"

"Yes," Laura said firmly.

"Forgive an older brother. I worry about you. I should know by now you can take care of yourself."

"Yes, you should," Laura said firmly.

And Alex didn't say a word.

CHAPTER FOUR

Jeremy sat alone in the library, staring into the fire as he nursed his whiskey. He was going to have to kill them all.

It had seemed so simple, so logical, when he first decided on it. William would be proud of him—the weakling son who had no blood claim to any of the Fitzpatrick boldness. He couldn't get the job done, the old man had told him years ago with blistering condescension. He was too weak, too civilized, not like the Fitzpatricks, who'd made their fortune and their power climbing over the dead bodies of the people they'd stabbed in the back.

Ah, but the old man had always underestimated him. He could backstab as well—better than—the next man. He was simply more subtle about it. Not for him the slice and dice.

He worked delicately. With a twist, and just the right amount of pressure, he could eviscerate an enemy and smile while he did it.

He'd been laying his plans carefully, knowing he had only borrowed time. They had to be dead before the old man finally breathed his last or it might all be for nothing. William was too strong, too mean, to die without a hell of a fight, but even he couldn't last forever. And during the past few days, Jeremy had made his plans.

It was to be enormously simple. A carbon monoxide leak from a faulty heater would wipe out his wife, his neurotic stepsister and his drunken brother-in-law. He wouldn't be there—he would be staying up at the big house, at a bedside vigil. In his grief he would be dignified, restrained. Oh, he might allow himself to break down at an opportune moment, just to play it through to the end. After all, Laura was no fool.

But she was gullible, innocent, and had no idea what he was capable of. She'd been spared, in many ways, by her previous affinity with death. There was no need for Jeremy to shorten her life with the others'. She wouldn't outlive the old man by long, and she would have no other heirs. All that money would end up where it belonged. With the strongest of them all. The man who could do what needed to be done.

Jeremy Fitzpatrick.

The storm was a mixed blessing. It cut off access to the rest of the world, and it would enable Jeremy to take his time, alter his plans, if need be. He didn't like the newcomer. Not the mirrored sunglasses or the faintly derisive smile on his mouth. Nor the interest he showed in Laura.

But in the end, it would make no difference. Even if the storm had brought them Alex, it kept others away. They were trapped at the mountaintop compound with far less than their usual complement of servants and outsiders. Only Mrs. Hawkins and the nurse were there now, and both of them were too centered on the old man to notice anything unusual.

William's unexpected rally gave him more time, but Jeremy didn't want it. He'd looked down into his stepfather's face and smiled a filial smile, but he'd wanted to wrap his fingers around the old man's wattled neck and choke the life out of him.

No, time for the Fitzpatrick family had run out. Ricky and Justine were asleep already—Ricky was drunk, Justine equally comatose from tranquilizers. Cynthia was asleep, as well, her beautiful face flushed and sated. He'd given her what she wanted, since the stranger had refused to succumb, and she'd taken it, clawing at his back, spitting at him when she peaked, her contempt and hatred complete despite her need. She thought he was weak, as well.

It was too bad she would never discover how strong he really was.

The carbon monoxide was already filling the cozy, airtight guest house. He was very proud of how he'd managed to jury-rig the heating system, but then, no one had ever quibbled about his brain. Just his determination.

Laura had gone to bed, though he knew perfectly well she hadn't wanted to go. She was infatuated with the stranger, and Jeremy almost considered encouraging her. It would add to the scandal in a most delicious way. Half of the Fitzpatrick dynasty dies in a freak accident while the younger daughter spends a night of passion with a stranger. And the noble stepson keeps a bedside vigil, unaware of the tragedy surrounding him.

He giggled softly at the notion, wishing he could risk it. But he didn't dare. The doctors had always warned them that any undue strain on Laura's heart would carry her off, and that included horseback riding, square dancing and making love. Jeremy couldn't afford to have Laura die the same night as the others—it would be too coincidental. Of course, it might have the added benefit of pointing suspicion at the stranger, but Jeremy didn't want to take that risk. He'd covered his tracks extremely well, but if someone were really determined to look into things, there was no telling what might be uncovered. Including the bodies of the three servants who'd disappeared over the years, buried in shallow graves on the mountainside. Or the women in Colorado Springs.

No, he would leave things as he'd originally planned. William's eleventh-hour rally wouldn't make the slightest bit of difference, either. The old man wasn't alert enough to cause problems; he would only feel the pain of loss. The notion was wonderfully soothing.

Jeremy poured himself another drink, exactly two ounces of single-malt whiskey. He knew to a quarter of an ounce the amount of alcohol he allowed himself. He watched his fat and salt intake, he never smoked, and he allowed himself to kill only when he'd planned every detail. Mistakes were made in the heat of passion, and he never allowed himself passion.

He walked back into his stepfather's bedroom. The nurse was dozing in the corner, nobly refusing to leave her post, despite William's improved condition. All well and good, he thought to himself. She would provide the perfect alibi. In the servants' quarters behind the kitchen, Mrs. Hawkins, who'd always tried to mother him, slept on. And somewhere overhead, Laura probably dreamed ignorant, erotic dreams about the stranger.

Alex Montmort was the only question mark, a risk that Jeremy found exciting. He didn't want to be excited. He wanted to sit coolly and calmly at the old man's bedside while most of his family died, and he wanted to keep his pleasure in the act under the tightest of reins.

Maybe the stranger would sneak out of the house and go in search of Cynthia. Maybe he would climb into bed with her—Cynthia was always ready for more. And then he would be found dead in the guest house, as well.

Carbon monoxide. An odorless, colorless gas. Lethal, undetectable. So very, very sad, Jeremy thought, composing his face into stolid lines of grief. And then he giggled again.

Alex stretched his legs out in front of him, watching the storm from the balcony chair. It was growing colder, he suspected, though he was impervious to it. The faint drizzle had turned to icy pellets dashing themselves against his flesh, and he felt the sting with a certain wry delight. Life was a painful process, apparently. He was unused to the elements interfering with him—they were usually his to command.

As were people. Laura Fitzpatrick's reaction to his high-handed ways amused him, as well. She seemed patently unwilling to do what he wanted, a fact that astonished him. He had no doubt that even with his diminished powers he could make the others obey him without question.

Perhaps Laura would be equally docile if he exerted himself. But he didn't want her docile.

A gust of wind came up, and a streak of lightning split the sky. He watched it moodily. He felt oddly restless, as if he should be doing something.

Of course he should be doing something. He should be following his ordained path, taking those souls who were ready to go. Instead, he was ignoring their cries, determined for once to listen only to his own selfish wants.

The calls were getting louder, nearer, and he wondered whose they could be. The old man, of course, but his voice, persistent, weak, was unchanged. Was it Laura's?

But if Laura called to him, he would go to her. He would end this sojourn, take her with him and never let her go.

Ah, but he didn't have that choice. Even for a creature as powerful as he, there were limitations. He could take her, of course, and he would. But then he would lose her, as she went on to fulfill her destiny.

No, it wasn't her voice. And there were no other voices he chose to listen to right now, only Laura's and his own. No other souls to deal with.

Except that he doubted he had a soul in the first place. That part had always been unclear to him, and by now he wasn't sure he wanted an answer.

He rose, wandering to the edge of the railing, and looked out over the thickly wooded hillside. He glanced over to the left, to the smaller, log-crafted guest house, and his eyes narrowed. The voices were coming from that direction. *How interesting,* he thought, wrinkling his forehead. *Unexpected.*

His shirt was stiff with ice. He moved back to the French doors that led to his room. There was a fire in the fireplace, a fact that amused him, and the down comforter lay on the high bed. He almost pulled it away, then thought better of it. He wouldn't need it.

But Laura might. When the time came for her to share the bed.

He stripped off his sodden clothes and tossed them over a chair, then glanced down at himself. It was the body he was used to. Strong, spare, without discernible weakness. It was a body men and women found attractive, and that was partly how he managed to persuade them to come with him. Those who needed persuading.

He wasn't sure about Laura. Whether she would need persuasion or force. Seduction, or simply the crook of his finger.

He knew only that he wanted her, needed her so badly that his self-control was close to shattering. Those voices crying to him wouldn't have long to wait.

Laura lay in bed, listening. She'd heard him on the balcony, and it had taken all her strength of will not to throw back the heavy covers and go to him. He was courting death out there in the freezing rain, and she wanted to bring him inside, to warm him, to find out what dark torments lay behind those mirrored sunglasses.

She didn't, of course. She knew all too well what Jeremy had said to him in his soft, mellifluous voice. If Alex had had any interest in her, it would have vanished instantly when Jeremy told him how sick she was.

But then, she'd already told him herself, and it hadn't seemed to shock him. Her father had always warned her of unscrupulous men who would come after her, try to seduce her, marry her, knowing that she would die and they would inherit her share of the

Fitzpatrick millions. Perhaps Alex was one of those. After all, what did she know about him? A French ski bum, appearing suddenly on the tightly patrolled slopes of Taylor Butte just as the world and the weather went haywire.

She thought she could feel something between the two of them. Some strand, some rope, of longing, of recognition. She was probably going crazy from the stress of William's last weeks and the demands of her own failing body. She had thought she would die tonight, alone in the forest. She'd felt the pain, the sudden cessation of breath and life and heartbeat, and when she looked up, she'd seen nothing but a clear white light.

And Alex, holding out a hand to her.

She hadn't taken that hand, a fact that stayed with her, oddly enough. She'd wanted to. With all her damaged heart, she'd wanted to.

But instead, she'd opened her eyes, struggled to her feet unaided and brought him home with her.

What would he do if she got out of bed and walked into his room? Would he welcome her into his bed? Would he expect knowledge and experience? Would he give her pleasure? Would she die?

She would never find out the answers to those questions. She would do as her family expected of her. She would die, sooner or later, a virgin, never knowing life or sex or passion. She would be a good girl, as the good Fitzpatricks expected her to be.

She punched the pillow, hard, before she turned over and went to sleep.

* * *

"You're up early." Laura poured herself a cup of herb tea, ignoring the tantalizing odor of dark-roasted coffee with a stoic effort. Her doctor had banned even decaffeinated coffee in the past few years, and the enticing scent was almost more torment than the sound of Alex had been, tossing in the bed beyond her wall.

Jeremy yawned, then rubbed his bristly jaw. "I fell asleep by Father's bed," he admitted. "Lucky for me, Cynthia isn't the type to worry."

Laura glanced out at the overcast morning. The wind still whipped through the treetops; the thunder still rumbled. "You've rather gone beyond that stage in your marriage, haven't you?" She took a scone, ignored the butter, and sat down next to her brother.

Jeremy managed a boyish smile as he drained his cup of fresh-ground coffee with unappreciative haste. "Well, we've actually been talking about a future."

Laura simply stared at him. "A future? You mean a reconciliation? I thought things were years past that."

Jeremy shrugged. "Life is full of possibilities, don't you think? On a morning like this, I feel incredibly alive. Like I could do just about anything I wanted."

Laura looked out at the stormy violence of the day, then back to her usually stolid older brother. "I think you should go down to the cottage and get some sleep," she said flatly. "I know why you stayed here, and I'm not very happy about it."

The change in his shallow blue eyes was startling, brief and oddly terrifying. "What do you mean?" he said in a completely expressionless voice.

"You wanted to play chaperon for me, didn't you? For some reason you thought I'd go traipsing off to bed with a perfect stranger, and you didn't even trust your heavy-handed warnings to make him keep his distance."

The tension vanished from his shoulders as swiftly as it had come. "You said he was an old friend," Jeremy murmured. "Not a stranger."

She wasn't used to lying. As a matter of fact, she didn't know where the lie had come from in the first place, or whether it was, indeed, a lie. Alex didn't feel like a stranger. He felt like part of her, and, in some strange, inexplicable way, bound to her past and her future. And now, suddenly, to her present, as well.

"I wasn't sure you believed me," she said, amazed at how easily she could prevaricate.

Jeremy reached out and put his hand over hers. It was a soft hand, with short, pudgy fingers, a hand that had never known a day's physical labor. "We're family, Laura," he said sweetly. "If not by blood, then by caring. We're the Fitzpatricks. We don't lie to each other."

She didn't move. She wanted to pull her hand away from his—an odd reaction, when physical touches were so scarce in her family that she'd always tried to cherish them. She let her hand rest beneath his and summoned up a semblance of a smile.

"It would be wonderful if you and Cynthia could manage to patch things up," she said, still not quite certain if she thought so.

"I'm ever hopeful," Jeremy said, releasing her hand to drain his coffee. "In the meantime, I think I'll grab a shower and a shave while I'm up here. The guest house has its own generator, but it's not as powerful as the one up here. Might as well save the hot water for the others." He rose, an affable expression on his face that suddenly froze when he looked past her shoulder to the door.

Laura didn't need to turn to guess who stood there. She'd felt his presence moments before, with an imperceptible tightening of her skin, a sudden, dangerous racing of her heart, a flush of heat across her face.

"Good morning," Alex said, his voice soft, husky, faintly accented.

"You're up early." Some of Jeremy's good cheer had swiftly vanished. "I thought the French slept late."

Alex's laugh was low and faintly derisive. "The French sleep however they wish to. I personally have little need of sleep."

The tension in the room was almost painful, and Laura dived in, determined to lighten things up. "Besides, Alex is a skier. They rise early so they don't miss the first runs. Or so I've been told."

God, what an incredibly stupid thing to say, she told herself, feeling the color flood her face.

"Very true, *ma chère,*" Alex murmured.

Laura turned to look at him. He was dressed all in black, his midnight hair tied back from his angular face. The mirrored sunglasses were firmly in place against the dim light of the day.

Jeremy stood there, rigid, unmoving, the empty cup in his hand, clearly loath to leave the two of them alone. Laura cleared her throat, but Jeremy didn't even spare her a glance—all his attention was trained on the man who'd just entered the room.

"Do you mind if I pour myself a cup of coffee?" Alex asked.

"Help yourself to anything," Laura said firmly. "And weren't you going to take a shower, Jeremy?"

"I can wait," her brother said stubbornly.

"Don't you think Cynthia might be worried about where you were last night?"

Jeremy gave himself a little shake, and his laughter sounded only slightly hollow. "You're right, of course. I won't be gone long."

If Alex heard the warning in Jeremy's voice, he chose to ignore it. He sat down next to Laura, a mug of coffee in one of his elegant, long-fingered hands. He placed a second mug of coffee in front of her.

She looked up at him, biting her lip. "I don't drink coffee," she said.

"You don't like it?"

"I love it. My heart can't take it. The doctors say even decaffeinated coffee has too much stimulant for my heart, and this is high-test. Mrs. Hawkins doesn't make coffee for wimps."

"Do you want it?"

"Yes."

"Then drink it."

She reached for it. The heat from the coffee warmed the handle of the mug, and she wanted it almost as much as she wanted him.

"Are you trying to kill me?" she asked, attempting to keep her voice light and humorous. It came out dead serious.

He shook his head, and she could see her reflection in the sunglasses. She looked pale, vulnerable, longing. "Nothing will harm you today," he said.

She believed him. She took a drink of the coffee, the bitter, smoky taste of it dancing on her tongue. And when she set the cup down she looked at him, feeling the energy dance through her veins.

He reached out and touched her, putting his cool fingers against her flushed cheek in a faint, almost experimental caress. Almost as if he were afraid it might hurt her.

She smiled at him, feeling the slight tremor in her lips, in her heart. "You see," he murmured. "Nothing will hurt you today."

She stared at him, breathless, as he moved closer, his cool, cool fingers stroking her cheek. His lips were damp from the coffee, as were hers, and she wondered what French roast coffee would taste like on the mouth of a French man. She knew she was about to find out.

His lips were cool, as well. Cool, damp, a faint, almost tentative pressure against her own firmly closed ones. He drew back, and she stared at him. And at her own reflection in his mirrored glasses.

"Open your mouth for me, Laura," he whispered. It was not a request.

She obeyed. His mouth covered hers, open, wet, possessive, and she tasted his tongue. She didn't know whether she would have pulled away, but his fingers had threaded through her hair, holding her head in place, and he deepened the kiss into a long, thorough caress of tongue and teeth and lips, heart and soul, enticing her, seducing her, until she caught her breath and kissed him back, letting him lure her tongue forward, dancing with his, the intimacy shocking, arousing, devastating.

When he pulled away from her, his hand was still tight in her hair. She opened her eyes to stare up at his mirrored face. "Is that why they call it French-kissing?" she asked dazedly.

He laughed then. The sound was soft, surprising, almost unbearably intimate. "Did you like it?"

"Yes."

"Do you want more?"

"Yes." The word was a sibilant sound in the quiet morning, and he moved closer again, his mouth hovering over hers.

The scream that tore through the house was blood-curdling in its horror. High-pitched, a hollow, keening, sexless wail of such abject terror that Laura tore herself away from Alex, knocking the coffee over as she jumped up. The liquid spread like a black stain, soaking into the white tablecloth, spilling onto Laura's jeans, burning her.

"Oh, God," she moaned, barely aware of her burned flesh. "It sounds as if someone died."

"I doubt it," Alex said in a dry voice. And he rose, taking her hand. "Shall we see?"

CHAPTER FIVE

Jeremy stood in the hallway, his color ashen. He was staring at the front door with an expression of abject horror, but the three people crowding inside the tiled entryway were too busy arguing to pay much attention to him.

"That damned heating system," Ricky grumbled. "I just about froze last night. Why the hell it picked last night to malfunction is beyond me. And then you have to scare the life out of me by screaming like a banshee! What the hell's gotten into you, Jeremy?"

"At least you had someone to sleep with," Cynthia said with a malicious purr, glaring at her husband. "A little body warmth must have made a difference."

"It would have if I'd been sleeping with someone other than Justine. She's about as cozy as an ice maiden." He glanced over at Jeremy, and his eyes narrowed. "What's wrong with you, man? You look like you've seen a ghost."

"It's Father," Justine cried in a piteous mew. "He's dead, isn't he?"

Laura moved swiftly, pushing past her motionless older brother, wrapping her arms around Justine's narrow shoulders. "He's still holding his own, Jussie. As a matter of fact, I looked in on him before breakfast, and Maria said he'd had a very peaceful night."

"Then what's wrong with Jeremy?" Cynthia murmured, moving closer.

Jeremy managed a rough laugh. "Nothing," he said. "I'm a little spooked, I guess. I don't like being cut off up here."

"Cut off?" Ricky echoed.

"Trees are blocking the road. The radio and telephone are still out. Not to mention the TV. We're isolated up here on the mountain, and it gets on my nerves." He moved toward the door, and Laura noticed a curious stiffness to his gait. "I'm going down to shower and change. I spent the night sitting up with Father. I'll see if I can figure out what's wrong with the heating system."

"Don't we have servants who take care of that sort of thing?" Ricky drawled.

"They're on the other side of the fallen trees," Jeremy snapped.

"Besides, Jeremy's always been terrific at mechanical things," Laura said, jumping in to try to soothe the tense atmosphere. "Father always used to say it was proof..." Her voice trailed off as she realized what she'd been about to say.

"Yes," Jeremy murmured, and there was no missing the twist of bitterness in his voice. "He always said it was proof I didn't carry any of the glorious Fitzpatrick blood in my veins. If my mother hadn't married him, I could have had a very happy life as a plumber."

Laura bit her lip. "You know I didn't mean that, Jeremy."

He shrugged, a wry expression on his usually bland face. "Don't worry about it, Laura. I stopped being offended by your father's gibes years ago."

It must have been the weather. The strange, stormy ether in the air or the tension that clung to them all, that suddenly made Jeremy's humorous excuse ring false. Laura glanced up, over her shoulder, to Alex. He was standing apart, watching them, rather as a scientist might observe a tribe of interesting bugs. The unexpectedly strong notion sent a chill of foreboding dancing across Laura's backbone.

"Well, go or stay," Cynthia snapped. "But make up your mind. I'm freezing to death." She cast a measuring glance toward Alex, letting her eyes drift past Laura for a brief, dismissing moment. "In the meantime, I'm bored, and I'm afraid it's up to you to entertain me, Alex. I'm sure Ricky's mainly interested in how much whiskey he can sneak into his coffee cup, and Justine's frightened of her own shadow. You and I can play blackjack for impossible stakes."

Laura held her breath, waiting. She wanted him with her, not the mesmerizing Cynthia. She wasn't sure what she longed for. A continuation of that too-brief, devastating kiss? Or escape from something too powerful for her to handle?

"Why don't you and Laura see if you can help Mrs. Hawkins?" Jeremy suggested. "With the road closed, she's shorthanded."

Cynthia cast a scathing look at her husband. "Sorry, darling, but Laura's even more tedious than you are. The poor girl's lived like a nun, and everything she knows she's learned in books. We hardly have a thing in common."

"True enough," Ricky drawled. "You've never read a book in your life, and I bet you were a tramp by the time you were twelve."

"Not getting enough, Ricky?" Cynthia cooed, unmoved by his insults. "Sorry, but I'm no longer interested in charity cases." She moved past him. She was dressed in a garnet velour catsuit that clung to her curves, and she stopped in front of Alex, her mane of blond hair rippling down her back as she stared up at him. "Do you like to gamble, Alex?"

Laura held her breath, wickedly longing for a put-down. But what man had ever been able to resist Cynthia's wiles when she focused them? "It depends on the stakes," he said, and his faint accent and husky tone made the words sound deeply erotic.

Cynthia's smile widened. "How delightful. You don't mind if I steal him, do you, Laura? I'm certain you have a million things to do."

"Of course," she said in a cool voice. "A million books to read."

Laura turned away, starting to move past them, and the unexpected threat of tears stung the backs of her eyelids. She didn't want them to see—she didn't want *Alex* to see—and she moved quickly, clumsily, toward the door.

It must have been an accident. The back of his hand brushed against hers as she went, and his skin was cool, firm, an odd caress so brief it must have been a mistake. And yet that momentary touch sent a thousand thoughts soaring through her, and there was no way she could believe where they'd come from. Except that she knew. They came from him. An apology. An assurance that all would be well.

She didn't want to hear apologies, assurances, but they slid into her subconsciousness through his touch, and she couldn't fight them. She had already moved past, out of reach, and she wanted to turn around, to catch his hand and take him with her. To warn Cynthia to keep her hands off him.

It was childish and absurd. If she'd been less troubled, it would have been amusing. As it was, she was barely able to summon a smile. And as her lips curved, she remembered the cool delight of his mouth against hers, and she shivered.

"There's coffee and breakfast in the dining room," she said with creditable calm. "I think I'll go check on Father."

Cynthia had already laid claim to Alex's arm. "Don't worry about our guest, Laura. I promise I'll keep him entertained."

He wasn't quite sure what he was expecting from the woman. She felt the coldness of his touch far more acutely than Laura did. She minded it, but she couldn't seem to keep her hands away from him.

He had no qualms about letting her experiment. He knew now that her voice had been one of those calling to him last night. For some reason, her appointment with death had been moved up, unnaturally, and he wondered idly what had caused the change. It wasn't of great importance to him. When the time came for him to return, he would take those who were still ready. Those whose reprieves seemed justified could wait their turn.

She drew him into a room he hadn't seen before, some kind of study, and she closed the door behind them and flicked on the overhead light. The glow was dim, and he suspected the generator might be failing. It made little difference to him, but it might bother Laura. He didn't want Laura bothered.

But he knew she was very angry with him right now. The emotion had sung through her skin, stinging him, and he'd had time for only the briefest of reassuring touches. She didn't know what he was trying to spare her.

This woman might serve as a substitute. Perhaps she could provide the answers he sought, perhaps she could quiet the emptiness inside him. And then Laura could wait a little longer.

Cynthia put her hand on his thigh. She had attractive hands, adorned with expensive rings. Experienced hands. He leaned back on the sofa and watched her from behind the mirrored sunglasses, curious as to how far she intended to go.

"I like playing dangerous games," she cooed, moving close to him. Her scent was dark and musky, erotic. "Anyone might walk in here at any time. You know that, don't you? They know we're in here, and they'll probably leave us alone. Unless Laura gets too annoyed. I'm sure you know she's got a crush on you, Alex. I've never seen it before—little Laura is usually too saintly for human passions. Her family has seen to *that*, as well." Her hand trailed higher, and he watched it curiously, anticipating.

"But you're quite an interesting man, aren't you? You make us poor women throw caution to the winds." She rose to her knees on the couch, hovering over him, and he could see the hardness of her nipples. "You're so cold," she whispered. "Let me warm you up." And she put her mouth against his.

She was very practiced. He could appreciate her technique, both with her mouth and her hand as it claimed him. His body responded as a normal body would, but that dark, quiet part of him remained unmoved. He could push her down on the couch and have her, and she would scream with pleasure. Loud enough for Laura to hear, of course.

He would do it. It would hurt Laura, but it would also spare her. He touched Cynthia's plump breast, and she shivered, drawing back, a triumphant smile on her pink mouth. "I thought you might be interested," she purred. "Take off your sunglasses," she said in a husky voice, unzipping her catsuit with shaking fingers. "I want to look into your eyes when you make love to me."

She'd pushed the soft velour down around her elbows, baring her torso, baring her breasts. He stared at her through the sunglasses and tried to tell himself that he wanted her.

But he didn't.

It was a simple enough matter to drive her away. He reached for the mirrored sunglasses and took them off.

The thud when her body hit the floor was muffled by the thick Oriental carpet. She looked absurd, sprawled there in a dead faint, her jumpsuit halfway off her lush body. If he'd had an ounce of kindness in him, he would have pulled her clothes back around her, propped her up on the sofa and left her to regain consciousness.

But he wasn't feeling particularly kind. He rose, putting the sunglasses back over his eyes. And, stepping over Cynthia's unconscious figure, he went in search of Laura.

The odd thing was, she'd never felt more alive. Last night when she'd lain in the forest, gasping for breath, she'd looked up and seen the bright white light and known. Known that Death, who had always hovered so closely, was reaching for her. She'd denied him too long.

But instead it had been Alex, looking down at her from behind his mirrored sunglasses, and life had come surging back, as she'd never felt it before.

She felt strong. Invulnerable. Fearless. Nothing could hurt her—she was charmed, safe, protected. And she couldn't rid herself of the notion that it was Alex, the stranger, who was protecting her.

She moved slowly down the winding path, her feet scuffling through the fallen pine needles. Overhead the sky was dark and stormy, the tops of the trees swayed in the angry wind. There was a chill in the air, a bite that promised a long, cold winter. And yet, all around her, plants still bloomed.

She hadn't been able to bring herself to stay in the house a moment longer. She knew Cynthia far too well—if she hadn't managed to seduce Alex by now, then it was only a matter of time. It didn't matter that Alex didn't seem the type to be seduced by Cynthia's obvious machinations. He'd gone with her willingly.

Laura paused by an aspen. The yellow leaves had been drifting down for days, but right now the remaining few clung stubbornly to the wind-tossed branches. She stared out over the golden hillside, bright against the dark sky, and took a deep, shaky breath. She'd always loved autumn best. It didn't matter that winter was coming, the long, endless darkness. For her there had always seemed to be hope and beauty in the fall, not in the spring.

She shook her head. It was no wonder she was getting fanciful. The freak storm was unnerving. The inevitable death of her father was even more shattering. And the advent of Alex in their enclave was the final disruption.

She couldn't rid herself of the feeling that nothing was as it seemed. Not with Alex nor with her family. Not with her. She felt strong, invulnerable, for the first time in her life. And yet she knew that twelve hours ago she'd been closer to death than she'd ever been.

She heard the noise from a distance, and she tensed, her instincts suddenly alert. Whoever was approaching from the house was a stranger, dangerous to her and all she cared about. It had to be Alex, the only stranger there, but she didn't think it was. She leaned back against the tree, holding very still, readying herself to dart into the teeming undergrowth at any moment.

Jeremy loomed into view, and she breathed a sigh of relief and surprise. It was nothing dangerous after all. "You scared me," she called out to him, her voice light and faintly teasing.

His response was a bland smile. "I don't tend to have that effect on people. What are you doing out here, Laura?"

"Going for a walk. I wanted to get out of the house for a bit. I felt . . . crowded."

"I know what you mean," he said gloomily. "Cynthia will never change. I don't know if there's a future for us after all."

"Jeremy..."

"But that's not why I followed you down here. You're the one I'm worried about," he said, his voice earnest. "I don't trust that man, Laura. I don't like the fact that he showed up here out of nowhere. I don't like the fact that he's been stalking you."

"Stalking me? Don't be ridiculous—no one's stalking anyone. Aren't you letting your feelings about Cynthia cloud your judgment?"

"Don't you think it's a little strange that he showed up just when we got cut off from the outside world?"

Laura managed a hollow laugh. "He doesn't control the weather, Jeremy."

"Something strange is going on, I can feel it. Something very odd. Those news reports, about people not dying. I don't like it."

"Don't like the fact that people aren't dying?" Laura echoed. "You're not making any sense." She stared at her stepbrother for a long, troubled moment. "Is there something else going on, Jeremy? Something you want to tell me?"

His own laugh was suddenly hearty. And annoyingly false to her ears. "I'm just being melodramatic," he said. "That's what comes of being trapped up here, then staying up all night. Lack of sleep will do you in."

"Maybe you should take a nap," she suggested quietly.

"Maybe I will. But I want you to promise me something. Keep away from him. I have a very bad feeling about him. He's trouble, Laura. Trouble for you, trouble for all of us."

"You're being ridiculous, Jeremy. He's harmless. A French ski bum with a lot of charm and not much money. He isn't going to hurt a soul."

"You find him charming? I don't."

Laura thought about it. The cool, mesmerizing power that flowed from him, that seemed to travel directly to her. The feel of his mouth against hers. He made her feel alive, she thought again. Pulsingly, heart-poundingly alive, as she'd never been before.

"The weather will clear, Jeremy," she said, in a deliberately calm voice. "Alex will be on his way, and you and Cynthia can try to work things out. Don't worry about me. I've already accepted the fact that I'm only going to have a limited life, and that doesn't include passionate interludes with strangers any more than it includes grandchildren or little country cottages with white picket fences. I've learned to accept what I have and leave it at that. When Alex leaves, everything will be as it was."

"What if he asks you to go with him?"

The flash of anger that swept through her shocked Laura. She wasn't used to rage, to fighting against the inevitable. "He's not going to," she snapped. "There's no reason why he'd want to burden himself with a woman who's dying."

"When that woman stands to inherit a third of her father's estate, he would."

"Flattery will get you nowhere," she said dryly. "It *is* possible for someone to be attracted to me, you know."

"Is he attracted to you?"

"No," she lied, remembering the kiss.

"And you don't look like a woman who's dying," Jeremy added with unusual frankness. "You look better than I've ever seen you. Your color's good, you've got more energy."

"Must be something in the air."

"It's keeping Father alive."

"It's keeping everyone alive, Jeremy. But it's not going to last, and you know it. I'm not going to last, either, but flirting with a stranger isn't going to make me die any sooner."

"You admit it?"

"That I've been flirting? Just a little bit. It's fun," she added.

"I want you to promise me you'll keep away from him. I don't trust him."

"Jeremy," she said with great patience, "I'm not going to promise you anything except that I'll take care of myself. That's all you really have a right to ask."

"If you don't keep away from him, then I'll have to do something about it."

She stared at him, and it was like looking at a stranger. The bluff, cheerful man she'd known all her life was nowhere near the pale, angry man who stood before her, eyes bulging, veins standing out. He looked like a man on the edge, and it wouldn't take much to push him over.

"Jeremy," she said gently, "get some sleep."

"I'm warning you." His voice trailed after her as she started back up the steep path. She wanted to run, and yet she knew she didn't dare. Running across a relatively level surface last night had almost killed her.

Even making her way slowly up the steep hillside would put untold strain on her heart.

She turned a corner, which put her out of Jeremy's view, and quickened her pace. She waited for the breath to catch in her chest, waited for the dull, omnipresent pain to sharpen. But she could feel no pain. The air was pumping through her lungs, the blood pumping through her heart, as if they weren't the damaged organs she knew them to be.

She moved faster. The wind rippled through the trees, tossing her long hair behind her, and she could feel the dampness of autumn on the heels of the breeze. Faster still, the energy spiking through her, soaring, faster and faster, until she was running, freely, effortlessly, up the steepest part of the incline, and a laugh rippled out of her throat, dancing over the countryside.

She saw him then, standing at the edge of the clearing, watching her. Waiting for her, as the restless light reflected off his dark glasses. He waited for her, alone, Cynthia nowhere in sight.

She came to a halt a few feet away from him. She was out of breath, flushed, and feeling dangerous herself. She thought of her stepbrother, with his threats and warnings. She thought of her shortened life, and she looked up at the man who stood there, waiting for her.

Again she felt that odd shiver of memory. She knew him. But she couldn't remember where or when she'd seen him before. He was a part of her life, a part of her, and yet she couldn't say how.

She knew only one thing about him. There was nothing to be afraid of. He wouldn't harm her.

Whether that extended to everyone, she didn't know. But the man in black, standing there in the storm-tossed shadows, would never hurt her.

"Do you believe in love at first sight?" she asked him, her breath caught in a small gasp.

"You might as well ask whether I believe in love at all," he countered softly.

"Do you?"

"I'm not sure. Perhaps for some creatures. In some circumstances. If one is very lucky."

"Are you one of the lucky ones?"

"No," he said gently. "And neither are you."

It was like a slap across the face. She stared at him for a long moment and saw the trace of Cynthia's coral lipstick on the side of his neck. The sudden clenching pain in her chest had nothing to do with her damaged heart and everything to do with her soul.

"True enough," she said brightly, after a moment. "In the meantime, I'd better check on my father." She moved past him, concentrating on maintaining a calm grace.

He reached out a hand to stop her, to touch her, but she managed to avoid him. He didn't pursue the effort, just followed her at a secure distance. "Are you worried he might have died while you went for your walk?"

She paused at the French doors that led in from the rough-hewn deck. "No," she said, staring at her reflection in his sunglasses. "No one's going to die for the time being. Are they?"

"How would I know?" he asked at last, breaking the silence.

"How stupid of me," she murmured. "You wouldn't have anything to do with it, would you?"

His smile was pale, cool, bewilderingly gentle. "Not at the moment," he said. And he put his hand on her elbow, and the force of the current they created shot between them.

"Who are you?" she whispered, unable to move.

He leaned closer, and she lifted her face to his, wanting his mouth again. Needing it.

"There you are, Miss Laura." Mrs. Hawkins's voice shattered the faint, dreamy mood as she appeared at the end of the hallway, an old dish towel in one hand. "Your father's been asking for you. Quite agitated, he is. Maria said to find you as quick as can be."

"Is he going?"

"Not so's I could tell. He wants to talk to you, though, and I don't think getting worked up will do him any good. You go on in, and I'll get Alex here a cup of coffee. There never was a Frenchman who could resist a good cup of coffee."

Laura waited for him to protest, but he said not a word. His hand dropped from her arm, and she felt burned, frozen. "Go see him, Laura," he said softly. "Maybe he'll have the answers to your questions."

But Laura wasn't quite sure she wanted to hear them.

CHAPTER SIX

William Fitzpatrick lay still and silent in the bed. Only the steady chirp and beat of the machines gave the lie to the appearance of death, and Laura moved quietly to his bedside, loath to disturb him.

The crepey, blue-veined eyelids shot open, and her father fixed her with the piercing look that had terrified her in her childhood. It still had the power to make her feel very young and very helpless.

"Why did you bring him here?" he demanded in a mere rasp of a whisper.

She didn't pretend to misunderstand. "I ran into him on the mountain," she said, trying to keep the defensiveness out of her voice. "I'd fallen, I was afraid I was dying, and then...he was there. He brought me back here, Father. Instead of you and Jeremy being so distrustful, you ought to thank him."

"Thank him?" William echoed in a hoarse laugh. "That'll be the day. Don't you know who he is? What he wants?"

She put her hand on his forehead. He was hot, feverish, and his faded eyes were burning with determination and something akin to madness. "He's no one," she murmured soothingly, stroking his brow. "A ski bum. He doesn't want anything but fresh powder."

"You're almost as stupid as your siblings," William snapped, with a trace of his usual malice. "He's fooled you, but he can't fool me. I *know* him. I've wrestled him too many times. I'm not going to let him win now."

Laura cast a desperate glance around the room. There was no sign of Maria, and her father's mind was clearly wandering, increasingly delirious, even though his body seemed uncharacteristically strong. "He won't win, Father," she said in a soothing voice.

"Don't patronize me. You think I'm off my head, don't you? I may be dying, but that doesn't mean I'm crazy. I know who he is, I tell you. I know what he wants."

"What does he want, Father?" she asked calmly.

"You. He's come to kill you."

Laura's gentle smile didn't waver. "I can't imagine why. He doesn't even know me."

"You don't understand!" Her father was getting more agitated by the second, and the monitoring systems began to chirp louder, faster, more erratically. "That's what he does. That's who he is. He's—"

"What's going on in here?" Maria bustled in, the picture of sturdy efficiency. "You calm down, Mr. Fitzpatrick, and don't say another word! You're agitating yourself, and if you want your poor daughter to stand there and watch you die, then just keep on the way you are."

"I'm going to die anyway," he said sulkily, leaning back. His color was a sickly gray, and he looked like Death himself, Laura thought.

"We all are, sooner or later," Maria said briskly, checking his pulse. "There's no need to hurry it along.

If the good Lord saw fit to grant you a reprieve, then you take it and be grateful.''

"Ha!" William Fitzpatrick snorted, but the sound was a hollow travesty. "I don't think the good Lord had a damned thing to do with it."

"Not another word, Mr. Fitzpatrick. Laura, why don't you go have a cup of herb tea or something? Leave this grumpy old man to get some rest."

Her father opened his eyes for a moment, staring at her malevolently. "Yes. Go away, Laura. Don't worry, I'm not going to pop off without any warning."

"I don't think anyone is," she murmured, half to herself.

Maria looked at her oddly, but William missed her cryptic statement. "Anyway," he continued, "I'm not ready to go yet. I promise you'll get to hold my hand and weep over my corpse. Unless your new friend has something to say about it."

"There are times, Father, when you are completely impossible," Laura said with affectionate exasperation, leaning over and placing a gentle kiss on his wrinkled forehead. "I'll come back when you've decided you don't want to bait me any longer."

"Knowing him, it might be a long wait," Maria muttered under her breath.

The dining room was deserted. Laura had lost track of time, and it gave her an odd shock to realize that it was already early afternoon. The remnants of a luncheon still lined the buffet table, and she instinctively went for the carafe of coffee. After all, she'd survived one cup without the slightest ill effects. Any racing of her heart had come from Alex, not caffeine.

She might as well live dangerously, she thought, pouring herself a cup. She took it with her as she wandered down the hallway in search of her family. She'd left Jeremy down in the woods, but she still had no idea where the others were. Ricky was probably drinking, Justine weeping, and Cynthia? What was Cynthia doing?

The door to the library was still closed, and Laura paused outside. If she had any sense at all, she would take her coffee up to her room and not even think about what lay on the other side of the door.

But she'd never been a coward. She didn't bother to knock. She simply turned the handle, pushing the door inward.

There were no lights on, and the murky sunlight barely infiltrated the shadows. At first she thought the room was empty. And then she saw Cynthia, huddled in a corner, her arms wrapped tightly around her knees, her pale face streaked with tears and runny makeup.

Laura forgot her jealousy. The hot coffee sloshed over her hand as she slammed the mug down on a table. Within seconds she was kneeling on the floor next to Cynthia, pulling her sister-in-law's unresisting body into her arms.

"What happened, Cynthia?" she murmured.

The room was warm, almost hot. Cynthia's body felt ice-cold, and she was shaking so hard Laura could barely hold her. Cynthia's teeth were chattering, and her attempts at speech were just a helpless stuttering.

"Did someone hurt you?" Laura persisted. "Was it Alex?"

Cynthia let out a small moan, burying her head against Laura's shoulder. A moment later, electric light blazed through the room, and Jeremy stood there, his face in shadows. "I'll take care of her," he said in a long-suffering voice.

Cynthia jerked, burrowing closer to Laura as if looking for a safe haven, and Laura's arms tightened around her. "Something's happened, Jeremy," she said. "Something frightened her."

"I can imagine what. Now do you believe me when I tell you that man is dangerous?"

"Don't be ridiculous!" Laura snapped back. "He didn't hurt her."

Jeremy reached down for his trembling wife. Cynthia tried to resist, but he simply pulled her upward, pushing Laura out of the way. "She'll be all right. I'll take her back to the guest house and get some hot tea into her. She could do with a nap. Don't worry, Cynthia. I'll take care of you."

Cynthia looked up at her husband of more than ten years, and her expression was one of complete horror. Before Laura could intervene, however, Jeremy had half helped, half dragged her from the room.

Laura watched them go, feeling helpless, frightened, confused. Nothing was as it had seemed. Not her autocratic father, not the fearless, amoral Cynthia, not the stolid, dependable Jeremy.

And certainly not the stranger who'd appeared on their mountain just as the rest of the world was shut away from them.

She slammed her bedroom door behind her, then locked it. She had no idea where Alex was, and she didn't want to know. She locked the French doors that led out to the small balcony their two rooms shared, and then she lay on her bed, bundling under a down comforter. The coldness was permeating the entire house; the lights were dimming, and outside, the storm was increasing in its intensity. It seemed as if the world were about to end. Laura pulled the covers over her head, shuddering, prepared to ride it out.

Poison was far more dangerous, Jeremy thought calmly as he put the mug of arsenic-laced tea in Cynthia's trembling hands. There would be an autopsy, and there was no way a toxicologist would miss the huge amounts of poison he was pumping into her system.

But he couldn't afford to wait. Or to make another miscalculation.

It was fortunate for him that Cynthia had had her fit of hysterics in front of his gullible stepsister. He had no idea what had set Cynthia off, and he didn't care. While a part of him thoroughly enjoyed the expression of abject terror in his wife's eyes whenever she looked at him, he couldn't afford to indulge himself. If Cynthia had inexplicably come to suspect him, it wouldn't take long before that suspicion was passed to others.

He would make it look like a suicide. She'd been restless, despondent, drinking too much. She'd had a nervous breakdown right in front of her fragile sister-in-law. The strangeness of the weather, the isolation, her despondency over her failing marriage—it was no wonder she'd succumbed to thoughts of suicide and taken a fatal dose of rat poison.

There would be less money for him this way. If only
Ricky and Justine had died as planned, it would all
have been his. But he was resourceful. He'd been
willing to wait for Laura's share, secure in the knowledge that she hadn't long to live. He could certainly
manage some misfortune for Justine and Ricky in the
next year or so.

And *then* it would all be his. The money. And the
knowledge that he'd been stronger, more determined,
than all of them. His only regret was that he would
never get the chance to throw it in the old man's face.

"Drink it all, darling," he urged gently, feeling
wonderfully calm and encouraging. After last night's
unexpected failure, things were finally coming together. All the old man had to do was hold on for a
few more hours, and then at least Cynthia's inheri-
tance would be his.

If he hadn't known better, though, he would have
thought Cynthia knew what was going to happen to
her. There was a bleak, terrified expression on her
face, as if she'd looked into the future and seen her
death. If she had, it wasn't enough to stop her fate.
She took the mug of poisoned tea from him and
drained it, then leaned back against the pillows and
closed her eyes.

He closed the door gently behind him. He hadn't
had time to concoct a suicide note, but he could take
care of that later if the need arose. In the meantime,
it was only a matter of minutes before he was free.

He carried the tray back into the kitchen, humming
under his breath.

* * *

When Laura awoke, her room was pitch-black. There was a faint tapping noise, a clicking against the windows, and it took her a moment to realize it must be the rain. Or even sleet, considering the icy, metallic click against the glass. She reached for the light beside her bed, but it wouldn't turn on. The generator must have finally given up the ghost, she thought, swinging her legs out from under the down comforter.

She almost swung them back. The room was ice-cold—the heating system must be down, as well. With luck, there would still be enough juice in the auxiliary generator to keep William's life-support system functioning, but there was obviously nothing to spare.

She should go downstairs and make sure everything was all right. That there were fires burning in the myriad of fireplaces that were usually more for atmosphere than function. That her father was still alive, that Cynthia had recovered from whatever had panicked her. She should see if Mrs. Hawkins needed help, or if any new disaster had befallen the Fitzpatrick compound. But she knew she wasn't going to do anything.

She reached into her nightstand drawer for the tiny flashlight she always kept there, turning it on. It remained stubbornly dark, and she shook it in frustration. She'd just put fresh batteries in a week ago—they must have been duds.

There were a pine-scented candle and a box of matches on the mantel overhanging her fireplace. She stubbed her toe as she made her way across the pitch-black room, and all the time the wind outside was growing louder, wilder, and the ice particles dashing against the window grew noisier.

The match flared, and the candle sent a tiny pool of light into the room. She knelt down, using the candle to light the kindling that was always in readiness in the hearth, then stood back as light and warmth began to fill the room.

A streak of lightning blazed outside, filling the room with a blinding glare before plunging it into darkness once more. It was followed by a clap of thunder so powerful it shook the sturdy log house, and Laura dropped the candle, watching as it rolled across the floor, landing against the French doors before guttering out.

Once more lightning flashed, and she could see him outside, his long hair caked with ice, his shirt plastered to his strong back. He was holding on to the railing, staring out into the night, and Laura watched in both fascination and despair as he seemed to reach into the night, becoming a part of it. She half expected him to leap off the balcony, to hurl himself into the darkness, and she stood, transfixed with pain and longing.

They were plunged into darkness once more, and finally Laura moved. She'd put a chair under the door handle in addition to locking it, and it took a moment for her to pull it away and fumble with the latch before flinging open the French doors. Letting in the night and the storm. Letting in the man.

He turned. Ice coated his face and his dark glasses and frosted his hair. The late-summer night had turned to winter, and she reached out for him, pulling him

back inside, into her room, shutting the storm outside.

She caught his icy shirt in her hands and was trying
to strip it off him when he stopped her, his hands covering hers, holding them still. And despite the chill of
his flesh, he was hot, desperately hot, burning against
her skin.

"You should never have let me in," he said in a
whisper. "Send me away."

For a moment, time seemed to stand still. It would
be so easy, she thought, to pull her hands free, to step
back. He would leave her then, and she would never
have anything more to fear. He would leave her, and
she would be alone.

"Why?" Her response was barely a breath.

"Because if you don't send me away, I'll take you.
And there will be no turning back."

She heard the words, the threat, the promise, with
her heart and her soul. The blatant sexuality of it. And
something more, besides.

He wouldn't take her untutored body. He wouldn't
take her innocence, her love, and her passion. He
would take far more than that.

He would take her soul.

Run. The word echoed in her head. *Run away, fast.*
And she knew the words came from him, as well as
her.

"I can't," she said, answering the unspoken plea.
"I've waited too long for you. I love you." And she
pulled her hands out of his restraining grasp, slid them
up his arms and began to pull off his ice-coated shirt.

He didn't stop her this time. He stood perfectly still
beneath her hands, and the flicker of the fire reflected

on the mirrored lenses of his dark glasses. She pulled the shirt free from his pants, and her arms went around him. She found herself pressed up tight against him, the hard sinew and muscle and bone, the icy heat of him. For a moment her heart clenched in longing; then it began pounding, fast, hard, as she stared up at him.

"Who are you?" she asked, one last time.

"A bad dream," he whispered. "A nightmare." And his mouth covered hers.

The ice had melted from his face, his lips, his hair. He kissed her with a ferocity that should have terrified her, but she was past terror, past second thoughts. She wanted to kiss him back, but she wasn't sure how. Then his thumbs cupped her jaw and gently opened her mouth for him.

He used his tongue as he had that morning. He taught her how to use her tongue, as well, to give, as well as to receive, and when he thrust his tongue into her mouth, her knees buckled.

He caught her effortlessly in his strong arms, holding her as she swayed against him. His mouth left hers to trail down the side of her neck, and then she felt herself swung dizzily in the air.

He took her through the night and the darkness, through the storm and the ice. He carried her back to his room, to the wide bed, and set her down. She lay back, staring up at him, and he was leaning over her, silhouetted in the darkness with only the flicker of the firelight piercing the gloom. Like the flames of hell, she thought as his hands slid up the front of her sweater, reaching for the buttons.

She watched him as he stripped off her clothes, deftly, efficiently, and she couldn't rid herself of the feeling that there was a grim purpose to his actions. That this was something he needed to do. Even though he regretted it.

She was so caught up in that odd sensation that she barely noticed the disappearance of her clothes. He leaned back and stared at her, and even through the mirrored lenses she could feel the heat of his gaze.

Suddenly she was self-conscious. She was too thin, too pale, too unfeminine, to please him, to—

As if he could read her thoughts, he stopped them, with the simple expedient of covering her naked body with his. His pants were cool and damp against her legs, his chest was strong and smooth, and she could feel him against her stomach, hard, wanting her.

"I should tell you . . ." she began breathlessly, but he put his hand on her breast, his long, cool fingers cupping it, and the sensation was so powerful that her voice trailed off in a strangled cry.

"I should explain . . ." she began again, but his fingertips encircled her nipple, tugging at her, and she felt the fiery reaction in a straight line down to the burning place between her legs.

"I should tell you . . ." she said—one final attempt—when his mouth closed over the tight bud of her breast, and she let out a soft, strangled wail.

She struggled to keep some portion of her mind intact. He was icy-cold, fiery-hot, and he lay between her legs as if he belonged there. She reached down to the waistband of his pants, pushing at them in mindless frustration, and from somewhere she felt his amusement.

He rose up, kneeling between her legs, and even in the flickering firelight she could see his hands reach down to the row of tiny buttons that strained over the front of his groin.

"Tell me what, Laura?" he asked, flicking the buttons open one by one.

She swallowed, suddenly panicked. "That I'm ... that is, they were afraid ..."

He released himself into the night, and if she hadn't been frightened before, she would have panicked then.

As it was, she was beyond panic. She lay beneath him, staring up in mute fear and trust.

"You're a virgin," he said, "and they were afraid that if you made love you would die. Is that it?"

She nodded.

He leaned forward, sliding his hands up her torso to cover her breasts, and the sensation was the sweetest torment. "Are you afraid of death, Laura?" he whispered against her mouth.

She found she'd been clutching the sheet beneath her. It was a simple enough question, with an obvious response. But she didn't want the obvious, she wanted the truth. And for some odd reason, she knew that her answer mattered terribly.

"No," she said, with no doubt whatsoever. "I'm not afraid of death."

"Then let me show you life," he said. And, moving down, he put his mouth between her legs.

Her reaction was so powerful and immediate that she tried to jerk away, but his hands cradled her hips, holding her there, as he used his mouth, his tongue, his teeth, driving her down a dark, narrow path that she'd never taken before.

The trembling began deep inside. She clutched his shoulders, her heels digging into the mattress as a rush of sensations swept over her. She was gasping for breath, her entire body in an ever-tightening knot, and she needed something more, but she wasn't sure exactly what.

The first wave hit her, a spasm of reaction that sent starbursts dancing behind her eyes. The second wave came, harder and stronger, and from a distance she could hear a gasping sob that had to be her own.

Before the tremors had died away he moved up, over her, between her legs, thrusting deep, breaking past the fear and the fragile barrier of her innocence, deep and hard and sure, and his hand covered her mouth, muffling her cry.

There were footsteps outside her locked door. A slow, measured pace. They lay in still, absolute silence, his body deep within hers, as the sound of those footsteps slowly died away.

He started to pull away from her, and she clutched at him, aware of a sudden, desperate panic. But he thrust again, deeper still, his pace slow, deliberate, driving her farther, deeper, faster, until she felt a new trembling begin to take over, and she knew that nothing mattered but this.

He thrust deep, so deep, and she felt a shudder ripple through his body. It hit her then, with the force of a mindless eternity, a pulsing, throbbing explosion so deep and powerful she thought she might shake apart. She tried to scream, but he shoved his hand against her mouth to quiet her, and she bit down, hard, as her body went rigid, taking him with her.

Reality and time seemed to have vanished into the maelstrom. She lay beneath him, listening for the pounding of a heart that should have exploded five minutes ago, listening as her breath rasped to a more reasonable pace. She reached up and cupped his face, and his long hair fell around her fingers. His sunglasses were gone, but it was too dark to see his eyes, his face. She could feel dampness on his cheeks, could feel the tentative movement of muscle that might have been a smile. She felt his love, strong, sure, unspoken. She didn't need the words.

"Did I hurt you?" he murmured, his mouth feathering hers.

"Only for a moment. Oh, God, I bit your hand," she said, memory flooding her.

She could feel the faint ripple of laughter. "I liked it," he said.

She sighed, settling beneath him, her hips cradling him, her arms tight around him. He was still hard, and growing harder, locked within her.

"I gather that was an orgasm?" she said, in what was supposed to be a casual tone of voice.

"It was. In France it's called *la petite mort*. The little death."

"Well," she said frankly, "if that's the little death, I hate to imagine what the big one is like."

And the sudden silence in the room was absolute, as even the fire died.

CHAPTER SEVEN

The voices were louder now, calling to him, plaintive, crying, and he knew his time was fading. She lay in his arms, sound asleep, replete, her heart beating soundly, and he wanted to pull her closer against him.

He had to let her go. He'd known that for an eternity. Time had little meaning for him—she seemed to have existed in some part of his being for as long as he had had memory. She would continue there, a part of him, forever.

But it was time. He slid out of bed, careful not to disturb her. It would have been remarkable if he'd awakened her—she had to be exhausted.

She would wake, alone, uncomfortable. A caring lover would have held back, but he hadn't had that choice. Tonight was his only night, and he'd made love to her repeatedly, each time drawing forth a stronger and stronger reaction. He'd bound her to him, body and soul. But in the end, he knew, he would have neither.

The long night would have to suffice. The memory of it would last him. The memory of it would leave her. She would go on to a new life, a healthier one. Her next life would be strong, blessed and lengthy, and she deserved no less. Her encounter with death would be nothing more than an erotic dream that would haunt her, unsuspecting, on stormy nights.

The sleet had halted, but the wind still blew wildly through the huge pines, and in the distance he could see the faint light of another storm-ridden dawn. He would leave, and when her time came again, he would be impervious to her and the siren call of weakness. He had tasted life, but he was Death. He would not forget again.

He dressed in the darkness, out on the balcony, covering his eyes with his dark glasses for the last time. He wouldn't even say goodbye. She would mourn, and then she would grow angry, but she would never know the truth.

The voices were calling him. The old man, fading, well past his time. Another voice, louder still. A woman's voice, nearby. He recognized it with a start. The other voices were a rumble in the distance, but this one, he knew, couldn't wait.

He could feel the change coming over him, and he knew there was nothing he could do, no bargain he could make, to stop the inevitable. He'd had his respite, his brief glimpse of paradise. It was time to return to the dark place where he ruled supreme.

He would take up his role once more. He would take the soul that called to him, and in doing so, he would be gone. And there would be no turning back.

Laura woke with a start. Murky daylight was seeping in the French doors, and she was in his bed. Alone.

She lifted her head, looking around with the futile hope that he was still there, but she knew in every cell of her well-loved body that he was gone. She sat up, pulling the duvet around her, listening to the strong, steady beat of her heart. The breath that filled her lungs, the blood that pumped through her veins. The sheer sense of strength and physical well-being. And then she felt it begin to fade.

She slid out of bed quickly, wincing at the aches in her body. She took a quick shower, throwing on clean clothes and shoving her fingers through her still-wet tangle of hair before she started out into the hallway in search of him.

He would be drinking coffee, she knew it. He would be cool and noncommittal, and she would have to do her best to be equally sophisticated. To convince him that last night she hadn't died and gone to heaven.

There was no smell of coffee permeating the downstairs, her first signal that something was very wrong. It was after seven—Mrs. Hawkins was usually up by five and on her second batch of coffee by then. The dining room was cold and dark—the kerosene lamps had burned down, and no one had replenished them. The fireplace held nothing but coals, and the silence was ominous.

Her first thought was to check on her father. He lay in his bed, scarcely breathing. He was alive, but just barely. He was also alone, with no sign of Maria or any of Laura's siblings.

"Mrs. Hawkins! Maria?" she called as she ran down toward the kitchen. It was empty, as well, dark and cold. Far in the distance she thought she heard a faint pounding, voices calling to her, but before she could go in search of the source, lightning flashed again, illuminating the darkened kitchen.

She looked out toward the ravine below, and she could see them. Jeremy, dragging a woman who could only be Cynthia down the steep pathway that led to

Nichols Ravine. And a tall, dark figure following behind them. Almost floating.

Somewhere along the way, she'd lost her strength. She slammed out the kitchen door, calling to them, but her voice was captured by the wind and whipped away. Yesterday she could run without pain—this morning her heart ached in her chest, and her breath rasped in her throat.

She started after them in a stumbling run, afraid of what she would find, but they couldn't, or wouldn't, hear her. Cynthia was fighting, screaming, but she was no match for Jeremy's unexpected strength. And the dark figure followed behind, saying and doing nothing.

She fell once, slamming down into the hard, cold earth, and she half expected the iciness of death to come for her. But there was no bright light, no explosive finale. She scrambled to her feet once more, and by the time she caught up with them they were at the edge of the ravine, the rustic deck of the family compound hanging over them, and Jeremy had his thick hands wrapped around Cynthia's throat as she kicked at him, struggling desperately.

"You won't die!" he screamed at her, and her body shook with the force of his fury. "Nothing kills you. Not carbon monoxide, not poison. I'm going to damned well choke the life out of you with my bare hands and then throw you over the ravine. We'll see if you survive that, you bitch. You can't cheat me out of the money. I earned it. I earned it sucking up to the old man, always being the good boy, doing what I was told. But I'm not going to anymore. It's all going to be mine, sooner or later. And I'm not going to give you the chance to get in my way.''

"Jeremy!" Laura screamed. "What in God's name are you doing? Let go of her!''

His hands didn't loosen their death grip around his wife's throat, and the hoarse, choking noises Cynthia was making filled the eerie morning. "What does it look like, you stupid fool? I'll kill you, as well. I was willing to wait—you were living on borrowed time as it was, but now I can't afford to do that." With a last, wrenching twist, he dropped Cynthia's body on the ground. Laura had no idea whether she was alive or dead; all she knew was that Jeremy was advancing on her, and there was no mistaking the purposeful madness in his eyes.

Alex stood at the edge of the clearing, surrounded by the morning fog, indistinct, watching, saying nothing, making no move to come to her rescue. "Are you just going to stand there?" she demanded of him, backing away from her murderous stepbrother. "Aren't you going to stop him?"

Jeremy halted his determined advance. "Who are you talking to?" he demanded in a bizarrely irritated voice.

"Is he part of this whole plan?" Laura demanded, backing away from him and his murderous, outstretched hands. "Did you bring him here to seduce me, to keep me busy while you murdered everyone who stood in the way of your getting Father's money?"

Jeremy followed her gaze to Alex's still, waiting figure. "I don't know what you're talking about. There's no one left alive here but you and me."

As if to refute his claim, Cynthia made a faint moan, but Jeremy just shrugged. "She won't survive a fall down Nichols Ravine," he said. "Nor will you. I can't imagine what people will think happened. Perhaps I'll tell them Cynthia was despondent. Maybe you came after her, trying to stop her suicidal desperation, and in the struggle you both fell. I think that would work very well, don't you?"

She turned to look at Alex. "Can't you stop him?" she cried again.

Jeremy's expression of affable determination vanished. "There's no one there!"

"No," Alex said, and his voice was deeper, richer, more unsettling. The sound of it drew Jeremy's attention, and suddenly he was able to focus on what he'd failed to see before.

"How long have you been there?" Jeremy demanded, his voice rising in panic.

"He followed you down here," Laura said. "Don't you realize you can't get away with it? Even if you're strong enough to throw Cynthia over the ravine, even if you managed to kill me, as well, I'll still fight you. I'll fight you enough to make you give me bruises, and then people will wonder..."

"You already have bruises," Jeremy said, pulling himself together. "Doubtless courtesy of your friend there. He's already told you he won't stop me, though I'm not sure why. Maybe he knows I can be generous. Or maybe he knows that he's a more obvious candidate if anyone starts to get suspicious, and he has the good sense to get the hell out of here."

"Why won't you stop him, Alex?" Laura whispered. "Do you want him to kill me?" She was half-afraid of the answer. He looked oddly indistinct in the misty gloom, almost insubstantial, and she couldn't begin to guess at the expression behind his mirrored glasses.

Alex moved forward through the mist, and overhead the lightning crackled in the gloomy sky. "He won't kill you," he said, and there seemed to be a built-in echo to his voice.

"The hell I won't," Jeremy said, lunging for her.

She was so mesmerized by panic that she didn't see Alex move. One moment he was halfway across the clearing; in the next he put his hand on Jeremy's shoulder, with seemingly the lightest of touches.

The white-hot light sizzled, illuminating the clearing with a blinding dazzle. Laura fell back, covering her eyes instinctively, and in the distance she heard a muffled cry, followed by a powerful clap of thunder.

She sank to her knees on the damp earth, terrified beyond coherence, shaking as the thunder shook the earth. It died away slowly, the brilliant white light faded back to the overcast morning, and slowly she opened her eyes.

Jeremy lay at her feet, his eyes open, staring, his face fixed in a grim rictus of death. She had no doubt that he was gone, nor did she question what had happened. She turned and looked at Alex, across the clearing. He looked as if he hadn't moved.

"You killed him," she said. "How?"

"I took him," he told her. "And it doesn't matter how. You'd better see to his widow."

Cynthia lay crumpled up against the lower railing, stirring slightly, a faint, choking rasp signaling that she was still alive. Laura sank down beside her, pulling her into her arms, stroking her tangled hair.

"It's all right, Cynthia," she whispered. "No one will hurt you. It's over."

Cynthia's eyes blinked open, and she stared up at Laura in uncomprehending horror. "Jeremy," she managed to gasp. "He was trying to kill me...."

"He's dead, Cynthia. He won't be able to hurt you."

Cynthia turned her head, her eyes focusing on the other figure in the clearing. And then she screamed, the choked sound eerie. "No!" she gasped. "Don't let him near me. Don't let him hurt me!" She clawed at Laura's arm.

"Cynthia, I told you. Jeremy's dead. He won't hurt anyone again."

"Not Jeremy." Cynthia's voice was choked. "That...that *thing*." Her voice was deep with horror and loathing as she stared at Alex's dark, shadowy figure.

"Laura!" She could hear her father's voice from the deck overhead now, and the babble of confusion, as Maria and Mrs. Hawkins were crying and talking. She released her hold on Cynthia, then turned and rose, confronting the man who stood there. Realizing for the first time just how insubstantial he was.

"What is she talking about, Alex?" she asked, her voice astonishingly calm. "Who are you? Why do I know you?"

"Don't let him touch you!" William shouted from overhead. She glanced up, just for a moment, to see her frail father leaning on the railing, shaking a fist down at Alex. "He can't have you, damn it."

She turned back to him, taking a tentative step toward him. "Who are you?" she asked again.

He retreated. One small step away from her, as if he were afraid of her touch. Which was odd, she thought, since everyone seemed to feel she was the one who should be afraid.

"Don't you know?" Cynthia spit out the words like a curse. "Don't you recognize him? He's Death. The Grim Reaper. And he's come to take you."

Laura raised her head, staring up at him. Oddly enough, she felt nothing more than profound relief. She *had* known him. Through her darkest times, he'd been there, a presence, a comfort. He was part of her, and now she knew why.

"No," he said, his voice echoing in the morning stillness.

"Don't lie to her." William's choked voice came from overhead. "She's too damned smart to be tricked. Take me instead. I'm an old man, a bad man. I've lived out my life."

"I'm not going to take her."

The words fell into the clearing like a stone into water. And then Laura spoke.

"Why not?"

The question was simple, almost childlike in its curiosity.

He seemed to be growing larger now, shimmering in the murky light, and his voice took on the echoes of a thousand years. "Someone else will come for you when it's your time," he said, and even so, she could hear the desperation in him.

"Why not you?" she persisted, taking another step toward him.

He backed away again. "Because it doesn't work that way. I'm a courier and nothing more. I rule in hell, and I serve in heaven. If I were to take you, it would only be to pass you on."

"And if I didn't want to go?"

She could feel his fury, his longing, in every fiber of her well-loved body. As the moments passed, she was feeling more and more certain, and the strange hope began burning inside her, between her breasts.

"You don't know what you're talking about."

"What if I want to stay with you?"

"Laura, no!" William cried out, but she ignored him.

"What if I wanted to come with you, be with you, forever?" she went on.

"Don't be a fool," he shot back bitterly. "We're not talking about a condo in Hades and a two-hearse garage. We're talking about eternity. An endless black ether, a vast cloud of emptiness."

"It wouldn't be empty," she said very simply. "You would be there."

She took another step toward him, but he had nowhere to retreat. "You have no idea what you're asking," he said.

"Listen to him, Laura," Cynthia begged. "Get away from him."

"No." It wasn't a word she had used very often. But she used it now, her eyes never leaving his face. She reached out her hand, and he flinched.

"Don't let me touch you," he said. "If I do, you'll die."

"You touched me before," she said. Her heart was racing too fast, but she didn't care. She willed it to go faster, to speed up and burst.

"I've gone back to what I really am."

"And what is that?"

"Power," he said flatly. "Energy. Death."

"And love," she said.

"It's not a fairy tale, Laura!" he cried, and there was no missing the desperation in his voice.

"You love me," she said, very certain.

"What does Death know about love?" He yanked the sunglasses from his face as he loomed over her. "Look at me, and tell me you're not afraid."

She heard Cynthia's piteous shriek, the babbled prayers of the women above her, her father's choked gasp. None of it mattered. She looked up at Alex, into his eyes for the first time.

They were dark, endless, and she knew why so many were terrified of him. In those bottomless depths she could see herself, quite clearly, and she could see the future. The endless night that held nothing but him.

"Why should I be afraid?" she asked gently. "You've always been there for me. You always will be, unless I let you go."

"Laura!" her father shrieked, but it was too late. She took a final step toward him and threw herself against his shimmering, vibrating body.

The white light filled the air, blinding her. The crackle of lightning singed around her; thunder shook the earth. And from somewhere far away his arms came around her, wrapping her tight against him.

They stood, bound together, in the midst of a tornado. She raised her face to his, and there was no horror in his eyes. No regret. Just the sheer, shining power of love.

"You've lost everything," he said, though there were no words spoken. "You've given me eternity."

She found she could smile. "That should be time enough," she said.

Then she closed her eyes as he kissed her. Forever was just beginning.

Dear Reader,

I've always been fascinated with the relationship between love and death. One is the ultimate light, the other is the ultimate darkness, and the joining of the two is deliciously, terrifyingly extreme.

This is a beauty-and-the-beast fantasy taken to the very limit—there's no pulling back from death, no settling down in an apartment with a two-car garage with the Grim Reaper. In order to love Death, you have to be willing to give it all, with no future, no past, nothing but a deep, velvet now. That kind of complete surrender, and triumph, can provide the ultimate satisfaction. Small things no longer matter—destiny is in force now, and the real world slips away.

For a woman to accept Death as her lover, she has to be very brave, selfless, loving.

For Death to succumb to human weakness, to a human female, he has to be willing to risk everything, as well. Human emotions are foreign, and dangerous. But Death, like his true love, is willing to chance it.

The happy ending for such a union is, of course, bittersweet. But the greatest victories are always so. Prepare to take a dark ride on life's most fascinating amusement park attraction. Death, and its polar opposite, love. And the mesmerizing union the two create.

Anne Stuart

Catching Dreams
Chelsea Quinn Yarbro

CHAPTER ONE

It was one of those peculiar shops at the end of the wharf-side restaurants, a slightly artsy souvenir-and-curio place with items ranging from postcards, sea-shell night-lights and blowfish made into hanging lamps to seascape oil paintings, Native American pottery, Pacific Islands masks and pendants stamped Made in USA and the genuine article for significantly more money. The weathered wooden sign over the French entrance doors proclaimed the shop to be Oddments. The whole place filled three large rooms, the last being an art-and-anthropology gallery, with tall windows overlooking the lovely, lazy curve of Monterey Bay, burnished now with afternoon sun-shine and lending the gallery its splendid light.

Dana found the owner in this third room, bent nearly double over a shipping crate, plastic packing worms strewn about like petals as he delved for new treasures hidden in its depths. There was already a collection of small wooden statues and masks standing around the crate, as if to witness its unpacking. For almost two minutes he continued to paw through the packing material, for all the world like a determined puppy after a bone. At last he uttered a cry of success and emerged clutching a small box, which he handled with care that bordered on reverence. He opened it with a glad chuckle and took out one of the figures contained within, holding it up and inspecting it carefully.

"Mister Styles?" Dana ventured, not wanting to startle him on their first meeting, but wanting to get off to a prompt start. Being completely on her own, she would have no one to blame but herself if she screwed this up, and very little to fall back on. She held her portfolio in place with the pressure of her arm. But thanks to the three blocks she had walked from her parking place, it was becoming a burden to her. She hoped that her sleek knot of brandy-colored hair had not suffered too much from the sea breeze; she had no opportunity to check the state of her panty hose, either, which she feared were springing a run. She rarely wore much makeup, and for once she was certain it was better this way.

He looked around abruptly, then fixed a smile on his face. "You must be Ms.... It's a bird name, isn't it?" He made no apology for his lapse in memory, and Dana could not help but like him for his candor.

"Piper," she supplied, holding out her hand. "Piper Designs—"

"A bird," he confirmed with a nod, interrupting her merrily. "One of those little, pretty ones." He was about five-nine and slight, with well-cut putty-colored hair and soft-green eyes. He wore black jeans, a black cashmere turtleneck and an unbuttoned, vibrant turquoise camp shirt over it. On his left wrist he had a silver-and-turquoise bracelet of superior quality and design. "A pleasure to meet you. I've seen your work. It's very good. Hamilton Styles, at your service." He held out the little figure he had removed from the box. "Exquisite, isn't it?"

She inspected the little wooden statue, which was about four inches long, a large-headed representation of a man with talons for fingers and formidable sexual endowments. Bits of glass embedded in the wooden visage gave the figure a brilliant, green-eyed stare. The craftsmanship was superb, and she said with sincerity, "It's marvelous. I've never seen anything like it. Where is it from?"

"South Pacific. From Malekula." He noticed her lack of recognition. "It's one of the New Hebrides group. In the middle. East of Australia, southeast of the Solomon Islands, slightly north of New Caledonia. I'll show you on the map, if you like." His smile was genuine. "Don't worry. When I first got interested in these things, I didn't know where anything was, either."

"Sounds exotic," said Dana, not wanting to take too much for granted with this man. She needed his account and was afraid she would put him off if she intruded on him now. "If it's not convenient to discuss—"

"Stationery and business card designs? And fliers for the exhibits in this gallery? I can't think of a better time. In fact, it's a *wonderful* time to discuss them; I couldn't have planned it better if I wanted to. I'm all enthused. Everything is going well. It's a good day." He grinned, and added, "I'm at my best when things are going well."

"Who isn't?" asked Dana, not expecting an answer, and fully aware that by his standards she was most definitely not at her best.

"There is that," said Styles. "Very well. Let me see what you have, and I will open us some champagne. Now don't say no. I hate to drink alone." He did not wait for a reply, but hurried off to the office, leaving Dana with the little idol in her hand.

Now that Dana had a chance to examine it more closely, she discovered it was truly beautiful, and a little frightening. Those long talons did not make her feel the figure was intended to be helpful, not given the possessive stare in the tiny carved eyes—how could anything carved in wood have an expression in its eyes?—and the determined stance of the figure. She turned it over in her hands again, admiring it even as she was slightly repelled by it. There were a number of tiny symbols marked on the body, as well, and it appeared to have clipped wings.

"Here we are," called out Styles, returning from the office with an open bottle of Schrammsburg in one hand and two champagne flutes in the other. "And I'm so glad I have someone to celebrate with. You have no *idea* how long I have been trying to get these little fetishes. It's been almost seventeen months since I made my first attempt to purchase them." He put the glasses down on an empty sculpture pedestal and poured out the sparkling wine.

"I...I don't know that..." Dana said, looking at her watch and calculating the time it would take her to conduct this meeting if champagne was factored in.

"You said on the phone I'm your last appointment of the day. You don't have to get back to your desk. And unless you've got kiddies at home waiting for Mumsy to make supper, you can have champagne with me, and then we'll go over to the Sea Chest and I will buy you a proper dinner. We'll have a chance to get acquainted, because we're going to be great friends." His face crumpled with dismay. "You can do this, can't you? Tell me you will."

In spite of herself, she smiled, liking Hamilton Styles. "I'm not married, Mr. Styles—" And not likely to be anytime soon not after what Kirk had done last month, she added to herself. How could he have treated her so callously?

"Hamilton. Please. And I will call you—?" He waited for her to go on.

"Dana. As for the rest of it: there are no kiddies waiting for Mumsy, only three very spoiled cats—Anthos, Porthos and Aramis. All for one and one for all. And I was going to rent a video or two and have a pizza delivered."

"You're free. Terrific. Everything's settled, then. We can take all the time we need. Come get your drink. And bring that fetish over here," he went on, handing her a flute. "I want to gloat."

Dana accepted the champagne, holding the crystal stem carefully, though with her portfolio tucked under her arm, this was awkward. As she tried to balance the things better, she accidentally spilled a few drops of the champagne on the fetish. "Oh, dear. I'm terribly sorry," she said, and worked at the wood with her thumb to get off the liquid. "I hope I haven't damaged it." Then she noticed that the glass of the eyes had cut two little frowns in her thumb; there were a pair of reddish smears to blend with the champagne. She started to apologize more profusely.

Styles laughed. "Not to worry. He's undoubtedly had worse. In fact, that's probably the classiest offering old Dream Catcher ever had."

"Dream Catcher?" Dana asked, looking down at the figure she held.

"That's his name. He's supposed to catch the dream you want and make it real for you. Those hooks on his hands are to bring the dream down to earth and hold it for you. And hold you to it." He lifted his glass. "To fulfilling our dreams. What do you say?"

"To fulfilling our dreams," she echoed, and touched the rim of her flute to his. It struck her that this afternoon was turning out to be almost as strange as this shop.

"And to new friends." He took a careful sip. "The nectar of the gods," he declared after savoring the wine. "And we must treat it with respect." He topped off both their glasses and favored her with a quizzical look. "Well, since you have made Dream Catcher an offering, you'd better tell him what you want." Dana had been about to hand the fetish back to Styles, but he waved her away. "You gave him the champagne. And you cut your finger, so it's your blood that gives him power. It's your dream he'll catch."

"I can't," said Dana, feeling very silly.

"Why not? I would, if I had dropped the champagne on him." His smile was wistful. "What a chance. I wouldn't waste it."

She held out the little doll to him. "Then it's yours."

He held up his hand and shook his head firmly. "Oh, no. It's your wish. You're the one who should use it. Otherwise, it's useless. Wish for something you really want. Something that's really important to you. It's what I'd do."

She frowned, not certain she should take this seriously. But it might help get Kirk out of her thoughts at last. She had said a week ago she'd do anything to banish him from her thoughts, as he had banished her from his. There were things you could do in front of strangers you would never do around your best friend, weren't there? Then she surrendered. "Why not?"

"What do you want, then?" Styles asked, interest making his whole body alert, like the ears of a startled fox.

"I don't know." She thought about what her week had been like. "Business could be better. A little security would be nice."

"Amen," said Styles. "But that's nothing really important, is it? Not dream-important. You're not the type."

It was tempting to ask what he meant, but she decided that was pushing first acquaintance too far. "And there are some improvements the house needs—" She took a taste of the champagne. It was excellent, as Styles had claimed.

"But that's not what you dream about—house improvements—is it?" His shrewd guess made her blush.

"No," she admitted. What was it about the little figure that made her think about where things had gone wrong with Kirk? Had forced her to consider what she wanted instead.

"There's something on your mind. I can see it. Go on. Tell him," urged Styles. "I won't gossip. Promise." He took another sip of champagne.

"You're serious, aren't you?" Dana asked Styles, feeling embarrassed for no reason she could identify. "You think I should tell this piece of carved wood what I want most—what my most treasured dream is."

He shrugged. "Well, let me put it this way—I wouldn't waste an opportunity like this. If it doesn't work, what have you lost, but a couple of minutes and a few drops of champagne and a minuscule trickle of blood. But if it *does* work, then you stand to get something you really want." He made a sign with his hand, with the index and little finger extended. "Unless you're afraid of the Evil Eye."

"No," she said quickly, then frowned. "All right." She held up the fetish where she could see it, and repeated, "All right, Dream Catcher. Here goes." Her ideas came readily, as if the little statue drew them out of her. "For once in my life I'd like to have a man love me whom I can love without upsetting him. A man who accepts me as his equal. A man who does not feel threatened by my competence. A man who wants me for me, and only me." Now that she had gotten started, she began to warm to her task. "A man who listens to me, and understands, and is willing to let me understand him. A man who lets me know what he is really thinking, and how he feels. A man who finds me really interesting, not just available. A man who does not belittle what I do. A man who enjoys my friends.

A man who doesn't want me as territory, but as a companion. A man who does not trivialize me. A man who meets my needs emotionally, as well as physically. A man I can find attractive the way he is and who finds me attractive the way I am. A man who isn't put off by my temper. A man who is drawn to me gladly. A man who does not think love is an intrusion into his privacy. A man who takes care of himself without too much vanity. A man who believes being with me is a privilege, not an imposition. A man who enjoys music and art and picnics and reading and conversation more than he enjoys football and basketball games. A man who does his share without thinking he deserves battle ribbons and a parade for it. A man who is generous with his time and his emotions, as well as his money. A man who wants an equal partner, not a servant. A man who doesn't think romance is laughable. A man who is willing to make serious commitments without resenting it. A man who is willing to go the extra distance for me. A man who takes my life as seriously as his own." She stopped suddenly, feeling very foolish. Had a single sip of wine made her tipsy?

"Sounds wonderful," said Styles with an exaggerated sigh. "Let me know what Dream Catcher brings you. If he even comes close, I'll give it a try."

Dana handed the fetish back to Styles. "There you are," she said, averting her eyes. Now that she had spoken, she wanted to flee. Until she had said these things out loud, she had not realized what trouble she had had with Kirk, how many things about him had actually displeased or disappointed her. Now that she knew, she felt sad in a way she had not since he had left her.

There was a brief silence between them. "It must have been a rough ride. I know how it feels. And I hope you get it." Styles put his hand on her arm. "Come on. Bring your glass with you, and I'll bring the wine. Let's go over to the Sea Chest and get something to eat. Bring the portfolio, too, and we'll look over your ideas while we gobble up scallops and prawns in pesto over fresh pasta." His eyes widened. "Don't tell me you don't *like* scallops and prawns in pesto. Hector will be crushed." Hector Ramierez was the justly famous owner and chef of the Sea Chest, whose recipes were often featured in *Sunset* magazine.

"No," she said, feeling strangely confused. Why had she let herself say such personal things in front of a near-stranger? "I like pasta and pesto and the rest." And she struggled constantly to remain a size ten. This admission to liking food left her feeling slightly guilty. She forced herself to smile.

"Good," said Styles. He fished his keys out of his pocket, saying, "I'll just need a minute to lock up."

Dana watched him set his various alarms before he snagged the champagne bottle and his glass and marched toward the front of the store. She followed after him, wondering if this had been a performance for her benefit, or if Hamilton Styles was always like that.

Dinner was a magnificent demonstration of why Hector Ramierez had such an enviable reputation. At the end of the meal, while they were finishing their coffee and flan, Ramierez himself came over to the table and sat with them a few minutes, graciously accepting the praise Styles offered. He was a middle-aged man, his dark hair shot with gray and his body beginning to thicken. His smile was wide, his voice soft.

"My kids go through school on people like you," said Ramierez, with an easy smile that cut deep creases in his face and narrowed his eyes with good humor.

"As well they should. I've never had a bad meal here, Hector," said Styles.

Ramierez smiled, as if at a private joke. "You are precisely what my partner and I run this place for. We want to keep you coming back." He glanced at the papers and printing samples spread out on the table, and asked, "Do you mind?" before he began to look over them with some interest. "Very nice. Superior quality papers and unusual presentations." He smiled at Dana.

"Thanks," said Dana, handing him one. "If there's anything you want to discuss, call me. Our prices are competitive and our work is—"

"Distinctive," finished Styles for her. "I like everything she's shown me. The only trouble was deciding which I liked best. And it's time you had a new menu designed, something more contemporary, with different colors than this pale blue. You've had this one for as long as I've been coming here."

"There may be something in what you say," Ramierez said thoughtfully, addressing Styles. "Let me see how her work for you turns out, and perhaps you, Ms. Piper, will make some designs for me, as well.''

''That would be very nice,'' said Dana, who knew better than to count on this kind of offer. She would be pleasantly surprised if she had any response whatever from Hector Ramierez.

''I'm getting this marbled-effect border on all my paper—stationery, business cards, fliers, the lot—with this typeface.'' He pointed out the one he had chosen to Ramierez. ''I think it's distinctive.'' He grinned at Dana. ''You did a great job. It's terrific, isn't it?''

''I like it,'' she said, trying not to feel too tired, for the day was catching up with her with fearful quickness. She thought, I'm twenty-nine. I have my own business, and things are starting to improve. I have the independence I want. I shouldn't be so worn out. She felt as if she had been working in the yard or struggling to move heavy furniture. But there was no reason for her to feel this way. Or to be so lonely.

''Look at you,'' said Styles, noticing Dana's fatigue, his concern as swift as it was unexpected. ''I shouldn't have kept you out so long. It's…after nine. But we got a lot done, didn't we.''

''Yes,'' said Dana. ''I'll be able to have roughs for you in three working days.'' She could actually have them in less, but she had learned it wasn't wise to be too quick with her work—too often, clients feared she had not given their work the serious attention it required if she did it too quickly, and would balk at the price she charged. She gathered up all her samples and put them in her portfolio once more. Her arms felt weighted down, and the sheets of paper were like slabs of lead.

"Good. Bring it by at the end of the day and we can have supper again." He put down bills for their dinner, held the chair for Dana and gave Ramierez a thumbs-up signal. "Where are you parked?"

"Off of Foam. The next block, halfway up the hill," she answered, hoping that she had not been given a parking ticket.

"I'll walk you over," said Styles as he held the door for her. He matched his pace to hers, saying, "I think we're off to a good start, don't you?"

"I hope so," she answered, and then said, in a different voice, "Mister Styles, I don't want you to think I'm doing this as anything more than good business."

He laughed outright. "I don't." They had almost reached the crosswalk when Styles went on, "When you were talking to Dream Catcher, I had the impression you had real trouble with a man. Or maybe men. Let me tell you, I know what that's like. Don't you let it get you down. And don't let him have another chance to mess you up. You go and catch that dream you asked for. Accept no substitutes."

The stoplight made them halt, but Dana was grateful for it. "I...I don't know what to say, Mister Styles."

"Well, you can call me Hamilton, as I told you to this afternoon," he reminded her. "And you can give me the best job you could ever do." His smile was quick as the light changed. "You can also stay away from the bastard who treated you so badly. Don't bother trying to fix it. Take my advice." He gave her a more serious stare. "You're okay to drive home, aren't you? You haven't had anything alcoholic for more than two hours, plus that big dinner."

"I'm fine, Mister Styles," she assured him. "I only had two glasses of wine all evening, counting the champagne."

"Hamilton. Remember." He held up an admonishing finger.

"I will," she promised as she reached her year-old Acura. "Thanks for dinner. I enjoyed it."

He stopped her flow of good manners with a chuckle and a gentle warning. "We'll do a lot better if you talk to me like a brother, not a date."

She said nothing for a few seconds, thinking that this man was much better company than her brother, Vincent. Maybe Styles had been serious when he announced they were going to be good friends. "All right. The food was wonderful. The evening was fun. I've enjoyed myself thoroughly. I'm glad we'll be doing some work together. I think we'll get some good things done. That's the truth. Besides, anyone who can get me to talk to wooden fetishes and drink champagne in the afternoon..."

He favored her with a wicked wink. "That's better." He stood aside so that she could open her door; he held it for her as she climbed in. "That man you asked Dream Catcher for—I hope you get him."

Dana was about to turn the key in the ignition when something her grandmother had said came back to her as loudly as if the old lady—now dead sixteen years—had spoken in Dana's ear: *Beware of your desires, for surely you shall achieve them.* She seemed to see

Dream Catcher grin at her from the shine of the streetlight on the windshield. Suppressing a shudder, Dana started the engine and fastened her seat belt as Hamilton Styles slammed the door. She saw him in the rearview mirror, waving her on her way.

She drove home in a state of pleasant good humor, telling herself that the day had gone very well, and that she had every reason to be proud of the progress she had made in the past two weeks—three new accounts. They were the first signs of security she had had in many months.

But as she tended to the cats, doubts began to creep back, and she could hear Kirk's voice asking her demoralizing questions, questions that sapped her vitality and confidence. She wished she could forget the way he'd had of manipulating her. He had never attacked her directly, but instead undermined her with sly innuendo: *You sure you can count on a flake like that? How do you know he'll honor the contract? What makes you think you're ready to compete with Martin and Grossman—they're big-league. Hey, I think you do great designs, but you know how trendy the market is—are you certain you can keep up?* or *"I wouldn't like having such a tight deadline. If they don't like what you do, there's no time to come up with something different, is there?"*

Resolutely she ordered the voice to be still, and she thought instead of what she had told that fetish during that afternoon—had she really done such a foolish thing?—and what she wanted for herself now. It was better to think about what was to come and not what was over. It was enough that Kirk was gone, she had a place of her own and she was doing her work successfully at last. And in time she might meet someone who had a few of the qualities she had asked Dream Catcher for. Someone who would be willing to take her seriously. Someone she could trust. With those thoughts for company, she finished up her household chores and took herself off to bed, only to lie awake for the greater part of an hour, staring at the ceiling, trying not to imagine the life she could have with someone like the man she wished for. Her emotions welled up, bringing her fresh reminders of what she sought in a man. These became a litany of wishes. Somewhere between her longing for easy demonstrations of affection that did not turn out to be nothing more than foreplay and the wished-for man's ability to laugh early in the morning, she drifted into sleep.

That night Dana slept on and off, restlessly, fragments of a song she remembered from her youth coming back to her.

> The water is wide—I cannot cross o'er
> And neither have I wings to fly.
> Something, something, something
> Deeper my joy, and deeper woe.

Kirk had been best at the woe department, she thought, as fragments of their arguments and long, simmering silences, came back to her in the fragmentary way of dreams. There were other images, too, images she could not identify, and the face of a man she did not know. This must be her way of getting rid of Kirk in her thoughts.

I leaned my back against an oak
Thinking it were a trusty tree

It had cost her nearly five thousand dollars to be rid of him, not including the cost of moving. But after she caught him with another woman for the third time, in spite of his promises to reform, her patience and her capacity to forgive were exhausted. Then he had walked out, saying she had become boring. Five thousand dollars seemed a reasonable price to pay to be rid of Kirk and his manipulative ways. Reluctantly she had to admit he was still one of the handsomest men she had ever met—movie-star handsome, almost, with dark brown hair and hot blue eyes, somewhere between Rob Lowe and an unscruffy Harrison Ford—and she could not call him to mind without a faint twinge of nostalgia. If only Kirk had been as nice as he was good-looking, life with him might have been heaven, instead of the nightmare it had been, filled with constant criticism and sly remarks that eroded her confidence.

At least they had not had children, no matter how he had hinted and pressured. How could he commit to a relationship, he had asked as if it were a reasonable demand, if she were not willing to give him children. She had resisted his manipulations, refusing to use children as a bargaining chip, or a test of devotion. She was grateful for that now, for she knew she had done the right thing. Now that she was free of Kirk, she realized how much he was like her older brother, Vincent, who had always tormented her.

The worse echoes of his coercions were at last fading. And her sense of wanting to hide away from the world was no longer as strong as it had been. If she could find a man like the one she had described to Dream Catcher, she knew she could still be happy in her life. She did her best to imagine what life would be like with that kind of man. Someone who would get her jokes and know when she was serious. Someone who would not dislike her cats. Someone who would lie in bed with her on Sunday mornings, reading the papers and drinking tea until noon. Someone who would be glad to see her at the end of the day. Someone who wouldn't mind going to the symphony once in a while. Someone who would trust her. Someone who would listen when he asked her opinion. Someone who would not call her boring. Someone who laughed with her and not at her. Someone she would not mind being around when she had the flu—or when he had the flu. Someone who would be patient with her, taking all the time she needed to wholly enjoy sex. Someone like the man she had described to Dream Catcher. Someone with clever, clear green eyes, powerful arms and a lived-in face.

But love turns cold when it grows old
And fades away like morning dew.

Dana's mother had liked that lament and had sung it often. Dana had never understood why, for her parents had a happy marriage that continued to this day. There had been no trace of unhappiness that Dana had ever seen, and yet her mother had loved those poignant lyrics of betrayed love. Her brother had thought such songs maudlin and sentimental and never hesitated to say so. She recalled his disdain with a shock, for it was so much like the things Kirk had said. Now it struck her as sinister that she should have the song in her dream so soon after the debacle with Kirk.

As the memories jumbled, she began to dream again: *she saw herself walking along the beach, looking toward the ocean. It was nearing sunset and there was a stiff breeze, so the air was damp with spray. Someone was walking beside her, his arm around her waist, someone she wanted to be with. She felt comfortable with him, with his nearness and the warmth of him. She trusted him, had nothing to fear from him. All his attention was on her, loving, open, playful and genuine. He spoke to her, and though she could not make out the words themselves, she could not mistake the passion in them. He had an accent, not quite English, not quite Australian, and big, square, calm hands that touched her with affection and desire.*

Finally she turned to his kisses, and her senses filled with him, her own need awakened by his caresses. He seemed to kiss her everywhere at once, the act as reverent as it was erotic. She had an impression of deep laugh lines around his green eyes, and rugged features that were not as handsome as Kirk's, but far kinder, far more real. She trusted him as she had never been able to trust any man before. He was safety, as well as passion, kindness and arousal at the same time. His lips were persuasive on hers, and as he held her in the haven of his arms, she felt that nothing bad could happen to her so long as she was close to him.

The last image from Dana's dream—that of the man drawing her down beside him on a gigantic bed—was supplanted by a strong impression of the fetish she had wished upon for the man she was making love with. Dream Catcher was gloating. It startled her awake. As she sat up in bed, finding Porthos waiting beside her pillow, she had the oddest impression that the fetish was in the room with her. She noticed that the two tiny cuts on her thumb were open again and decided she had better bandage them.

Athos, Porthos and Aramis were littermates, three of seven. Their mother was a huge Maine Coon Cat, but their fathers were obviously varied: Athos was blocky and melancholy, a big cat with a big head carried tiger-low, and massive shoulders; he was a sooty brown color. Porthos was the clown of the outfit, curious and mischievous, a dark marmalade shade, and a whopping twenty-seven pounds. Aramis was a splendid silver tabby with a large white ruff, tufts on his ears and a refined face, who had a way of looking at Dana as if he understood every word she said. All three of them accompanied her to the kitchen, tails up, ready for breakfast. She opened two cans and a large bag of Iams, listening to her cats wheedle, order and cajole her.

The daily ritual did much for Dana, dragging her back from her dreams to the real world and the welcome ordinariness of her life. As she doled out food into three bowls, the cats butted their heads into her hands, purring loudly. Once the cats were eating, she put on the kettle for herself and got three crumpets out of the freezer and put them in the toaster oven, then turned the heat on under the teakettle.

Dana yawned and ran her hands through her hair, trying to decide whether she wanted to keep it long. Kirk had liked it that way, which was now reason enough for her to change it. She decided to call Yolande that afternoon and make an appointment to have something done to it. Before the weekend would be nice, if Yolande could fit her in.

As the toaster oven heated the crumpets, Dana got the nonfat yogurt from the refrigerator and measured out her vitamins and the allergy pill she took every morning. It was a routine Kirk had mocked from the first, telling her pills couldn't cure anything, and that vitamins were a waste of time unless you wanted to work out at a gym, and he couldn't see her bench-pressing sixty pounds, let alone more, or doing curls until her biceps bulged. He would smile at her as he spoke, so they could both pretend he was not hurting her.

The teakettle shrilled, and Dana jumped up to make her morning tea—English breakfast, very strong—and take down a plate for her breakfast. There were two spoons in the drying rack by the sink, and she snagged one of these, along with an oversize mug in pale yellow ironstone. She put these on her kitchen table.

Absentmindedly she took the box of bandages from the drawer by the stove and bandaged her thumb. Her dream was still with her, and still strong. It held her like a force-field, interfering with her concentration and slowing her morning. Had she finally let go of her longings where Kirk was concerned? All her friends had told her she would know she was getting over Kirk when she began to have fantasies about someone else. And certainly there had been passion in her response to the man with green eyes. Could a figment of her imagination really excite her so much? She found this disconcerting, but tried to ignore the faces and music that had filled her sleep. But who was that unknown face? Was he anyone real, or the figment of her imagination, the embodiment of all she sought in a man? Could she dare to hope he might be real? She kept trying to place him, without success: a strong face, more used to laughter than frowns, with green eyes and a firm jaw, a mobile mouth, springy light-brown hair, and a shade too much nose to be truly handsome.

She was startled to hear the phone ring. Glancing at her watch, Dana wondered who would be calling her so early, and at home. "Piper residence," she answered.

"Oh, thank goodness I caught you," said Hamilton Styles. "Look, I'm very sorry to disturb you at home and so early, but I have to ask—did you notice where I put that fetish I showed you last night?"

"The fetish?" Dana repeated, trying to gather her wits about her. "I...I thought you put it back with the others."

He sighed in exasperation. "That's what I thought, too," he said. "But I've been looking for it for the last half hour and it hasn't turned up." He paused. "I don't mean this offensively, but I'd appreciate it if you'd check through your things. If it dropped out of the box, it might have fallen into your purse." He coughed and hurried on. "I don't think it is there, but since I've been looking for it."

"You mean you think I took it?" Dana asked, shocked at this suggestion, and indignant that he should say baldly what he suspected. "Well, I didn't—"

"No!" he exclaimed, chagrined. "Nothing like that. I didn't mean that at all—but it's not very big, and if it fell, it could have landed in your bag, couldn't it? You had your bag set on the floor with your portfolio, as I recall, right next to the pedestal where I had the fetishes." He sounded very concerned. "Don't worry, Dana. I haven't any doubts about you, I have them about me."

"Oh," she said, feeling awkward for her reaction. "All right. I'll look around before I leave for work."

"Call me if you find anything," he said, his voice apprehensive. "And if you find it, wrap it up in something, will you please?"

She remembered the piece was valuable, and said, "I'll take good care of it, if it turns up here."

His response surprised her. "I'm more worried about you than it. I don't think you ought to touch it too much."

"Skin oils," said Dana, aware of how damaging they could be to paints and dyes.

Now he spoke in a whisper, as if afraid of being overheard. "No. Don't laugh. Emanations."

"Emanations?" she repeated, as if she had not heard right. "What kind of emanations?"

"Fetish emanations," he said nervously, then attempted a laugh. "You don't believe in such things, do you? I don't blame you. Well, at one time I didn't, either. And I would have said exactly what you're saying now," he assured her.

"Okay," said Dana, suddenly uncomfortably aware of the way her dream had lingered into her waking thoughts. "For the sake of argument, tell me what you think is going on."

"I can't," he protested. "Not now. Just look for the fetish and be careful not to touch it if you find it. You don't want its hooks in you."

This caught her attention. "Wait a minute. You said it hooked a dream and brought it into the world."

"Yes, it does," said Styles, more nervously than before, "and I told you it hooks you to the dream, as well." He tried to chuckle and made a mess of it. "So please, Dana, check around for it."

"All right," she said, and glanced at the clock over the stove. "Oh, Lord, look at the time. Hamilton, I've got to go. I'm going to be late as it is."

"Oh, yeah. Sorry." He was about to hang up, but added, "You be carefully, Dana. You hear me?"

"I'll be careful," she promised, knowing already she would not have much chance to look for the fetish before leaving for work.

The crumpets were almost too brown to eat. She managed to get two down with yogurt slathered on top of them, and ended up tossing the third one out. While her tea steeped she rushed through dressing, and alternated putting on clothes with taking long, hot sips, welcoming the caffeine and the warmth equally. She left her plate and mug in the sink, gathered up her portfolio and purse and headed out the door, pausing to lock up before using the garage-door opener. She tossed her things into the passenger seat, then got into the car and drove off to work. The garage door descended as she pulled out of the driveway, as if it were waving goodbye.

CHAPTER TWO

"Sorry I disturbed you for nothing, day before yesterday," said Hamilton Styles as he welcomed Dana back to Oddments. Today he had on an oversize natural linen shirt over his black turtleneck and jeans. A Maori pendant hung from a thong around his neck.

"Then it turned up," said Dana, with more relief than the circumstances warranted. Perhaps it would be the end of her dream lover. The sense of that little idol had remained with her the last two nights, invading her dreams with visions she found as distressing as they were thrilling—visions of herself in passionate and erotic and occasionally perverse abandon with the man with the not-quite-handsome face. She was beginning to have a sense of him, and against her better judgment he was becoming real to her, a man who fulfilled all her wishes without damaging himself. It was easy to think of him as a part of her life. And it was dangerous, for he was the embodiment of a wish, not anyone she actually knew.

"No," he said, a little frown puckering his brow. "But it's got to turn up. I think maybe the cleaning service knocked it under something, or behind something. I'll find it." He did his best to make light of it, and failed.

"I don't doubt it," she said, her mind still on the man in her dreams. It was probably folly to let him take over her imagination in this way. She should be looking for someone alive and breathing, not a fantasy.

"By the way," he went on in a different tone, "I like what you've done with your hair."

Dana tossed her new cut. "Thanks. I just had it done this afternoon, and I'm trying to get used to it." She put her portfolio down on the top of a glass display case and zipped it open. "I've got your preliminary designs. If you like them, I'll take your order this evening." She could not stop herself from wanting the man in her dreams to like her new look, and chided herself for it.

He came to her side. "Good. I've got a show opening here in five weeks, and I need to get the fliers out quickly."

"We can arrange all of that for you, if you like." She habitually said "we," though Piper Designs was only herself and a part-time secretary. "I can work out the quotes and call you back tomorrow."

"Good. I want to get moving on this." He grinned at her. "You'll come to the opening, of course. Won't you?"

Dana did not know what to say. "If . . . if you want me, certainly I will. Thanks for asking me."

"Great." He pointed to a stack of shipping crates. "Two more and they'll all be here. All South Pacific pieces. Easter Island, Niue, Samoa, Fiji, New Caledonia, the Solomons, New Guinea, Sumatra, Java, a couple of historical pieces from Tasmania. Sounds like

locations for a bad movie, doesn't it? With Hedy La-
mar or one of those stars lounging about in a sarong
while Jeff Chandler fights the jungle." He tapped the
crates, as if to show them his approval and affection.
"Given that I'm a small gallery and I don't have a big-
money clientele or a huge display area, I think it's going to be a show to be proud of."

"That's terrific," said Dana, looking around un-
easily in spite of herself, wondering what had become
of the fetish; she had the peculiar sensation that the
thing was *watching* her, tracking her the way a hawk
tracks a rabbit. She made herself pay attention to
business. "How many fliers will you want?"

"I have a mailing list of six hundred, my own, plus
a list from the library, and I'm buying another thousand names from Pat Harding." He was boasting, and
was delighted when Dana responded the way he had
hoped she would. "That's a good base to start from,
don't you think?"

"Pat Harding? The cultural antiques expert? The
guy who does all the testifying?" she asked, trying not
to sound too astonished. Perhaps she had underestimated Styles' expertise.

Styles answered modestly. "Luckily, I've known Pat
for fifteen years. We met when I was taking his semi-
nar in college, before he got famous and gave up aca-
demia for full-time commercialism." His color
heightened, as if he had been caught doing something
he ought not to. "He was the one who got me started
on these artifacts." He indicated the crates.

For no reason she could identify, Dana felt a chill go
up her spine; she was certain that someone was

watching her, though no one was. She decided that one of the windows must be open a crack: that would account for it. "So you'll want what? Two thousand fliers?"

"Better make it three thousand. I want a stack of them here, to give out to customers." He glanced at his watch. "There's supposed to be one more crate arriving today."

"More fetishes?" asked Dana, wishing she didn't sound so apprehensive. She thought she had best account for her uneasiness in some way. "It's bad enough you've . . . mislaid one valuable piece."

"No, not fetishes, nothing historical or folk-art," said Styles with visible satisfaction. "These are modern works, done mostly in wood. The sculptor is flying in next week to help me set up the display. I'm driving up to San Francisco to pick him up. Wednesday afternoon."

"Oh?" said Dana, her voice rising for no reason she could think of. "From where?"

"New Zealand. Trevor Davidson. Wonderful name, isn't it? Trevor Davidson. I never thought I could pull it off. But I asked, figuring he wouldn't accept if I didn't. You may have read about him?" He studied the way the light fell from the north-west-facing windows. "It's no good," he muttered to himself. "I'll have to put up shades."

"To protect the artwork," Dana finished for him.

He looked directly at her. "Yes. And because I don't want my opening-day patrons going half-blind because the sunset is in their eyes. It slows down sales." He gestured toward the main display wall, which reached up two stories at the highest point. "At least nothing will get on the paintings and drawings. Direct light can ruin them, you know."

"The same thing's true with good graphics," she said as she zipped her portfolio closed.

He understood her meaning. "Don't worry, Dana. We can get down to business shortly."

"I don't want to tie you up, if you have other things to do," she said. "Tell me when it's convenient, and I'll come back—"

"Oh, for God's sake, don't go all noble on me, please. I get enough of that from the artists I show here. Just give me a little time and we can get out of here. I can't tell you how much I'm looking forward to the designs." He spoke with great sincerity, and she felt a pang of shame go through her.

"I didn't mean anything critical, Hamilton," she said quickly. "Really. Sorry I sounded bitchy."

At that he laughed aloud. "Honey, you don't *know* bitchy." He motioned her to a stool. "Make yourself comfortable, and once the crate arrives, ten minutes later I'm yours."

"Okay," said Dana, and climbed onto the stool, leaving her portfolio and purse leaning against the packing crate.

Not quite half an hour passed before the last crate was delivered. The driver of the step-van had a number of papers for Styles to sign, and went through the ritual automatically. Then he took his dolly and left the crate to Styles' enthusiastic care.

"You want to look?" asked Styles, indicating the crate.

Part of her longed to explore, but another part was frightened. She hung back. "I think I'll wait until you have it displayed. That crate isn't the best setting to view the works, is it?"

"True enough," said Styles.

"And I'd just slow you down," she added, aware that this assertion was one he would accept. "Let me know when you've finished."

Twelve minutes later, Styles turned to her and bowed. "Done. Let's go let Hector feed us. On me, of course."

She got down from the stool and picked up her things. "You don't have to."

"I know that. But I enjoy it, and I can take part of it off my taxes legitimately. I'd rather look at designs over good food than in the middle of packing material. Wouldn't you?" His grin had impish charm. "There is one thing you could do for me," he said as he started toward the door, setting the alarm system as she joined him.

"What's that?" she asked with genuine interest.

"I wish you'd tell that fetish to turn up," he said. "It makes me nervous, having it crawling around out of sight that way."

His suggestion made her feel queasy; then the moment passed and she was able to smile. "All right. Dream Catcher," she addressed the gallery, trying not to pay attention to the long shadows angling from the brilliant splash of sunset coral. There was something unnerving about the contrasts between the light and dark that bothered her. She had a sensation that she was calling into a darkness deeper than the coming dusk. "Dream Catcher, come out, come out, wherever you are."

"Very good," Styles approved. "It won't have the nerve to stay away now."

In spite of her best intentions, Dana trembled, and the skin on her face and neck prickled.

"Here. You're cold," said Styles. "Where's your coat?"

"In the car," she told him. "It's not worth bothering to get. We aren't going any farther than the Sea Chest, are we?"

"If you're sure..." he faltered.

"Food will warm me up better than the coat will. I haven't eaten anything since my morning yogurt." It was the truth, but she did not tell him that the reason for this was that she had had no appetite all day long.

Once they were in the restaurant, Hector Ramierez seated them in a booth toward the back. "Where you can talk privately. No one will disturb you; I'll serve you myself, so you can speak confidentially," he promised them, his gaze lingering on Dana. "Have you done something...new? Whatever it is, it suits you."

"I had my hair cut this afternoon. Thanks for noticing," Dana replied, blushing.

"It's very nice," said Ramierez, and handed them menus. "There's prawns with olive oil and three kinds of mushrooms. We have halibut with an orange salsa. And I've made seviche."

Styles waved grandly. "Bring us whatever you think is best tonight," he said as he slid into the booth. "And a couple of glasses of Far Niente Chardonnay." Belatedly he added, "And a basket of focaccia. Dana needs something to sop up the wine."

"Leave everything to me," said Ramierez gallantly, and went off in the direction of the kitchen.

"Now," said Styles, rubbing his hands together. "Let me see what you have."

Dana had lifted her portfolio onto the table, and she unzipped it carefully, trying not to disturb the tablecloth. As she opened it, she had a moment of panic, fearing that Hamilton Styles would not like her designs, certain now that Kirk had been right and she was no more than a dabbler in a tough, competitive world. These megrims evaporated as she handed the preliminaries to Styles, who grinned with profound satisfaction.

"This is just what I wanted," he said as he looked at the sheets. "The business card will reduce all right, won't it?"

"Yes. And still be readable." She showed him a set of variations. "These aren't quite as effective, but they cost a third less, as you'll see on my price sheet."

He nodded several times. "I don't care if it costs more, I like this color scheme best." He held up the first set. "We'll work out numbers." He paused, taking an oversize envelope out of his zipper case. "One more thing. Can you include this picture in the fliers for the show?"

Expecting to see a statue or a print, Dana turned the photograph over and stared down into the not-quite-handsome face with the springy light-brown hair and green eyes that had haunted her dreams. A sensation of vertigo came over her, but reversed, as if she were

being drawn up from the ground, not spiraling down
toward it. She tried to convince herself it was all an
odd coincidence. As if he were speaking from a great
distance, she heard Styles tell her, "That's Trevor
Davidson."

He filled her dreams that night, Trevor Davidson
did. *He came to her, seeking her out in a place that
was neither her office nor her home, but some of both.
He brought her a bouquet of flowers she did not recognize, and a wine that was clear and red as the sky
before a night wind. He touched her as if he touched
something sacred. And when he took her in his arms
she felt she was made of light. Every sinew and fiber
of her body resonated to his passion. He let her set the
pace, never showing impatience or petulance, encouraging her with caresses and lazy kisses. He awakened
something in her she had begun to fear she did not
possess. She could not encompass the joy he gave her,
so vast did it seem. Never in her life had she so wanted
someone to be real as she did now.
    And she could not rid herself of an echoing sound
of mocking laughter.*

The following Monday, Styles called and asked
Dana if she wanted to ride up to San Francisco with
him to pick up Trevor Davidson. "There's room
enough in my Pathfinder. It isn't going to be
crowded."
    "I don't think I can," she said, not wanting to ex-
plain her meaning to Styles. She hoped he would assume she was too busy.

"I know how that is." He hesitated. "Well, what about coming along this evening for supper? It won't take the whole evening. The poor guy's going to be jet-lagged anyway, and a couple of friendly faces will make it more pleasant to unwind and get back in line with the clock."

"I guess so," Dana said reluctantly, torn between her desire to meet this man who haunted her dreams—and half her waking hours, as well—and her fear that he might be nothing more than another version of Kirk. The dream of him had promised so much that the reality might well disappoint her. That would surely dash all her hopes, if the man she had imagined so vividly, and had invested with every virtue she longed for, turned out to be nothing more than another male opportunist.

"Hey, Dana," said Styles, teasing her, "I'll be there to chaperon. If it turns out that he's one of the brooding, silent types, I won't make you hang around much longer than it takes to eat a plate of nachos. If you want to run off early for an important last-minute appointment, I won't stop you."

In spite of herself, she could not keep from chuckling. "All right. Tell me where and when."

"Well, Wednesday night. Probably earlier than later. I'll give you a call at your office after I pick him up. You can figure it will take us about two hours from San Francisco Airport, if we don't run into rush-hour traffic in San Jose." He paused. "His plane is due in at 12:20, and assuming it's on time, I don't think traffic will be a problem. But customs can take a long time."

"True enough," Dana agreed, trying to think of what she should wear, and whether she ought to cancel her three o'clock appointment on Wednesday.

"I'm estimating we'll arrive fourish." Styles laughed, a little nervously. "I'll have all that time in the car to find out about him. They say he's a very odd man—not bad or unpleasant, but odd." Again, he laughed. "But he's an artist. What else are they going to say?"

Dana could not summon up a response; she put her free hand to her forehead, as if trying to press her thoughts back inside her skull. "Where were you planning to take him? For supper, I mean?" She assumed it would be the Sea Chest.

"Oh, I thought we'd go someplace easy," he said, with a guarded tone to his voice. "Probably El Gallo Dorado. He can get everything there. With lots of variety."

"El Gallo Dorado?" Dana asked. "I haven't been there in years." Kirk had considered it too low-class for him, and had refused to go there.

"It's lots better than it used to be—the decor isn't plastic grapes and sugar skulls anymore, and the salsa is fresh," said Styles, and answered her unvoiced question. "I'm saving the Sea Chest for when he's rested, if it turns out he cares about good food. Besides, Hector wouldn't let him out for at least two hours, and if Davidson is zonked, he won't want to spend all that time over a meal."

"Oh," said Dana. "Yes."

"So. I'll give you a call when I've collected him and we'll work out when you're supposed to meet us at El

Gallo Dorado." He was about to hang up, then said, "I still haven't found the fetish. And I've been looking for it."

"Oh, no, Hamilton." For Dana, this news was disturbing. "Has it been really lost? Or stolen?"

"I don't know," he answered, his voice now sounding troubled, in spite of his single pop of a chuckle. "There are times I think it's hiding."

That last word struck Dana like a fist. "Why would you think that?"

"Because sometimes I think he's *taunting* me. I feel like he's just out of reach somewhere, making my life miserable and enjoying it." He paused and brought himself to order. "It's probably just nonsense."

And the face in Dana's dreams was probably not Trevor Davidson, it was too unreasonable to think it was anything more than her own projected longings, but the eeriness of the experience lingered, along with the sardonic laughter. "I know what you mean," she said. "I occasionally think it could be trying to... influence me some way."

Now Styles' sigh was truly one of relief. "I'm glad it isn't just me. I was beginning to worry that I had worked myself up into... a state."

"Maybe this is one of those hysterical things, a shared delusion," said Dana, wanting to find an explanation that did not make her spine go cold.

"Pretty strange for hysteria," said Styles. "Nothing in my Master's prepared me for this."

"Masters?" Dana asked, startled and ashamed of being startled. Why shouldn't the owner of Oddments have a Master's degree? "In what?"

"In psychology, of all things. I did a study of cultural symbolism and psychology in primitive art. Most of it was overintellectualized hooey, but the core of it was sound. I wish I had had more time on it, so it wouldn't have been so superficial." He fell silent for a long two seconds. "The research was great—I barely scratched the surface."

"I can imagine," Dana said with feeling.

"Anyway," he said briskly, "it's nothing for you to worry about. I'll find the thing eventually, and you can let him know then what a lousy job he did on your dream."

It was on the tip of her tongue to tell him about the dreams, but she said nothing. Not only would it sound absurd, Styles might think she wanted to make brownie points with his New Zealand sculptor. She made her voice as bright as his. "If you find him, I will."

It took Dana ten minutes to get up the courage to leave her car and go into El Gallo Dorado. She had found a parking place just half a block from the restaurant. Ordinarily this would have pleased her, but she felt now as if she were being drawn into a trap. Nervously she ran a comb through her hair, checked her lipstick for the third time, then ordered herself to open the door. She fed the parking meter, making the most of these last few seconds of freedom. Sternly she chastised herself: This meeting was no big thing, nothing more than a favor to a friend. It was only her fears, based on a ridiculous wooden figure and the things she had said to it, that made her so jumpy. She should regard it as an opportunity, a first time back in the pool since Kirk left. She had a chance to meet an interesting man, not a dream lover who brought her ecstasy. Trevor Davidson, she told herself sternly, was a sculptor from New Zealand, here for a show. Period. He did not visit her in the night. He was not the culmination of the desires she had told to Dream Catcher. They had not spent the past three nights making love—that was her fantasy. The real man was someone entirely different. Whoever he was, Trevor Davidson was not the lover of her dreams, much as she might wish he were. He was not here on some supernatural summons, but through a practical arrangement with Hamilton Styles. The rest was spooks and silliness. As she crossed the courtyard of the restaurant, she wished fervently she believed her own pep talk, that she was not afraid to meet Trevor Davidson because she was certain she would once again be disappointed.

The hostess was an attractive woman of about forty. She smiled at Dana and asked how many in her party.

"I'm joining Hamilton Styles and his guest," said Dana, not wanting it to appear that she was alone.

"Mister Styles called a few minutes ago and said he would be about ten minutes late." The hostess's smile was professional, without interest. "If you would like to wait in the patio bar?"

Feeling nonplussed, Dana managed to gather her thoughts. "Yes." She fussed with the zipper on her purse. "That would be fine." Actually, she thought, it would be awful, sitting alone, waiting, while all her newfound courage drained away in fidgets.

"I'll have Matteo bring you some salsa and chips," said the woman as she indicated a high-backed rattan settee with tropically bright cushions on it. "I'll tell Mister Styles where you are when he gets here."

"Thanks," said Dana, wishing she could vanish and reappear after Styles and Trevor Davidson arrived. There was always the option of gong to the ladies' room, but that was too obvious an out, and it made her feel more apprehensive than ever, like a high school girl hiding out at the prom. She took her place and pulled out a paperback from her portfolio, which she had brought along just in case. Ordinarily the story, which was a complex tale of love, betrayal and politics at the start of World War II, would have held her attention, but now she found she was reading the same paragraph three or four times before any of it made sense.

When the waitress came to ask her if she wanted a drink, she almost ordered a margarita, and then thought better of it. She would need all her wits about her when Styles arrived with the sculptor from New Zealand. She reminded herself that there was no need for embarrassment. Trevor Davidson had not been in her dreams. He did not know what she had imagined them doing together. But she also hated looking as if she was waiting, so at last she ordered a pot of tea and hoped she could nurse it and the chapter along until the men arrived.

She had just reached the part where the young Jewish musician had successfully eluded the Gestapo and was making plans to escape in the hold of a Norwegian ship when she heard someone speak her name.

"Must be one hell of a yarn," said Styles, coming to plunk himself down opposite her. He indicated a man still standing. "This is the man from Wellington—Trevor Davidson. Trevor Davidson, this is Dana Piper."

His green eyes were brighter than she had imagined, Dana realized as she held out her hand to him. "Mister Davidson." It was hard not to stare at him. He was sturdy, his body solid without being fat. His arms and shoulders were well muscled—from work, not honed by hours in the gym. He was in a loose cardigan of natural wool over a turtleneck in a dark sage shade. His slacks were a color between pewter and brown. She knew how his big, square hands felt, and the scrape of his day-old beard on her skin.

"I thought you Yanks always started with Christian names," he said, engulfing her hand in his. There was a twang in his deep, peaceful voice that was not quite Australian, not quite English.

"California is a long way from Yankees," said Dana, astonished that she would be so rude, especially to this man, who had taken over her dreams.

But the New Zealander smiled without a trace of offence or annoyance. "Point taken. So do I call you Dana or Ms. Piper?" Before she could answer, he went on. "I'd better warn you that Hamilton has been telling me all about you on the way from San Francisco, and so I feel we are already acquainted. I hope I won't offend you by saying there's something familiar about you."

Chagrined by her own bad manners, and flushed with the feelings his presence excited in her, Dana tried to repair the damage she was sure she had done. She said, "Well, then I suppose it should be Dana. After all, Californians are supposed to be the most casual of all of us." She could not bring herself to smile—she was too amazed by his reality to do that—but she relaxed enough to make a gesture inviting him to take the chair on her left.

"That's what everyone tells me." He settled down on the small settee, taking over the whole thing by putting one arm across the back of the magenta cushion. "But, to be honest, I like being asked which I'd prefer first."

Dana saw Styles give her a hidden thumbs-up. She had not insulted him after all. She could feel her cheeks turn rosy, which made her blush more deeply. "So do I," she admitted.

"And you haven't said yet which it is to be," he reminded her.

"Nor have you." She wanted to bite her tongue before she made a complete fool of herself with this man. Where did she get off, fencing with him this way?

"I never thought Americans were such sticklers for form. All right. You may call me Trevor, unless you're introducing me, and then I would prefer my whole name. For obvious reasons." The last was done with a nod to Styles. "We don't want all his lovely publicity to go to waste."

"It would be a pity," Dana agreed, trying to match his bantering tone. If she could keep up a contest with him, perhaps she would not give herself away. "That being the case, I think the same arrangements will do for me. I don't want to lose the chance to put in a good word for Piper Designs.''

Styles was smiling like the Cheshire Cat.

"No, indeed," said Trevor at once. "From what I've seen, you do excellent work, and you ought to make the most of it."

"Thanks," said Dana. She put her book back in her purse as she saw the waitress approach. It felt like giving up her last protection against—what? She did not want to have to name it, for fear of what it would mean to her. Trevor Davidson was paying very little attention to her. She had no reason to think that this would change when he was rested. Why should she feel so exposed?

"How hungry are you, Trevor?" asked Styles.

"I haven't the least notion," he answered amiably, and stifled a yawn. "I don't know what time it is. I hardly know what *day* it is. If you're ordering for me, I want appetizers only. Travel is catching up with me."

Styles grinned at Dana. "You heard him. Let's get a pitcher of margaritas and an order each of quesadillas, nachos grandes, and flautitas. That will hold us, I think." He winked at the waitress. "And if you'll bring the guacamole, we have to have some with chips. Soon."

"Certainly," she said, scribbled a few words, then left them alone.

"I'm going to sleep for the next sixteen hours," Trevor announced to Styles. "And as soon as I figure out where I am, I will come to your gallery and help you set up."

"I'd appreciate that," said Styles. "I think you'll find that for a smallish place, the exhibit area is very good."

Dana realized she was staring at his hands, trying to decide whether they were like the ones that touched her so magically in her dreams. With an effort of will she dragged her gaze away.

"So you've told me," said Trevor, energetically running his hands through his springy light-brown hair. "If I drift off, neither of you should take it personally. This is nothing but jet lag. I always have it when I travel."

Dana watched him closely, thinking how much she liked his face, and how familiar it was. Right now he needed a shave, but often in her dreams he had been courteous enough to shave and bathe before, or to apologize for the marks he left ... She looked across the room, afraid her eyes would give her away if he saw them. Keep your wits about you, she ordered herself sternly. He's probably got a wife and kids at home. Probably a nice house, with a studio in the back. Men like him don't remain single forever. This bracing notion did not improve her state of mind as she had hoped it would.

"Would you like me to order coffee for you?" asked Styles.

"No, thank you," said Trevor. "I want to sleep, not spend the night or whatever-it-is going dotty." He made himself sit up straight. "I'll take you up on coffee tomorrow night, if I may." He made his suggestion include Dana.

"How does seven sound?" asked Styles, looking directly at Dana. "I'll call you in the afternoon and tell you where."

"Great," said Dana, as if listening to the order for a firing squad.

The waitress returned with the pitcher of margaritas with three glasses and two bowls, one of guacamole and one of chips still warm.

Athos was curled up at the foot of the bed, Aramis draped over the other pillow, and Porthos was lying alongside her, his large ears almost touching her chin. As tired as she was, Dana was almost afraid to fall asleep. For the past three hours she had remained awake, her mind repeatedly going over her meeting with Trevor Davidson. Now that the lover in her dreams had a real body, and a voice she liked to hear, she felt awkward in her desire, slightly ashamed that she had permitted herself to enjoy everything in her dreams. As long as he was a figment of her imagination, it was easy to give her fancy free rein, but now, having met the man, she could not rid herself of the sense of intruding.

She adjusted her position, and Porthos gave a soft yow of protest, then did what he could to restore his comfort.

By 3:00 a.m. she could not keep herself awake any longer. She drifted off into dreams that were more intense than any she had had so far. Trevor Davidson filled her dreams with a passion so burning that Dana half expected to find marks on her skin when she woke. That she would have such all-consuming fulfillment with this man. That she could succumb to a need with so much joy. In back of the dream was her own good sense, reminding her that dreams could do all kinds of things that people could not, and that just because her dreams offered gratification of her every wish, it did not mean that any of it would happen while she was awake. Let alone with a man she had met only a few hours ago.

She feared she was becoming obsessed with him, and he was a stranger to her. *And once again he was in her dreams, but this time so vividly she felt her sheets less immediately than she felt his skin. She could hear him talk to her in his warm, deep voice, though she could not make out the words. He was the air she breathed and the support of her bed. He was the whole world, as compelling as the need for nourishment. He sustained her. He had weight now, and smell, and taste that was so much more than it had been before they met. And for the first time that frightened her, for she dreaded what might become of them both if she could not rid herself of his dominance of her dreams.*

Morning brought her awake with a start half an hour before her alarm, and gave her an odd, engulfing sense of shame. As long as Trevor Davidson were only a figure in her dreams, it did not matter to her what form those dreams took. But now that she had met him, had touched his hand and heard his voice, she could not rid herself of the feeling that her dreams were somehow intrusive, a way to break in upon him and demand an attention that was not hers, from a man who might not want her.

Porthos came and nudged her with his head, purring encouragement as he did. He angled his head to allow her to scratch him in a better spot. Taking notice of this display of affection, Aramis sauntered up the bed and sat very neatly in front of Dana, too polite to require her to do anything, but close enough to make it easy for her to pet him.

"If only people were as easy to deal with as cats," she said to hers. "But people are tricky, aren't they?"

Porthos gave a kind of chirp and pressed his head more firmly against her fingers.

"All right, all right," she said, and spent a few minutes pampering him with one hand and petting Aramis with the other. Then she looked down at the foot of the bed, where Athos lay, all curled up and apparently indifferent to what was going on. "You don't have to sulk," she told him, reaching down and dragging him toward her. He pretended to ignore her but managed to lift his chin to just the right height for her to take proper care of him.

"Very good," she approved as she went to work on his jaw and jowls. Then she made herself get up; she drew on her robe and straggled to the kitchen in her tangled escort of cats. She began to shake off the embarrassment that had claimed her. After all, she reasoned as she turned the toaster oven on, it was only a dream. It wasn't as if anything real happened.

This steadiness stayed with her all the way to midmorning at the office. A phone call shattered the calm she had been able to restore for herself.

"Ms. Piper?" said the deep, musical voice on the other end of the phone. "This is Trevor Davidson. I hope I'm not interrupting your work."

"I...I was just about to take my coffee break," she lied, having trouble breathing. She had never before felt such an intense response to anyone.

"Oh," he answered, as if suddenly uncertain of what to say. "I...uh...wanted to thank you for being so cordial last night. Hamilton told me that you postponed another engagement to join us."

This was news to her, but she said, "No trouble, Mister Davidson, I assure you."

"I thought we'd settled that. I hope you will call me Trevor, Ms. Piper, so that I may call you Dana." Whatever part of his confidence had faltered before, it was back now. "I realize you're busy, but I was hoping you might have some time free later today. I'd like the chance to take you out, to make up for my behavior yesterday."

"You don't have to do that, Mister Davidson." She knew she was blushing; her dreams were suddenly terribly clear to her, so specific that she was afraid to close her eyes for what she might find there. He might be the object of her dreams, but that did not make him the man she had wished for, she reminded herself sternly. She could feel herself shivering and knew it was not from cold or fear, but from the aftermath of intense physical desire.

"But I'd like to, if you'll permit it." He paused. "I was afraid I'd got off on the wrong foot. And I'd like to make amends for any...poor impression you might have received."

She opened her calendar, although she knew everything in it, and looked at her schedule for the day. "My morning's booked, and I have a luncheon at 12:30, and then I have to go by the printer's at three, to check color separations. But if 3:45 isn't too late in the day, I could meet you then."

"Then 3:45 it is. Where shall we—"

"How about the entrance to the aquarium?" she suggested, choosing a well-known and very public location. She wanted to make certain they were not isolated together, not with her feelings in such confusion.

"The aquarium entrance would be great," he told her. "I'll be wearing a roll-top pull-over in dark green wool. Slate-colored twill trousers."

"A roll-top pull-ov— Oh, you mean a turtleneck sweater," she said, mentally translating from New Zealand English.

He chuckled. "Didn't your Mark Twain say something about the barrier of a common language?"

"Sounds like him," said Dana, trying not to feel too giddy. It was only a dream, she reminded herself sternly. Her dream, not his. What would she do when she saw him? When she had to face him with her dreams of him still fresh in her mind? She wasn't sure she could touch his big, square hands without remembering what they had done to her in her dreams, the way they had molded her flesh and shaped her passion. And what would she do then?

"Well, very good, then. I'm looking forward to it, Dana." He said her name as if it was delicious on his tongue.

"See you then." She could not bring herself to say his name, for fear of what it would reveal to him. She hung up quickly so that she would not be tempted to linger on the phone. If she spoke to him too long, she might say... anything.

CHAPTER THREE

A thin line of fog so white it turned the horizon to a band of glare hovered beyond the edge of the bay, imparting a chill to the brisk wind that tweaked the waves into whitecaps and sent most of the visitors to the aquarium off the decks to the warmth of indoors, and the wonders of the enormous tanks of marine life.

"It's a handsome place, from what I can see from outside," approved Trevor, hitching his thumb at the aquarium as he came up to Dana. His smile was tentative. "It doesn't feel as big as it is. Makes it comfortable. I want to have a proper tour of it." He was dressed in a light khaki windbreaker very like the ones recreational sailors wore out on Monterey Bay. Beneath it was his roll-top pull-over, as he had described it, and his dark twill slacks showed enough use to prove they were not new for this trip. His shoes were sensible, and, she realized, expensive Mephistos.

Dana glanced over her shoulder at the building. "Do you want to go in? It's worth seeing." And they would be safely surrounded by a crowd.

"Not today, thanks. If we can walk on the beach instead..." he answered, looking at her with such directness that she blushed and hoped he would think the wind had colored her cheeks. "I don't think I'm ready for crowds yet. I need a couple of days to get acclimated.''

''All right. There's a walkway down that direction,'' she said, trying not to sound flustered. She realized it would take very little to panic her. ''It leads to the beach on Point Cabrillo. It's not far.'' She hitched her purse strap a little higher on her shoulder.

''Let's go that way, then,'' he said, and started out at a pace that was not too fast and not dawdling, either. ''It's a magnificent day, isn't it?''

''Yes,'' she said, wishing she didn't feel so self-conscious. She indicated the paved walk. ''That's what we're looking for. It leads around the point.''

''Very good.'' He smiled at her, something so winning that she felt her heart leap in her chest. She was beginning to think that she should not have agreed to come. It was too embarrassing to think of this man she hardly knew in the way she was thinking of him now, with his hands making a sculpture of her body, and the weight of him on her.

They had just turned off the main walk onto the narrower path leading to the sand. Three teenage boys in wet suits came rushing toward them, all but oblivious of their presence. They all carried scuba gear; they were laughing.

As she stepped out of the way of the boys, Dana coughed, and tried to think of something to say that would not offend Trevor. ''We're almost at the place where Monterey Bay becomes the Pacific Ocean. The tide's pretty high just now.'' Did that sound as inane to him as it did to her? But what was she going to say to him?

"So Hamilton informed me. He has agreed to lend me his tide table, though I suppose I could buy one readily." As they rounded the point and the Aquarium vanished behind them, Trevor slowed his walking to a friendly amble. "Look, I don't want you thinking I've lured you here on false pretenses."

She made a motion with her hand that meant everything from *It's nothing* to *I would never think such a thing of you*. With Trevor so close to her, she could not help but be acutely aware of his body, and that led to more troubling recollections of the passion of her dreams. She was afraid she would blurt out something to him that would give her away.

"Actually, when you think of it," he went on in a detached way, "all pretenses are false, aren't they? So the phrase is redundant." The wind ruffled his springy light-brown hair as he left the packed earth of the path for the first low hillock of blowing sand. He gave a single laugh. "I'm babbling. Sorry. That's because I'm nervous." He looked directly at her.

"So am I," admitted Dana before she lost her courage completely.

"You?" He sounded amazed. "It doesn't show."

It was her turn to be amazed. "Really? I thought you... I mean, I'm so edgy... It was just so..." She let her words trail off. "Why?"

"Why what?" he asked, genuinely puzzled. He had to speak loudly to be heard over the rumble and crash of the waves.

"Why would you be nervous?" She had stopped walking now, and as the sand blew around her shoes, she put all her attention on him.

"Well, I don't know you yet. I don't know how things stand with you, if I'm putting myself at a disadvantage by speaking so candidly. But you're a very beautiful woman, for starters," he said with frank appreciation. "And I don't know how you Yank—er...Californians go about things like this, but I find you very attractive."

"Oh." She remained very still as her short hair whipped around her face. "I...I don't know what to say."

"You don't have to say anything. Unless you don't want to hear anything more." He waited for her response.

Her dreams returned in a sudden rush, and she blushed more deeply. Somehow she was able to answer him. "If you say something I don't like, I'll tell you." Where had she found the courage to say that?

"I know I'm probably going too fast. I don't have a lot of time to do this right. You don't have to say anything unless you want me to stop. I hope you'll hear me out. Let me do the first talking." He did his best to smile at her, though now he was as bashful as a kindergarten kid at his first party. His voice was rich and warm, just as she had dreamed it. "I know it's not always wise to act on these chemical responses, I know, but...I don't expect anything from you. This isn't meant to soften you up. But I don't have a long time here, and I'm not willing to wait until the night before I leave to talk about this with you. Hamilton told me you're not involved with anyone just now, and that you would like to be. I hope that's true." He stared out at the waves. "So there might be a chance for..."

Dana wasn't sure she had heard correctly. Could it be that she was not alone in the thoughts and images that haunted her? For an instant she was angry with Styles for talking about her to this foreigner, but her annoyance vanished almost as soon as it was sparked. She tried to convince herself that Trevor was being direct with her, and had no ulterior motives for his confession. But she could not shake off the kind of doubts Kirk would have put into her mind, had he any inkling of this. *Well, he's a man away from home. He doesn't want to spend the whole time in an empty bed, and the cost of a dinner is a lot less than a safe professional,* or *It isn't real, you know, it's only the influence of that thing Styles gave you.*

"Is there?" Trevor prodded in her long silence. "A chance of something happening?"

What sort of something, she wanted to ask—an affair? marriage? debauchery? tennis?— But the very thought of questioning him opened doors she did not want open. She tried not to look as upset as she was, wrestling with equal amounts of hopes and doubts, with cynicism and romantic dreams. This man was real, not a fragment of her dreams, and she had to keep that firmly in mind. It would be so easy, she thought, to let herself lower her guard with this man because of what went on in her sleep, to assume he had all the qualities she sought because he resembled the man in her dreams. It would be easy, and it would probably be a mistake. The trouble was, she liked him; he was attractive and interesting, so she didn't want to turn him off completely. "I might like that, if it turns out that way," she said uncertainly.

He resumed walking slowly, continuing along the beach, parallel to the waterline. "Good." The single word was almost lost in the noise of the ocean.

Dana followed after him, her mind on the force of the waves so that she would not wreck everything by asking too many questions. She wished now she had remembered her dark glasses. The wind and the sun off the water made her squint. It was nippy, and she realized she should have brought a heavier sweater than the cotton-ramie one she wore. She had chosen it for its color, a soft rosy brown that brought out the best in her skin and hair. Her old jeans were so faded as to be as pale as the distant fog.

"I suppose I had best tell you a little about myself." He kept his green eyes fixed on the luminous swath of fog out to sea. "I am thirty-six. I have a thirty-three-year-old brother who teaches anthropology in Sydney, and a sister of twenty-eight who raises show dogs—her husband is a statistician for the government, and they have twin boys, age four. My mother's father's father was Maori. My father was a cruise-ship navigation officer; he died when I was at university. My mother remarried last year. She runs a commercial nursery. Her new husband is a retired barrister. I took a degree in engineering before I decided to try my chances on art. Everyone thought I was bonkers to throw away the security of engineering for the uncertainty of art. I've been sculpting full-time now for five years. Before then, I divided my time between working on bridges and working in wood.

The day I quit my job was the happiest and scariest of my life.''

He said this as if he were speaking to an interviewer, giving the standard biographical information that was usually sought. Now his manner changed, and he spoke with circumspection. ''I was married for three years, shortly after leaving university, but it didn't work out. Once we were out in the world, we discovered we had almost nothing in common except intellectual curiosity. We divorced as amicably as people can, without bitterness or sorrow. She had a great deal of her own money, and as we had no children, the break was total. We've gone in radically different directions, which is probably fortunate for us both. We haven't spoken in six years, largely because neither of us has anything to say to the other. I read last year she had married again. I wish her every success. Truly.'' He met Dana's eyes with his own. ''I don't want you to think that I would abandon Alicia. Had she needed alimony, I would have kept at bridge design as long as necessary, but, fortunately, that wasn't the case. She wanted everything finished, and I agreed with her.''

''Why tell me? Why does this matter so much to you?'' asked Dana, because she could think of nothing else to ask him.

The deep note was back in his voice. ''Your good opinion is important to me. I don't want to be misunderstood. I don't want you crying foul later on.''

Dana stared at him, trying to make sense of everything he was saying to her. ''What is there to 'cry foul' about? Why should I misunderstand?''

He shook his head, his eyes directed at the sand. "There is something more," he went on awkwardly, adding to himself, so quietly that Dana could hardly hear him, "Damn. I rehearsed all this so I wouldn't muck it up. And I'm mucking it up." He made fists of his hands. "Please, Dana. Don't interrupt me now. Let me get it out or I'll never have the nerve again."

"Why did you rehearse it?" asked Dana.

"Because... I'm worried you won't believe me. I want you to know I'm not the kind of man who goes around with lines about..." His green eyes revealed the depth of his feelings, like little living flames. "You see—promise me you won't laugh at this—I've been... well, I've been dreaming about you for the last week or so. I won't distress you by telling you about the dreams, but they did emphatically catch my attention. I know it isn't... You're not my dream, but I can't help but hope you might..." His nervous smile faded, and he turned suddenly and took both her hands in his. "In fact, when I met you, I was... I can't describe it."

Now Dana was shivering, but not entirely from the bite of the wind. It was troubling to think that something was set in motion between them, something they could not control or change. She tried to pull her hands away, but without much effort and no success. "I think I know," she confessed, and felt a deep rush of warmth spread swiftly through her.

"If I hadn't been so jet-lagged I might have said... something foolish then, like, haven't we met before?" He released her hands, and squinted down at the sand. "Instead, I saved it for now."

"What makes you think it's foolish?" asked Dana, surprised at her own audacity. "It doesn't feel that way to me." What had come over her, she wondered, that she let herself answer him so boldly?

He turned his green eyes on her, hope brightening them once again. "Do you mean that? You had a similar feeling?" He was reassured by her nod. "That's a relief," he said, and sighed, as if ending a long effort. He went on a short way, saying nothing, watching the sand move ahead of the toes of his shoes. Then he stopped and asked her once more. "You mean it? Really? You felt you had met me before?"

She could deny it now, and it wouldn't mean anything. She heard herself say, "Yes."

He regarded her intently, with a look between hunger and speculation. "How? Do you know how you met me? Or thought you met me?"

"In dreams," she answered, and was lost.

They had supper together at a small, uncrowded restaurant at the back of a courtyard, about a quarter mile from the beach. The fog had come in, turning the evening clammy and chilly, so they were glad to sit near the free-standing fireplace and linger over port and cheese.

Dana had been able to subdue the most frenetic images of her dreams, and she was able to look Trevor in his bright green eyes without embarrassment. She was trying to work up her courage to explain to him about Dream Catcher when he saved her the trouble.

"Hamilton told me about that peculiar incident you had in his gallery the first time you went there," he said, as if he was discussing nothing more than tomorrow's weather. "That's how he came to explain about your circumstances, your being on your own, and all that. He said you deserved better than you'd got so far. He wasn't just gossiping, or trying to make a match, or anything of that sort."

"What incident?" she asked, although she knew.

"With the fetish. Want to tell me about it?" prompted Trevor. "According to him, you cut your thumb and spilled a little champagne on it. He suggested you ask the demon for something—"

She interrupted. "Demon?"

"Sure," said Trevor. "All those dream dealers are demons, bent on possessing humans to do their will. At least that's what the missionaries said, and this time, it could be right. The fetish demons snare their victims by luring them with the things the victim desires most. There are about a dozen of them in the mythology of the New Hebrides." He laughed, but the sound rang hollow to Dana's ears. "I wish I knew which one you'd been talking to."

"Hamilton called it Dream Catcher," said Dana, feeling queasy.

"They're all called that. That's like calling a native of Paris French. They come in all sorts of inclinations and temperaments, however. What one does in one fashion, another does in another. Some are more benign than others. The question is, which version of Dream Catcher was it?" He looked at her and saw she was becoming upset. "Sorry, Dana, truly," he told her, at once contrite, but with a promise of warmer feelings in his green eyes. "I didn't mean to trouble you. If I didn't feel a certain stake in this, I wouldn't pursue it."

"That's okay," she said, her voice flat. "I shouldn't put any credence in such things, I know, but I . . . that is, you . . . And I thought about . . . everything that mattered to me, things I wanted to have." She made herself sort out her impressions. "From what I can tell, you are so much what I wished for, that's all. And that makes me worried. I don't want this to be because of a wooden carving, but because . . . because we are who we are." There. She had said it. It was out in the open now. There was no going back.

His response ended her doubts. "Great! That's *great!*" His smile made creases in his cheeks and deepened the lines around his eyes.

"Why?" she asked with determination. "If the Dream Catcher is a demon, why should you be so pleased you fit the bill of what I wanted? Wouldn't that make you suspicious instead?" It was the thing she feared the most, and now she said it, she was more uncomfortable than before, as if he had read her diary or eavesdropped on a private conversation.

"On the contrary. You've complimented me highly, because you . . . It has nothing to do with the fetish." He lifted his chimney glass to her in a silent toast. "I was afraid at first you were amusing yourself with the visiting artist, enjoying a fling." Abruptly he looked very serious. "There are women who do that, you know. They like a little of the artistic ambience— whatever that means—from time to time. They look upon this kind of fling as a sexual vacation with culture. Something like the way certain men always go after models or stewardesses, wearing them like trophies. And not that there aren't artists out there who like getting caught by women wanting flings.''

"Has that happened to you often?" Dana asked, astonished to realize she was feeling jealous.

"No, not very, thank God. I don't like to think of myself as that kind of entertainment. So I'm fairly adept at spotting such women. The last time I was caught up in something of the sort was four years ago." His features softened once more. "You don't have the look about you, but I couldn't help but wonder. If I hadn't been dreaming about you for a week, I might have been more reserved."

"I know I would have been, if I hadn't been dreaming of you." This was not much more than a whisper.

He leaned forward to speak to her, and to look directly into her eyes. "I don't know about your dreams, but mine have been wonderful. So wonderful that I couldn't believe you were real when we met. I don't think I can tell you yet how the dreams make me feel." He managed a slight smile that was as mischievous as it was shy.

She felt color mount in her face and neck, and she wanted to flee almost as much as she wanted to stay. "So have mine, and I can't describe how, either," she confessed, and put her hand to her eyes, as if that would protect her from all she sensed in him.

As he took her hand in his, he said, "Don't worry, Dana. You have nothing to be afraid of from me.

Nothing will happen you don't want to happen. And I won't think the less of you, no matter what you decide." He kissed her fingers and released her. "But don't hold it against me if I hope."

"No, I won't," she said, trying to think of what she was hoping for from him. Was it the steamy stuff of her dreams, or was it something else? And if so, what?

"Listen, Dana," he said softly, "I don't want to put pressure on you. Tell me if I'm going too fast and I'll back off."

"You keep saying that," she pointed out. "Are you protesting too much?"

"God, no," he assured her. "I don't want you to think of me as someone who coerces you into things." He read something in her expression. "What is it?"

"Are you saying that because Hamilton told you what I asked the fetish for?" She disliked herself for making the accusation, but she knew she had to have the answer before she could trust herself to spend more time with him. "Are you trying to shape yourself into the thing I want?"

He looked genuinely baffled. Showing no trace of offense, he said, "No. I'm saying that because I don't want to screw up my chances with you." He drank the last of his port and indicated the last of the Stilton. "Do you want anything more?"

"Not tonight," she answered, reaching for her small purse and drawing the strap up to her shoulder. The gesture seemed so final. "Thank you for dinner."

"Ta. And let's not do any more of the polite dance, shall we? I asked you because I want your company and it pleases me to do it for you. Yes, I am a stranger here, and a little friendly company is very welcome. But I'd want to spend time with you in Wellington. Or Timbuktu, for that matter." He drew on his windbreaker again and nodded in the direction of the door. "I'd ask you about tomorrow night, but I think Hamilton wants to begin setup at the gallery, and I haven't a clue when we'll be finished." He held the door for her. "If you're willing to have a late drink or coffee with me, time as yet uncertain, I'd be thrilled."

"I was planning to go to San Luis Obispo tomorrow." As she said it, she felt a keen disappointment. "I made the arrangement six weeks ago, and my cousin is expecting me. My brother and his family are arriving from Akron for a short vacation. I don't think I can postpone going there—the visit is a quick one. It'll be the first time in three years that we'll see each other. I really ought—"

"I understand," he said, lifting his hand to silence her explanations. "When will you be back?"

"Saturday, fairly late," she answered, hoping he would not comment on the brevity of the visit. "I don't know the hour, but not before nine, certainly." She looked pleased. "I can call the gallery when I leave San Luis, if you like."

He grinned at her. "That would be terrific." He indicated the thickening fog. "I'm just three blocks away. Are you going to be safe driving home in this soup?"

"I live here, remember?" she asked, fighting off the giddy feeling that his concern sparked in her. "My car knows the way. If you like, I'll call you after I've fed the cats."

"Please," he said, and offered her his arm to cross the courtyard.

As family reunions go, this one was a bust, Dana thought as she drove up highway 101 toward the Monterey turnoff. She had been tempted to take the coast road, but with dense fog reported, she knew it would not be possible to drive safely along its narrow, winding course. Highway 101 was wider and faster, and right now she needed speed to ground the ire that crackled in her. That Vincent should have taken that attitude with her! And lectured her on how foolish she was being, having her own business when she could have a larger and more regular income in the employ of a corporate sales-and-promotion division. With this raging discontent for company, she rushed through the farmland, doing her best to ignore the hurtful and hateful things Vincent had said to her. Vincent had been unusually cutting, even for him. She cringed at some of the things she had said back to return hurt for hurt. Poor Elaine, caught in the middle of all this, had deserved better. Dana vowed she would find some way to make it up to her cousin.

At King City she remembered she was supposed to call the gallery; she pulled off, filled her car with gas, then pulled into a nearby restaurant for coffee. She used the phone outside the ladies' room to let Styles and Trevor know she would be arriving in a couple hours.

"How'd it go?" asked Styles. "I've had my share of shell-shocked family gatherings, and you sound like you've been through one."

"I'll tell you about it tomorrow evening. I'll be by after six-thirty," she said, feeling a dull ache at the back of her head, as if she had been coshed when she wasn't looking.

"Sounds good," said Styles. "I'll be waiting."

As she paid the bill, Dana ordered a second large coffee to go, so that she would have its bitter taste with her to keep her alert while she drove.

"There's road repair going on outside of Salinas—there are delays," said the woman at the cash register. "Be careful going through there. Keep an eye out for work crews and flagmen. You don't want to have an accident."

"Right," said Dana. "Thanks." Back in the car, she concentrated on the funnel of brilliance created by her headlights. It was better than letting herself mull uselessly over the deteriorating relationship between Vincent and her. But what could she expect, she wondered, with fourteen years' difference in age? He had long since got used to being an only child. And then, just as puberty got its hooks into him, along comes this baby sister, and Vincent was not ready to deal with infant Dana and pimples at the same time. The family had just been transferred from St. Louis to San Jose, and Vincent was resentful of being taken away from his school and his friends. To be exiled and asked to tolerate an interloper at the same time—that was the way he saw those years. He had blamed her for every unhappiness in his life. She sighed as she recalled how he had bullied her all through her childhood.

"Don't dwell on it. It's over, for now. He'll be two thousand miles away next week, and he won't be back in California for another four years," she said aloud to the unpleasant memories. In a little while, she told herself, you will be home. You'll see Trevor again. It was so much nicer to think about Trevor. Vincent was the past, a brother who had always resented her, and that couldn't be changed. She let herself lapse into a kind of freeway dream, in which she anticipated everything that would unfold with them. Most of the images were erotic without being specific, a montage of hands and lips and fused senses. But occasionally, like a sour note in a beautiful song, there would be sharp, clear moments of pain, of deliberate harm. When these happened, Dana winced, swallowed against the humiliation that rocked her, and tried to convince herself that they were the result of her anger with Vincent, not part of the allure Trevor offered her.

By the time she reached the turnoff for Monterey, she was rattled and uncertain. Her headache was big enough to kill her appetite; she felt shaky. As she drove home, she promised herself she'd have a long bath and make an early night of it.

The sound of her doorbell roused her from the gentle stupor of her bath, where she had spent the past hour trying to ease the tension from her body. She looked around at Aramis, who was curled on the back of the toilet, watching her with slitted eyes. "What? What was that?" It seemed unlikely that anyone would be stopping by at this hour.

Aramis had no answer for her as the bell rang again.

"Just a moment!" she called out, rising from the hot, rosemary-scented water. Her skin was rosy as she drew her terry-cloth robe on and fumbled for her slippers.

The third ring came as she padded into the living room. A glance at her mantel clock told her it was too late for a casual caller—10:34. If it was an emergency, there should be other indications, such as sirens or... She kept the chain on as she opened the door just enough to see who it was.

"Sorry to disturb you so late," said Trevor Davidson, without any indication that he was distressed about what he was doing. He was casually dressed, but did not appear to take his welcome for granted. "But I was worried when you didn't call. I was afraid something might have happened to you, so I thought I'd better make sure you were all right." His smile came and went. "I know that sounds lame, but—"

"You could have used the phone," she said, returning his smile in spite of herself. This was the kind of concern she had hoped to find in a man—had wished to find in one. If only she weren't projecting her desires onto Trevor Davidson, who might only be showing the kind of courtesy anyone would expect of a friend in New Zealand.

"So I could," he agreed. "But then you would have had the option to tell me you didn't want company tonight." His green eyes grew serious. "And I think we need to talk."

"About what?" she asked, trying not to feel nervous.

"You know about what," he said, his voice deep and gentle. "Well? Do you want me to leave?"

Dana shook her head, for the thought of him leaving now was desolating. She was suddenly acutely aware of how she was dressed, and how she must appear to him. She blushed, but closed the door to take the chain off. "Come in," she told him as she stood aside.

He glanced around. "Very nice, Dana," he approved as he looked at the wood paneling of the living room and dining room, and the large, deep built-in bookcases that flanked the fireplace. "I particularly like the Chinese chairs." He thrust his hands into the pockets of his anorak. "I'm not much good at California architectural styles. How old is it, sixty years or so?"

"Built in 1909," said Dana. "Rewired twenty years ago, and with a new furnace, as well. Thank goodness," she added. "New roof eight years ago. Kitchen remodeled in 1964. Track lighting put in in 1983. The landlord is the grandson of the original owner."

"You rent it, then?" he asked.

"Lease with purchase option," she answered. "The landlord is getting old, and his kids are well established in other parts of the country." Why, she wondered, was she telling him all this?

"I hope you buy it." He smiled at her, his manner becoming awkward as she continued to stare at him.

Thinking she had to say something, Dana offered, "Would you like a cup of tea, or coffee?"

"Coffee would be lovely," he said, grateful for her tact.

"Just a moment. I'll put the water on," she said, going toward the kitchen. She would have a moment to escape, she decided, so she could throw on her sweats and feel less naked than she did in her bathrobe. It was the lack of underwear, she realized, that gave her the sense of exposure, that and the way the terry cloth folded back from her legs when she turned, as if she wanted to give him more than coffee and a little of her evening.

He followed her, nodding his approval at what he saw. "A very nice place."

Porthos came rushing into the kitchen in the fond assumption that he was about to get a second dinner. He slid on the linoleum as he saw Trevor, all but somersaulting to avoid running into the newcomer.

Dana had rarely been more pleased to see her cat. "That's Porthos," she said.

"And where is Athos, and Aramis, and d'Artagnan?" he asked her as she began to measure out coffee into a clean filter.

"No d'Artagnan. Just the Three Musketeers. Athos and Aramis are around somewhere." She filled the coffeemaker with water, put the pot in place, then turned to look at him. "You said you wanted to talk?"

Trevor was bent over, scratching the back of Porthos' head; the cat purred encouragement.

"I don't have anything other than coffee to offer you, unless you want some nonfat yogurt," Dana went on, trying to behave as if there was nothing strange about having Trevor in her kitchen at this hour of the night. Trevor, of all people in the world, she added to herself, her face reddening.

"Coffee's fine," he said, standing up. Porthos made a loud protest at this shameful neglect.

Abruptly Dana said, "Look, I'm going to go change. I don't feel comfortable dressed like this." The admission made her blush again.

"Whatever you want," said Trevor.

Dana shot him a dubious look, and discovered he was sincere. "I won't be long." She fled before he could say anything more.

Three minutes later she was in her faded, comfortable sweats, with a knit cotton cocoon jacket pulled over for extra warmth, and to hide her body more completely. She made her way back to the kitchen and discovered that all three cats were now preening for Trevor. "You've made a hit. They don't like everyone, like most cats. Especially Athos."

"The glum brown one," said Trevor. His smile was as warm as the beach on a July afternoon.

"That's right." She checked the coffeemaker, then took down two large stoneware mugs, setting them on the counter in anticipation.

Now that he had this opportunity, Trevor was hesitant. "I don't know quite how to begin this," he said, abandoning the cats to come to her side.

With him so close, all she could think of was how much he was like the man she had wished for. And if not for the terrible turn her dreams had taken, she would be delighted he had sought her out. She indicated the living room, needing to put some distance between them. "Would you like to sit down while you figure it out?" That was sharper than she had intended it to be, and she bit her lower lip.

"Thanks, yes," said Trevor, though he remained where he was. "You need any help? Is there something you'd like me to do?"

"Help with two mugs? Not really," she answered with a nervous giggle. With him so close to her, she felt as if her nerves were on stalks.

"If you change your mind, call me," he said as he went off to the living room and chose a place on the long sofa. Aramis and Porthos followed after him; a short while later, so did Athos.

As soon as the coffee was ready, Dana filled the mugs and carried them into the living room. She hesitated before taking her place at the other end of the sofa, ostensibly not to disturb the cats. "I hope black is okay."

"It's hot, that's what counts," said Trevor. He looked down into his coffee as if he might find secrets revealed in it. "About the dreams," he said, and fell silent.

"What about them?" Dana asked, when she could not stand the suspense. It would be so easy to reach out and put her hand on his arm. She forced herself to remain still.

"They started before I came here. I saw you." He looked directly at her; suddenly her sweats felt transparent. "And there was more. I know you understand what I mean by that. Don't you?"

"More," she repeated, the breath catching in her throat. Why did he have to come here on the same day she had fought with Vincent? She was feeling rocky enough without this.

"If you don't want to talk about it, I'll shut up," he said, aware of her anxiety.

She shook her head. "Let's get it over with." As soon as she heard herself, she knew she was handling it badly. "Forget I said that. It wasn't what I meant."

He studied her profile before he went on. "I've never experienced anything like this before. I feel out of my depth. Most of the time, it's wonderful, what happens in the dreams. I won't deny that, but there are times...I get frightened what I dream. There are things I am compelled to do in the dreams—" He broke off, unable to go on.

She nodded. "The...painful things?"

This time he faltered. "That, and liking it. Seeking out humiliating, disgusting things. Liking those perversions is the worst part. It...shames me." He took his mug in his hands, as if it would protect him. "I don't know where that comes from—and that worries me. I don't want to do anything like— I don't want to think I could ever—"

Dana saw the sadness and longing in his eyes, and some of her apprehension faded, and again she had to fight her inclination to touch him. If she did, she would give way, and then she would... Unbidden, her fears struck again. "It worries me that I could ever want things like that done to me." Then she looked away.

"I know what you mean," Trevor said, with such utter conviction that Dana took courage from him.

As the coffee in their mugs went cold, they talked, he at one end of the sofa, she at the other, the cats between them as furry, purring chaperons. And by the

time he left, at two-forty in the morning, most of her
fear was gone.

There was a parking space directly in front of Oddments, next to Styles' Pathfinder. Dana pulled into it
gratefully and parked; she did not relish a long walk
by herself tonight. The car seemed to hum even with
the power off, and the feeling was disorienting to her.
Dana fumbled for her purse and knocked it onto the
floor. She cursed herself for her clumsiness, then
leaned down to reclaim the contents that had spilled.
As she scrabbled under the seat for her pen and lipstick, her hand closed on something that was almost
a familiar shape. Slowly she pulled it out and stared
down at the Dream Catcher fetish. So Styles *was* right:
she had had it all along. She had somehow or another
got it into her things and removed it from the gallery.
Had it been on the floor of her car all this time? She
ought to have checked her portfolio more carefully
that first time she came here. She would owe Styles an
apology, that was certain.

As she opened the car door, the fog leached the
warmth out of her and left her shivering as she made
her way to the darkened front of Oddments. It was
disconcerting, arriving to find the lights out and the
area deserted. She wanted to rub her hands together,
but with the fetish in her left fist, she dared not do
anything that might damage the little figure, and she
decided to shove her hands into her blazer pockets.

Her rap on the door was opened quickly by Styles,
who was in his customary black, this time with a rich
brown leather jacket over it. "Thank goodness it's

you." He waved his hand. "I don't want people to know I'm here, so I keep everything but the security lights off in front."

"Sorry I'm late. I had to see a new client, and we ran late," she said, and was about to present him with the fetish when he broke away from her.

"Just give me a couple minutes, will you? I'm up a ladder, doing a tricky part of the lighting." He winked and made his way through the darkened front rooms to the rear, not waiting to see if she would follow him.

"How's it going?" she asked, following after him, moving far more carefully than he in the gloom.

"It's coming along. Trevor is a big help. He has a good eye for light placement, and for color balance. You'll see what I mean. The display cases are almost done. Tomorrow evening we start on his stuff, setting it up and lighting it. I want it to look great for the opening." He was already halfway up the ladder in the gallery. "And speaking of Trevor, you'd like to know where he is, wouldn't you?"

"Well, yes," she admitted, watching Styles adjust his track lighting to show off the case where many of the artifacts were displayed.

"Hector is preparing him a fabulous meal. We'll join him just as soon as I get this done." He took another step up, and the ladder swayed. "Do me a favor—hold it steady for me, will you? Please?"

Dana set her purse and the fetish aside and hurried to take hold of the ladder. "Do you think you ought to be doing this alone?"

"No, I don't think I ought to be doing it alone, which is why I am not, anymore. I did ask for your help," he said testily as he continued to climb until he was almost at the top and could reach the fixtures. "A *liiittle* more to the right and it should be fine," he said, more to himself than to her, as he aimed the small spotlight at the largest of the glass cases. "What do you think? Does that do the job?"

"It looks fine," she said, a bit distantly, then turned her full attention on the display. "There's a pretty sharp shadow cast on the left side of the items."

He pursed his lips. "That's what I was afraid of. I'm going to have to get a brighter light for the front of the case and hope it does the job." He made another minute adjustment of the small spot, and glared down. "Any improvements?"

"I think so." She regarded it critically, her head cocked to the side as she held on to the ladder.

In the next second, the whole room rocked like a small boat in a sudden squall, the walls moaned, the glass cabinets rattled and jiggled, exhibits in them fell and rolled with the pitch of the building, and the ceiling fixtures yawed in their places. In the front rooms of Oddments, things clattered to the floor. A minor shiver followed after.

At the top of the ladder, Styles clung like a limpet, silent and tenacious. Only when the room stopped swaying did he trust himself to speak. "Definitely a rolling quake. Not more than five seconds, tops. I make it a 4.7 or 8. Five starts breaking windows."

Taking the same nonchalant tones as Styles used, Dana said, "Depends where the epicenter is; that sounds about right for here."

"Right," said Styles, making his way gingerly down the ladder. "I think," he said in a clipped manner, "that it is time I stopped for the evening. I can tend to the rest of it in the morning."

"What about cleaning up?" Dana asked, trying to be as calm as he was.

"I'll do it in the morning. When I can hire some help, and bring my video cam for the insurance company. I want to have a complete record of what happened." He dusted his hands off against his thighs.

"The lights are still on. No sirens yet, just a lot of car alarms. That's a good sign," Dana remarked. She glanced around the room, looking for obvious damage, and noticed that the fetish she had set aside had fallen to the floor. Though she felt she ought to look for it, she was relieved that it was back in the gallery, and could be located tomorrow.

"Come on," said Styles, taking her by the elbow. "Let's get out of here before San Andreas tries anything more to amuse us."

They made their way across to the Sea Chest, slipping up to the hostess' station in order to get a glimpse of the main dining room, where the diners were all talking too loudly and quickly in the wake of the quake.

Hector appeared a few minutes later with four large bottles of cabernet sauvignon in his arms. "Good evening, Hamilton. You come in good time."

"How are you? Is everything okay?" Styles asked, hurrying from one question to the next. "Any damage here? Nothing broken? No trouble in the kitchen?

None of the help hurt?'' He ran out of words all at once.

"I am fine. A few of my patrons..." He shrugged. "So tonight the wine is on the house. I am certain my partner will not object, and the patrons will appreciate the gesture." He indicated the second dining room. "Your friend is in there. Table by the window."

"Is he all right? Did the quake—" Styles broke off, not wanting to appear too concerned about Trevor.

"He has ordered a second appetizer of guacamole, crab and cheese with peppers and cilantro. He said he was not worried, because the water in the Bay did not change." He gave another hitch of his shoulders. "It may be so. I did not watch the water."

"Thanks," said Styles, and led the way into the second dining room, where they found Trevor staring out at Monterey Bay, a half-empty wineglass in his hand and a few squiggles drawn on the napkin in front of him.

"There you are," said Trevor as Styles and Dana came up to the table. "I was beginning to think I should come and find out if you were all right. I didn't think you were in any real danger, though. I trust I made the right decision." He rose to help Dana to her seat, and noticed she was pale. "Are you all right, Dana? Were you hurt?" His worry was followed by a self-effacing smile. "I thought Californians were supposed to be used to quakes."

"Just a bit rattled," she admitted, trying to chuckle at her own feeble joke. "I'll be over it in a little while."

"We are—used to quakes," said Styles. "But we have enough experience to be...careful." He picked up his napkin and snapped it into his lap.

"You wouldn't have been able to prove it, not the way they were carrying on in the main room," said Trevor with faint amusement. "Not that it wasn't frightening, but it didn't deserve screams or..." He took another sip of wine. "Probably tourists," he suggested as he set his glass aside.

"Like you," said Dana, and wished she did not sound so critical.

He was unfazed by her manner. "Hardly like me. I've known my share of minor quakes. There are hot springs and mud pots and other volcanic-related phenomena in New Zealand, so there is seismic activity, as well. And it wouldn't be a real visit to California without a single quiver. I did have a bit of a qualm when it began, but it passed soon enough. A jolt of the old adrenalin is good for the appetite, I've found." He took his place once more. "I've been listening to Mister Ramierez talk about food, and it's made me hungry. What about you two?"

"You're doing well with the appetizer," said Hamilton, eyeing the second order with the look of one who has starved for a week.

"Help yourself," offered Trevor. "I haven't decided on dinner. In fact, I was toying with the idea of ordering appetizers. They all look so good, I can't decide which one I want most."

"I've done that," said Hamilton. "It's fun."

"Appetizers," said Dana, and disliked the petulance she heard in her voice. "Oh, well, I suppose the calories won't matter this once."

"I really like the artichoke-and-garlic puree with lime and shallots served on Mexican corn bread," Hamilton enthused. "It's *very* good."

It was bad enough she had had the barbecued pork Elaine had prepared at lunch yesterday, thought Dana, and the Green Goddess salad dressing, she was now faced with cheese and butter and all these delicious, forbidden temptations she liked much better than barbecued pork, which was Vincent's favorite. Usually she was careful about what she ate, and never more than when she had already let herself go. But as much as she wanted to refuse to indulge herself in these goodies, she could not bring herself to turn them down. She glared as Styles threw her a kiss.

"It's not the end of the world. You're not going to turn into a size sixteen overnight, Dana," he said, with such uncanny recognition of the very thing that was troubling her that she almost wanted to kick him under the table for giving her away.

"Ah, yes, the well-known American preoccupation with skinniness," said Trevor, smearing a cracker with the crab-guacamole-and-cheese. "Not that we don't suffer from it to some extent. But for me, charm, warmth, intelligence, grace and kindness have it all over boyish-girlish figures and masses of wavy hair. But then, I'm old-fashioned enough to like women who look like women—grown-up and female. I've always been partial to hips and thighs and breasts, myself. The best model I ever had weighed in at more than fifteen stone, and let me tell you, every ounce was beautiful.''

"How much is a stone?'' asked Dana. She knew it was more than ten pounds, but could not remember how much more. Even at ten pounds a stone, the model was built generously.

"Fourteen pounds,'' said Styles before Trevor could answer. "Meaning she weighed in at over two hundred ten pounds.'' He looked down at the folded napkin in front of him. "I'm good at numbers.''

There was a reminiscent look in Trevor's green eyes, a relish that was not for the food. "Half the artists in New Zealand were in love with her, and sometimes I was one of them. She was a marvel to work with.'' He shook his head once. "She was—and still is—joyously married, had three children, and didn't give a damn about how many artists fell for her.''

Dana listened to this with a mixture of satisfaction and uncalled-for jealousy. She was pleased at what she heard, after all those times Kirk had compared her to other women, liking their bodies more than hers. At the same time, she resented the regard Trevor still felt for this unknown, overweight woman living happily in New Zealand with her husband and children.

"What do you want this evening?''

This question, coming from behind her, nearly brought Dana out of her chair. She swung around and saw Hector Ramierez standing over them. "I... haven't made up my mind,'' she said.

"I'll take care of this. We're going to have the full run of appetizers, including the asparagus salad with sesame oil and walnuts,'' said Styles for all of them.

"And those chicken-thigh things, with the pine nut, spinach and sweet onion stuffing. And some of those wonderful broiled mixed shellfish—you know the ones I mean—and your Monterey salad for three, with extra salsa. I leave the wine up to you, so long as it's good. You know my tastes." He handed the menus back to their host, adding, "You should talk to Dana about these things, Hector. You really should."

"I am considering it—I may take it up with my partner," said Ramierez, and added to Dana, "Ms. Piper, I will call you and make an appointment."

"Do you think he means it?" asked Dana as Ramierez walked away toward the kitchen.

"Of course he does," said Styles.

"I'd like the work," said Dana in a burst of candor. "Not just for the money, though that's part of it, but for the exposure." She felt an inexplicable embarrassment at this admission, and she tried to account for it as best she could. It had to be left over from seeing Vincent yesterday. He always made her feel inappropriate and foolish.

"Penny," said Trevor quietly.

Startled, she swung around to him. "What?"

"For your thoughts," he added. "You looked . . . I don't know . . . sad."

His obvious concern only added to her chagrin. "I'm not very good company tonight."

"It's all right," said Trevor. "So long as I haven't offended you."

She stared at him in disbelief. "You? You mean because of last night? Not a chance." She made herself smile. "Nothing like that. It's been a hard day, that's all." Her explanation sounded inadequate even to her. She thought of the night before again. "It's not you. Not either of you," she continued, including Styles in her gesture of apology. "It's—"

"Family," said Styles for her.

"Family," Dana confirmed. "The ones you can't choose, as my brother was good enough to remind me."

"Ah," said Trevor knowingly. "Relatives can be a trial, can't they? I have a few like that, myself, cousins who think I went round the bend the day I took up sculpting. It's the way they want to see me."

"Yes," said Dana, certain that Vincent would feel betrayed that she would admit it. She was about to modify her assertion when Hector Ramierez brought a large tray and began to unload the selections. Dana felt she had been spared making an idiot of herself. It was better to eat these luscious appetizers than to try to sort out her relationship with her brother. Or to straighten out her feelings about Trevor Davidson, who was the most compelling man she had ever met, and at the same time was potentially the most frightening.

She forgot entirely about Dream Catcher, now laying half-under a display case back in Oddments gallery.

CHAPTER FOUR

"It's a wonderful turnout." Styles all but crowed with delight as he looked over the crowd milling in his gallery. Then he added to Dana in an undertone, "I couldn't have done it without you. I mean that, Dana." Tonight he was wholly in black, his slacks of rich velour, his shirt of silk, his blazer light-weight wool.

"Oh, yes, you probably could have, but it would have been more expensive," she said, feeling emboldened by his confidence.

"True enough. You're talented, you're on time, and your prices are reasonable. You're a *miracle*. Stick around and let me give you a lift to the buffet afterward, so we can debrief." He cocked his head to the side. "Don't mind me mentioning it, but you look a little peaked—" he pronounced it with two syllables "—tonight. Something bothering you?"

"I . . . didn't sleep . . . very much." She had forced herself to stay awake for most of the past three nights, after her dreams took on a kind of sexual obsessiveness that made her cringe to think of it. As the sensations came back, pale wraiths of the straining flesh that had haunted her nights, she thought of how Kirk had insisted that what she, as an independent woman, really longed for was male domination. It was nature's way of keeping the relationship between the sexes in balance, Kirk had claimed: the more self-sufficient a woman was, the more she longed for sexual subjugation. She had never believed it until her dreams of the last two nights fixed increasingly on images more cruel than romantic. Pleasure had not been the objective in the dreams—endurance had, and suffering. Last night there had been a ruthless wash of sensation, so intense that she could almost believe it was real. Most disturbing was the malign pleasure her dream lover took in her pain, the lover who looked like Trevor Davidson but could not—oh, please, could not be. Or was it that she was more afraid of what she wanted, and was doing her best to screw it up for herself by making Trevor seem a worse monster than Kirk was?

"Nerves? For this? I wouldn't have thought it would get to you so much," he prompted her, and lifted his champagne flute to a distinguished man in an expensive suit.

"Not really," said Dana, trying to sound indifferent.

"Does Trevor have anything to do with it?" Styles asked, with a directness that startled her.

Dana shook her head and repeated, "Not really."

"Too bad," said Styles. "I thought you two were getting along pretty well. He was at your place night before last, wasn't he?"

"You know he was." She did not want to sound irritated at this intrusion, though she did. "I think he might be avoiding me tonight," she added reluctantly.

"I also know he didn't spend the night with you, night before last," said Styles, ignoring her second remark. "You're *interested,* aren't you?"

"Oh, yes," she said with unguarded candor, then tried to minimize her exposure. "But it hasn't ... We haven't ..." She could not make herself go on.

"No kidding." Styles was at his most blasé. "Maybe you should. Time's a-wastin'."

"Hamilton, you're outrageous," she said, teasing him lightly.

"We try to please," he responded with a quick grin.

She said nothing to him for a moment so that he could greet new arrivals and point them in the direction of the cheese and champagne. When she was sure of his attention, she said, "Are you being a match-maker?"

"*Moi?*" Styles inquired, his eyes huge and inno-cent.

"Yes. You." She kept her voice low. For the last two days, she had wanted to talk to Styles about his role in her flirtation with Trevor. This was turning out to be difficult.

"He's very interested in you," said Styles. "As if you didn't know."

She wanted to demand to know how Styles could be so certain, but that seemed like the stunt of a girl in high school with a crush. Instead she remarked, "He's an interesting man."

Styles laughed. "How diplomatic you are."

"I am, aren't I?" she countered, trying to break away without being obvious about it.

"He said he liked your cats." It was a clever opening, but Styles did not pursue it. "Get out there and hand out business cards. I'll catch up with you later."

Feeling spared, Dana offered him a little salute. "Aye, aye, sir. Crass commercialism it is."

Another group of guests arrived and claimed Styles' attention. By the time he was finished with them, Dana had been drawn into a conversation with Hector Ramierez and a long-headed man who owned the largest independent bookstore on the central California coast. Then a landscape gardener joined them and the conversation shifted to the sorts of woods Trevor used in his sculptures. Dana wondered suddenly if Styles had found Dream Catcher, and made a mental note to herself to check the display case. But a retired Coast Guard engineer and his schoolteacher wife came up to Dana and began to ask about fliers for their new Victorian bed-and-breakfast inn they had opened in Aptos. Dana listened to their questions, and the fetish was relegated to the back of her thoughts. And for the next two hours, Dana met strangers, rather than let herself notice that Trevor was watching her as he shook hands and made polite small talk.

"It went pretty damn well, if you ask me. Even if you don't ask me, I think it went pretty damn well," said Styles to Dana and Trevor as the last of the guests were thinning out. "We'll head out in another half hour. Give the others a chance to get there first."

"If their enthusiasm here is something more than good manners, I'd agreed it went well," said Trevor, who was looking tired and a little jittery. "It's awfully hard to tell about that."

"Oh, I think it was fairly genuine," said Dana carefully. "Not all of them, of course, but most of them liked what they saw."

"I'll trust your take on it—I'm a terrible judge of public reaction," said Trevor, and did his best not to yawn. "Sorry. These dos take a lot out of me." He rubbed his chin. "Is there somewhere we can sit down? I need to get my second wind."

"There's the storeroom," said Styles unexpectedly. "I've got two chairs and a sofa down there, along with my desk and my Mac." He came back from locking his front door. "That's the last of them." Then he indicated a door in the second room, one that Dana had not noticed before. "Downstairs. It's where I have my office." He linked arms with Dana, saying, "Let me take you away from all this."

"I hope your maintenance service is up to this mess," she said, looking around at the stacks of discarded paper plates, napkins and plastic champagne flutes that littered the three rooms of Oddments. She disengaged her arm from Styles so that she could retrieve her purse from the counter where she had set it a few minutes before.

"They have been warned," said Styles. "Come on, Trevor."

The stairs were sturdy and utilitarian, and the store room was half filled with neat stacks of crates and a few cardboard boxes. A narrow path led through the stacks to the office area. Two good Oriental carpets marked the place.

Styles went to his antique rosewood desk and sat in the ergonomic chair behind it, waving his hand at the leather-upholstered furniture. "Make yourselves comfortable." He patted his computer affectionately. "This baby's got a lot to do tonight when I come back from the buffet."

"How do you mean?" asked Dana, trying to find a comfortable position in one of the two deep chairs. Now that she was in it, how was she to get out of it? The question triggered recollections of the helplessness she had felt in her recent dreams, and the things that had been done to her because of it. She felt a bit queasy and decided she was getting too tired.

"Oh," said Trevor as he reached into the pocket of his dinner jacket and brought out the fetish. "I noticed this lying under my *Equinox*. It must have been dislodged by the quake."

Styles paled and came around his desk. "It was under your sculpture?" he asked distantly.

Dana was staring at Dream Catcher, remembering how she had come upon it on the floor of her car. At the time, she was satisfied with her own explanation of the event, but now, with the baleful figure lying on Trevor's outstretched hand, she was no longer so certain. Belatedly she spoke up. "Oh. Yes. That." Her edginess made her breath a little short and her words abrupt. "I found it. In my car. Under the seat, in fact. I brought it in. The other night. I meant to tell you, but the quake..."

Now Trevor looked shocked. "This is the fetish you told me about?"

"Yes," Dana answered as Styles took it from Trevor, his silence ominous.

"Thought you could get away, didn't you," Styles said to Dream Catcher.

"Not that fellow, not as much as you might want him to," said Trevor with feeling. "Once he gets hold of you, he doesn't let go until you are his or you're dead."

"What do you mean, 'you're his?'" Dana asked, cold and hot washing through her.

Styles stared at that fetish, as if trying to see what it was that Trevor saw in it. "Why do you say that?"

"Because he's an obsession figure; there are about a dozen of them. You know he's a demon because his wings are clipped. He can't fly. All you can do in his power is fall," said Trevor with a hint of discomfort. "He magnifies every sexually exploitive, possessive feeling until that's all there is left. Greedy Eyes is a reasonable translation of his name." He coughed once. "I'm not a superstitious or credulous fool, but I have a healthy respect for those things. They represent some very powerful and disturbing part of the human psyche."

"How do you mean?" asked Styles with a glimmer of apprehension.

Trevor yawned, shook his head to apologize, then sat forward. "All right, here's one explanation: human beings are full of things we dislike or fear in ourselves. So we externalize them."

"Basic Psych 112," said Styles. "We tend to make these projections wholly the thing we are externalizing. All-wise, all-corrupting, all-furious, all-protective, all-despairing, and the like, with none of the contradictions that balance out the personalities of people."

"You include the positive, as well," said Trevor. "It's overwhelming to think you would have to be completely accepting of frustration all the time, or endlessly merciful all the time, or truly compassionate *all the time*. So those are gods and angels and other qualities we aspire to, but cannot sustain."

"Make me holy, God, but not yet," Dana quoted softly, recalling something she had read in college.

"Saint Augustine," said Trevor. "And he was right. And demands of such . . . narrow-focused living is beyond what most of us are prepared to do. And because we sense such potentials in ourselves, we seek to get a handle on them by disowning them, moving them outside ourselves. Hence all those patron saints and all the demons. Including this one." He nodded toward the figure Styles held.

Styles added with a slight shudder. "But doesn't that mean these things are batteries, holding psychic energies? The refusal to accept the human component in the demon gives it more strength because it makes you have to resist a part of yourself?"

"Hamilton," said Dana, truly disliking the direction the conversation was taking as she remembered dreaming terrible, degrading, painful things. How could she want anything like that for herself, and from Trevor? "Don't you think that's going a little far? You can't—"

"No, it isn't going 'a little far'; that thing can be dangerous," said Styles bluntly. He turned to Trevor. "Do I seem to be overreacting to you?"

Trevor gave his answer some thought. "No, you don't. There are cases on record in regard to these figures, cases of obsession. You'd have to be irresponsible not to pay attention to them."

Dana looked at him blankly. "Not you, too?"

Trevor nodded. "Me, too, I'm sorry to tell you."

"But why?" she asked. "They're just wood and glass." She recalled how her finger had been cut, and it was hard not to shiver.

"It's what they represent. Hamilton's right. Nothing frightens and angers us so much as the things we dislike in ourselves." He indicated the figure with obvious distaste. "This fetish creature sums up all the force of sexual obsession. You know what people can do when they become obsessed."

Dana looked around the basement office. "If I didn't know better, I'd think you'd both been watching too many Stephen King movies."

"Then you'd be trivializing something important. This isn't about entertainment," said Styles seriously. "I'll put it under lock and key and—" He turned around and stared at Dana, dismay banishing his usual impish good humor. "Oh, God, Dana. I'm sorry. I should never have encouraged you to tell this guy anything. It was a bad idea."

Until Styles said this, Dana had not realized how much she was troubled by just that consideration. "What can it do to me? It's not big enough to knock me out, or anything else." She felt a jolt of fear go through her, and did her best to convince herself she was being foolish. "You don't think that it really has anything to do with...my interest in Trevor, do you?"

"I hope it doesn't," said Styles, and rocked back on his heels, just enough to make Dana think he was trying to escape. "Truly."

"How could it?" Dana asked, worried what the answer might be.

"Whether it does or it doesn't," said Trevor with purpose, "we are the ones who will determine what becomes of us, not Greedy Eyes, not the Archangel Gabriel, no one but us." He looked directly at Dana and did his best to reassure her with a smile.

Dana thought of the green eyes and said nothing.

Styles reached for his overcoat. "Come on. Let's get off to the buffet. They'll send out search parties if we don't get there soon."

Reluctantly Trevor rose and offered his hand to Dana to help her out of the deep leather chair.

It was shortly after two, and the city was still; streetlights were fuzzed in halos of fog, and the occasional car moved slowly in the gathering mists that rolled in slow-motion imitation of waves across water. It seemed the most sensible, comfortable, natural thing in the world to do, walking this way through the fog. Making their way along the gentle curve of Ocean View Boulevard in Pacific Grove, heading toward the Los Piños Lighthouse, Dana and Trevor walked slowly, more concerned with being together than reaching their goal. They had begun their stroll almost two hours and six miles ago. They were prepared to walk all night long and fetch up wherever the dawn found them, so long as they would not be apart.

"There's one thing that still bothers me. I don't want you to equate what you feel about me—whatever it is—with that Dream Catcher," Dana said softly as they crossed the T-intersection of Sea Palm Avenue.

"I wouldn't do that," Trevor said, his deep, tranquil voice as gentle as a caress. "Because I don't want you to do it, either, about me."

This had been bothering her for the last few days, and she said, "I was afraid at first that I had... invented you. You know, when I described what I wanted, that it did something to you, because of the wish. I was afraid that I could not see you for what you are. That made me very apprehensive."

"Why?" he asked, surprised at her answer.

"Because then you wouldn't be real. And what is happening wouldn't be real. And I want you to be real, more than anything in the world. I want the things you make me feel to be real." Her eyes flickered as she thought of the dreadful things done in her dreams by something with a malicious version of Trevor's face.

"What is it?" he asked.

She smiled and shook her head, thinking, *if only Trevor did not have green eyes.* She could not bring herself to say it aloud.

He accepted her silence. "I don't blame you for not jumping in with both feet. I know all the cautions about the excitement of new people. I don't want to be misleading, for you or for myself. But I like your cats, and surely that makes me less foreign," he went on, his voice like the pedal note of an organ. "I don't want to be a stranger to you. Or to think I'm amusing myself on vacation. To have to come all the way to California and find what I have wanted for a decade."

How great it was just to listen to him, Dana thought, like being wrapped in very good, warm bittersweet chocolate. "It's something to think about, spending time with you," she agreed, wanting him to talk more, about anything.

"And if it's one of those sudden things, that comes and goes like fireworks, that'll be okay with me," he said, and added, "But it won't be what I want."

The twinge of doubt she had felt vanished. "I don't want it, either."

"But it could turn out that way," he warned her. "And if it does, I'll be glad all my life long that I've had this time with you."

Dana felt herself flush. This was better than anything she had hoped for when she touched Dream Catcher. This was sustenance to her soul. She tried to find a way to tell him, and could only say, "This is the best time of my life." A frisson went through her as she spoke, but whether from her burgeoning excitement or from something more sinister, she did not know.

His hand tightened on hers. "Of mine, as well."

She could not find the courage to tell him what she felt. Wouldn't it be wonderful, she thought, to be with a man whom she could trust? Who would not resent her, as Vincent had, or belittle her, as Kirk had? Wouldn't it be wonderful to be with a man who valued her, and wanted to have her a part of his life, not as an intruder, or a convenience, but as a complement to all he was? To all she was?

"Do you think anyone noticed when we left the buffet?" Trevor asked, amusement in his words.

"Hamilton did," said Dana. "But he was watching us."

"True," said Trevor.

They walked more than half a block in silence, content to be near each other, neither willing to admit to fatigue.

Suddenly Trevor said, "It's probably too soon to say this, but we don't have a lot of time, and I have to make the most of my opportunity." He took a deep breath and went on. "I know you have your business to run, and professional commitments to meet and cats to take care of at home, but if you could arrange a week to come to Wellington, I'd be delighted. Not immediately. We could make arrangements you'd accept. Say, in a month or so, maybe six weeks? It would give us a little time apart to think, to decide." He held up one hand. "No expectations. I can put you up in a hotel if you'd like. Or not." He stopped and looked down at her. "Would you think about it, at least? Don't make up your mind just yet. Think about it."

"All right. I'll think about it," she said as she felt his arms go around her. "You aren't going back tomorrow, are you? We still have another eight days before you leave. The show just opened, less than twelve hours ago. You can't go now."

"No," he said. "I certainly can't." And kissed her, tentatively at first, but with growing intensity as he felt her response the length of his body. His lips were eloquent and persuasive without recourse to speech; how could this sweet delirium be anything but the fulfillment of her dreams? What danger was there in believing?

Aramis put his ears back and showed his teeth; Athos hissed and drew away, big head low and threatening; even the ever-genial Porthos declined to be petted, avoiding Trevor as he came into the living room behind Dana.

"Must be something I'm wearing, or the weather; sometimes storms can upset them," said Trevor, perplexed by the response of the cats. He tossed his tweed jacket aside and sank down on the old-fashioned settee in front of the fireplace, at right angles to the sofa. It was a few minutes after seven, and outside, stormy rain battered, making all of Monterey huddle indoors for shelter.

"It probably is the storm," said Dana, too pleased to have a whole evening with Trevor ahead of her to be upset by her cats. "Either that, or they're jealous of you. Cats can be very possessive of their people." They had never been before, but they had never before had cause, she told herself. She was glad to have small talk to fall back on; having him in her house was making her feel vulnerable, which she had never been with him after their first meeting.

"That could be dangerous, given the size of this trio." He indicated the formidable bulk of Porthos. "I don't think I've ever seen a house cat that size. It's not just bulk—he's like a cat version of a draft horse." He held out his hand to Porthos, who declined to notice the invitation.

"He was the largest kitten of the litter—not that his brothers are small," Dana said as she began to put together what she hoped was a reasonable tea from what she had read about in books and seen in films. It had taken a good part of her afternoon to round up all the essentials. She had even found a place that had clotted cream and fresh scones, and she planned to make them the centerpiece of the not-quite-meal. She had tried to assemble all the right things for a real tea, to please him, but now she had doubts, anticipating his disapproval. "When I had them neutered, the vet said pretty much the same thing."

Athos had gone to the door and was waiting patiently to be let out; Aramis had curled up on one of the dining room chairs. Only Porthos stayed in the living room with Trevor, though he did not approach the New Zealander, as he had done on Trevor's previous visit. He hunkered down and watched the foreigner, as if expecting the worst. Occasionally he gave a low, musical growl.

"I hope they'll get over it, whatever it is," said Trevor as he looked at the magazines on the coffee table. There was an appreciative gleam in his eye as he picked up a small book of photographs of Hopi and Navaho fetish jewelry. He thumbed through it quickly, pausing now and again to admire the pieces he saw.

In the kitchen, Dana was measuring out tea into her only earthenware pot, trying to make sure it would be strong enough, but not too strong. *Always tea to the kettle; never kettle to the tea,* her grandmother had taught her. At the time it had seemed useless information, but now she was grateful for it. The tea strainer lay on the sideboard. Two halved lemons covered in cheesecloth were set out on a salad plate. It would have been nice to get a jar of quince preserves, but since Dana had never tasted them and she did not know if Trevor liked them, at $5.29 for less than a pint, she had passed them up. She had put the scones into the microwave to heat, and crumpets in the toaster oven, and was doing her best to make sure everything was hot at the same time.

There was a sound like concentrated gunfire outside, and the whole of the house went dark.

"What—?" Dana cried out, then realized the electrical power was out. She swore at it for breaking down now.

"There's a tree branch fallen, two or three houses down the street," said Trevor calmly. "I just looked out. This whole end of the block is out of electricity, from what I saw."

Again Dana swore. "That's the second time this year," she said. "They won't cut any trees down on this block—some kind of city ordinance against it—and so every now and then this happens. At least the stove is gas. I better report this, in case there are live cables down." She reached for the phone and discovered that—not too surprisingly—that it, too, was out.

"We might as well make the most of mischance. Tell me where the candles are, and I'll set them up for you." Trevor offered. He was standing in the door of the kitchen now, watching her with unconcealed interest that bordered on smugness. "If I haven't mentioned it before, it's a nice little house you've got here.

Unaccountably nervous, she began to babble. "I found it on a fluke; a friend knew the landlord would need a long-term tenant, one interested in a lease-purchase option, and I was looking for a new place," Dana said as she took her scones and crumpets out of her now-useless appliances and arranged them on baking sheets for the oven. "This is going to take awhile."

"I'm in no hurry," he assured her in a tone that was more suggestive than before. "Take all the time you want. I'll watch."

This made her a little flustered, but she did not object. It was flattering to think that he wanted to be with her, but she would be more comfortable if he did not stare at her all the time. She indicated a cabinet near the back porch. "It might be a good idea to get the candles out. I've got a couple of boxes of long-burning ones. They're marked with a green *X*. The candle holders are on the lower shelf."

He moved to accommodate her, not-so-accidentally brushing up against her as he went past her. He murmured appreciatively as his thumb tested the resilience of her breast, and then he was busy with candles.

Dana was startled by this, and offended. She was also embarrassed by what he had done and could not think of a suitable rebuke. Nothing Trevor had said or done had suggested he might take advantage of her in so deliberate a way, as if auditioning her for other erotic possibilities. As much as she wanted to say something, she decided that it would make too much of what was a very minor incident. And perhaps he was a bit put off with the lights out.

Five candles were set in the kitchen when Trevor was done with his task. Another four gave the dining room a soft glow. Nine more were in the living room, where Trevor was busying himself at the hearth getting a fire going as Dana brought in the mugs and teapot. He glanced over his shoulder and nodded his approval. "Looks like we'll do fine."

"It'll be better in here by the fire, anyway. The house will get pretty cold in a couple of hours." She arranged the cups and the teapot on the coffee table.

"But you said you have gas heat," he reminded her.

"Yes, I do. But the thermostat is electric. I can use the stove, keep it turned on, but it's an expensive way to take the chill off. Better to build up the fire." She went back into the kitchen, pausing to let Athos out at last. The scones were looking about ready, and the crumpets would be okay. She got the clotted cream and two kinds of marmalade for their condiments, and put them on her good red-lacquer tray. She was feeling increasingly edgy—the evening was not going as expected, which bothered her more than she liked to admit. On her way back to the living room, she saw that both Aramis and Porthos were curled up in the far corner of the dining room.

Trevor was sitting in front of the fireplace, nursing his kindling into proper flames. Two large sections of oak limbs were proving slow to catch, and so Trevor was sliding in twigs and bits of paper to keep the fire going. As he studied the wood, the oak began to smolder and bright points like luminous insects appeared in the dry bark.

"It isn't the style I was trying for," said Dana as she put the tray down. "I wanted to do the linen-and-china look, in the dining room. Though this is cozier. And the scones and crumpets should be good to eat. They better be. I haven't had anything else all day, so this won't destroy my diet too much."

"There you go again, worrying about skinniness. Believe me you have nothing to worry about." He swung around and looked at her. In the subdued light of the flames, his green eyes shone like lanterns.

"I can't help it," she confessed, dropping down on the rug beside him. "It's indoctrinated from the first Barbie doll to the ads on TV."

"So your Barbie dolls are skinniness fetishes," he said, half-playfully, sitting back against the coffee table.

She looked at him in astonishment. "I never thought about them that way, but you're right." Her laugh was shaky. "Somehow you don't think of countries like this one having fetishes."

"I'd say Barbie was pretty strong magic, if you're still held by her years after you stopped playing with her. You're still trying to live in her image, though you aren't a child any longer," said Trevor, an edge of nastiness in his tone. He dropped his arm over her shoulder and pulled her close to him. "It's easy to catch you. You're so willing to be shaped, aren't you?" he asked before his mouth closed on hers.

Of all the possibilities she had entertained anticipating this evening, such a ruthless beginning had not been among them. Dana stiffened and tried to break away from him, but his arms were stronger than anything she had imagined, and she flailed at him, panic rising in her. What was the matter with him? Why was he doing this now, when all it could do was wreck things between them? Had she been so wrong about Trevor? Was this a lapse, or a revelation of his character? Had her dreams told her the truth, after all? Did he want nothing more than someone to terrorize? Would he attempt anything more, and what would she have to do? She kept her teeth clamped together against the intrusion of his tongue. How was she going to get out of this? Would there be bruises on her arms from his fingers?

Suddenly he let go of her and fell away from her. "Good Lord, Dana," he said in a voice nearly as dismayed and astonished as she felt. "I didn't ... I don't know what came over me. It wasn't..." He sat up, and put about eighteen inches between them on the floor. "I didn't mean what that felt like."

Though she was shaking, Dana kept her answer calm. "It's the power being out," she offered for an excuse. "It's ... unnerving."

His single laugh was shaky. "Thanks for the try. It's not the power being out, it's worse than that," said Trevor, and ran his hands through his hair. "Christ, I hope... I apologize, Dana. I never intended... I don't know what else to say. It wasn't ... me." The last was the most helpless thing he said.

"Not like you at all," she agreed, with a spurt of temper. "Unless this is something you keep hidden from your friends." That, she knew, was unfair. But how dare he ruin everything? Unless she had caused... She decided to try to salvage the evening. Give the guy a break, she told herself inwardly. Everyone is entitled to one mistake.

"No, not *like* me, not *me*. I would never do anything like that to you, Dana. Never. It was as if I became someone else." He ducked his head. "I wouldn't hurt you for the world, please believe me. I wouldn't do anything to make you distrust me." He stared into the fire. "It was like being in a trance, I reckon."

Dana had pressed her hands together to steady them, and now she reached out to pour the tea. Anything to retrieve their evening together from disaster. Once the tea was poured, she thought, everything would be all right. Little as she wanted to admit it, she was afraid to speak, and went about restoring the illusion of normality as quietly as she could while Trevor continued to gaze into the fire.

She had put the strainer into place on Trevor's mug when she felt him lunge at her, knocking the teapot from her grip. Hot tea scalded her hand and his forehead and nose, but he did not seem to notice. He wrapped himself around her, bearing her down to the floor.

"I will have you, or no one will," Trevor vowed through his teeth in a voice like an avalanche, and grabbed at the neck of her shirt.

"Trevor!" she cried, striking out at his shoulder and neck with the heel of her hand as she had been taught on her Women's Self-Defense Weekend two years ago. She wanted to reach his nose, to twist it or break it. If she'd had on high heels, she could scrape his shin with them. How dare he do this to her, after so wonderful a beginning! She wanted to cry with vexation. It shocked her to feel anger welling in her, sharp as razors and just as lethal. She felt more than saw her cats hovering on the top of the sofa, watching, tails a-twitch, mewing in distress. He was pawing at her clothes, grunting as he pulled at them. "Stop it!" She had to get away from Trevor, for both their sakes. She had to. "Trevor! Stop!"

The neck of her shirt tore, and buttons scattered across the rug and floor. "You. Are. Mine." His big hands went to work on her bra, pressing the rise of her breasts with blunt, impatient fingers, as he had in her dreams when they turned into nightmares. His eyes were fixed on her with ferocious desire.

"*Trevor!* Stop it!" Dana boxed him soundly on the ear and was able to wriggle away from him enough to land a solid kick to his knee. She had the satisfaction of hearing him grunt with pain.

This time he rolled halfway across the living room floor, halted only by the old rocker she had inherited from her great-grandmother. He drew into a huddled crouch, knees pressed against his chest, his forehead almost touching the small Oriental rug. Very quietly he began to sob.

Dana staggered to her feet, looked about the room for a weapon, settled on the fireplace poker and, clutching it firmly, approached Trevor, ready for anything. She was determined not to scream. She would hit instead.

He forced himself to be silent as she came up to him. "You won't need that, Dana; please believe me—not now. I think it's over," he said, indicating the poker with the jut of his jaw. "I'm...myself again." He wiped his face with his hands, abashed. "I . . . don't know what to say."

This time Dana was not convinced. "I'll hang on to it, if it's just the same to you."

"Please," he said with feeling, and began to straighten up. "You landed quite a kick," he said as he winced at the pain in his leg. "That's what did it. It broke the hold."

"The kick?" she repeated, warily keeping her distance.

"Yes," he said, sounding exhausted and beaten. "I don't think it will happen again. Not tonight." There was such despair in his green eyes that she was tempted to forget how dangerous he had been less than two minutes ago. "I'm going to need some ice; to keep it from swelling."

"For what?" she asked. This sudden shift in subject caught her unaware.

"My knee. You can see it's starting to swell; if it gets much worse, I won't be able to walk out the door, and I don't think it would be prudent to ask you for assistance." He pulled himself up into the rocker. "I'm not going to try to reach you. I'd be fool to try. But if I don't give this thing a rest, it will be the size of a soccer ball come morning, and I'll have to get treatment for it." He extended his leg gingerly, teeth set against the ache. "I think Greedy Eyes likes to give pain, but he doesn't like to receive it very much. He won't come back as long as this hurts." He deliberately did not look at her.

Dana heard him out skeptically. "Then why should I get you ice, to make it better?"

"Because it hurts," he answered matter-of-factly. "I'm not asking for aspirin, or brandy. Just ice, to control the swelling. I don't want to lose the pain just yet. Not while you're still with me. I don't want anything more to happen."

Porthos came up to him and sniffed at his cuff, then began to purr.

"Whatever it was he didn't like is over," said Dana, beginning to get the cold, shaky aftermath of fury. She backed up to the settee and more fell on to it than sat down. She could not let go of her poker, and she watched Trevor narrowly as she fought off nausea and tears. "It wasn't you again, right?"

"Right." He sounded defeated. "You probably don't believe me. I'd probably feel the same, in your place."

"Not entirely, no, I don't believe you," she said, lifting the tip of the poker as a reminder of her doubts.

"Probably wise of you," he said quietly as he scratched the cat. "I don't have any way to excuse...what happened." He lowered his eyes again in a gesture of capitulation. "It... I wanted to do such things that... I can't describe them to you. I don't *want* to describe them to you. They're too terrible. It disgusts me that I could consider such things—I wouldn't really do any of them. It would make me sick if I tried to. That's what I want to think, anyway." He added this last in so dispirited a way that Dana felt alarmed. "But some part of it has to be in me, or Greedy Eyes could not do this to me. I don't want to think... Part of me that I cannot face wants to do those...those hideous things. Or Greedy Eyes wants me to assume that I could do them—" He could not go on.

"So you're sure it's Greedy Eyes," said Dana flatly.

"It's that or I've run mad," Trevor answered in the same tone. "In which case, you are well rid of me."

The lights flickered on. For a moment, the room was dazzling, as their eyes adjusted.

"Power's back," Dana said, grateful for the obvious.

"I'd better call a cab," he said, blinking against the brightness. "I should leave before..." He did not say before what.

"I can give you a ride," Dana protested. She was beginning to feel responsible for the swelling in his knee, which was becoming more apparent minute by minute.

"I don't think that's a very good idea," said Trevor. "I wouldn't want to chance it." He forced himself to his feet and limped heavily over to the telephone table at the entry hall. "If you think of some way I can make amends—"

"Tell them to come up Martin Street instead of Pacific; it's easier to find coming that way." Dana said as she heard him punch in the number.

He did as she suggested, and then reached for his jacket. "It's probably best if I wait on the porch. There's enough shelter. I won't get wet."

She nodded absently.

"I'll call you tomorrow?" he ventured as he opened the door.

"Um," she responded, to show she had heard. She would not let herself cry while he could hear her. And then she was alone with the now useless candles, the wreckage of their tea and evening and everything else before her.

CHAPTER FIVE

"It's my fault," said Styles to Dana the next morning as he came into her office unexpectedly. He paced the small office where she did her work. "I really screwed things up for you. I apologize, Dana."

"Why? You aren't the one who...attacked me." She swallowed hard and did her best to sound composed. "You didn't encourage him. And I don't care what you say about fetishes, Trevor Davidson isn't the kind of man who gets taken over by anything."

"It doesn't sound like him, though, doing something like that," Styles persisted. "I mean, going after you the way he did, it's not his style, is it?"

"I don't know—maybe he has an evil twin. It certainly seemed like it, last night," said Dana forlornly, and started silently to weep. "Maybe it's all a con job, suckering in gullible females. Maybe he's the kind of man who has to keep women guessing and off balance. Maybe he's a Don Juan, wanting to add another notch on his bedpost. Maybe he likes to find out how much he can get away with. Maybe he gets off on drawing women to him and then taking them over. Maybe he thinks he's got a God-given right to—" As Kirk had. Just when she had let herself start to trust a man with more than being on time. Anger stirred in her, and beneath it, an abiding sorrow. She had hoped for so much, and it had all seemed within her grasp. "Sure, he didn't seem that way at first. What man does? At first he was so charming. What if he is really like the way he was last night? What if he has to take over any woman in his life? There are men who can be really sweet one instant and living hell the next."

"But still..." said Styles, holding out a handkerchief to her.

Dana reached for the handkerchief and wiped her eyes, hoping she was not making a mess of her makeup. She didn't need to deal with her clients looking like someone out of a soap opera. "Don't start on the fetish thing again, okay? He's a grown man. He wasn't jerked around by a South Pacific demon. That's just an excuse."

"Maybe. But what if it isn't? What if Dream Catcher is doing its work on you right now?" Styles was being his most persuasive.

She remembered the way she succumbed to the increasingly violent demands of her dreams and was appalled. "He said something about it, and I...I was ready to believe him." She suppressed a shudder of revulsion. "But what if it doesn't have anything to do with that fetish?" she pressed on. For the last hour, she had been considering this unhappy prospect. "Maybe it *is* what I want, deep down inside. Kirk thought so. And my brother Vincent, too. Maybe these are the kinds of men I attract because they're what I really want."

"Better the devil you know?" said Styles. "I doubt it."

"Don't I have to face the fact that this could be *my* doing?" She looked at him, demanding an answer with her eyes.

"If you want the blame..." Styles said, then added, with a greater sense of purpose, "Don't worry. We're going to get to the bottom of this. I'm going to see Trevor. It's all arranged."

"Oh, God, Hamilton!" Dana objected. "You can't!"

"Yes, I can. I don't want my graphics designer unable to work around my imported sculptor." He laid his hand on her shoulder. "I'm worried about you."

"Just keep him away from me, and you won't have any reason to worry," she said, wadding the handkerchief into a ball. "He sure had me fooled."

"Maybe there's more to it than that," Styles suggested. "He told me that he didn't want to do the things he tried to do. He said he felt sickened. I believe him. I've heard enough bull from men to know when I'm hearing the truth."

"Yeah," said Dana with conviction. "He can be very convincing when he wants to be."

"Now, listen to me, Dana. Ordinarily I'd agree with you every step of the way, but not this time." Styles was firm with her. "It's been hard on him, too. Now, I know that's easy to say, but if you'd heard how he sounded... He's just as worried as you are—he said so when he called this morning. He wanted to talk to you, but he couldn't work up the nerve, so—"

"That's pretty glib," said Dana, knowing her cynicism was fake, and that it hid her growing sense of betrayal. It could have been so wonderful, and now...

"We'll get to the bottom of this. I'll arrange something," Styles assured her, and did not wait for her to try to talk him out of it before he left her office.

Dana braced her elbows on her drafting table and let herself sob.

Trevor looked terrible—there were hollows in his face Dana had not seen before, and his eyes were livid as guttered candles. His hands were sunk in the pockets of his rumpled tweed jacket. He had nicked himself shaving, leaving a small line of blood on his chin. He rose as Dana approached along the corridor of packing crates, looking shamefaced and weary in response to the suspicion in her entire demeanor.

Styles offered Dana the chair on the far side of the desk so that she would have its rosewood bulk as protection. This was not lost on either Dana or Trevor, though neither gave any sign of noticing. He poured coffee for all of them, saying nothing.

Dana sat with her back very straight and did her best to avoid looking directly at Trevor. She did not want to feel sorry for him, and given his enervated state, it would be easy to become sympathetic. After last night, she found it difficult to believe anything about him, or her dreams. She sipped her coffee and stared at the packing crates.

"I think," said Styles after the silence grew intolerable, "that I owe both of you. You've gone through quite a lot because of me, and I don't mean because I introduced you. I set you up. I didn't know it was happening. But I did it, and it's my responsibility to fix it, if I can." He addressed a blank section of air halfway between Dana and Trevor, doing all that he could to show he was not taking sides. "It's my turn to talk—I don't want any interruptions." As he continued, he drew something out of the pocket of his safari jacket that he wore today over his usual black. He held up Greedy Eyes the Dream Catcher. "Given what I've been told, there are things happening between you two that are not explainable in any other context but that you have been influenced by this thing. Ordinarily you'd get a shaman to help you, but under the circumstances, I'm afraid you're stuck with me."

"What do—" Dana began, only to be cut off.

"I said it's my turn to talk," Styles reminded her. "I'll let you know when it's yours." He set the fetish on the arm of his chair. "I've been doing some more reading up on these guys, and I've made a couple of calls to some experts I know; I should have talked to them before now. I don't like what I've found out."

"Don't believe everything you're told," said Trevor, his voice now more flat than calm.

"Ah-ah. You can talk or ask questions in a little while," Styles informed them. "When I'm finished telling you what I know. Until then, hold off." He drank the last of his coffee and put the mug on the floor beside his chair. "According to what I have found out—thanks to a very distinguished anthropologist who was willing to talk to me this afternoon— your Dream Catcher is a killer. Quite literally. According to Professor Asche, this demon grants the heart's desire and takes life in payment, usually through sexually obsessive murders," he went on, holding up his hand to forestall any comments. "I know that neither of you put much credence in the effectiveness of idols of any size. But you cannot deny that things have been happening to you both that are . . . shall we say uncharacteristic of you both?"

"Yes," Dana admitted reluctantly.

Trevor only nodded.

"And I think that this fetish has something to do with how things are going." He pointed to Trevor. "Aside from what came over you last night, would you say that you are generally interested in and becoming fond of Dana?"

"God, yes," came his answer at once. "I couldn't have asked for anyone better. She's everything I've ever hoped to find in a woman."

Styles gave a single, satisfied nod. "And Dana, had Trevor not attacked you, would you say he fit the bill of what you told Dream Catcher you wanted in a man?"

Dana hesitated before answering; when she spoke, she felt her way through her answer as if through a garden of thorns. "I think so. I haven't known him long enough to find out all of it, but . . . if it weren't for the dreams and how he acted—" She stopped abruptly.

"Ah, yes," said Styles. "The dreams. They're very disturbing, aren't they? And very convincing. You could almost swear they were real. Especially the bad parts, the exploitive, humiliating parts." He gave her a moment to answer; when she did not, he continued. "They took all the things you wanted and perverted them, didn't they? They made you ashamed of your desires, and made you afraid that you were bringing something hideous upon yourself. They made you feel that everything was your fault, that you sought it out, that you invited, that you *deserved* the terrible things you dreamed. Am I right?"

"Wait a minute!" Trevor protested. "You're upsetting her."

"Good. I meant to." He motioned Trevor to sit down. "Let me finish. The dreams you've been having," he went on to Trevor, "are not so much different than hers."

"I can't remember them," he answered sullenly.

"Exactly. And *that's* why you did what you did last night. You denied what was in the dreams, so you had to act them out. That's what Dream Catcher does. Not to sound all psychological on you, but that's what Professor Asche said was typical." He got out of the chair without effort and began to pace the limits of his Oriental carpets. "Don't interrupt me yet," he warned as he bent to retrieve his mug and filled it with coffee. "I'm taking off for Hawaii a little after midnight. I'm booked on a flight to Suva in Fiji, and from there I'll have a ticket waiting to get this monster home. Once it's back in Malekula, it can't do anything more to you. He'll be far away then. His wings are clipped. He can't fly."

"Hamilton." Dana was confused and worried that he should think such extreme steps were necessary, or that Styles should place such credence in a four-inch-high wooden figure with eyes of green glass. "For heaven's sake, it can't be that important."

"You don't have to do that. I'll take it for you, when I go back to Wellington," offered Trevor listlessly.

"No way," said Styles. "For one thing, it's not safe for either of you to touch it again, and for another, you've got work to do here. I'll do the shaman's part if you'll do yours. And given that I'm gallivanting all over the South Pacific for you, I expect you to do what Professor Asche said you had to do to break its hold. And, frankly, you've got the tougher job."

"But why go all the way to the New Hebrides: leave him in Honolulu," suggested Dana. "That should be water enough, if, as you say, he can't fly." Am I actually talking as if I believed this? she asked herself inwardly. And why did the prospect of having the fetish far away from her make her feel so much safer? Was she so thoroughly taken in, or so shocked by all that had happened that anything, including this crazy project, seemed better than doing nothing?

"Nope. Professor Asche said it would only rest where it was made. So I'll get him there." Styles fiddled with his mug. "It's the best way, believe me."

"You're kidding," said Dana. "I can't believe I'm listening to this."

"Not everything in the world makes the same kind of sense," Styles told her. "Not all sense is rational."

"All right, we'll assume for the moment there's some... influence it has. But if the fetish, the demon, is doing what you say," Dana reasoned, doing her best to go along with his absurd notion, "surely going to all the trouble you intend to go to is enough to make it stop. Getting it away from here is enough, isn't it?"

If there is anything in the fetish to stop, and this isn't all just a lot of superstitious nonsense to account for a man's need to domineer, she added silently to herself.

"It's already working on you. You've both admitted as much. So it's important for you to break its hold on you while I take it away from here. Lucky thing you didn't end up with one of the winged fetishes," Styles said to Dana, in so light a tone that she was not certain he was really serious. "Those winged guys can cross water easily, according to Asche. And then you *would* be in trouble."

"Sure," said Dana in outright disbelief. "Do you expect me to take this on faith? This is the end of the twentieth century. Demonic possession doesn't happen anymore, except in movies. Look, Hamilton, if you want to go off to the South Pacific, you don't need this as an excuse. You're a dealer in folk art. You can do anything you please."

Styles stopped and faced her across the desk. His manner was wholly serious. "I'm not doing this to get folk art. I'm not trying to be a hero. I'm doing this to make up for what I'm afraid I've done to you and Trevor. As much as I can, anyway, as a makeshift shaman. The rest is up to you. You have to…exorcise Dream Catcher from your lives. And you're going to need my help to do it."

"How?" asked Trevor. "I know the tradition is to drive yourself to the brink of death as a kind of purging—"

"And if we do nothing?" Dana challenged. She could not make herself believe that she was being influenced by a New Hebrides demon fetish.

"Then you risk destruction," said Styles.

Dana wished she could bring herself to laugh at so portentous a statement. "From Greedy Eyes."

"You saw what happened to Trevor when he denied the dreams. Dream Catcher was given free rein. He terrified you, and he terrified himself. He's afraid now that it will happen again. Well, that's just the start—your dreams will reach a point where you won't be able to deal with them, either, and you'll end up acting out the very thing you find most loathsome. That's the hold that has to be broken. It exaggerates your feelings and—" He regarded her steadily, letting his words sink in "—and sooner or later it will kill you."

"When he goes home, it'll stop," said Dana. "If you're right, that is."

"No." Styles looked from Dana to Trevor and back again. "Dream Catcher has already influenced you. According to Asche, you could be in New Zealand, or California, or Greenland, for that matter, and you would continue to dream, and the dreams will become more obsessive and demanding unless you break the hold now."

"All right," said Trevor, as if waking from deep sleep, "assuming there is something to this, what do we do? Is there a rite of exorcism?" His sarcasm did not work.

"Trevor!" Dana cried out, acknowledging their shared predicament for the first time.

"Well, I'm willing to try," he said. "Almost anything. For me. For you. For a decent night's sleep." He folded his arms and sighed. "What do we have to do?"

"This is silly." They sat huddled in wet suits, side by side on the sand, facing the Pacific and the west, that last radiance of twilight fading in the sky as the sun continued its westward course. The tide was advancing, and would rise above them in a matter of two hours unless they moved. Dana had been growing uneasy about their task since they delivered Styles to San Francisco International Airport the previous night. Now it seemed to her the height of all things ludicrous that Styles should be on his way to bury a fetish in a South Pacific beach and that she and Trevor Davidson should be sitting here, preparing to exorcise a sexual-obsession demon from the New Hebrides—or drown in the attempt.

"I don't want to do this, either, but I don't like the alternative, and if feeling foolish is the worst that happens to me, I'll be damned lucky," said Trevor in a remote way. "But, Dana, I can't go through life wondering if I'm ever going to treat you, or any other woman, the way I did at your house. I don't want to have that hanging over me for the rest of my life." He tilted his head back and squinted up at the sky, studying the stars. "Is that the Great Bear? We can't see it in New Zealand."

"The Great Bear?" she asked, looking where he pointed. "Oh, you mean the Big Dipper. That, and the Little Dipper. And that's Draco. And that thing like a broken *W* is Cassiopeia.'' She showed him where to find them overhead, taking a curious comfort in the familiar night sky.

"It's almost dark," Trevor said gently. "We ought to get started."

An abrupt shiver, like a small, intense, personal earthquake, went through her. "It seems so... strange."

"Do you want to stop the dreams?" he asked her, looking at her for the first time since they sat down, forty minutes before.

"Yes," she answered with emotion. "But what if this doesn't work?"

"We drown, I suppose." He smiled a bit. "What if it does?"

The wind was out of the north, polishing the sky and whipping the waves to white frills. On the beach, their wet suits grew shiny; their hair was spangled with droplets, and their faces were becoming damp. Their place was no longer quite so secure on the sand as the ocean advanced.

She did her best to shrug. "Well, we're here. And we know what's supposed to work. So we might as well." She drew up her knees and rested her forearms around her legs. "How do we get started? Who goes first?"

"You know what we were told." He put his arm around her shoulder. "According to Professor Asche, we start at the beginning. That would be what you told Greedy Eyes you wanted."

"I don't know if I can remember it all," said Dana. For some reason she could not fathom she had trouble getting started. "I told you a little about Kirk—the man I lived with? I'd been thinking a lot about what was wrong with our relationship, and what I wanted to have—"

"Yes," Trevor interrupted gently. "So what did you ask for?"

She sighed and got down to it, trying to ignore the subtle rising of the water. "I asked for a man who wanted to be loved, who didn't resent it or use it or minimize it. A man who was willing to have a loving equal. A man who liked me as a person, to have around for more than service and sex. A man who wanted a partnership. A man who wouldn't resent my abilities or undermine my confidence. A trustworthy and trusting man. A man who...liked more than macho sports for entertainment." She faltered, disliking the emotions being stirred up in her as she spoke.

"You asked for someone with a little art and culture in his soul," Trevor filled in for her. "Is that what you mean? Is that what you are looking for?"

"That's right, and a little romance," she finished. "There were a couple other things, like a sense of humor and playfulness, but that was the gist of it, I think."

"You're certain?" he prompted. "You shouldn't leave anything out."

She nodded twice vigorously. "I'm certain."

"Is that really what you want?" Trevor asked, following the instructions from Professor Asche. "Including the sense of humor and playfulness, and the romance?"

"Yes. That's really what I want." There were other things besides, things that she had not spoken aloud but that remained in her thoughts so vividly that she was aware of how close they sat together, with the tide coming in.

"Are there any more?" He recalled how they had been warned that the unspoken wishes were often the most potent. It would be these secret wishes that would give Greedy Eyes the greatest hold on them.

Dana shifted uncomfortably. "Two, I guess. I want a man I can be comfortable with, whom I can rely on and who relies on me. And someone who... lets us both enjoy sex together. I want to have him care as much for my... fulfillment as his own." Her words could hardly be heard over the tumult of the surf.

"Kirk must have been a real charmer," said Trevor dryly, departing from their instructions.

"Yes," said Dana seriously. "That was the trouble. He could be. But not when it really counted."

Trevor took a moment to bring his attention back to what they were doing; he had heard enough about Kirk that he had developed a hearty dislike for the man, and not only because of what Dana had said, but what he knew about his fellow males, and it troubled him. He reminded himself the tide was coming in and their time was limited. At least they were not hanging off the side of a cliff, as the New Hebrides tradition usually required to exorcise Dream Catchers. "The things you say are your wishes—are they really what you want? And is that all of them, as you can remember?"

"Yes, they are," she said, with more force than she had expected.

A wave broke over them as he went on to the end. "Good." Trevor remembered the specific Professor Asche had provided them on the phone that morning. "Do you truly want to do those things?"

"Yes, yes I do," she said, and was glad for the comfort of his arm.

"The dream or the reality?" The undertow was strong enough to be frightening to them both. It was not easy to hang on to one another in the churning water.

"The reality," she said with intense feeling. "And you? What do you want?" she asked.

He knew the question was coming, and was somewhat unprepared for what he heard himself say. "I want ... passion. I don't mean lust or possessiveness or jealousy or any of the rest of the things that are called passion to make them more acceptable, but that abiding commitment that sustains everything else. I don't want half-measures. I want all of you there is to have. I had enough of the other designing bridges."

The waves no longer retreated beyond them as they eddied. Now they were constantly in water, and it rose around them.

Dana listened with a mixture of amazement and ill-defined uneasiness. She remembered it was her job to ask him more. "Is this what you really want?"

"Yes, it is." He stared out at the last pale line at the edge of the horizon, where daylight finally vanished.

"Is it what you want to do?" she asked.

"Yes." The deep, calm note was back in his voice for the first time since the disastrous evening at her house. The next question was his. "What do you fear may come of having your wish?"

Dana angled herself so that she was not quite so close to him as she had been. Her elbow was pressed between them, a potential wedge. "That it will turn against me and I won't be able to walk away." Those last two years with Kirk had been that kind of nightmare. This reminder made her want to cringe at how readily she had accepted his manipulation. She had bartered her self-respect for Kirk's attention, and she dreaded the same thing happening again.

"Do you want that to happen?" asked Trevor, as required.

"No." She wanted to sound more certain, to feel the denial in her like strength.

"What do you think those things would be?" How would the things you don't want be expressed?" He found his mouth was going dry. Whatever she said, he would have to listen to, and face what it meant for them both. "The things you don't want to happen?"

"I think they would be...discouraging at first. And I would want to make up for the discouragement, so I would be more accommodating," she said, trying not to stop herself from describing her growing discomfort. For the first time, she drifted a bit with the movement of the waves. Her hands tightened in his. "After a time, I would be looking for things to do to keep the disappointment from beginning, and that would mean I would be giving up parts of myself in order to hold the disappointment at bay. I would anticipate his next demands and accommodate them before he could make them. It would become a cycle, and it would grow more destructive. I would seek out ways to damage myself so that he—you—would not catch me unaware." For the first time a wave broke over their heads.

"What would you do?" asked Trevor, coughing and steeling himself for the answer.

Very slowly Dana began to describe all the hideous things that had happened to her in her dream. "I would encourage abuse in order to control it. I would...suggest things. Hateful things."

"What things?" he asked, as neutrally as he could. He had to hold her more tightly now, or she would start to drift away from him.

"Painful things. Disgusting things. Perverted things." She went carefully, mindful of the careful warning Professor Asche had given them about exposing all the demon's secrets, all the dark places in her soul. The degradation she felt at having the thoughts at all made her horrified of what she had to say. "Don't...don't despise me for...any of this," she pleaded, holding him with brittle strength.

"I won't," he promised, and did his best to keep it. When she was at a loss to describe what she experienced, he coaxed her through to the end as the tide rocked and tossed them several feet farther up the beach. The most heinous images she could express served to make him more determined to protect her from what Dream Catcher would use to coerce her into her own ruin.

"Okay," she said when she had completed the whole of it. She was sweating inside her wet suit and shivering at the same time, as if she had a fever. "That's all of it." She shuddered, hoping she would not be sick. "What's wrong with me? How can I think such things?"

"People think all kinds of things, all the time. It's what people do." He resumed their improvised rite of exorcism. "Do you know those were your thoughts?"

Dana nearly gagged on her answer. "Yes. I know it. I don't like it, but I know it."

"Do you want to act on any of them?" Trevor persisted, hanging on to her as tightly as he could in the backwash of another wave.

"No!" Her answer now had the strength she had wanted to hear all along. She felt her body come vibrantly alive. She did not have to live in a constant state of chagrin and apology for being Dana Piper. The malignant specter of self-betrayal lifted from her. Enjoyment no longer had to mask debauchery, and concern was no longer a polite term for control. She looked at Trevor, trying to find words to express the vitality that coursed through her, as enduring and stalwart as the ocean. "How could you stand it, the way I've been?" she whispered.

"What was so awful?" He strove to hold her more close, filled with amazement at her transformation. "God, you look— Asche was right!" he marveled, shaking his head. "You're not just beautiful, you're... Something has changed in you, beyond words. I'd have to sculpt it."

She slid her arm around his back. "Tell me about how what you want can go wrong," she said, feeling unaccountably serene. She gave herself a sharp mental reprimand for thinking it was all over. He had held her, and now she would have to do the same for him, for if either let go, they were both in danger. And Trevor still had his bonds with Dream Catcher to break, and he would need her compassion and insight to succeed. It was unbearable to imagine being freed himself and have him still in the grip of the demon of the fetish.

The waves continued their steady progress, flinging Dana and Trevor about with the lazily deceptive power of a cat with mice.

He began confidently enough, but as he described more of the desolation of spirit he felt when caught in the throes of the obsession, she had to ask questions that urged him on. When his descriptions became morbidly graphic, Dana implored him to reveal the worst of it, like lancing a festering wound. She wondered if he had been as appalled by what she told him as she was by the things he said. It was tempting, and simple, to be shut of it all, to let him go, and surrender to the ocean. It was hard to hold him, and harder to trust him—the echoes of Kirk's manipulative phrases murmured with the roar of the Pacific.

"Dana!" His shout cut through the distractions.

To her horror, she realized she had almost let go of him. The specters of her past had clouded her sight. She had almost failed him. And herself. The despair she saw in his face then would have proven too devastating for her just an hour before, but now she reached out to him through the very heart of his anguish. "Do you know these thoughts are yours?"

"Yes," he said. "They're repulsive, but they're mine." The admission was bitter as gall. He realized now why she had been so distressed by her own explorations; his were an ordeal.

"Do you want to do any of them?" She felt his answer before it came from him.

"No!"

"Do you want the dream or the reality?" The water toyed with them, pushing them toward safety, then tugging them out toward the deep.

"The reality! The reality! You!" he gasped, coughing, as they broke through to the surface, tossed away from the wet, cold darkness. And they clung together for courage and life as the Pacific Ocean surged around them, to leave them tangled together like driftwood, high up the beach.

"We're going to have to put an addition on the house for your studio, assuming we can arrange purchase ahead of time," Dana said as she signaled for the San Francisco airport turn-off. It was shortly after midnight, and Hamilton Styles was due to arrive in forty minutes. The past two days had been filled with plans. They had used most of the two-hour drive to the airport to try to stick to pragmatic problems and had almost succeeded.

"We can arrange for that later," Trevor said; his seat was on half recline and he was gazing at her, smiling slightly, his green eyes shining. "I can rent facilities for the time being. Besides, you may not want my studio at the house. Sculpting in wood is messy work. Shavings and sawdust everywhere." He paused, and added mischievously. "However, the cats would love it."

She jockeyed for a lane into the parking lot. "You sure you want to make the move?" She did not feel afraid when she asked. There was none of the sinking sense of failure that had haunted her before, no unspoken dread that she would have to make up for asking such a question. It was four days since they had stumbled out of the ocean, shaken to the core and changed.

"Don't you want me to?" he countered, and went on. "I don't want to be away from you. And this is a beautiful place. I can sculpt anywhere. Hell, most of my commissions come from the States. Your business is just starting to take off. It makes more sense for me to move." He laid his hand on hers as she toggled the window control.

She loved the sound of his voice and the touch of his hands. All the fantasies of erotic pleasure that had consumed her had been completely eclipsed by the reality of their lovemaking. The blandishments of her dreams were nothing compared to the warm, breathing presence of Trevor Davidson. Passionate, tender and playful, Trevor had proved to be a generous and secure lover who had already banished the worst of Dana's qualms about herself as a woman, freeing her from the eroding doubts Kirk had instilled in her. Reluctantly she pulled her hand away and took the steering wheel once more. "So long as you're not giving up too much. Your family..."

"There are planes. We can visit. California isn't Mars." He glanced at the sign indicating which airlines were reached from that area. "United—"

"North terminal," said Dana as she continued around the roof of the garage. "Hawaii flights usually come in at the same group of gates."

"You know this airport—I don't," he conceded as she swung down one of the parking aisles in search of a space. "Not yet, anyway."

As she parked, she said, "Stick around and you'll get the hang of it, when we come to pick up your relatives." It was easy to be lighthearted now, and to revel in what she had found at last.

"I'm planning to," he reminded her as they got out of the car. "Stick around, not pick up my relatives."

The airport was not as busy as it was during the day, but there was still the anonymous rush around them as they made their way through security and out the long pier to the gate where Styles' plane was due to come in.

As they waited, Trevor took Dana in his arms and gave her a long, thorough, friendly kiss. "Don't worry," he said. "People are always kissing in airports. No one pays any attention."

Dana had not been worried, but she grinned as she saw another couple meet at the end of the moving walkways and embrace. "I see what you mean." She saw the display at the desk change, indicating the flight would be ten minutes early.

"He's going to be worn out," said Trevor, remembering his own arrival not so long ago.

"Good thing he gave himself an extra day in Hawaii, coming home," said Dana. "He'd be in awful shape if he hadn't done that."

"What a trial for him, an extra day in Hawaii," Trevor consoled. "We'll have to try the same thing, when we go to New Zealand."

"Christmas," she said, confirming the plans they had made.

A crackly, disembodied voice announced that the United flight from Honolulu was arriving and passengers could be met at the gate. A few of the people who had been milling about the gate now gathered with greater purpose.

Trevor took Dana's hand as they found a spot near the gate where they could stand with their backs to a pillar.

Styles had on an outrageous Hawaiian print shirt of blossoms in neon-brilliant colors over his usual black turtleneck and slacks. He carried one large leather valise and looked immensely pleased with himself as he came up to Dana and Trevor. If he was surprised to see them together, he gave no indication of it. After giving them a hug, he said, "What did I tell you? Uncle Hamilton was right?" There was a look in his eyes that had the same lucid depth as both Trevor's and Dana's.

"Bloody hard way to be right," said Trevor firmly.

"No argument; and I'm a good swimmer." His tone was eloquent; whatever he had experienced was nearly as harrowing as what they had endured. Deliberately he took a bantering tone. "But now you're through it, it was worth the effort, wouldn't you say?" The arch of his brow was deliberately provoking.

"Absolutely," said Trevor.

"No question," said Dana at the same time.

"I just wish it wasn't necessary to come near drowning in order to be rid of it," said Dana. She felt Trevor's fingers tighten on hers. "If either of us had let go—"

"But we didn't," Trevor said quickly.

"Oh, that." Styles chuckled a little, but without a trace of mirth. "That was for intent. You have to mean it, really mean it, to do the job right. If you cannot put your life on the line, the demon will always have its hooks in you. The ocean was the most obvious way to get you through. It's like graveyard dirt—it's the same as most other dirt, but it takes more determination to dig it up."

Trevor nodded. "Of course. I should have seen that."

"No harm done," said Styles. "Since you got through it." This last was less confident, and once again Dana wondered what his journey had been like when he reached Malekula. One day, she realized, he would tell them, but not yet.

Styles stepped between them. "Come on. This is all the luggage I've got, so we can go now. Speaking of now, I don't know what time it is, but I'm famished. Let's call and wake up Hector and have him cook us something. He should be able to have something ready by the time we arrive."

As they strolled off beside the moving walkway,

Dana said, "Regular customer or not, don't you think
that's a bit much?"

"Regular customer, hell!" Styles exclaimed cheer-
fully. "Who do you think his partner is, anyway?"
With that, he linked arms with both of them and
headed for the parking lot.

*   *   *   *   *

Dear Reader,

As the dedication on this novella suggests, I wrote this for an old friend who died February 15, 1994, of acute double pneumonia, at age forty-six. Kathy lived out in western Marin County, on the bluffs overlooking the Pacific Ocean in the remote town of Bolinas, an hour and a half away from my home in the East Bay in good weather; we phoned each other several times a week. She was a voracious reader and loved what she called "thrill-romances" more than any other subgenre. She was delighted when I told her about the chance to do this one, and I asked her to describe to me the stories she liked and why she liked them. She answered with great enthusiasm, "Oh, you know, they're the kind of stories where you can have the fantasies without the nightmares."

There is nothing like the word *nightmare* to start a writer to ruminating, and the next day I called Kathy again and asked her what themes she thought were too overused to be interesting. She immediately told me what she thought about the current state of the field, and recommended a few titles to me. I asked her what she hadn't seen so far that she would like to see. Again she had a quick answer, "Real shamanism, but without the real shaman, so mistakes can be made without a sudden attack of the stupids. One of those person-who-learned-better stories. And not European in origin. That's getting too common." She gave me another piece of advice that day: "The heroine's got to be a good fighter."

So I went to my books on shamanistic traditions and came upon dream fetishes of the New Hebrides in the South Pacific. They sounded interesting and could cause 110 manuscript pages of trouble, or so I hoped. When I told

Kathy about this idea, she said, "That's drool you hear coming through the phone."

A few days later she went, protesting, to the hospital, and was immediately placed in intensive care. She asked me to hurry up on the story so she could have something interesting to read while she was recuperating. I was on manuscript page 38 when she died.

Chelsea Quinn Yarbro

Beyond Twilight
Maggie Shayne

To Lisa, my littlest angel

CHAPTER ONE

He twisted away, but her hands were still there. Burning him. Whispering across his chest like wind over water. He shivered. He sweat. He gasped for air but inhaled only her scent. He reached for sanity and found his fingers entangled in short, satiny hair. He opened his eyes and found them captured by hers. Huge, dark, innocent. Imploring, hot, sexy eyes, staring down at him as he lay trembling with desire on his bed. And he knew he was lost. He lifted his arms, slid them around her small body to pull her down to his chest. Parted his lips to taste her succulent mouth...

And there was nothing there. He lay panting and alone, his torso and face coated in a slick sheen, his arms wrapped around themselves. He sat up fast, blinking in the gathering dusk, grabbing the first thing his fist closed on and hurling it into the opposite wall. Both hands pushed through his hair. Dammit, he was still shaking, still hotter than hell for some fantasy woman; a dreamworld pixie who looked more like Peter Pan's Tinkerbell than a swimsuit-issue cover girl. What the hell was the matter with him?

"Pressure." He muttered the word to himself and slid naked from the bed for his ritual cold shower. The dreams had been coming for months on a regular basis. "Stress," he added, stomping into the hotel bathroom, flicking the light, twisting the knobs. It was the job. Hell, it would get to anyone. He'd failed his last mission, damned near got himself killed while he was at it.

His latest assignment had been handed down eight months ago, and he still hadn't had any success. So many close calls, so many near misses. Every time he thought he had her, she pulled some trick out of her sleeve and slipped right through his fingers. And *almost* didn't cut the mustard with DPI. An agent for the CIA's secretive Division of Paranormal Investigations had to deliver the goods. He was closer than he'd ever been to doing just that. She was here, in this small, middle-of-nowhere town in northern Maine.

Stephen "Ramsey" Bachman was a hunter of sorts, but his quarry wasn't human. She was a vampire.

It was her house and she had finally come home to roost. The place was like something out of an old Vincent Price movie. Big and gothic and sadly in need of a coat of paint. The front door was unlocked. It was just before dusk.

Finally, he had her cornered, right in her own backyard. She'd been on DPI's Most Wanted List for more than a decade. He didn't know why. It wasn't his business to know why, just to bring her in. And he had a feeling he was about to do it.

He gripped a small leather satchel in his right hand. Inside were three syringes, each containing a dose of tranquilizer developed by legendary DPI researcher Curtis Rogers. His original formula had been lost when he had been killed, probably by one of *them*, though no one had ever proven it. But Bachman didn't need proof. They were all the same, ruthless killers who preyed on the innocent.

DPI's scientists had been painstakingly working to recreate Rogers's tranquilizer and they thought they'd finally succeeded. He swallowed hard. Tonight would be its first actual test.

The huge, darkly stained door groaned when he pushed it open. His steps echoed on the dusty, time-dulled parquet. He ignored the baroque furnishings, the dark woodwork, the cobwebs, the dust, and he headed straight for the spiral staircase. It creaked with every step.

He'd cased this house early on, as soon as he'd learned she owned it. He knew the basement was prone to flooding and that there was only one room in the place with no windows. That room was where he was heading right now. It had been empty the first time he'd seen it, but he had a strong feeling it wouldn't be vacant tonight.

He reached the top of the stairs and started down the tall, narrow corridor, moving right past the rows of closed doors. He knew which door hid his nemesis. When he reached it he paused with his hand on the knob.

His first inkling that something wasn't quite right came when he turned the knob and it gave without resistance. His feet planted, he stood still a moment, listened, *feeling* the very air around him for a warning, a sound.

Nothing.

He pushed the door inward and stepped slowly inside. Nightmarish candlelight illuminated the entire room. A hundred tapers danced and flickered, casting lively shadows on the walls, the ceiling, the floor. And there was music. The melodramatic chords of a ghostly pipe organ floated softly on the air. A little chill raced up his spine. Not one of fear, induced by the music and candles. But one of foreboding, as he wondered just what in hell she was up to this time.

The coffin gleamed black with shining brass trim from atop a flower-strewn bier. He stepped forward, noting the dead roses at the head and foot. Nice touch. If he found her, he thought he'd choke her before he ever took her in. He was tired of this, tired of her games and jokes, all of them seemingly designed to make him look like a fool.

He approached the coffin, glancing over his shoulder every second or two, just in case.

A thick curtain of cobwebs stuck to his face and he swept it aside with an angry gesture. The music swelled a little louder, he thought as he put his hands on the lid.

Jaw clenching, he opened it.

Then he stood there, blinking in shock as he stared down at the most horrendous creature he'd ever seen. She had hair like a matted rat's nest, tight facial skin tinted blue, with black rings encircling the sunken, closed eyes. The cheeks were hollow, gaunt. The lips were pulled back in an almost snarl, baring the pointy tips of yellowed incisors. He could count the bones in the narrow hands that lay crossed upon her chest. The gruesome image, along with his own, was reflected in a mirror on the inside of the lid.

Ramsey poked a finger into the skin of her arm, then let his chin fall to his chest as he blew every bit of air from his lungs. She'd done it to him again, damn her. The body in the coffin was made of wax. And Cuyler Jade was probably a hundred miles away from here by now.

Soft laughter, like crystal water bubbling over smooth stones, filled the room. He stiffened and spun around. The woman stood in the doorway, her hand over her mouth, her mischievous eyes twinkling with candlelight and mirth.

"If you could have seen your face..." She laughed some more, closing her eyes and tipping her head back.

She was tiny. Her gleaming black hair was cut short, with spiky bangs on her forehead and jagged ends laying on her neck. She brought her head level and tilted it slightly as she studied him. She looked like a pixie, like Peter Pan's Tinkerbell.

Impossible. It's your imagination, dammit. She's not the woman in your dreams.

He said nothing. She stepped into the room, bold as brass. "I'm kinda tired of this endless chase, Ramsey."

He blinked. "What did you call me?"

"Ramsey. Isn't that what all the guys in military school dubbed you? Stephen Bachman from Ramsey, Indiana, became Ramsey in the tenth grade, if I remember correctly." She smiled and moved closer.

"Don't look so surprised. Isn't the first rule of all you secret agent types to know your enemy?"

He watched her approach until she stood only inches away from him. She wasn't the one he was after. She couldn't be. She was the imp from his dreams. The erotic, sexy, innocent-eyed devil that smiled as she touched him. The one that drove him half out of his head with pure animal lust. She wasn't a monster.

She offered a tiny hand, and as he closed his huge one around it she told him the last thing he wanted to hear. "I'm Cuyler Jade. The one you've been chasing all over the country for the past eight months."

He swallowed the sand-covered rock that seemed to have lodged in his throat, and quickly dropped her hand.

"So here I am," she told him. The impish light in her eyes was tempered with a hint of uncertainty. The brazen smile on her lips, a little unsteady. "Question is, Ramsey, now that you've got me, what are you gonna do with me?"

He stiffened his back. Okay, so she was a vampire. And he'd had recurring, wildly erotic dreams about her for the past several months. Almost as long as he'd been after her. So what? He had a job to do, and that was his priority—not his unruly libido.

"I'm going to arrest you." His voice sounded cold, harsh. Good. "You're now a federal prisoner, Ms. Jade. I'm taking you back to New York, to our headquarters in White Plains."

"Are you?"

God, her eyes were big. And dark. And those thick lashes made him think of Bambi, made him feel like the heartless hunter.

"Afraid so."

"And what if I won't go with you? You going to overpower me?"

She knew he couldn't do that. Remarkably, she stood still while he opened the satchel and brought out one of the syringes. "I could tranquilize you."

She frowned at the hypodermic. "That stuff work?"

He shrugged. "One way to find out."

He reached for her arm, but she danced away from him before he could grip it. Tapping her chin with a coral-tipped finger, she faced him once again. "Suppose I was to come along peacefully?"

He studied her through narrowed eyes, all too aware of her knack for tricks and pranks. "Why would you do that?"

Her black eyes narrowed. She came back to him, leaned in so close her breath fanned his throat. One of her small hands came up and her fingertips danced over his nape. "'Cause you're not going to go through with it, Ramsey."

He swallowed again, hoping she wouldn't press any closer and accidentally discover the effect she was having on him. He shifted his stance and tried to remind himself what she was. She only looked like a woman. Beads of sweat popped out on his forehead, and he tried to summon the will to jab the needle into her arm before she could slip away again.

Instead he only managed, "What makes you think so?" His voice sounded coarse. Not at all as intimidating as it ought to.

Her lips curved upward just a little. "I know about the dreams," she whispered.

He didn't let it shake him. All right, it shook him, but he didn't let it show. "Because you caused them? Another one of your tricks?"

She shook her head. "I don't know *what* caused them, Ramsey. But I've been having them, too."

CHAPTER TWO

She watched him, waited to see his reaction to her words. She truly believed what she'd told him, that he wouldn't be able to take her into custody. But she didn't think he was fully aware of it. Not yet, anyway. Ramsey Bachman had a thing or two to learn about himself. And Cuyler had decided she was the only one who could teach him.

He was speechless for a long moment. Then he shook his head, staring at her from wary, deep gray eyes. "You're a good liar, Cuyler. But not that good. You haven't had any dreams about me."

"No? Want me to describe them to you?"

"No." He said it too quickly.

She smiled. "I get to you, Ramsey. You know I do. It's not a big surprise, really. You get to me, too. I'm not afraid to admit it."

"Dream on, Cuyler." Still holding the syringe in one hand, he clasped her arm with the other and turned her toward the door. "Come on, if you're so eager to surrender. My car's out front. You want to pack a bag?"

"Not just yet." She resisted the urge to pull her arm away yet again. She couldn't do that, couldn't let him think she was up to something. But the big boys from DPI were getting restless waiting for Ramsey to bring her in. Much longer and they'd come for her themselves, and she'd rather take her chances with Ramsey than with them. She had to play her cards fast and well.

The wariness had never left his eyes. It only intensified. "You're trying to pull something on me."

"I have a deal to offer you. Take it or leave it, it's up to you."

"No deals. You're coming with me. Now."

"No. I'll come in with you in a few days. Without a peep. No tricks, no struggles, no fuss. I promise."

"And I'm supposed to believe you?"

"You want me to write it in blood?"

He released her arm, let his own hang loosely at his side, and stared at her so hard she could feel the touch of those eyes. More than that, she could feel the anger behind them, and the pain. And her arm still tingled where he'd held it. It still baffled her, this awareness between the two of them. This attraction. She'd felt it before she'd even laid eyes on him.

"What do you want in return?"

"Hmm, a hunk with a brain. You're a rare specimen, Ramsey."

"What do you want?" he repeated, impatience giving an edge to his voice.

She tilted her head, shrugging delicately, walking in a small circle with a happy bounce in her steps. He was faltering. He wouldn't even have asked unless he was considering giving in. "Nothing much. Just a little bit of your time. Three nights of it should be enough."

"Three—"

She stopped, spinning on her heel and pointing at him. "You spend three nights with me. At dusk on the fourth, I'll be ready and willing to head off to Nazi headquarters with you. Okay?"

He shook his head slowly. "Three nights... doing *what* with you?"

She rolled her eyes, threw her palms up. "Not that, for crying out loud. Crimey, if *that* was all I wanted from you, I could have had it months ago!"

"The hell you could."

"Forget it, Ramsey. I'm right and you know it. Picture it. You wake from one of those hot and heavy dreams to find the real thing naked in your arms. You tellin' me you'd roll over and go back to sleep?" She moved closer as she spoke, leaned into him, stood on tiptoe until her nose nearly touched his chin. "I don't think so."

"I don't give a damn *what* you think."

She shrugged, but backed down and resumed her circular pacing.

"So if you don't want me sleeping with you, then what are the three nights for?"

"I *sleep* during the day." She ruffled the short layers of her hair with both hands. He was exasperating. She hadn't expected it to be this difficult. She turned away from him, picked a slender white candle from its holder and tilted the flame to an incense dish, igniting the cone in its center. She inhaled the sweet fragrance. Just because she hadn't expected difficulty didn't mean she hadn't prepared for it.

"Look, Ramsey, I need to spend some time with you if I'm going to figure this out, that's all. I just want to get to the bottom of this . . . this *thing*."

"What thing?"

She made two fists, held them near her temples and squeezed her eyes tight. She was going to hit him if he didn't stop acting so obtuse. She took a step backward, and he very logically advanced an equal distance. He stood near the incense. A spiral of scented smoke rose around his head.

"You know I could have killed you months ago, or hurt you so badly you would have been off my case for a long time," she told him. "I could have closed my eyes and given one good mental scream and had half a dozen older, stronger ones here to get rid of you for me."

"Then why the hell didn't you?"

"*I don't know!* That's the *thing* I want to get to the bottom of! I can't even think about hurting you. Hell, I've got this off-the-wall notion that I ought to be looking out for you, but—"

"*You?* Looking out for *me?* That's a laugh."

"Damn straight, when I know you're planning to haul me off to a death camp."

"It's not—"

"Don't bother, Ramsey. DPI's research techniques are well documented. Look, I made you an offer. What's your answer?"

He shook his head slowly, then pinched the bridge of his nose with two fingers and shook it again. Glancing down at the syringe in his hand, he straightened a little. "Sorry, Cuyler. I've been the butt of too many of your tricks. I don't believe you for a minute, and whether it's three nights from now or not, I'm still taking you in. Why delay the inevitable?''

She lowered her head, looked at the floor. "Well, I'm sorry, too. But I'm afraid you don't have a choice in the matter.''

He lunged toward her, but she'd known he would. She was ready. Before he could blink, she snatched the offensive little hypodermic from his hand. She snapped the needle with her thumb, dropped it on the floor and crushed it under her foot. Facing him, she lifted her palms. "Try again?''

"Damn you...'' His voice trailed off. He squeezed his eyes tight, opened them, closed them again.

She stepped closer to him.

"What...what did you...'' He swayed backward.

Cuyler gripped his shoulders, held him steady. "You'd better sit down, Ramsey.''

He did. His legs folded and he hit the floor hard, but remained upright, one palm pressed to his right temple. He lifted his head to look at her, the gleam of anger in his eyes dulling. "I knew...I couldn't...trust one of you.''

"You can, Ramsey. I promise, you can.'' She knelt beside him as his eyes closed. His body fell backward, but she caught him and eased his shoulders and head to the floor. She bent close to his ear and whispered, "You'll see.'' She stood and snuffed out the drugged incense.

He opened his eyes slowly, warily, and registered surprise that he was still able to do so. The throbbing in his head was enough proof that he was still alive. So she'd only drugged him. But for what purpose?

He struggled to sit up, only to feel her hands on his shoulders pressing him back down. "Lie still for a while. Here, this will help." She laid a hot cloth across his forehead.

He blinked her into focus, then looked beyond her. The room was dim, but he knew with a glance that they weren't in her tumbledown house. He'd been all through it. There'd been no canopy bed surrounded by sheer black curtains. No stone walls. No fireplace snapping and crackling with red-orange heat.

"Where the hell am I?"

She pursed her lips. "My hideaway. I can't tell you where, exactly. Just in case I'm wrong about your inherent sense of decency. I wouldn't want you running back to DPI with directions to my one and only haven."

He grated his teeth. He'd strangle her as soon as he got his strength back. He didn't think he could stop himself. With an angry snarl he sat up, brushing her hands away. His feet swung to the floor and he got up, swayed a little, caught himself. Then he walked unevenly toward the arched window cut into the thick stone wall. He braced himself against the cold sill and stared through the thick, tinted glass.

All he saw was snow. Gentle hills and valleys of it, without end, unrolling like a lumpy sheet beneath a starry sky.

He turned toward her again, dazed with disbelief. "Where the hell am I?" he repeated.

"North. You are definitely north."

"North of what?"

"Just about everything." She ended with a little laugh, those eyes of hers glittering with mischief.

"Dammit, Cuyler—"

"Look, all you need to know is that you're miles from another human being. There are no roads, no transportation, and no phones. Nothing. Just you and me, together for the next three nights. Just like I told you."

Letting his head fall backward, he stared up at the vaulted ceiling, the gaslights glowing in the chandelier.

"Don't look so upset. I'll take you back when I know what I need to know."

He shook his head, met her gaze. "If there's no transportation, then how the hell did we get here?"

"That doesn't really matter."

He pushed one hand through his hair, scanned the room, spotted the open door and left her standing there. She followed him. He heard her steps on the ceramic-tiled floors as he moved quickly through the corridor, glancing into rooms furnished as if for some fairy-tale princess. Satins and ruffles and lace. Trinkets he didn't take time to examine littered every surface.

He found the stairway, broad and stone with a gleaming hardwood banister, and he hurried down it. Another fireplace. More gaslights, more stone. More expensive-looking antique furniture.

The front doors were huge, and double, with stained-glass panes in starburst patterns centering each of them. And they were unlocked. He flung them wide and stepped out into the biting wind, bitter cold. There was nothing. As far as he could see, there was just nothing. A sense of doom settled on his shoulders like a thousand-pound pillar.

She touched him again. Her small hands closed around his upper arm and tugged at him. "Come back inside, Ramsey. It's going to be all right, I promise you."

He lowered his head. The wind stung his face, his ears. He let her pull him back inside, but he was shaking his head. "It isn't."

"It will." She closed the doors, turned to face him.

"There are things I need . . ."

"I know. The insulin."

His head came up fast. "How do you—"

"I brought everything from your hotel room. Your clothes, the medicine, everything. The only thing I didn't bring was that nasty drug you were planning to inject me with." She closed her eyes, shook her head slowly. "That really disappointed me, Ramsey. I didn't think you'd do it to me, but you were going to."

"Immoral bastard that I am, right? I notice you didn't hesitate to do the same to me."

Her brows rose, then she smiled a little and gave a shrug. "Guess you have me on that one. But, honestly, the incense is harmless. It just lasts a few hours and the only side effect is a bad headache."

He rubbed one throbbing temple with his forefinger. "Tell me about it."

"You want something for it? Aspirin or—"

"I don't want anything except to get the hell out of here." He was angry. He hated feeling trapped, forced into a situation he didn't like. And he sure as hell didn't like this. Being locked away in a miniature castle with the object of his most vivid, graphic fantasies. Knowing he couldn't lay a hand on her. Hell. That's what this was. Hell on earth.

"And you will. Soon. But, Ramsey, there are things I have to know."

"If you think you can pry any DPI secrets out of me—"

"Not about your precious organization. About you." She reached out to him, took his hand, drew him into the huge room, and pressed him into a chair near the fire. "Relax, Ramsey. Please, just try to accept that you're going to be here for a few days, so we can get on with this. Think of it as a minivacation."

He looked up into her innocent eyes, marveling that they could hide so much deceit. "A vacation?"

"It's warm and safe. There's plenty of food. I have wine, too. Your favorite kind. You want some?"

"So you can knock me out again?"

"I don't need to knock you out again."

She turned and walked away from him, fishing a bottle of white zinfandel from an ice bucket on a nearby pedestal table. She poured some into a glittering cut-crystal glass and brought it to him, pressing it into his hand. He'd had time to get up and run, but what was the use? There was nowhere to go.

She knelt down in front of his chair, her hands resting on his knees, and stared up at him with more intensity in her eyes than he'd ever seen. He braced himself against that look. He wasn't going to believe a word that fell from those full, moist lips. And he wasn't going to entertain a single erotic thought about her current position.

"I want to tell you something, and I want you to listen to me. I'm out of tricks and tired of games. Everything I say to you from here on will be nothing but the truth. I'd like for you to return the favor."

She paused, waiting. He said nothing.

"Ramsey, if you take me to that research lab in White Plains, I'll die. And I won't be the first."

"That's bull. DPI isn't in the habit of murdering—"

"But they are."

Ramsey shook his head hard. "They're scientists. They want to learn all about you—"

"They want to eradicate us from the planet."

"Yes." He sighed, admitting that much. "Yes, but not by killing you. By finding a cure."

Her eyes flashed with anger and for just a second he felt the force of her rage. "A cure. Where do you get this stuff, Ramsey? It's not a disease. We don't need a cure for what we are any more than you need one for being tall or for having gray eyes."

He was skeptical. "You wouldn't like to be human again, to *feel* again?"

"I'm as human as you are, dammit. And what makes you think I don't feel?"

She stared up into his eyes, her own brimming with so much emotion he almost wondered if she might somehow be an exception to the rule. But her eyes narrowed and she looked at the floor.

"The good ol' DPI handbook, right, Ramsey? We're all animals. Emotionless, cold-blooded killers."

He swallowed the lump in his throat. "Aren't you?" He wasn't asking. Not really. He knew what they were.

She bit her lower lip, blinked fast. "No. But they are. Do you have any idea how many of us have died at their hands, in the name of their so-called research?"

"And yet you promised to go there with me, willingly, after these three nights." If he sounded skeptical, then he was. He wasn't as gullible as she apparently thought he was.

"Yes. If you still want to take me there."

"Why?"

"Because I know that you won't. I'm as sure of that as I am of my own name, Ramsey. I don't know why, but I am."

He shook his head slowly. "That doesn't make any more sense than dragging me up here."

"I think it does." She closed her hand around his, held it there, and he felt the warmth of her flowing into him, through him. A tingling awareness skittered along his nape, up his spine. Something odd happened to him. He felt invaded, as if her very soul was seeping into him, or his into her, or something.

"Do you feel it?" she whispered. "There's something between us, Ramsey. You know there is."

He shook his head in denial and tugged his hand away from hers. It was no more than another of her tricks.

"It's more powerful than the connection I feel with one of the Chosen." She said it softly, eyes downcast.

"The Chosen...that's your term for humans with that rare belladonna antigen in their blood?" He sat forward a little, thinking maybe he'd get something out of this forced incarceration, some kernel of knowledge to take back with him. If he ever *got* back.

She nodded. "They're the only ones who can be transformed. We all had that antigen as mortals. But you don't have it. I'd have known right away if you did."

"How?"

She rose, chewing her full lower lip with even, white teeth. "We sense them. I can't explain it, but we always know. We have an instinctive need to watch over them, protect them—"

"Make them into what you are?"

She shook her head. "No. Never, unless they want it and we're sure they can handle it. Most couldn't deal with it, I think."

He leaned back in the chair, studying her face for a long time. She was telling him things she didn't have to tell him. And she was being honest. He'd read up on the connections between certain humans and vampires. What she said matched the research DPI had done on the subject. So, was she serious about not lying to him, or was she just trying to gain his confidence?

Stupid to even consider that she was sincere. She was just baiting her trap.

"There's usually one person in particular to whom a vampire feels the strongest connection," he said, quoting almost verbatim from the studies he'd read. "Is that right?"

She paced away from him, nodding as she went.

"So, who's your pet mortal?"

She stood right in front of the fire, her back to him. "You are."

Ramsey blinked, then forced the shock into submission and tried to keep a logical, analytical mindset. "That doesn't make any sense, Cuyler. I don't have the antigen."

"You think I don't *know* that?" She shouted it as she whirled to face him.

He stood and slowly moved toward her, searching her face for a sign she was lying. He saw only turmoil and frustration in her eyes, as real as if she were honestly experiencing those feelings. She had him completely confused, and he didn't like it.

"Then why do you think—"

"I dream about you, Ramsey. I think about you when I'm awake. I know when you're angry, when you're sick, when you're in pain."

She grasped his shoulders, and he couldn't believe that there was moisture in her eyes.

"I want you to the point of madness, but it's more than that."

She wanted him. And that should scare the hell out of him, because he knew that with her kind, sexual desire was so closely entwined with the bloodlust that the two became inseparable. If she wanted him, then she not only wanted him in bed. She probably wanted to drain him dry, too.

Another reason to keep his mounting desire under control. Hell, if he gave in to it, he'd end up dead.

"You're out to destroy me," she went on, her voice catching in her throat. "I ought to be running away from you as fast as I can go. But all I feel is this longing to be as close to you as I can get."

She released him, looked at the floor, and he saw the way her lips trembled.

"My rest is torment. I wake up frustrated and confused instead of rested and strong. It's driving me crazy, Ramsey. All I want to do is figure out why. Can you really blame me for that?"

Ramsey had trouble swallowing when a single tear spilled onto her cheek. Not a manufactured one. She quickly turned away from him, brushing the back of one hand over her face to wipe it away. For some reason he had the urge to wrap his arms around this suffering pixie and make it all right for her. He grated his teeth, stiffened himself against the softening that seemed to be happening inside him. She was the enemy. She was a master of lies. She had murder on her mind; his murder. He had to remember that. He didn't know what she could possibly have to gain by convincing him of all this bull, but there had to be something.

In a private office on the fifth floor of a building in White Plains, N.Y., three men stared at a small, lighted screen, watching the little red blip flash on and off incessantly.

"It has to be a malfunction," Stiles said.

"No. No, it makes perfect sense. It's dark there eighteen hours straight, this time of year," Whaley argued. "Perfect for one of them."

"But why would she take him there?"

The third man hadn't spoken yet. He removed a pipe from his teeth and tapped spent tobacco into a plastic ashtray on his desk. "I knew he'd turn on us. Hell, it was a given. A matter of time. I'm just glad we planted the tracking device in his suitcase."

"A matter of time?" Stiles frowned, puzzled. "You sound as if you were expecting this."

"I was," Fuller said.

"But, Mr. Fuller, I don't—"

"Until you need to know, don't bother asking."

Stiles sighed hard, but nodded his acceptance. "So, what do we do?"

Wes Fuller paced the room for a moment, his bulk making his steps fall heavily. Then he calmly began refilling his pipe. "We get some maps, some more information, some equipment, and we go up there. Get ourselves two research subjects for the price of one."

CHAPTER THREE

It wasn't the castle it at first appeared to be. It was actually no bigger than an average house, all made of stone, blocks of it two feet in depth. Deep gray here, lighter there. Sometimes nearly white. It had the huge rooms and high ceilings of a mansion. But the place wasn't what it seemed. The ground floor consisted of only three rooms. The palatial front one with the fireplace, a dining room fit for a king, and a tiny cubbyhole of a kitchen with a fridge and stove that appeared to be gas-powered, like the lights. He tried the faucets, found they worked. Hot and cold. The place had every comfort.

It was a whimsical place. Made him think of the castles and enchanted cottages in fairy tales. Everywhere he looked there were crystals. Huge blocks of quartz with jagged points like countless fingers, sparkling at him. Glittering purple amethysts. Lapis lazuli, so blue it hurt your eyes to look at it too long. Tiger's eye, flashing and winking yellow and gold at him as he passed. And a hundred others he couldn't identify. Tiny pewter statuettes peered up at him from every inch of space not occupied by a stone. There were fairies, unicorns, dragons, wizards, castles on high. My God, there were hundreds of them. And the art that adorned her walls held similar themes. No pastels, though. Grim colors, grays and browns and dull blues. Lots of charcoal sketches. Pegasus. Pan. An ugly creature that might have been a troll.

Interesting.

"Looked your fill yet?" She sat on a beanbag chair near the fire—a beanbag!—with her legs curled beneath her. She hadn't followed him, seeming content to let him explore the house on his own. More evidence there was really no way out. If there was a chance he could escape, she wouldn't have let him out of her sight.

"I haven't looked upstairs yet."

"Three bedrooms, with a bathroom between two of them. No big deal. Can we sit down and talk now?"

"The place is smaller than it looks. The size of the room is deceptive."

"Astute observation. Please, Ramsey, I have so much I want to know." She sat a little straighter, pleading with those big, round eyes that seemed to want to suck him into their depths.

"How'd you ever find this place?" He poured himself some more wine, his back to her. He had to avoid looking at her if he was going to manage to remain in control, maybe get her to let something slip, like how the hell he could get out of here.

"I had it built. Always wanted a castle all my own. Ever since I was a little girl."

That tidbit made him turn to face her. His next question was impulsive and not at all what he'd intended to ask. "How old are you, Cuyler?"

"Ninety-nine." She smiled fully when she said it. Her smile was something to see. Made her eyes crinkle at the corners and sparkle with mischief. "Pretty spry for my age, huh?"

"How long have you been—"

"Didn't do much research on me, did you, Ramsey?"

He shook his head. "Research isn't my job."

"Right. I forgot. You just hunt us down and bring us in."

"I'm not going to apologize for it."

"Who asked you to? I just wondered why you suddenly wanted to know about me." She turned to stare into the firelight. It made her eyes glow, and gleamed its reflection on her multilayered ebony hair.

"I'm curious."

"Is that all?" She didn't look at him. Just sighed softly before she went on. "I was twenty-five. My sister and I danced at a gin joint in Chicago during the height of Prohibition."

He stopped with his wine halfway to his lips and just stared at her with his mouth gaping. "You were a flapper?"

She shrugged, looking at him, grinning. "I was young and I needed the money."

He laughed. He couldn't help it, she was funny. She'd always been funny. Every time she'd pulled one of her pranks on him and slipped out of his reach, she'd done it with a stroke of humor that couldn't be ignored. More than once he'd been in the midst of anger and frustration, only to find himself smiling and shaking his head at her wit. That dummy in the coffin at her house had been just one more example of her impish streak.

He stared at her, tilted his head a little. He could see her very clearly in his imagination, wearing a fringe-covered sac dress and a headband with a feather. Then his laugh died. He wasn't sure he wanted to hear any more. Seeing her as a real person with a life and a past would only make this harder.

"Honestly, I loved to dance. We both did. And we were good at it."

"I'll bet you were." It slipped out before he thought about it. He averted his eyes, cleared his throat. "So, what happened?" He could have kicked himself. Hadn't he just decided he didn't want to know?

"There was this woman, the most beautiful woman I'd ever seen in my life. She was elegant. No, regal is a better word. But she was fun, too. She used to come in all the time, bugged us to teach her the dances. One night she came in dressed as a flapper and joined us on stage." Cuyler shook her head slowly, smiling, the movement drawing his gaze against his will. "She was something. Every man there wanted her, but she never seemed interested. And when the lushes got a little out of hand with us, she'd step in and scare the hell out of them."

Ramsey wondered what man in his right mind would be interested in any other woman when Cuyler was in the room, then frowned and reminded himself what he was doing here. "Who was she?"

Cuyler only leaned back in her beanbag, drew her knees up to her chest and wrapped her arms around them. She ignored his question. "One night there was a raid. FBI. G-men as we called 'em back then. The owners fought back, naturally. The rest of us got caught between machine guns."

She released her legs and rolled to her feet with a little bounce. She walked toward him, stopped when she stood right in front of him, then caught the hem of her blouse and lifted it.

Ramsey licked his lips and tried to deny his instant reaction to the sight of that taut skin, her flat belly, the curve of her waist, the dark well of her navel. He stiffened when she took his hand and pulled it toward her, but he didn't pull away. And then his palm was pressing to her warm flesh and he felt odd puckers that shouldn't be there. They barely showed, but he could feel them.

He frowned, moving his hand over her waist, feeling more of the puckers, and more on her rib cage. Slowly, it dawned on him just what these scars had to be, and for some reason his stomach convulsed, twisting into a knot, and a hot fury came to life in its center. He set the wine on a stand and stood, both hands on her warm skin now. Clasping her waist, he turned her slowly and ran his palms over the small of her back, as well, then higher, slipping them beneath her blouse and up to her shoulder blades.

He tried to swallow as he felt the scars left on her smooth flesh where the bullets had passed through her body. But he couldn't. His throat had closed off. He had a sudden image of her, with her short ruffly hair held in place by a feathered headband, her fringed dress filled with holes, her small pixie's body riddled by bullets.

His hands stilled on her skin. He closed his eyes, trying to block out the image.

She leaned back just slightly, pressing herself closer to his touch. "My sister was killed, and I wasn't far behind her. But that woman found me in the chaos. She took me out of there while the bullets were still flying. I don't know how, but she did. She laid me down in the alley and she asked me if I wanted to live."

"And you said yes."

She turned to face him and somehow his hands ended up on her shoulders. He ought to move them away. He really ought to.

"What would you have said?"

He shook his head slowly. It wasn't a clear decision between good and evil. It wasn't an easy question to answer. Not the way he'd always thought it would be. He couldn't get the image of it out of his mind, her small body jerking like a marionette's as bullets tore hot paths right through her. Her lying still, the life seeping away from her. Why was this so vivid to him? Why did he feel as if he'd witnessed the whole thing? His hands tightened a little on her shoulders, a natural reaction to the sensation of her life slipping away. "I don't know."

Her hands rose in slow motion, came to rest lightly on his chest. "I probably wouldn't have known, either, if she'd asked me while I was strong and alive. But I was bleeding. I was dying. I couldn't even feel the pain by then. And I said yes."

He couldn't blame her. He couldn't imagine himself in the same situation doing anything differently.

But the decision, that single moment in time, was only the beginning. And he found himself wanting to know more. "What about afterward? When you were changed, a completely different being? Did you regret your choice?"

She closed her eyes, smiled softly. "But I wasn't a different being. Ramsey, the changes were physical. I was the same person inside. A little flaky, maybe. A believer in fairy tales. A practical joker. I was the same. I still am."

His stomach clenched. For a second he wondered what right he had to drag this woman off to DPI's research center. He stared down at her wide eyes, her moist lips, and felt her lean toward him. His hands tightened on her shoulders. She rose on tiptoe and tilted her head up, fit her mouth to his . . .

The hiss of resin seeping from the firewood got louder just as he caught her lips, began sucking at them, tracing their shape with his tongue. A loud snap worked like an electric shock, jarring him out of the spell she'd woven around them. He wouldn't have fallen so easily unless she had. He deliberately called up the image of his mother's lifeless body and unseeing eyes, focused on it to remind himself of why he'd joined DPI in the first place.

He lifted his head and pushed her away. Dammit, she was playing with his mind, making him feel things he had no business feeling. Those dreams he'd had of her, these pictures she was drawing for him, it was all part of her plan.

He looked at her. She was biting her lip, shaking her head, looking everywhere except at him. "I'm sorry.

I didn't mean to—" She spun in a circle, pushing both hands through her dark hair, ruffling it until its short layers resembled the feathers of a flustered raven. "It won't happen again. That's not why I brought you here."

She was apologizing. He gave his head a shake. Why the hell was she apologizing?

"Look, Ramsey, I'm not trying to seduce you into anything. If we can come to an understanding, I want it to be because you've thought things through and listened, and you believe me. Not because your libido was too strong to resist."

He blinked twice, more confused than ever. Seduction would be her best weapon here. Did she mean to tell him she wasn't even going to try? And why did that idea feel like such a letdown? Hell, he ought to be relieved. At least he wouldn't have to worry about her passions taking over and him ending up dead.

Glancing at the grandfather clock in the corner, he felt his eyes widen. They'd been talking for a couple of hours, yet it hadn't seemed more than a few minutes.

She followed his gaze, shook her head. "You ought to eat, Ramsey. And take your insulin before you get sick."

He frowned, glancing through the windows where the pale winter darkness still reigned. "Just how far north are we, Cuyler? Shouldn't it be light by now?"

She shook her head. "Dawn around 9:00 a.m. Dusk again by three this afternoon. That's part of what I like about this place in the winter."

"Don't you get tired on so little rest?"

"Hell, Ramsey, since you've been on my tail my rest hasn't been very restful, anyway."

He knew she was referring to the dreams. Maybe she really *had* experienced them. He doubted it, but there was probably a slight chance. And there was also a slight chance, he conceded at last, that she was being straight with him about her reasons for bringing him here. For, even though he couldn't admit it to her, she'd been haunting his life the same way she claimed he'd been haunting hers. Only difference was, he hadn't known who she was. Just the pixie with the big sexy eyes that seduced him in his dreams. So maybe she did want to understand this thing, and maybe she would let him go when she had her answers. Maybe she was telling the truth.

But he doubted it.

Wes Fuller held the lighter to the tobacco in the bowl and inhaled until it caught. He puffed appreciatively, then held the pipe in his hand and blew smoke rings as he studied the maps tacked to the wall.

"Only way in will be by helicopter. And then they'll hear us coming." It was Stiles, his chief aide. Stiles, always the cautious one, always wary. "We could land a few miles away, though, and hike in. But we'll want to be sure we can get in and out by daylight. We want to be well out of there before dark."

"What's the matter, Stiles? Afraid the three of us can't handle her?" And that was Whaley, the intrepid. He wanted a battle. It gleamed from his eyes like a fever.

"Stiles is right in this case," Wes said slowly. "We have no way of knowing whether she's alone up there or not. There might be half a dozen others with her."

Stiles's eyes widened. "I hadn't thought of that. My God, do you supposed Bachman is still alive? I mean, what if they just took him up there to—"

"He's alive."

"But, sir, how can you—"

"He's alive. There's not one of them who'd hurt Bachman. If there was, he'd have been long dead by now. God knows, I've given him the riskiest assignments, sent him up against the worst of them. But he's never been hurt beyond repair, and he's never brought one in."

Stiles blinked.

Whaley frowned. "You telling me you've deliberately put Bachman in high-risk situations with them? Including this one?"

Fuller nodded. Whaley wanted to hit him. Fuller could see it in his flashing eyes. But he wouldn't. He was a subordinate and he knew his place. "You'll understand in time, Whaley. Till then, you'll just have to trust my judgment. Bachman's been one long experiment. And his usefulness to us has just about run out. Don't trust him, whatever you do. He's never really been one of us. He just didn't know it."

CHAPTER FOUR

He'd eaten, injected his insulin, and searched the house from top to bottom. For what it had been worth. The most interesting thing he'd found had been a sled in the basement and some harnesses hanging on the wall. No dogs, though. No outbuildings where any might be kept. So the sled was useless. Everything he'd found had been useless.

Interesting, but useless. He'd left her bedroom for last. He figured the longer he waited, the more deeply she'd rest. Now he stood at the foot of the fanciful bed and stared at her through the sheer red bed curtains. She lay uncovered, curled on her side, hugging her pillow. A gossamer bit of a nightgown hid very little. Her legs were not long, but so shapely he caught his eyes roaming them from her exposed slender hip to her small toes.

He blinked fast and forced himself to look somewhere else. He'd come to see if she had secrets hidden in her bedroom, hadn't he? Well, he ought to be looking for them, not gawking at her perfect little body and wondering if she would wake up if he went over there for a better look. He hadn't expected this. He didn't know what he'd expected. Maybe that she'd seem like a corpse as she rested, lying flat on her back, hands folded over her chest, not breathing, cold, white. Instead she looked just like any other woman. Relaxed. Warm. Breathing deeply and steadily. No, not like any other woman. Much better. Almost irresistibly innocent and vulnerable right now.

He swallowed hard and walked to the dresser against the stone wall. There were three black-and-white framed snapshots of Cuyler and another young woman in full flapper regalia. He didn't like looking at her that way. He knew she'd been mortal when the photo had been taken. Vampires didn't show up in photographs. But, honestly, he couldn't spot a single difference in her. Mischievous grin, sparkling black eyes, innocence and sex appeal all wrapped up in the most appealing package imaginable.

He turned from the photos to examine the books. There were at least a hundred of them lining the shelves that stood against the wall, and as he scanned the titles, he noted they were all high fantasies. Sword and sorcery stories, with knights and dragons and magic. She was really into that stuff.

He gave up on the bedroom, because no matter what he chose to investigate, he found his gaze drawn back to her again and again. He couldn't stay in that room with her. It was dangerous. God, could she weave spells even in her sleep?

He headed back downstairs into the dining room. He hadn't examined the books on the shelf there, but as he did, he noted they were the same. Fantasy stories about other worlds where good always won over evil. Ironic.

Then he spotted a few that were different. He pulled one out, frowning. He grinned as he scanned the blurb. It was about vampires, of all things! He slipped the book back into its place, wishing he had time to read a little of it, see what the latest fiction writer had dreamed up and whether it compared with the real McCoy. But he had to catch a few hours' sleep while he had the chance. From the looks of things, there wasn't much else he could do right now.

She writhed in her bed, knowing all of this was just a dream, but dying of sheer, tormented pleasure all the same. He was kissing her. His mouth was warm, wet, eager as it moved from her fingertips over her wrist, along the inside of her arm and into the hollow of her elbow. He tickled the sensitive skin there with his tongue, then moved higher, up to her shoulder, over it to her neck. She tipped her head back, closed her eyes, moaned softly. Her fingers buried themselves in his hair as he pushed the nightgown from her shoulders. Then he moved to her breasts, taking one in his hungry mouth, feeding on it like a starving man while he tormented the other with his fingers. His knee moved between her thighs, nudging them apart.

She touched his unclothed chest, raked her nails lightly over his nipples until he panted. Then her hand slipped lower, finding the smooth, rigid core of him, encircling it, squeezing, running her fingers over the tip.

He stared down at her, saying nothing, just watching. Then he closed his eyes, and she knew his need was almost painful. She opened to him, and he settled himself on top of her, nudged against her slick opening. She lifted her knees, desperate for him, for fulfillment. She needed this, needed him. No one else could fill the emptiness inside her. And she knew that he needed her just as desperately. Only she could soothe his wounded heart, erase the pain that darkened his soul, replace his anger and hatred with tenderness and love.

Her hands reached for him, to pull him to her...

But there was only air. Her eyes flew wide and she screamed in frustration, tugging at her hair. She punched the pillow, threw it, knocking half a dozen pewter figurines from the stand beside the bed, then pressed balled-up fists to her eyes and moaned like a wounded animal.

Her door banged open and he stood there, staring at her. His face was flushed, beads of sweat stood on his brow. His breathing was uneven. He looked at her, and when their eyes met she knew he'd had the same dream. Every image she remembered was reflected in his eyes. He must know it, because he averted them, as if that would stop her from seeing.

"You cried out. Are you okay?"

She drew three open-mouthed breaths, closed her eyes, and finally shook her head. Her palms rose to her face and she lowered her head. "I can't take this anymore, Ramsey. I can't. I'm gonna go stark raving—"

His weight made the mattress sink, and then his hands gripped her shoulders. "You think I don't know? It's driving me to the edge, too, Cuyler."

She sobbed, and he drew her head to his chest. She felt the warm skin, the muscle, smelled him, wanted him. She slipped her arms around his waist and clung tighter.

"Dammit, Ramsey, why'd you come in here? You're only making it worse." She turned her face to his chest, pressed her mouth to his skin and tasted it. She kneaded his shoulders with her nails as her pulse thundered in her temples.

One of his hands lowered to her waist. The other crept over her nape, up into her hair, and he tipped her head back. Then his mouth came to hers. She parted her lips, and his tongue dug into her, stroking deep and pulling back in an erotic pattern. She fell backward on the bed, and he came down on top of her, feeding on her mouth, crushing her body to his. She felt his arousal pressing hard between her legs, and she arched against it.

Then he stiffened and rolled off her. Sitting on the edge of the bed with his back to her, he pushed both hands into his hair, clenching fistfuls of it, and swore in a voice rougher than tree bark.

"Damn you, Ramsey...." She rolled onto her side to face the other way and tried to stop the flow of frustrated tears.

"I can't. I can't do this."

"Then why did you—"

"I didn't mean to. Hell, Cuyler, I was still half-asleep, probably having the same dream you just had."

He got up and paced away from the bed, the front of his jeans poking out like a tent.

"This is crazy. It's crazy."

She blinked, sitting up and fighting the tears into submission. "Maybe if we just did it, the dreams would stop..."

He turned slowly to face her and his eyes were hard, cold. "No."

The finality in his tone cut to the quick, and for a second she thought she saw the reason. "You're afraid of me, aren't you? You're afraid I'll take more than just your body."

He faced her head-on, not flinching. "Wouldn't you?"

Cuyler closed her eyes, grated her teeth. As much as she wanted him, who was to say she wouldn't lose control of her deepest desires in the heights of passion? Bracing her shoulders, she forced herself to be honest. "Maybe I would. But I'd never hurt you, Ramsey. You have to know that. I couldn't if I wanted to."

He searched her eyes for a long moment, and she felt as if her very soul were being scoured. "If you'd been capable of hurting me, I doubt I'd still be breathing. So I guess I have to believe that."

"Then why—"

"Look, I told you, I can't. It'd be unnatural for..." He stopped midsentence, maybe due to the shock and pain that must have shown on her face, or perhaps it was the involuntary cry she uttered. "That isn't what I meant. Wait—"

"Go to hell, Ramsey!" She was on her feet and through the bathroom door almost before he could blink. She slammed it so hard she loosened the hinges, then she turned the locks.

She didn't say a word to him when she came out, freshly showered, dressed in dark gray stirrup pants and a long, fuzzy, white sweater. She didn't have to say anything. He could see the hurt in her eyes. He felt like an assassin's bullet, like a cobra's venom. He felt like the lowest, meanest form of being in the universe for blurting what he had. Worst of all, he hadn't meant it. It had been his own voice of self-preservation trying to convince *him* to keep his hands off her. It had been desperation, searching for any excuse that would pull his hormones off the scent and tame his libido. Hell, he'd been holding himself back by believing she'd do him some kind of harm if he took her. But he hadn't believed it. Not really, and once his conscious mind admitted that, he'd had to come up with another reason to abstain from the erotic feast he imagined every time he looked at her.

Unnatural. He'd blurted it and she'd looked as if he'd just kicked her right in the gut. It hadn't been what he really thought. And that was kind of odd, when he considered it. Because it *used to be* what he really thought. When had his spin on things undergone such a radical change?

She plopped down onto the bed and leaned over to pull on slouchy white socks. He walked over and sat down beside her. The second his backside touched the mattress she shot to her feet as if she'd forgotten something in the bathroom.

"Cuyler, listen for a—" The whir of a battery-powered hair dryer cut him off.

Ramsey blew air through his teeth and went into the bathroom with her. She sat on the vanity's padded stool, hair flying all over the place as she whipped the dryer through it. There was no mirror. He wanted to say something. He just wasn't sure what. He didn't want to make amends, exactly. Hell, she was still his enemy. The fact that he was burning up inside for her didn't change that. But he'd hurt her. And despite his years of learning that vampires had no feelings, he regretted it.

Opening the cabinet, for want of anything better to do, he found his kit right where she'd left it. He unwrapped a fresh needle and took out a color-coded strip. With a quick, practiced flick of his wrist, he poked the forefinger of his left hand, squeezed a fat drop of blood out, and smeared it on the strip. Then he watched for the color change. He was moving like a robot, doing the things that came automatically, without really giving any thought to them.

He felt her gaze on him, heard the hair dryer flick off, and looked at her.

"Are you sick?" If her eyes got any bigger, they'd swallow him whole.

"Just checking the blood sugar." He glanced at the strip again.

"And how is it?"

"Fine." He put the used needle and strip back into the container. He'd dispose of them properly when he got back to civilization.

"Do you have to do that every day?"

He nodded as he held his finger under the cold water tap for a second or two.

"Has it ever been out of whack?"

"My sugar level? No. It's always within normal range. I have a good doctor who keeps me in great shape. Hell, I'm the healthiest diabetic I know."

Her eyes narrowed to slits as she studied him. "And who is this Marcus Welby of the nineties?"

"Just one of the best hematologists in the country."

"Don't tell me. A DPI staffer."

Ramsey shrugged, wondering about her line of questioning, but relieved she'd apparently forgotten his earlier slam. "Yup. One of the perks of being an agent."

"Kind of balances out against having to work around us animals, doesn't it?" She got up and brushed past him, going back into the bedroom, yanking a pair of huge, fluffy slippers with unicorn heads on them from under her bed.

"Look, I didn't mean that."

"Sure you didn't." She lifted one foot, put a slipper on it. "Ramsey, if you didn't mean it, then why are we both dressed and vertical?" She never even looked at him. Just hopped on the slippered foot and dressed the other one.

It came out before he could order it not to. "Because I know damned well it'll do me in. Cuyler, once wouldn't be enough. I'd be addicted, and I know, as sure as I'm standing here, that I could OD on you. You really think I could take you to bed and then take you in? If I had you once, I . . ."

He glanced up at her, saw her blinking rapidly, staring at him in something like childish wonder. "What?"

Her lips curved upward a little. "I just didn't know you wanted me that much."

And she shouldn't have known. It didn't do any good tipping his hand to the enemy. But he'd been honest, if nothing else. He was determined to take her in, and he knew he couldn't do it if he ever made love to her. He lowered his head, refusing to meet her eyes. "I didn't say I did—"

"Sure you did, Ramsey. Don't try and take it back now." She took his arm in her warm hand and tugged him along beside her back into the bathroom. "Come on downstairs after you've had your shower," she told him softly. "I'll get you some breakfast. I don't want you getting sick."

Then she left him. And he had to wonder when he'd stopped seeing her as something abnormal, something frightening, and started seeing her as a woman with a few special needs. One of which he'd really love to fulfill for her.

CHAPTER FIVE

"I'll keep this impersonal, Ramsey."

"What?" He finished the whole-wheat muffin, washed it down with a gulp of remarkably good coffee.

"As long as you find the idea of laying a finger on me so frightening—tempting, but still frightening—I'll try and make it as easy on you as I can. But we have to talk."

"We *talked* last night. I don't see that it's helped matters any." He wanted to correct her, tell her he didn't find the idea frightening at all, anything but, in fact. But it was probably better to let her hurt a little, let her hate him. And he wasn't satisfied with what he'd gotten out of her last night. He wanted to know more.

"I talked, you didn't."

He stiffened a little, watching her. "What do you want to know?"

"How you wound up working for DPI. When did they approach you, Ramsey?"

"My senior year at military school." It was a lie, but he figured the less she knew about the truth, the better off he'd be.

"And don't you find that a little odd? DPI's a secret organization. Even most of the CIA's top dogs don't know about its existence. They obviously don't make a habit of announcing their presence, or drafting high school students. So why you?"

He took another sip of the coffee. "How do you know so much about DPI?"

"Their exploits are well documented. I probably know more about them than you do."

"How? Where is all this documentation you keep mentioning? Where's the proof that they're guilty of all the crimes you accuse them of?"

She sighed and got up from her seat. Walking to the bookshelf he'd so closely examined last night, she pulled several titles from it, brought them to the table and set them in front of him.

The vampire books. He frowned up at her. "You call this proof? It's *fiction*."

"The world in general seems to believe that. Those of us who know better have good reasons to let them keep believing it."

He glanced down again at the books, shaking his head in disbelief. He picked one up.

"You ought to read them, Ramsey. See the whole hunt through the eyes of the prey for a change, instead of the predator."

He riffled the pages, scanned a few, felt his blood chill. "There's classified information in here! Hell, this is a blow-by-blow account of a DPI investigation!"

She only shrugged. "Like I said, the world thinks it's fiction."

He slammed the book down on the table and stood, facing the bookshelves. "What about the rest of them?"

She smiled slightly, lifted her eyebrows. "What, my fairy stories? Who knows?" She turned to a shelf lined with pewter figurines, picked up a winged dragon and lovingly stroked its fierce-looking head. "I like to think they could be real, that there could be some other world where fairies and magic exist. I mean, why not? Vampires are real, and most people consider us fantasy."

He should be angry. He had been for all too brief a time. Why, then, was he feeling so enchanted all of a sudden? Couldn't DPI have sent him after a monster? Why the hell did they have to pick a beautiful pixie who believed in fairy tales? He cleared his throat and tried to focus on business.

"Does DPI know about these books?"

She shrugged. "I don't know. Are you going to tell them?" She looked at him with those huge dark eyes, all innocence and beauty.

He lowered his head. "I have to, Cuyler."

She was standing in front of him before he knew she'd moved. Her small hand lifted his chin a little, and she stared up into his eyes. "Why are you so dedicated to them? What did we ever do to you to make you hate us so much?"

He only shook his head. He couldn't tell her. It was bad enough that these traitorous feelings for her assaulted him with every breath he drew. His betrayal stung, and if he spent much more time with her, it would be complete.

"Tell me about your childhood, Ramsey. What was your family like?"

He stiffened. Was she reading something in his eyes, his thoughts? "There's not much to tell. I was my mother's only child. Never knew my father."

She lowered her head, walked slowly away from him, then reached for a battery-powered boom box on a low shelf. She pushed a button and soft, hauntingly beautiful music filled the room. A woman's voice, like a gossamer strand wavering in a slight breeze, singing in what sounded like Gaelic. New Age stuff.

Cuyler closed her eyes for a second, listening. Softly, she prompted him. "Tell me about your mother."

Hot blades ran through his chest. "She died when I was twelve." He turned his back to her, walking into the front room and sitting down in a chair near the fireplace. He stared into the flames, remembering.

Her hands closed on his shoulders. "She was all you had, and you lost her. No wonder I see so much pain in your eyes."

He said nothing, and tried not to feel her soothing touch as she began a rhythmic massage.

"How did she die?"

"I don't remember." His eyes wanted to close. He hadn't slept much, and when he did, he didn't rest. He only dreamed about making frantic, hot, imaginative love to Cuyler.

"Why are you lying to me, Ramsey?"

Her fingers kneaded the sides of his neck. He let his head fall sideways to give her more access. "I'm not going to talk to you about my mother," he said, but his voice lacked conviction. He sighed as the image of her danced through his memory. "She was beautiful, all carrot-colored curls and pale blue eyes. And she'd sing... Sometimes, right before I fell asleep at night, I can still hear her singing to me. *Wild Irish Rose,* that was her favorite." For a few seconds his mother's lilting voice played in his memory. Then he felt Cuyler's lips on his head. She bent and pressed her cheek to his, and he felt the dampness on her skin.

"I'd take the pain away, if I knew how."

"I know you would." Why did he say that? And why did it sound so true? He swallowed and tried to regain his strength. "We all have pain, Cuyler. Just part of life. You must have hurt, too, when you lost your sister."

She sniffed, and her hands slid down his chest to rest near his heart. "For a while I wanted to die. Then I wanted vengeance. I thought about hunting down every man involved in that raid. But it wouldn't have eased the pain. It wouldn't have brought Cindy back."

"Might have stopped them from snuffing out another life, though."

She straightened, came around the chair and knelt in front of him. He shouldn't have been surprised at the tears on her cheeks, but he was. Her kind wasn't supposed to have human emotions, wasn't supposed to care. Wasn't that what he'd been taught? And hadn't that particular bit of DPI doctrine been losing validity with every second he'd spent near Cuyler?

"What happened to you then?"

"A military school. Some benevolent organization foot the bill. I lived there, stayed with relatives who'd rather not have had me during vacations. Then the DPI academy, for training.''

''And indoctrination.''

He shook his head slowly, staring down into her beautiful face. ''It wasn't like that.''

But it was. Since he'd been twelve years old, he'd been educated under the organization's watchful eye, beginning with the debriefing right after his mother's murder. They were the ones who'd paid for his education, who'd provided a private tutor to teach him the things he wouldn't learn in any school. He'd been filled with hatred already, and that hatred found validation in his secret lessons, the ones he'd been warned not to talk about. He supposed now, that they'd seen him as the perfect candidate. He'd had a score to settle. He'd been seeking vengeance all his life. They'd known that, and offered him the means to achieve it.

And now he was sitting here with one of those he'd spent his life hating. He was sitting here wanting her with every cell in his body, talking to her like a cherished friend, finding a kind of understanding he'd never expected shining from her teary eyes.

But it was all a lie. It had to be.

''I don't want to be here with you, Cuyler. You're too damned convincing.'' He pushed her hands away from him and got to his feet. Leaning against the hearth, he closed his eyes.

''Why do you hate me so much?''

Lifting his head, he looked down at her, still kneeling in front of the chair. ''My mother was killed by a vampire. One of you. Someone that feeds on the innocent without a hint of remorse. A killer.'' He hoped his words would rekindle the hatred in his soul, reinforce his resistance to Cuyler and her wiles.

Her eyes widened and for a moment she only stared at him in stunned silence. Finally she shook her head. "It wasn't me."

"You're all the same." He looked away from her. Dammit, he couldn't spout DPI policy while he was looking into those eyes. "So now you know. Nothing you can say is going to change it. You can pretend to be just like us all you want, Cuyler, but I *know* what you are. And I'll never stop hating you."

She rose slowly, anger beginning to simmer in her eyes. "You're lying. You don't hate me. If anything, you hate yourself for not being able to—"

He lifted a hand, cutting her off. "Don't bother. You're only trying to convince yourself."

"But it's so stupid! Ramsey, one of *your* kind murdered my sister and pumped enough bullets through my body to kill an elephant. But I don't hate *you* for it. I don't lump all mortals in with the few truly evil ones. I don't go out hunting them down like animals to exact vengeance."

"Don't you?"

She flinched as if he'd slapped her. "How can you ask me that?"

God, the hurt in her eyes... He looked at the floor, at the beanbag, at the fire. Anything but at that pain he'd caused. "Look, you got what you wanted. We've talked. Do you think we can get the hell out of here now?"

She stood so still, stunned maybe. "I don't have what I wanted. I still don't know why there's this connection between us. I still don't know what misguided force makes me give a damn about a man like you."

"Let's chalk it up to physical attraction and call it even."

"It's more than that and you know it!"

He faced her, forced his expression to remain hard as stone. "Maybe for you it is, but not for me, Cuyler." He strode to the stairway, started up it. "I'm packing my things. You line up whatever means of transportation got us here, and have it ready."

"I won't."

He never broke his stride. "Then I'll go on foot."

"I won't let you!" She came up the stairs behind him.

"You have to sleep sometime, Cuyler. One way or another, I'm out of here." He went into the bedroom, slammed the door and turned the lock. He couldn't look at her, listen to her, for one more second or he'd break. It was all a game, some mind game she was playing to win his trust, and it had been working all too well. Until he'd brought the memory of his mother's death back to burning life, anyway. Damn Cuyler for making him talk about his mother, for stirring up that old pain, and especially for acting as if she cared. Damn her.

CHAPTER SIX

Like a potent corrosive, his rejection burned through her. But he didn't hate her. She knew better. It was in his eyes, in his voice. She was so attuned to his feelings that it was impossible to be fooled by his stubborn resistance. He liked her, in spite of his determination not to. He wanted her, though it went against everything he'd ever believed in. But she also knew that the conflicting emotions were slowly tearing his soul apart. She sensed his every emotion, even the ones he denied; frustration, confusion, anger, desire. Bringing him here, forcing him to see her as she was, instead of as DPI had painted her, was the same as torturing him. It was cruel to put him through this, especially now that she knew where his hatred originated. To see Cuyler as a woman and not a monster was, in Ramsey's mind, to betray his mother. To side with her murderer.

Maybe she ought to just take him back, let him go.

She twisted the doorknob, freeing the lock with her mind the way Rhiannon had taught her. Ramsey was asleep. He reclined on the bed, his back against the headboard, his head cocked to one side until his ear touched his shoulder. He looked as if he'd sat down there with no intention of going to sleep.

Cuyler walked softly to him. Even in sleep, he seemed strained. A slight frown puckered his brows. His lips were tight. His pain showed in his face, a pain he'd felt for a very long time. For a moment, as she looked at him there, she saw the image of the boy he'd been. A boy whose innocence and mischief had been stolen from him along with his mother. A boy forced to become a man before his time, a man who'd forgotten how to love.

She stared at him, sending silent, soothing messages from her mind to his. She focused her energy on relaxing him into a deeper sleep and chasing his worries from his mind the way an autumn wind chases fallen leaves. Then she leaned closer, clasping his sturdy shoulders and easing him lower until his head rested on the soft pillows and his back wasn't bent so severely. She tugged a blanket from the foot of the bed to cover him. Then she bent and brushed her lips across his, a whisper of a kiss.

When she straightened away from him, his hand reached toward her. He whispered her name.

She ran a hand over his cheek, into his hair. "I'm here. Rest now. Just rest."

His body relaxed again, and he sank back into his deep slumber. Cuyler sighed softly, shaking her head in remorse. She couldn't let him go. Not now. DPI had targeted Ramsey for their vile organization from the second his mother had been killed, she was sure of it. They must have known of his anger, his fury and feelings of helplessness. The guilt even a boy of that age would suffer; that he hadn't been there, hadn't been able to help her. Those ruthless men had stoked the

fire of Ramsey's anger, built it into the blazing inferno that was rapidly devouring his soul. They were
using a young boy's pain as a weapon against Cuyler
and her kind. And she couldn't shake the feeling that
they intended to use it against Ramsey, as well. DPI
would see both of them destroyed unless she could
find a way to fight them.

She understood so much more now. But still not
enough. There was no explanation for the connection
between her and Ramsey. She sensed the solution to all
of this hinged on her discovering the cause of that
emotional, mental link. And until she did that, despite the pain it caused him, she had to keep Ramsey
here, with her.

Ramsey trudged through the snow, half-blinded by
the brilliant sun flashing from its pristine surface into
his eyes. He had to find a way out of this mess. He was
desperate, and this was his last-ditch effort. There had
to be some means of transportation, somewhere. A
plane, a snowmobile, something. Clever as she was,
Cuyler had probably hidden it a distance from the
house to keep him from escaping. He didn't know why
he hadn't thought of the possibility sooner.

He hadn't meant to fall asleep. He supposed the
stress and sleepless nights were beginning to wear on
him. It was only when he woke to see bright winter
sunlight slanting through the window that he'd realized just how tired he'd been. Oddly, he felt rested,
refreshed even. No dreams, for a change.

But that wasn't right, was it? There had been
dreams, just not the usual wildly erotic ones that left

him exhausted. He'd dreamed of Cuyler. She'd been leaning over the bed, touching his face, stroking his hair and whispering softly to him. Her touch had been soothing, her voice like a salve on his oldest wounds. He hadn't wanted her to leave.

He stopped walking and closed his eyes as a shaft of pain bisected his chest. There'd been a blanket over him when he woke. He didn't remember putting it there. Had Cuyler really come to stand over him, touched him that way, whispered so lovingly, so gently, as he'd slept?

She'd kissed him. Her soft, moist mouth had touched his for the barest instant, and he'd wanted to pull her into his arms, into his bed. He'd wanted to feel her smiling lips caress every inch of him, and then he'd wanted to do the same to her. The hell with the danger that she might go too far. The hell with the fact that they were sworn enemies. He wanted her with a passion above and beyond all of that. Above and beyond everything.

He opened his eyes and drew a deep breath, steadying himself. He had to get away from her. She was bewitching him, using her mental powers to make him forget his life's work, driving him so mad with desire he'd gladly exchange his every principle for a night in her arms. He was in danger with her, and he had to get out or lose his mind.

But now that he had, he almost wished he hadn't. He'd trudged a couple of miles, he figured, and the scenery hadn't changed in the least. Nothing but white. No trees. No vegetation of any kind. Hardly any hills. He was pretty sure what he was looking at could be described as tundra. He hoped to God he found some form of aid soon. He wasn't exactly dressed for long periods of exposure. Only thin rubbers separated his shoes from the hard-packed snow. His ski jacket was hardly sufficient, and he didn't even have a hat with him. The wind whipped hard out here with nothing to break its progress.

He walked a little farther, then frowned and tilted his head. What was that sound? A motor of some sort growled in the distance. He turned slowly, trying to gauge the source, then realization dawned. A snowmobile. No, more than one. And the sound came from the direction of the house, though he couldn't see it anymore. His first thought was that Cuyler was coming after him, using a machine she'd had hidden somewhere.

But that thought was quickly banished. It was still daylight. She wouldn't even be awake yet.

He blinked slowly as that thought sunk in. She wouldn't be awake. She'd be lying in her bed, behind unlocked doors, thinking she was completely safe up here in the middle of nowhere.

The motors died abruptly. They didn't fade away, but simply cut out. The snowmobiles had stopped, and as near as he could guess, they'd stopped near the house. Someone was there, and with a churning in his gut, Ramsey thought he could guess who.

It made no sense to think DPI had somehow tracked them here. But it made less sense to think some harmless folks had just decided to take a snowmobile ride north of the Arctic circle and happened upon her house. Cuyler was there, alone and completely helpless. Her stories of torture and murder were utter fabrications. He knew that. But they were echoing through his soul all the same as Ramsey started walking back the way he'd come. Then he started running.

He followed his own tracks for several yards, hands shoved deep in his jacket pockets, shoulders hunched against the biting wind. But the tracks got harder and harder to see as he went. He frowned hard, and whispered a little prayer they wouldn't disappear entirely before the house came into view. Damn, he'd been an idiot not to take windblown snow into account. It had been filling his tracks behind him all the way out here.

And then he couldn't see them at all. Not even the tiny depressions he'd been following this far. Dammit to hell, he couldn't see the house. Everything looked the same in every direction. The wind was blowing harder, its bite sharper with every gust. It would be dark soon, and colder than ever. He tried not to think about what might be happening in the house right now, but images danced through his thoughts anyway. Cuyler's warnings about DPI's tactics rang in his ears, no matter how he tried to tune them out. He hadn't believed her. He'd told himself she was just trying to convince him not to take her in. But he now found himself wondering if there was even the slightest chance of truth in her horror stories. He didn't want to believe that, wouldn't let himself believe it. But the idea that anyone might deliberately hurt her...

Why the hell did it drive him to the brink of madness to consider it? Why?

The motor sounds came to life again. He was closer. He tried to run faster, but the frigid air burned his lungs and throat. They were moving, fast, in the opposite direction.

"Ah, God, no..." He tried for more speed, but he was out of breath. His muscles screamed in protest. His legs gave out just as the house came into view, and he dropped to his knees in the snow, scanning the horizon where the sun hovered, about to set.

And then he spotted them. Three snowmobiles zipping over the tundra in the distance. One pulled something behind it. Something long and narrow that looked like a box. He groaned in anguish as they moved out of sight.

He wasn't sure how long he knelt there. Emotions raced through him, so potent and confusing that he felt dizzy. Hadn't he been determined to take Cuyler in himself? Hadn't he vowed that he'd never stop hating her and everyone like her for what they'd done to his mother?

Why, for God's sake, was he racked with guilt that he hadn't been there to protect her? The frustration was as bad as what had consumed him as a result of not having been there to protect his mother. Why? Why was he kneeling in the snow, burning inside with the urge to go after them, to somehow get her away from them? He cursed softly at the thought of riding in like some knight on a charger to rescue his damsel from villains. It wasn't like that. *She* was the villain of this piece.

Wasn't she?

He got to his feet and made his way back to the house, not even bothering to stomp the snow from his shoes as he ran through it and up to her bedroom, already knowing he wouldn't find her there.

The empty bed was rumpled, the drawers and closet gaping wide, clothes strewn everywhere. When he went back downstairs, he found more of the same. The place had been searched, hurriedly and recklessly, before they'd taken her away. Her pewter figurines lay strewn everywhere. Her crystals had tumbled helter-skelter to the floor. The bookshelves had been emptied, her precious fairy-tale stories trampled beneath uncaring feet.

He bent to pick up the first of the vampire books she'd shown him, and bit his lip against the burning in his throat and eyes.

He couldn't hope to hike out of here tonight. He'd die of exposure before he reached help, and then Cuyler would be on her own. He had to wait, though it would damn near kill him to do it. At first light, he'd go, with as many provisions as he could carry. He'd get out of here, somehow. And he'd find her.

After that, he didn't have a clue what he'd do.

For now, though, he had to sit tight and await the cold dawn. He sank into a chair, weak from turmoil, and opened the book in his hands.

It took him two hours to read the entire book. And Cuyler had been right. The entirety of one of DPI's most disastrous investigations had been documented there, from the viewpoint of its subjects. It was quite a different take on things from the one in the official records. Oh, the facts were the same, but DPI's methods and motivations and the characteristics of the subjects of that investigation, couldn't have differed more. Ramsey had to believe it was all propaganda. Because if it were true...

He groaned in undisguised agony. If it were true, then Cuyler had been right about the torture involved in DPI's research. Even several deaths, all detailed here in these pages.

But it wasn't true. It couldn't be.

He knew, though, that it very well could be. He'd never been involved in the research end of things, never actually witnessed the so-called harmless studies performed on the subjects. He wasn't a scientist. And while he'd been told that the prisoners brought in would be kept for a week or two and then released, unharmed, he'd never actually seen that happen, either.

DPI believed Cuyler and her kind to be no better than animals. Beings without emotions, incapable of caring. Heartless, soulless beasts who preyed on the innocent with no sense of remorse. That much he knew. And it wasn't so farfetched to think that an organization who believed that about a group might want to annihilate that group. Was it? So why hadn't he known about it? And would it have made a difference to him if he had?

Up until a few days ago he'd believed everything DPI said about the undead. And he'd had a personal vendetta, to boot. But not against Cuyler. Everything he'd ever believed had been a lie, at least where she was concerned.

He got up, intending to go to the little kitchen and begin packing supplies for his trek out. He was no longer so certain he could wait for dawn to break. There was a new urgency eating at his soul. He had to get to her, just to prove to himself that she was all right and not being subjected to the torments described in the book. With every second that passed, those scenes embedded themselves more deeply in his mind, only the victim wore Cuyler's beautiful face.

He stopped halfway to the kitchen, stiffening at the scraping sounds coming from the front door.

"Cuyler?" Hope surged in his chest as he sprinted and yanked the door open.

A big, furry dog stood there, staring at him. It barked twice when he only stared back in confusion. Where the hell had it come from? More barking followed, and he looked up in amazement to see three other dogs, identical to the first, sitting patiently in the snow. Huskies, all of them. Silvery fur and ice blue eyes. Magnificent, wide chests.

Sled dogs?

The one at the door barked again. Ramsey frowned, thinking of the sled and harnesses he'd seen in the basement. Was this how Cuyler had brought him here? Were these dogs hers? But what were they doing here now? Where had they been?

It didn't matter. He saw the means to get out of there, and he knew he had to take it. Leaving the door wide, he ran into the basement and hauled the awkward sled up the stairs. He dragged it outside, and went back for the harnesses, praying he could figure out how to put them on properly, hoping the dogs would allow it. Hell, he didn't know what good it would do. He had no idea which way to go, even with transportation.

When he brought the harnesses outside, the dogs surrounded him, barking excitedly, tails wagging. They seemed impatient as he stretched the straps out, trying to see which way they went. But they stood motionless when he draped the things around them, and he knew they were used to this procedure.

Once he got them hooked to the sled, he ran back inside long enough to get his coat. That was all. His thoughts of bringing provisions had fled. All that remained was his urgent need to get to Cuyler, to make sure she was all right.

He stood on the back of the sled and picked up the reins. The dogs were off like a shot the minute his feet touched the narrow platform, nearly jarring him off into the snow. He didn't try to guide them. They seemed to know exactly where they were going. All

Ramsey could do was hang on and pray that they really did know.

He wasn't sure his prayers were answered until several hours later when the dogs stopped and stood barking like a raucous group of soldiers celebrating victory. A huge, barnlike structure stood in the middle of the perfectly flat, snowy plain. As Ramsey tried to adjust to the oddness of finding it here, a gruff voice called out to him.

"I expect you'll be wanting to fly out of here, after that other plane."

Ramsey turned and gave his head a shake. A grizzled old man, his face completely obliterated by a massive gray beard, came from the barn and bent to expertly release the dogs from their harnesses.

"Who are you?"

"Just call me Kirkland. Did they take Miss Jade?"

"How do you—"

"Miss Jade, she told me there might come some men someday to try and take her. Warned me not to tell a soul about her house out there. And I never did." His tone suggested he thought Ramsey might have.

He couldn't believe this old man knew the truth about Cuyler, couldn't imagine her entrusting him with it. "Did she tell you why they would want to?"

"Nope. And I never asked. Ain't my business." He slung the harnesses over his shoulder, absently stroking the heads of the dogs who milled and danced around his legs. "Knew there was trouble, though, soon as I spotted that other plane. Miss Jade's a good woman. Kind of heart. Nursed one o' my dogs after he'd tangled with a wolf. Took care of him as if he'd been her own. Even sat up all night with him, didn't she, Duke?" He ruffled the fur of the dog in question before turning his attention back to Ramsey. "So are you gonna help her?"

Ramsey could only nod mutely.

"Good, then." He walked into the barn and Ramsey followed, watching him hang the harnesses on the wall. A small plane sat like a giant bird at rest, taking up most of the space. The old man tugged a large, sliding door and Ramsey helped him open it.

"I don't get this. What are you doing up here?" Ramsey followed him, getting into the plane behind him. He ducked his head and settled into the seat beside Kirkland in the cockpit.

"Livin', mostly. I fly folks in and out for hunting and such. Transport supplies for the Inuit village a few miles off." He slanted a sideways glance at Ramsey. "Best buckle up. Takeoffs are rough."

"Do you know where they went?"

The old man nodded, but didn't say a word as the engines came to life and the craft rolled slowly out of the barn.

"Where is he?" The man blew his offensive tobacco smoke into her face, and Cuyler turned her head as much as she could. It wasn't much.

She was handcuffed to a chair in what she took to be a bedroom, with three cruel faces watching her every move. Ordinarily she'd have simply snapped free of the cuffs, knocked the men on their arrogant backsides, and made her escape. Unfortunately she'd had the extreme displeasure of proving their newly developed tranquilizer did, indeed, work. She'd been injected just as she'd begun to rouse with the sunset. And now she was as weak as a mortal. A tired mortal. Her mind was murky at best.

Not so murky that she couldn't wonder about Ramsey, though. At first she'd thought he might have been involved in her capture. The relief that filled her when they'd begun asking her for his whereabouts had made her weaker than she already was.

"Miss Jade, don't make us resort to drastic measures." The fat, white-haired man had cruel eyes, like two small blue buttons on his face. Emotionless, snake's eyes. "We all know how sensitive your kind is to physical pain. Don't make us hurt you."

When she averted her face, he caught her chin and forced her to look at him. Another gentle puff of smoke in her face. She coughed.

"Tell me where Bachman is."

"I told you already, I don't know what you're talking about. I was alone in the house."

The man—the others called him Fuller—smiled grimly and shook his head. "His suitcase was there. We know he was with you."

"I stole it," she lied. "He'd been hounding me for months. I thought I might find out why if I took his things and went through them." She tried to keep her chin up, defiantly. She forced her sagging spine stiffer. She had to be strong, but she couldn't help but wonder where Ramsey had gone. Maybe the dogs had come early. Maybe he'd found them and run away from her while she'd slept. God, she hoped that was the case. She'd arranged with old Kirkland to turn the dogs loose on the third day, knowing they'd make a beeline for her home. If Ramsey found them, if he knew how to use them, he'd be okay. They knew the way to Kirkland's hangar as well as they knew each other.

Fuller turned to the thin, dark one. "What do you think of that, Whaley?"

"I think she's lying."

"I'm not." She blinked and tried to think of a way to convince them, but only came up blank. "Why are you after him, anyway? I thought he was one of you."

"So did he—" Whaley began, but his reply was cut off by a swift look from Fuller.

The third man sat in a chair, silent. He didn't appear to have the same stomach for abuse his two colleagues shared.

"You're going to have to tell us, Miss Jade. We can't go back to headquarters without him."

She sagged inwardly. They were taking her there. And if they did, she'd die. She could have called mentally, begged others of her kind to come to her aid. But with this tranquilizer in DPI's arsenal, any who tried to help her might end up sharing her fate. She didn't want to die with that on her conscience. God, if only she knew Ramsey was all right.

Fuller's hand disappeared into his pocket. It came out with a big, shiny pair of pliers. He opened and closed their ridged teeth slowly, right in front of her face. Then he handed them to Whaley, who moved around behind her.

"Begin with the little finger of her left hand," Fuller said matter-of-factly. "Crush it."

She felt the cold instrument touch her finger. "Wait! All right. All right, I'll tell you the truth."

The tool moved away from her hand. Fuller looked down at her, smiling grimly. "That's more like it. Where is he?"

Kirkland brought the plane in expertly at a small airport.

"This is it? This is where they landed?"

"Nope."

Ramsey drew a sharp breath and waited. Kirkland had already explained that he'd been able to track the other plane with the sonar equipment back at his hangar. But the guy was a man of few words.

"Landed at Loring, not too far off. Couldn't very well take you to an air force base now, could I?"

Grating his teeth, Ramsey prayed for patience, and time. He kept telling himself that Cuyler was fine. They wouldn't hurt her. But more and more, his own voice of reason sounded like a liar.

Kirkland opened the hatch and Ramsey jumped to the ground. He took a look around, but apart from the runways and hangars and small planes, there was nothing to give him a clue. "Where the hell are we, Kirkland?"

"Northern part of Maine."

Northern Maine? Why the hell would they bring her here? Why not go straight on to White Plains? He scanned the place, sifting his mind for answers.

"Nearest city's Limestone," Kirkland continued. "Caribou's a little farther. You got any idea where they took her?"

"Limestone?" He almost sagged in relief. DPI had safehouses scattered all over the country, kept them at their agents' disposal. If an operative got into trouble, he could take refuge at one of them. They had security systems like Fort Knox, and direct phone and computer links to headquarters. Like the obedient, devoted agent he'd always been, Ramsey had memorized the addresses of every safehouse in the northeast. There was one just past Limestone.

He didn't know why they'd have taken her there. Capturing her had been their goal, and now that they'd done that, what could they have to gain by delaying their return?

Unless she wasn't their only goal? Maybe there was something else, something here, that they were after.

Ramsey faced the grizzled man beside him. "I need a car."

CHAPTER EIGHT

It was ridiculous to be going about it this way. He worked for DPI. He was one of them. He could punch in the code, walk right through the gates, up to the front door, and demand to see the prisoner.

But something held him back, made him cautious. Crazy, vague suspicions clouded his mind. He'd put them to rest when he saw that she was okay, but until then, he figured he'd be better off erring on the side of caution.

He'd had to argue with Kirkland to get him to stay behind. Hell, the guy had no idea what he'd be getting into if he came along. DPI was big. Powerful. It was dangerous to get on the wrong side of them. It was bad enough Kirkland was going to make the call.

Vaguely, she heard the phone and the low muttering from beyond the closed bedroom door. Two of the men remained with her. One, the one called Fuller, had gone out to answer it. Seconds later, he returned.

"We've got him."

Whaley rose from where he'd been comfy on the bed. "Bachman?"

Fuller nodded. "That was the hospital in Caribou. Seems Bachman was brought in, unconscious. They found this number on him."

Cuyler bit her lip to keep from gasping. God, what had happened to Ramsey?

"What the hell was he doing in Caribou?" Whaley asked.

"Probably trying to make his way here, to the safe-house. I still think you guys are wrong about him." That was Stiles, the most gentle of the three. "How bad is he?"

"Doesn't look like he'll make it through the night. We'd better get over there."

Pain tore through her heart. Dying? Ramsey was dying? She squeezed her eyes tighter to stop the tears that burned in them.

"What about her?"

Fuller glanced at Stiles, who stood unspeaking in the corner. "Can you handle her?"

The pale man nodded.

"She gets too lively, just give her another shot. We'll call in from the hospital."

She didn't lift her head as the two walked out. Just let it hang. She'd be damned if she'd give them any reason to inject her with more of that awful, debilitating drug.

Ramsey crouched behind a shrub near the gate and waited. Two men came out of the house. Their car started up, headlights came on, and he cringed lower. An electronic hum, a metallic groan, and the gates swung open. The car rolled through, and they began to close again.

He watched the car accelerate as soon as it hit the road. The gates were still closing. Taillights disappeared around a bend, and Ramsey lunged to his feet and dove. The metal scraped his sides as he threw himself in, then banged solidly as his body hit the ground. Closing his eyes, he drew three steadying breaths. Night birds slowly resumed their nightly serenade. A few seconds later, frogs joined in. The wind rustled the trees again. Other than that, Ramsey heard nothing. He got to his feet, brushed himself off, and started toward the house.

The numbered panel beside the door stared at him, the System Armed light glaring like an evil eye. If they'd changed the entry code and he punched in the wrong numbers, an alarm would tell anyone inside of his presence. And he was certain there *was* still someone inside. They wouldn't leave Cuyler unguarded.

His tongue darted out to moisten dry lips, and he tasted the sweat on his upper lip. There was no other way. If he opened a window or door without entering the code, the alarm would sound anyway. His hand rose slowly, hovering at the panel. He wiggled his fingers, grated his teeth, and entered the four-digit code he'd committed to memory.

The red light blinked out. A green one came on instead.

Ramsey pressed his ear to the door, listening. Only silence came from within. He gripped the knob and his hand slipped on its surface when he tried to turn it. Rubbing his palm against his pant leg, he tried again.

The door opened without a creak, and Ramsey ducked inside, closing it quickly and quietly behind him. He didn't hesitate, but went directly to the staircase and up it, straining every cell in his body to be quiet.

At the top, he froze as heavy footsteps sounded. Pressing his back to the wall, he waited and watched. A door opened down the hall. In the muted light he recognized the man who emerged. Ron Stiles. Ramsey had worked with him before. He'd personally thought the guy lacked the grit to be with DPI. Tonight, though, he was secretly relieved the mild-mannered agent was the one guarding Cuyler.

Stiles crossed the hall and ducked into a bathroom, never once glancing Ramsey's way. When the door closed, Ramsey hurried to the room Stiles had exited and slipped inside.

Cuyler sat in a hard chair, her arms pulled severely behind her. Her head leaned forward unnaturally. She wasn't moving, and Ramsey felt his pulse skid to a stop. Dropping to his knees in front of her, he caught her chin and lifted it.

Her eyes were tear-swollen and closed. A vivid purple bruise marred her cheek, and her lower lip was crusted with dried blood. He just stared at her, unable to form words.

Weakly, she tugged her chin away from his hand. "Leave me alone," she murmured. "Please, just leave me alone."

"Cuyler . . ."

Her eyes opened, but they were unfocused. She stared at him from somewhere behind that drugged haze. "Ramsey?"

The toilet across the hall flushed and a second later steps came toward him. Ramsey fell back a few steps, so he'd be behind the door when it opened. Stiles came inside.

"If you twitch, I'll have to shoot you, Ron." Big words, he thought, for a man with no gun.

Stiles's narrow back stiffened, but he didn't move. His hands rose slowly on either side of his head. "Bachman? I thought you were—"

"Never mind what you thought." Ramsey came closer, reached around Stiles and took his side arm. "Now get me the key to the handcuffs. Quick." He prodded the man's back with his own gun, glad Stiles had fallen for the bluff.

Stiles nodded hard, dipped into his pants pocket and brought out the key. He held it up, and Ramsey prodded him again. "Get those cuffs off her."

"Damn."

"Do it!"

Stiles moved slowly around to the back of Cuyler's chair, bent down and unlocked the cuffs. He stood again, dangling them from one crooked finger. "I didn't believe Fuller when he said you'd turn on us." He shook his head. "Guess he was right."

Ramsey moved forward, keeping the gun leveled on his former colleague. "Why did he think that?"

Stiles just shook his head. "I'm not saying any more. Kill me if you have to."

"Okay, if I have to." Ramsey nodded toward the man. "Snap one of those cuffs to your wrist, Stiles." He waited while the other man complied. "Good. Now turn around, hands behind your back. Come on, you know the drill." Stiles turned. "On your knees." When he complied, Ramsey moved quickly to slip one cuff through the foot of the bed, around the frame, and then snapped it around Stiles's other hand.

"You won't get far, Bachman. Fuller and Whaley will be back here just as soon as—"

"Fuller?" Ramsey gave his head a shake, stuffing the automatic into his waistband. Fuller was his immediate superior, a man he'd trusted. And Whaley was the cruelest s.o.b. ever to walk the planet.

Ramsey went around in front of Cuyler again, kneeling. She sat limply, rubbing her wrists. Ramsey's anger grew when he saw the way the cuffs had cut into her flesh. He grew still more angry when she lifted her head to look into his eyes and he saw the pain in hers.

"Which one of you did this to her, Stiles?"

Stiles only glared at him and shook his head.

"And why, for God's sake? It's pretty obvious the tranquilizer works. Why'd they have to hit her?"

Stiles swore viciously. "She wouldn't tell us where you were. You'd think she was human the way you're carrying on. Hell, Bachman, she's only one of them. An animal, like the rest." At Ramsey's glare, he lowered his head. "I forgot, though. You are, too, aren't you? Just like them."

"What the hell do you mean by that?" Ramsey rose, towering over the man on the floor, his fists opening and closing at his sides.

Stiles clamped his jaw and refused to say another word. Ramsey turned back to Cuyler, bent over her, gripping her shoulders. "Can you stand?"

She nodded, and tried to rise to her feet, only to have her knees buckle as she collapsed against him.

Ramsey caught her, slipped one hand beneath her legs and lifted her. He carried her across the hall and into the bathroom. Propping her against the sink, he ran cold water onto a washcloth. Carefully, he bathed her bruised face, her swollen eyes. He dabbed the blood from her lip.

"Here, hold this to that bruise and I'll look for something to put on your wrists."

She took it, but shook her head. "We have to get out of here, Ramsey. Those other two..." Her words trailed off and she swayed a little.

Ramsey found a tube of ointment and some bandages in the cabinet and stuffed them into his pocket. Then he bent to scoop her up again. He carried her down the stairs, toward the front door.

Cuyler's eyes had fallen closed again. The damned drug. And God only knew what else they'd done to her. His fury was beyond anything he'd felt in his life. The closest he'd come was the rage he'd felt when his own mother had been murdered. But that had been a child's rage. It didn't compare to the full-blown tempest whirling inside him now. He wanted to kill the DPI bastards for hurting her this way.

He carried her out into the chilly autumn night, marveling at the way her small body fit in his arms. He cradled her to his chest as if she were something precious. Hell, she was! Why was that so hard for him to admit? Cuyler was special, no matter what else she might be, and she didn't deserve what they'd done to her.

His shoes ground over gravel as he ran to the gate, opening it. He didn't care that it set off alarms inside . . . it didn't matter now.

Ramsey reached the twisting, narrow road and started up the opposite direction from the one Whaley and Fuller had gone. The car sat off the roadside where he'd left it, surrounded by scraggly brush and branches. He managed to open the passenger door with one hand and lower Cuyler to the seat. He forced his hands to remain steady as he snapped the safety belt around her, but it wasn't easy. She looked bad, and he had no idea what to do for her. She might be dying for all he knew.

Gently he pushed her hair out of her eyes. Why had he left her the way he had? Why the hell hadn't he been there when those bastards had shown up? Why hadn't he believed what she'd told him about DPI?

Her eyes opened, mere slits fringed by damp black lashes. "Hurry."

Nodding, he slammed her door and raced around to the driver's side. Seconds later the car reversed out of its hiding place and onto the road. Grinding gears in his haste, Ramsey shifted, and spun tires as they sped away from the safehouse, away from DPI, away from everything Ramsey had known in his life.

Ron Stiles twisted and squirmed until he managed to work the extra key out of his back pocket. It took some maneuvering to fit it into the lock without being able to see what he was doing, but he did it. The cuffs sprang free and he automatically brought his hands around in front of him and rubbed his wrists.

Then he stopped and looked down at them. Cuyler Jade's wrists had been rubbed raw, bleeding. There'd been no reason for Fuller to put the handcuffs on so tightly. But he had, and it had pricked Stiles's conscience to see it. Still, he hadn't said anything.

And there'd really been no reason for Whaley to hit her. Not once, but twice. And they hadn't been slaps. The bruises on her face had come from Whaley's knuckles when she'd told them more lies about Ramsey's whereabouts. Once again, Stiles hadn't voiced his objections. If Ramsey cared about her at all, Stiles supposed it was little wonder he'd been furious to see her that way.

But that was the question, wasn't it? Why on earth did Ramsey care about her? How had he gotten so mixed up with her that he'd toss his career—his life—in the toilet by coming to her rescue that way? God, he knew she wasn't human. He *knew*. So what was going on in his head?

Stiles hadn't wanted to believe what he'd read in Ramsey's files. He'd balked against what Fuller had said. That Ramsey had turned on them. That he was the enemy now. But now that he'd seen the proof of it with his own eyes, he couldn't doubt anymore. He just wished he understood.

Stiles left the bedroom, jogged down the stairs, and picked up the phone.

CHAPTER NINE

She couldn't believe he'd done it. As Ramsey drove the car through the night, Cuyler forced her heavy eyes open and looked at him. His knuckles were white on the steering wheel. His jaw tensed as if he were grating his teeth. Perspiration made his forehead shiny in the glow of the dash lights, and dark stubble coated his face. Gray eyes, intense with concentration and maybe a little fear, darted her way every few seconds. And when he saw her gaze on him, one side of his mouth pulled upward slightly and briefly. An almost smile, meant to reassure her. No more.

"You really came for me."

"Don't tell me you're surprised." He shook his head, sighing. "You've been saying all along I wouldn't take you in."

She bit her lower lip, unable to take her eyes from his face, from the strength she saw in it. And the turmoil. "You risked everything..."

He turned onto a larger road and increased his speed. Then, licking his lips, he glanced her way again. One hand left the steering wheel and he brushed it lightly over her bruised cheek. His lips thinned. "I'm sorry, Cuyler."

"Sorry? You just saved my life—"

"If I'd listened to you in the first place, I wouldn't have had to. If I hadn't left you there, alone..." He blinked slowly, lowering his hand and focusing his vision on the road once again. "I tried to get back when I heard the snowmobiles, but—"

"It doesn't matter." She slid her hand over his on the wheel. "You came after me. You got me out of there."

He shook his head. "It's not over yet, Cuyler. They aren't going to let us go without a fight. And they're after both of us now."

"They were always after both of us."

He frowned, slanting her a sidelong glance.

"Ramsey, they kept asking me where you were. The fat one, Fuller, he told the others that you were never really one of them, that it was only a matter of time before you turned on them."

Ramsey blew all the air out of his lungs. "That doesn't make a damn bit of sense. Why would he say something like that? I've never given them any reason to question my loyalty."

"I don't know."

Ramsey swore under his breath and hit the brakes, snapping the headlights off as he pulled the car onto the shoulder. Cuyler followed his gaze and saw the flashing lights ahead, on the ramp to the highway. A roadblock.

"Do you think they're looking for *us?* Already?"

"DPI works fast." He pulled the car around in a U-turn and slowly drove back the other way, flicking the headlights back on when they were out of sight. "We'll have to take back roads out of here."

"To where? Ramsey, where can we go?"

He closed his eyes slowly. "I don't know." He turned onto a side road, and then another. "There's a map in the glove compartment."

She took out the map, unfolded it on her lap, and tried to keep her still-clouded mind focused on finding out where they were, and on discovering a safe route. "Okay, at the end of this road, turn left. That one runs parallel to the highway."

He followed her directions, but even before they reached the road she'd pointed out, Cuyler saw the glow of more flashing lights in the distance.

Ramsey swore. "They've got us boxed in." He stopped the car, shut it off, and turned to face her. "We're not gonna get by them in this car. How do you feel? You up to a walk?"

She lifted her chin and swallowed her fear. She had to be strong to help him through this, even though the pain they'd inflicted and the blood she'd lost made her weaker than she'd ever felt in her life. "I'm fine. Let's go."

With a nod, Ramsey shrugged out of his jacket, then used the sleeve to wipe the steering wheel and gearshift, the headlight button, and anything else he might have touched. "No sense leaving them any clues."

She nodded, taking the map with her as she got out of the car. Then he got out, and came around the car. He put his jacket around her shoulders, folded his big hand around hers, and led her into the woods at the roadside.

* * *

The darkness worked in their favor as they made
their way from one small patch of woods to another,
keeping the road in sight but staying far enough away
from it to remain concealed by the trees.

She was exhausted. He knew she was. And frightened. Hell, he couldn't blame her. He was scared
himself. DPI was not going to be easy to elude. Besides, he had other reasons to worry. He didn't have a
drop of insulin on him. And if he didn't get some
soon, he fully expected to start feeling the effects.

His watch told him there was an hour before dawn,
when Cuyler suddenly stopped, clutched her stomach
and doubled over. She fell to her knees, groaning and
then retching violently.

Ramsey knelt beside her, held her shoulders. Fear
made him shudder as he wondered what could be
wrong. God, she was so weak, already.

She rose, unsteadily, leaning on him for support.
"It's all right. I'm all right."

"No, you're not. Cuyler, what the hell is it?"

She sniffed, still not standing very steadily. "I don't
know. Maybe the drug they injected me with. I don't
know. It's all right now, though."

It wasn't. It was perfectly clear that she was anything but all right. She was pale, trembling, cold. She
needed someplace warm to rest and. . . Hell, he didn't
know what else she needed. But whatever, he was determined to get it for her. They were approaching a
town, of sorts. A small grouping of neat little houses,
with cars and the occasional bicycle in short, paved
driveways. Supporting Cuyler with an arm around her

shoulders, tucking her body close to his, he took her toward them, scanning for someplace, anyplace, where she might lie down for a while.

She stiffened when he pulled her out of the sheltering trees and toward clipped back lawns, all of them littered with colorful leaves. "It's all right," he whispered. "Come on, trust me."

She did, but hesitantly. They crossed three backyards before they found one with a prefab shed standing in it. Ramsey sighed in relief and started toward it, only to come to an abrupt halt when a huge dog lunged out of its doghouse and began barking loudly.

He took a single step backward, ready to duck back into the trees, but Cuyler caught his arm, stopping him. She didn't say a word. Just moved closer to the dog, staring at it with an intensity that was palpable. The dog stopped barking. It stared right back at her, ears pricked forward, head tilted to one side. Then its tail wagged. She bent forward to stroke his big head. Ramsey only stood, dumbfounded, watching.

She turned to face him, smiling weakly. "He'll keep quiet now."

Ramsey shook his head. "So, should I start calling you Dr. Doolittle?"

"It doesn't always work. But sometimes, I can let animals know I'm a friend."

He took her hand again and led her to the shed, thanking his lucky stars there was no lock on the door. It opened easily, without a creak, and he pulled her inside. When he closed the door behind him they were in total darkness. He held her close to his side as he moved to the back, tripping once over what felt like a lawn mower, knocking over a shovel. Against the back wall, he urged her to the floor, then went back, feeling his way. He found a tarp that covered some piece of small machinery, and tugged it away. He returned and settled beside her, tucking the tarp around both of them for warmth.

"We could have gone farther." She snuggled close to him, resting her head on his shoulder.

"You're barely putting one foot in front of the other, Cuyler. You're sick and you know it." He ran one hand through her tousled hair. "What can I do to make it better?"

He felt her hesitation, could almost feel her deciding not to tell him. "Nothing. It'll pass."

"Funny how I can tell when you're lying." He drew a breath. "It's not just the drug, is it, Cuyler?"

She didn't answer.

"Cuyler, if there's something I can do to help you, I want to do it."

Her hand touched the side of his face. "No, you don't."

It was her tone, more than her words, that tripped the knowledge in his brain. "It's the blood loss, isn't it?" He felt her stiffen, knew he'd hit on it. "Your wrists bled, your lip. Quite a lot from the look of your blouse."

"The injuries aren't that bad, Ramsey. We tend to bleed a lot. That's all."

"So you need to replenish it."

"Tomorrow night. We'll find a blood bank somewhere or—"

"You could take some of mine."

"Ramsey, no—"

"You'd feel stronger, better, wouldn't you? Cuyler, it's all right. I trust you."

She sighed and sat up a little straighter. "That isn't the point. Look, Ramsey, it would make us even more connected than we already are. The link between us is already tearing you apart inside. I don't want to make it even stronger."

He sat up, too, gripped her shoulders and turned her toward him. "I don't go ten minutes without thinking about you, Cuyler. I've gone against everything I've ever believed in just to make sure you're all right. I don't see how it can get any stronger."

He felt her shake her head. "It's the situation. Ramsey, you'd made up your mind to get away from me. You struck out through the frozen wilderness on foot, you were so desperate to leave. And if those men hadn't shown up, I don't think you'd have come back. You'd have found a way out, gone back to your old life and stayed as far away from me as you could get. You still might want to do that, if we survive this."

He closed his eyes and drew a steady breath. "I was still fighting what I felt. Dammit, you can understand that, can't you? One of you killed my mother, for God's sake. How could I—"

"One of us. You see? You still see it that way. An individual killed your mother, Ramsey. I had nothing to do with it."

"I know that—"

"I could get help for us. I could summon others to help us out of this mess. We could stay with them until the danger passes. I could do it right now, Ramsey."

He went utterly silent at her words. Others. Others like her. Vampires. The beings he'd been taught to hate for most of his life. He breathed deeply, and shook his head. He couldn't trust his life to them. Just because he'd finally realized that Cuyler wasn't a heartless predator, didn't mean the others weren't.

She sighed deeply, and he thought he heard sadness in the sound. "It's all right. I won't do it. I wasn't considering it, anyway. I wouldn't want to bring anyone else into DPI's sights. I only wanted to make a point."

"Cuyler, you can't expect me to put my life in their hands."

"No. And I don't. But, Ramsey, they're just people. We were all human once, just like you. There are good and bad in any group, and you can't just write off an entire race because of one incident. It's bigotry, can't you see that?"

"No, it's not. It's different—"

"It's different because *we're* different, right?" She leaned against the wall, turning her back to him.

He knew he'd hurt her, angered her. But, dammit, it had been a major leap for him to see *her* as less than a monster, as a caring woman with thoughts and feelings like any other. Now she expected him to accept the entire race as just ordinary folks with a slight aversion to sunlight and solid food? They'd been different, even as humans. That damned antigen in their blood *made* them different.

No, dammit, he wasn't ready to concede that *everything* he'd ever learned had been wrong. DPI may have gone too far in their persecution, but they'd had reasons. Ramsey had reasons, too. His mother. She was his reason, and he couldn't let go of his old anger so easily.

Ramsey dozed, and it was full daylight when he woke. Cuyler slept in a corner, far away from him. It was the darkest spot in the shed, and while no sunlight touched her body, he covered her entirely with the tarp, just in case. There were no windows in the metal shed, but light spilled through seams in the tin here and there. He worried about the beams moving as the sun did.

Sounds of life—motors, air brakes—floated toward him. He opened the door a crack and peeked outside, checking first to make sure the light didn't touch Cuyler. A school bus rolled to a stop in front of the house. He couldn't see who boarded, since the house itself blocked his view, but a few seconds later it rolled away, followed closely by the two cars that had been in the driveway.

God, could he be so lucky? A two-career family with all the kids in school? He slipped out of the shed, glancing in both directions to be sure no one could see. He gave the dog a cursory glance, but the huge Newfoundland was busy devouring a fresh supply of kibble and didn't even look his way.

Swallowing a healthy dose of anxiety, Ramsey walked up to the back door and knocked as hard as he could. What better way to find out if anyone was home? He waited, rehearsing what he'd say if someone answered. He figured he could pretend he was at the wrong house. But no answer came. The lock was a snap for any government agent worth his salt. In a few seconds he was inside, carefully and quietly searching the place just to be sure no one was around. Sighing in relief when there wasn't.

It was too much to hope that one of the residents might be diabetic and have some insulin lying around. But he checked anyway. Not finding any, he was extremely careful when he raided the fridge. He had to eat, but God only knew what his system would do with whatever he put into it. He made do with a few stalks of celery and a sugar-free rice cake. There was a little coffee left in the pot, and he heated it in the microwave and gulped it down. Then he headed for the living room and snapped on the television, only to stumble a few steps backward when he saw his own face and a composite drawing of Cuyler's on the screen, with a 1-800 number beneath them.

He only heard the words "Armed and extremely dangerous," before the picture changed and the reporter launched into another story.

His initial reaction was to head for the shed, gather Cuyler up, and run as fast as they could go. But he couldn't do that. He had to wait until sunset. There was no other way.

He got another rice cake, and sat down to work out the most immediate problem. Cuyler's condition. She was weak, sick. He knew what she needed to feel strong again. And he knew she wouldn't take it from him no matter how often he offered.

So he had to come up with some way to convince her. And there was only one that came to mind.

CHAPTER TEN

She woke to the warning vibrations skittering over her nerve endings. The tarp slipped from her shoulders as she sat up, calling out to Ramsey.

"Right here. I'm right here." There was a click, and then the beam of a flashlight bathed the space between them. One side of Ramsey's mouth curved upward before the other, but she got the feeling his smile was hiding some new turmoil. "Found a few treasures in the house."

She sat up straighter, but dizziness swamped her. He saw it, frowned at her, and she tried to change the subject. "You were in the house?"

"Yeah. No one was home." His smile died slowly. "I only took what we needed. They won't even notice it's missing."

Her breath escaped in a rush. "Just what did we need so badly you had to steal for it?"

His head came up fast, a look of surprise on his face.

"Didn't mean to shock you like that, Ramsey. I forgot, my kind isn't supposed to have any moral values at all. You're not going to faint on me, are you?"

His brows drew together. "You wake up cranky, anybody ever tell you that? You still don't feel very well, do you?" She refused to answer. Ramsey scanned her face. "You sure as hell don't look as if you do. Anyway, I didn't steal this stuff, exactly. I left some money. Stuffed it under the sofa cushion."

She rolled her eyes. "Wonderful. But it still wasn't worth the risk. You could have been seen."

"But I wasn't. And I got us a much-needed flashlight. Ought to come in handy, since we can only travel by night."

"I have excellent night vision."

"A sleeping bag, so we don't catch pneumonia."

"I *can't* catch pneumonia."

"Some food—"

She crooked an eyebrow at him.

"Yeah, right. I forgot. How about this, then?" He handed her some folded clothing, and she took it.

"What—"

"One pair of jeans, size six, petite. They must have a teenager about your size. And a warm sweater. Now put them on and quit griping. We have to move."

She got to her feet, set the clothes aside, and grabbed the hem of her blouse. Then she paused. "Well?"

Ramsey blinked, breaking his intense stare. "Well, what?"

"You going to turn off that light?"

"Sure." There was a soft click, and the shed was once again bathed in darkness.

Cuyler heeled off her shoes, pulled her blouse over her head, then stepped out of her pants. She reached for the clothing she'd set aside, but Ramsey's hand closed over hers, stopping her.

She drew a quick breath, looking behind her. "What is it?"

"Not dark enough in here, I guess."

He stood closer, his shirt brushing her back. Then his hands crept around her waist, pulling her back against his strong chest. "I still want you, Cuyler. I'm still having those damned dreams."

She closed her eyes tightly, stiffening herself against the onslaught of desire that rocked her. She couldn't let this happen, not now, not when her hunger was so strong. She hadn't fed in such a long time. Didn't he realize what would happen if they...

"I can't..."

"Why not?" His head bent over her shoulder, his lips finding and nuzzling her neck. The brush of his new whiskers scraped over her skin, and she shivered.

Any excuse would do. She had to stop this craziness. "You still see me... as... Stop, Ramsey." Her head tipped sideways as his mouth moved over her shoulder. Warm fingertips trailed upward, along her spine. "I don't want..." The words became a sigh.

"Yes, you do. And so do I. Hell, I'm tired of fighting it, Cuyler. I'm tired of trying to deny it, hoping it will go away. It won't. I think we both know that."

"But..." His palms came up beneath her breasts, cupped them, squeezed. "Ramsey," she breathed. "Ramsey, you still believe..."

"The hell with what I believe. This is physical. Beliefs don't enter into it." His fingertips closed on her nipples. She caught her breath. He applied more pressure and she sighed. In one quick motion he turned her around, caught her mouth beneath his, dug his tongue into her. She responded, sucking it, running her hands up his back, under his shirt.

He gripped her buttocks in his hands, lifting her as he sat down on the seat of a lawn tractor, pulling her onto his lap so she was straddling him. Then he attacked her breasts with his mouth, sucking, biting, licking at them until she writhed against the hardness she felt poking up through his jeans.

"This isn't fair," she whispered.

"It was your idea. You said back at the house that if we just did it once, we might get over it. Well, here we are, Cuyler. Let's test your theory."

He devoured her nipples again, one after the other, all the while holding her hard to his lap and moving his hips against her. Then his hands closed on her waist and he lifted her, higher, until her backside rested in the curve of the steering wheel.

"What—?"

"I did this in my dreams, Cuyler. I want to try it for real." His hands slipped up the insides of her thighs, and he pressed them open. Then he dropped kisses along them, moving higher, ever higher. Finally his mouth found its goal and he pressed his face to her. His tongue parted her and found its way inside. Cuyler's head fell backward as she felt him licking her, scraping her with his teeth, sucking at her until she trembled all over.

Her hands tangled into his hair and he lifted his head, staring up at her as his hands moved to his jeans. Then he returned them to her waist, to pull her down to him. As he filled her, she felt the current that moved through both of them. Twining her arms around his neck, burying her face there, she sank lower. He clasped her hips, lifting her, lowering her again, plunging deeper inside her with every thrust.

Her lips caressed his neck, and her need mounted, beginning to build as she'd known it would. Every step she took toward fulfillment fired the hunger. She tasted the salt of his skin, felt the blood rushing beneath it.

He moved faster. Ecstasy hovered just beyond her reach, and the thirst raged. She tore her head away from his muscled neck, averting her face.

His hands slid up over her back, captured her face and turned it toward him again. He kissed her, deeply, desperately. "It's all right, Cuyler." His lips moved over hers as he whispered. He guided her head to his neck once more. "It's all right. Do it."

Her lips trembled on his skin, then parted. Only a sip, only one small taste of his essence. Just enough to get her through this night.

He stiffened, moaning deep and hoarse as her teeth pierced his throat. His hands pressed to the back of her head even as his body rocked harder and faster in time with hers. The climax claimed her, held her in its shattering grip for an instant, and forever.

As it slowly faded, the ripples of pleasure smoothing and stilling, Cuyler lifted her head away and closed her eyes to prevent the tears from spilling over. "God, what have I done?" She couldn't look at him, couldn't bear to see condemnation in his eyes. She began to rise, but he held her to him.

"You had to, Cuyler. You needed—"

Her sudden stare stopped his words. She searched his face, not believing what she was thinking, not wanting to think it. "You knew, didn't you? You knew the way desire would heighten the need until I couldn't fight it?"

He nodded once. "Yeah. I knew. And I also knew you couldn't take another night on the run without it." He shrugged, his hands moving into her hair, stroking it. "I offered earlier. You refused. I couldn't think of any other way."

That's all it was, then. Physical needs that needed fulfillment, just as he'd said. Only he'd been referring to hers, not to his own.

She slid to the floor, pulling from his grasp when he tried to keep her with him. Without a word, she picked up the clothes and began to dress. He got up, as well, but she didn't look at him. She couldn't. Making love to him had filled her heart to overflowing. Realizing how little it meant to him had broken it in two, and she could almost feel the fragile contents spilling onto the floor.

Cuyler heard him moving around, packing up his treasures, she imagined. Then he stood still, and she felt his gaze on her.

"I hurt you," he said softly. "I didn't mean to."

Blinking her eyes dry, she fixed her face into a smiling mask, and turned to face him. "No, Ramsey. It was physical, right? No feelings involved."

His eyes probed hers, reaching through the darkness, it seemed, into the depths of her soul. "Maybe..." He stopped speaking, his head coming up slowly. "What is that? Sounds like a flock of geese, or..."

Cuyler listened, and then her broken heart froze inside her. "Dogs! God, they've got dogs!" The crying of what sounded like a hundred hounds filled the night, louder when she flung the door open and ran outside.

Ramsey grasped her hand and headed for the street. She knew there was no use creeping through the woods, not now. Speed was what mattered. Calming one family pet with the power of her mind was a simple trick. She knew better than to try it with an entire pack of vicious hounds.

Cuyler's heart hammered with fear as she ran beside Ramsey. The baying drew nearer, louder. In moments the dogs would burst out of the woods where they were searching. They'd be on them seconds later, and it would be over. Everything—life—would be over.

"There! Look!" Ramsey didn't slow down. He kept running, but veered into a driveway, only stopping when he came to a mean-looking black motorcycle leaning on its kickstand. Releasing her hand, he straddled the seat. One kick, two. The motor roared and Ramsey twisted the accelerator, revving it. Puffs of black smoke belched from twin pipes at the back. Cuyler leapt on behind him, clinging to his waist as he released the clutch and the bike lurched into motion. Inexpertly, he turned it around, lowering one foot for balance. Then he shifted, gunned it, and they shot out of the driveway and down the street.

She might be killed on this suicide machine, she thought vaguely. But at least she couldn't hear those damn dogs anymore.

Okay, so he'd hurt her...again. He could only pray there would be time to make it up later.

When he'd decided to make love to Cuyler, he'd told himself he was doing it for her, so she wouldn't wilt and die of her brand of starvation before he could get her to safety. The problem was, what he'd told himself had been a lie. And not even a very convincing one. He'd wanted her. Hell, he still wanted her. Instead of dulling this rampant lust he felt, being with her had only sharpened it to a razor's edge. It hadn't been physical, dammit. It had been something more, something deeper, almost...almost spiritual. And when she'd finally done what he'd wanted her to do...

He shook his head in wonder. For a few brief seconds he'd felt everything she was feeling. He'd experienced her thoughts, known her emotions, felt every sensation that rippled through her body. It had been as if their minds had melded into one. He'd had the shocking sensation of her heart beating beside his within his own chest.

All of that had combined with the passion he felt for her and exploded into something he'd never felt before. It wasn't like sex with a...with a normal woman. It was above and beyond, a whole other world.

And so what had he done with all this newfound knowledge about her? Nothing. He'd ignored it, pretended it hadn't happened, let her go on thinking the entire exchange had been his own clever plot to get her to drink.

She was hurting over that, now. There was a real, physical pain where her heart lived. She felt as if her soul was bleeding, and she was battling tears.

Ramsey blinked in shock as those emotions flicked through his mind just as clearly as if they were his own. What the hell?

A police car blocked the road ahead. Ramsey leaned left, turning the handlebars and heading the bike over someone's back lawn. They bounded up and down on the seat as he drove over what felt like a washboard, up a shallow hill, and onto another road, then continued in the direction he'd been going. The ploy worked. The police couldn't get ahead of him in time to block his way, and he realized he could get to the road that ran parallel to the highway in the same manner.

This time, though, he didn't wait for a cruiser with flashing lights to force him off. He drove across a farmer's field, rutted and rough all the way, and he had to struggle to keep the bike upright. The cops would converge on the road where he'd been. But he would zip right past them by another route. For the first time tonight he thought they just might get out of this mess alive.

Cuyler was beginning to think so, too.

Ramsey frowned, glancing at her behind him. Her arms tightened a little at his waist, and her head rested against his back. He supposed he could no longer doubt that she had feelings and emotions. Not when he was experiencing everything she thought, everything she felt. This must have been what she'd meant when she'd told him that the connection between them would be even more powerful if she drank from him.

He felt her emotions. She was scared. But beyond that, a profound sadness made her keep fighting back tears. She thought that maybe she'd been wrong about him, all along. She thought that he'd never be able to see that his mistrust of her kind was a mistake, a product of the hatred he'd nurtured for so long. And she thought...

Ramsey blinked in shock and nearly dumped the bike. She thought she might be falling in love with him.

"Have we lost them?" She had to yell close to his ear to make herself heard over the motorcycle.

"Only for the moment," he shouted back. "Once they get a chopper up, they'll spot us again." The road they were on veered away from the highway, but he followed it anyway. It took her a moment to realize where he was going, but when she saw the sign, she stiffened. Limestone 5 Miles.

"Ramsey, you're going the wrong way! This is where we started!"

"Exactly what they'll be thinking," he told her. He took a turn, then another, and within a few minutes they were on a road Cuyler recognized. Ramsey stopped the bike, and when they both got off, he pushed it into the trees at the roadside. Taking her hand, he pulled her along beside him, right up to the gates of the house where she'd been held prisoner such a short time ago.

CHAPTER ELEVEN

She shivered uncontrollably as Ramsey pulled her through the gates, along the path, right through the front door. He knew what she must be thinking. That he'd lost his mind, or that he'd decided to turn her over to DPI after all. It amazed him that she didn't argue with him, just came along, completely trusting a man who'd given her nothing but reasons not to.

Sensing her turmoil, he gave her hand a reassuring squeeze as he closed the door behind them. "It's gonna be all right, Cuyler. This is the safest place we could be right now. The last place they'd think to look for us. And you can bet Fuller and his men won't be back here as long as they think they're on our trail."

She bit her lip, her gaze scanning the living room. The place looked like the home of a wealthy, tasteless individual. Not a branch office for a government agency. But then, that was the whole idea. DPI's anonymity was vital to its success.

Ramsey armed the security device, then began fiddling with the buttons, programming a new entry code, one Fuller wouldn't know. Cuyler walked slowly away from him, and he heard her exhausted sigh. Fortunately, though, her wounds had healed with the daytime rest. Her wrists were no longer cut and bruised. The purple mark on her face had vanished, and her cut lip had healed.

But some wounds were tougher to heal than others. And he still felt her pain, the one he'd caused himself. He'd have to find a way to remedy that soon, or he'd lose her. He wasn't sure they could get out of this alive, but if they did, and if they went their separate ways the way Cuyler seemed to have decided they must, he was going to hurt for a very long time.

He paused in punching buttons, to slant her a glance. "Cuyler, you're wrung out. Why don't you go upstairs, take a nice hot bath, relax for a while?"

She blinked slowly, and he knew she was tempted by the suggestion. "No, Ramsey. Two sets of eyes are better than one. Suppose I go up there and a swarm of agents kick the door in?"

"I don't think that's likely to happen anytime soon."

He finished punching in the new entry code. No one would open this door, or the front gate, without him knowing about it. Then he turned to her again, saw the uncertainty in her eyes. "Go on, Cuyler. Ask me."

"Ask you what?" Her chin lifted a little, and he saw her trying to mask her doubts.

"Why I brought you here," he said softly. He ran one hand over the side of her face, cupped her cheek. God, her skin was soft. "Not to give you up, Cuyler. If they want you, they'll have to go through me."

She bit her lower lip, nodding, but he knew she wasn't as sure of that as he was.

"You don't believe it?"

"I . . ." She shook her head, paced away from him. "How can I believe you'd lay your life on the line to protect someone you still see as some kind of inferior species?"

"That isn't—"

"I know. That isn't what you meant to say." She shook her head, turning to face him again, her gaze steady, strong. "But it's how you feel."

He shook his head slowly. "You're wrong, Cuyler. There's nothing inferior about you."

"Just the rest of my kind, right, Ramsey? So what does that make me? An exception? A freak?"

He lifted his hands, palms up, struggling to find words that would convince her how wrong she was, but she gave him a single glance that told him it would do no good. She wouldn't listen. He let his hands fall to his sides, sighing in defeat.

"So, why *did* you bring me here?"

Ramsey closed his eyes, tried to find some patience. It would take time to get her to trust him again. She'd believed so strongly in him before, and his fall from grace must have been a damaging one. But not fatal. "Come here. I'll show you."

He took her hand in his and laced his fingers with hers. Such a small hand, silky soft, steady now, despite her fears. He thought about the way that hand had felt tangled in his hair, those fingertips sinking into his shoulders. He glanced down at her, caught her staring up at him, but she looked away fast. He cleared his throat and pulled her with him to the door at the far end of the room. When he stepped through, he waved an arm at the equipment that covered every inch of the counters that lined the room. Computers, faxes, phones, radios, an entire bank of video screens, each showing a steady view of a different room within this house.

He heard the air escape her in a rush, heard her murmured exclamation. Ignoring it, he moved forward, snapping on the police band receiver, and then the more sophisticated radio. The one DPI used to keep in touch. He listened for a minute, heard nothing but static. Then he sank into a chair and flicked on a computer.

"What are you doing?"

He glanced sideways at her, but his attention shot right back to the screen. "I'll know everything they do, every move they make from here on in, Cuyler. We'll figure a safe way out of here before morning. Meanwhile, this system is a direct link to the main one in White Plains. I'd like to see what they have on me, find out why Fuller's been doubting my loyalty."

He heard her move, then turned to see her leaning against a wall, chewing her lower lip. "There's not much you can do here, really. I'll be on top of things. Take that bath."

Cuyler bathed. She didn't do as Ramsey had suggested, though, and lounge around in steaming water for hours. She made it quick and efficient. Then she scoured the house for extra clothes, finding none. She made do with the jeans and sweater she'd been wearing. After she'd towel dried her hair, she wandered back down to the first floor, located the kitchen, and brewed a pot of coffee.

With a cup in her hand, she went back to the room, tapped once, and walked in. Ramsey's face did a lousy job of hiding his emotions, and the look it wore made her heart trip over itself. He faced her when he heard her come in, tried to mask his bewildered expression, but still failed miserably.

She crossed to where he sat, pressed the mug into his hand. "How bad is it?"

He licked his lips, lowering his eyes. "Pretty bad."

"Tell me."

He glanced at the screen in front of him. It showed a spider web of lines that looked like a map, with little red lights glowing at intervals. He pointed to one of them. "These are the roadblocks. There's not one route out of here they haven't plugged tight. They're checking every vehicle that passes."

"So we can't get out by car. We can go on foot."

"They have choppers up, scanning the ground for us. And the dogs are working the woods. Cuyler, I don't think—"

The front door slammed and both of them went stiff, whirling toward the sound.

"You don't *think* at all, Bachman. That's part of the problem."

The deep voice was one Ramsey had heard before. He recognized it, and rose slowly.

The dark form filled the doorway, nodding once to Ramsey. "Hello again, Agent Bachman."

Ramsey tried to swallow, but found his throat blocked by a brick of hatred. This man was a killer, a killer Ramsey had been sent to bring in. But he'd failed. "Damien."

"Aren't you glad to see me, Bachman? Thought you'd be overjoyed, after chasing me all those months, trying to capture me for your bosses at DPI."

Ramsey took a single step forward. "You killed two women, you bastard. And you—"

Damien glared at him, his black eyes glittering with unconcealed dislike. "I killed one man. A vampire. The one responsible for the two murders you were sent to investigate."

"Liar!" Ramsey lunged toward him, only to have Cuyler leap in front of him, her palms flat to his chest.

"It's true, Ramsey! There were witnesses. I've read the whole account, and he's telling you the truth."

Ramsey glanced down at her, then at the man he'd spent months trying to capture, the man who'd made a beautiful young woman into a creature like himself.

Damien blinked and held his gaze. Some of the fury left the vampire's eyes. "She was dying," he said simply. "I loved her, Bachman. I couldn't just stand by and let her go."

Ramsey narrowed his eyes and shook his head.

"Check your precious DPI files, if you don't believe me." Damien lowered his head and paced in a small circle. "They know now it wasn't me who murdered those two. They know it was Anthar, the vampire I killed. Yet the hunt for me continues." He stood still, shot Ramsey a glare. "Go on, check. You have the information at your fingertips. Or are you afraid of what you'll find?"

Ramsey blinked twice, and stared at him, stunned speechless. "Anthar?" he finally managed. He glanced toward Cuyler, and she nodded confirmation. Sighing hard, Ramsey sank back into his chair. He closed his eyes. "All right. I believe you."

Cuyler sighed in relief, but Damien only cocked his brows in surprise. "You don't need to see the proof?"

"No." Ramsey shook his head slowly. "No. I've found quite a few surprises in my own DPI files. Enough to show me what they're really about." He shook his head, meeting Cuyler's gaze. "You were right all along. I just wish I'd believed you sooner."

Cuyler blinked moisture away from her eyes, and faced Damien. If she looked a bit awed, Ramsey figured it was natural. She was in the same room with the man reputed to be the oldest of all of them, the first. "Why are you here?" she asked him.

"To get you out."

"But how did you know—"

"No time for that, child. You must come with me now." He took her hand and tugged her toward the doorway.

She pulled free. "I'm not leaving him."

Damien's eyes took on a feral gleam. "He's not worth your devotion, Cuyler. He's one of them, those same bastards who make our very existence a game of hide-and-seek. The ones who see to it we never know peace. If they've turned on him now, then all the better. Poetic justice, if you ask me."

"I didn't ask you!"

His glare grew sharper still.

"They had me, Damien. He got me out. He risked his life to do it."

"Too little, too late. What good did it do? He's one of them, Cuyler! Leave him here and be rid of him for good."

"*Damn* you with your us-and-them mentality! Don't you see that's exactly the bigotry that got us to this point in the first place! Damien, your way of thinking is just as twisted as DPI's. Can't you see that?"

Ramsey touched her shoulder, his hands squeezing gently, but his gaze remained on Damien. "Can you get her out?"

"There's no doubt."

"No!" She twisted her head to stare into Ramsey's eyes just before he slammed them shut.

"Go with him, Cuyler."

"I won't! Dammit, I won't!"

"There's no time to argue," Damien said softly, though his eyes had lost some of their anger, and a frown that might have been one of confusion had taken up residence between his brows. "Have you noticed the radio silence, Ramsey? The sudden stop in all radio contact?"

Ramsey opened his eyes and turned slowly to stare at the computer screen that glowed like an all-seeing oracle.

"They knew the second you turned it on and began accessing information," Damien said softly. "They're probably already on their—"

A bullhorn-enhanced voice apparently shattered the slight grip Cuyler had on her composure. She screamed at the first words, but Ramsey still heard them.

"Bachman, we have the house surrounded. There's no way out. Give yourselves up."

Ramsey lowered his head. "Can you still get her out, Damien?"

"Ramsey—"

"If we can get to the roof," Damien replied, cutting her off.

She threw her arms around Ramsey's neck. "No! I won't do it. I love you—"

The bullhorn-enhanced voice came again. "We'll give you ten minutes, Bachman. Then we come in shooting."

The sharpshooter in the tallest pine tree whistled, and when he had Fuller's attention, he whispered loudly, "There's a third person in there, Fuller. A man, tall, very dark complexion."

"How the hell—" Fuller nodded, and hurried toward the DPI van, glancing as he did at the miniature dish on the top. "Can you get this thing up and operational? I need to hear what's being said inside."

The technician only held up one hand for patience, adjusting his headset and fiddling with dials. Finally he nodded and smiled. He handed the headset to Fuller, who held it up to one ear. Then his eyes widened, and he smiled.

"It's *him!*" He shook his head slowly. "We've hit the damn jackpot this time, fellas. Get me a line to Bachman. It's time to make a deal."

CHAPTER TWELVE

Damien studied Ramsey as if seeing him for the first time. "Hard to believe we have one common goal, after all this. We both want to see Cuyler get out of this alive."

Ramsey lowered his eyes. "We have more in common than you know, Damien."

The other man frowned, parted his lips to ask something, but Ramsey cut him off. "Look, it's no secret that I don't like you."

"You're not exactly my favorite person, either, Ramsey."

"Unpleasant as you are, though, you're not a killer."

"Thanks so much for informing me."

Ramsey blew air through his teeth. "You want to shut the hell up and let me apologize!"

"Is that what you were doing?"

Damien's stare was as hateful as ever, and Ramsey knew the one he sent back was as bad, or worse. Ramsey wanted to deck the guy, but he restrained himself. There was another part of him that wanted to shake Damien's hand, call him friend.

"The one you killed, Anthar..." Ramsey swallowed the lump in his throat and shook his head.

"What about him?"

Clearing his throat, stiffening his spine, Ramsey answered. "He was the one who murdered my mother." He heard Cuyler catch her breath. "DPI knew all along. It's in my files, along with a lot of other ..." He bit his lip, shook his head. "Doesn't matter now, I guess. I just thought you ought to know."

"Know?"

"That you're not quite the bastard I had you pegged as being, all right? Now, if you don't mind, can we quit talking and get Cuyler out of here?"

Damien tilted his head to one side. "You aren't a bit afraid of me, are you?"

"Oh, *hell* yes, Damien. Scared witless. Don't you see my knees knocking?"

Damien chewed his inner cheek, eyes narrow. "You're an unusual mortal."

"You're both idiots!" Cuyler shouted the words as she crossed into the living room and peered through a curtain. "And insane, to boot, if you think I'm leaving here without you, Ramsey." There were tears glittering in her eyes. "We go together or not at all."

He went to her, unable to stop himself. Vaguely he was aware of Damien tactfully slipping out of the room, but his mind was focused on Cuyler. Her heart was breaking. He could feel it. Or was that his own? His hands slipped around her waist as she turned to him and he pulled her close.

"I'm not worth dying for," he whispered. "Cuyler, you have to go with him."

She threaded her fingers in his hair. "You love me, don't you, Ramsey?"

His eyes devoured her face. Her turned-up nose, her huge, dark eyes. That ruffly jet hair.

"Say it, just once, say it."

He nodded, his mind reeling with the force of what he felt. "I don't think love is a strong enough word. Hell, Cuyler, you've turned me inside out. Before you, I swear there was ice running in my veins instead of blood. A big hunk of granite hatred where my heart ought to be. You changed that." He lowered his head, captured her sweet mouth one last time, kissed her the way he'd been wanting to all night long. When he pulled away, he licked the taste of her from his lips. "Yes, Cuyler. I love you."

Tears flowed like rivers on her cheeks. "Then don't ask me to go on without you." She sniffed, swallowed, her voice became tight and thin. "'Cause I don't think I can."

"You'd have to sooner or later anyway." His thumbs swept the moisture from her cheeks. "You're immortal. I'm not and there's no way I can be." God, how it tore him apart to utter that lie. There was a way. He knew that now, was still jolted by the knowledge. But he couldn't tell her. She'd never leave if she knew.

She shook her head fast and hard, but he caught her face between his palms, held it still. "It's the truth. We would have had to face it eventually."

"I don't want to hear this!" She whirled away from him.

Damien reentered the room, clearing his throat to announce his presence. Ramsey met his probing gaze. It was knowing, that look.

"There's a door to the roof through the attic," Ramsey said, fighting for a level tone. "I want you to go with Damien now. They won't wait patiently much longer."

Damien went to Cuyler, took a gentle hold on her arm, and started for the stairs. The telephone jangled and Ramsey went rigid. It rang again, and this time the voice on the bullhorn shouted at him to pick it up.

His hands damp with sweat, he did.

"Bachman?"

His lips thinned. The voice belonged to Wes Fuller, his trusted superior. "What the hell do you want?"

"Wouldn't be a good idea for your two pals to go up on the roof, Bachman. We have sharpshooters high enough to hit them there."

He swore his heart turned to ice in his chest. He covered the mouth piece with one hand, waved to get Damien's attention. Damien halted halfway up the stairs and waited, watching Ramsey's face intently.

Ramsey cleared his throat. "What makes you think anyone was thinking about going to the roof?"

"Oh, we don't think. We *know*. I've been listening in on your touching little conversation."

"Maybe you'd like to meet me one on one, Fuller? Maybe you need a little dental work done, hmm?"

Fuller's laugh was low and throaty. "No, thanks. Look, I know you've been sniffing around in your files...among other things. How much do you know?"

"About what?"

The other man hesitated, then went on. "Your diabetes, for starters."

"I know I don't have it. Never did."

"And your insulin?"

"An experiment. To mask..." Ramsey glanced toward Cuyler on the stairs, and decided not to say any more.

"Go on, Bachman. Tell me, do you know about your blood type?"

"I know," he said softly, slowly.

"So you know all that crap you just fed the...*lady* was bull. You could join the ranks and live happily ever after with her. You realize that?"

Ramsey stiffened. "What's your point, Fuller?"

"I could let you go. Her, too. I could pull back and let you both walk out of here, right now. I have the authority."

Just like that. Fuller let the words hang in the air for a long moment. But Ramsey wasn't stupid. There was more. It was either a trick to get them to let their guard down, or Fuller wanted something. He wasn't certain which.

"What's the catch?" He tried not to let the sudden surge of hope come through in his voice.

"Finish the assignment you had before this one. That's all. Not so much to ask, is it, Bachman?'

Ramsey closed his eyes, knowing exactly what Fuller wanted. The job before this one had been the capture of Damien Namtar, the most powerful, the oldest, probably the first of all vampires. Ramsey had had no qualms about hunting him down a year ago, when he'd believed with everything in him that the man was a heartless predator, a killer. But now he knew better. He'd wronged Damien with his persecution. And he owed the man. More than ever, Ramsey knew what would happen to Damien if he were turned over to DPI. *They* were the heartless killers, not him. God, it was all so clear now. Why had it taken so long?

"How do you expect me to do that?" he asked, just to stall, trying to think of some way out of this trap.

"The tranquilizer, Bachman. There are filled syringes in the desk, bottom drawer. Just stick him, and leave the rest to us. You and your pet can walk away and never look back."

Ramsey turned and met Damien's steady gaze. Not looking away, he replied, "It might take a little while."

"I can give you an hour, Bachman. Not a minute longer." The connection was broken.

Ramsey licked his lips and put the phone back in its cradle.

"What?" Cuyler whispered. "What's going on?"

"Nothing." His gaze shifted to Damien's and he got the odd feeling the man knew every word that had been said. "I bought us some time, is all." He reached for a piece of paper and a pencil, and scribbled quickly. "They can hear every word we say, so be careful."

When he held it up, Damien and Cuyler came back down the stairs. Cuyler looked at it, blinked in surprise, and showed it to Damien.

Ramsey looked around the house, feeling more trapped and helpless than he ever had before. More, even, than when he'd awakened in Cuyler's castlelike hideaway. The thought made him close his eyes and wince inwardly. He'd give a limb to be there with her right now. He'd let so much time go to waste, time when he'd been alone with her in that magical place.

They could never go back there now.

Inspiration struck, and Ramsey tilted his head so they'd follow, and headed for the basement. The place was solid, lead-lined and secure. Ramsey didn't think they'd be heard down here. Still, he whispered what he had to say.

"Damien, we need to exchange clothes."

Damien lifted one brow, then lowered it, his eyes narrowing in understanding. "Why?"

"There's no time to go into it," Ramsey lied. "Look, there are sharpshooters out there. If you head for the roof, they'll pick you off so fast it'll make your head spin. I have a plan."

Damien nodded thoughtfully and lowered himself to the bottom step. "Tell me about it."

"I told you, there isn't time."

Cuyler looked from one to the other. "I don't like this, Ramsey. Tell me the truth, what did that bastard say to you on the phone?"

Ramsey looked away, chewing his lip. "Nothing you need to be concerned about."

"No," Damien agreed. "He simply offered to let you and Cuyler go free, in exchange for my capture. That's it, isn't it?"

Ramsey's head came up and his eyes flashed angrily. The jerk was going to ruin everything.

"And you planned to put on my clothes, pretend to be me, and give Cuyler and me time to escape."

"Ramsey, you can't!"

Ramsey clasped her hands in his, squeezing to calm her, while glaring at Damien. "You had to spill it all? You couldn't just take her and go?"

Damien gave his head an almost imperceptible shake. "An unusual mortal," he said again, as if to himself.

"I've had enough of both of you!" Cuyler tugged her hands from Ramsey's and stalked through the basement, peering through the narrow windows, whose bottoms were level with the ground outside. One after another, pacing back to the first again as Damien and Ramsey continued their silent battle of wills.

"Here!" Her shout caught both men's attention. "Okay, see that DPI car right there? It's the closest one to the house."

Damien glanced at Ramsey. Ramsey only shook his head.

"I won't bother trying to explain to you two. You're too busy with your own tug-of-war to listen. Ramsey, get Fuller on the line again. Tell him you agree to his terms, but he has to pull all the police off the highways. The chopper has to land. Tell him you'll surrender Damien only to him and those two clowns he has with him. Everyone else has to leave. Especially those sharpshooters. I can see one from here, up in a tree. We won't stand a chance unless we get rid of them."

Ramsey frowned, rising, gripping her shoulders. "Honey, I don't know what—"

"We'll need a distraction. Then we make a run for that car. We'll squeeze through this window, and..."

Her words came to a stop as she pulled free of Ramsey, clambered onto a wooden box, and pried the window from its opening. Ramsey could only watch in wonder as she wrestled it free, and very quietly climbed down, setting it aside.

"Look," she whispered, even more softly than before. She pointed to the shrubs growing between the house and the car. There would only be a few yards without cover.

She nudged Ramsey's shoulder. "Go on, get up there and make that call."

CHAPTER THIRTEEN

They hovered at the open window as Ramsey conversed via the cordless phone with Fuller. No one was in sight outside now. Only two DPI cars and three agents. They must want Damien very badly, Cuyler mused, to take such a chance.

Either that or they were playing a huge bluff. Maybe the others were only out of sight, waiting. Maybe Fuller and DPI had no intention of letting any of them go.

"He's out cold, Fuller," Ramsey said into the phone. "Apparently your tranquilizer works. Cuyler and I want transportation out of here. Now."

Ramsey held the phone away from his ear, and Cuyler leaned in close to hear the reply. Damien didn't bother. Cuyler wondered if perhaps he didn't need to. She had no idea the extent of his powers.

"You and *Cuyler* stay put. We're coming in. When we see for ourselves that he's incapacitated, we'll let you go."

Ramsey covered the mouthpiece with his hand. "Lying through his teeth." Removing his hand, he said, "All right, Fuller. But you better keep your word."

They waited, all of them pressed to the opening in the window. Cuyler knew Damien could leave if he wanted to. He had the ability. But he stayed, all the same.

When they heard the front door open, and Fuller calling Ramsey's name, Ramsey made a stirrup of his hands, and bent. Cuyler stepped up, pushing herself through the window. She emerged kneeling, concealed by the shrubbery, still close enough to hear Fuller's voice raised in alarm.

"Where the hell are you, Bachman?" Then, "Dammit, he's up to something. Search the place."

Damien was beside her a second later. Then Ramsey himself crawled through. She bit her lip as Damien reached back, offering a hand, which Ramsey took. Sandwiched between the two men, she glanced toward the car.

"We move as one," Ramsey said, his body shielding hers on one side. Damien nodded. Bending low, they ran toward the car. Just as they reached the end of the shrub cover, the front door of the house burst open and several shots rang out.

She felt Ramsey stiffen beside her, but he never faltered. One arm came around her and he moved faster, around the far side of the car. Ramsey opened the back door, bending over her body as she threw herself inside, facedown on the floor. The window above her exploded and glass rained down into her hair. She tried to turn, tried to see Ramsey and Damien, but the bullets whizzed near her face, bringing back a flood of horrifying memories, until she could only lower her head again, covering it with her hands. She heard the door slam and felt the car jerk into motion. And then the bullets stopped ringing in her ears. She chanced lifting her head, only to see Damien on the back seat, sitting calmly amid the gunfire, his gaze so intense... and then glowing as he stared at something behind them.

Curious, even while shaking all over, she sat up a bit, following his gaze. She saw the DPI men running toward their car. But before they reached it, it exploded in a ball of blinding white flame.

Shielding her eyes and gasping, she glanced at Damien. But he didn't notice, still too focused on what was behind them. He stared at the house now, even as the confused men turned to scramble toward it.

All three flew backward when it exploded. This time, the ground beneath the car rocked with the impact. She heard Ramsey swear, saw him twist in the driver's seat to look at the sight. Then she was looking, too. The entire house was nothing but a flaming framework, rapidly disintegrating to ash. Great beam-shaped lengths of fire fell in slow motion, disappearing into the mouth of the inferno waiting below to devour them.

She still felt the vibrations of the explosion, and the house was all but gone already.

My God.

They rounded a bend. The car weaved in and out of its lane and steadily lost speed. Cuyler frowned, clambering over the seat. "Ramsey, what's wrong? What's—"

She bit off the rest of her words, seeing the blood that soaked the front of him. His grip on the steering wheel was white-knuckled, his eyes steadily glazing over, his back bowing more and more as his right leg began a spastic dance. The car jerked with his foot's movements on the accelerator.

"Ramsey!" She swung her leg over his, jamming her foot down on the brake and jerking the gearshift into Neutral. She gripped the wheel, guided the car to the roadside, slammed it into Park, and grabbed Ramsey's shoulders, shaking him. "Dammit, Ramsey, don't do this to me! Ramsey! *Ramsey!*"

He focused on her eyes, and she could see it was a struggle. One side of his mouth pulled into that half smile of his, and he managed to wink. "Maybe Damien oughta drive, hmm?" Both his legs trembled now. Then they stopped, and his eyelids fell closed.

Cuyler buried her face in the crook of his neck, crying uncontrollably. "It isn't over, Ramsey. Damn you, it isn't over. Not yet, not like this!"

A firm hand on her shoulder drew her gaze upward to look into Damien's solemn eyes. "No, Cuyler. It isn't over. Not yet." He got out of the car, opened the front door, hauled Ramsey out, then carefully placed him across the back seat. Cuyler got back there, too, and lifted Ramsey's head as she slid in, so she could cradle it in her lap. Damien got behind the wheel. "Hold on to him, Cuyler. I'll drive you somewhere safe. And the rest..." He glanced over his shoulder at the man she held, his eyes narrow. "The rest, I guess, will be up to Ramsey."

Ramsey woke to the most incredible, burning pain he'd ever felt in his life. But at least he woke. He supposed he ought to be grateful for small favors.

His chest was bandaged. His legs had gone numb. But there was warmth, softness. His head was pillowed on what felt like satin. Small hands were running over his face, through his hair. A musical voice, like the wind, begged him to wake up. Salty tears rained down on his face. Trembling lips pressed to his over and over again.

He opened his eyes. Hazy, everything was so hazy. His body felt weak, drained. And there was this incredible urge to just close his eyes again and float away.

"Ramsey?"

God, but he didn't want to float away. Not if "away" meant away from Cuyler.

"Right here." That didn't sound like his voice. It sounded far away, echoing back to his ears from the other end of a hollow tunnel. Man, he was fading fast. He tried to look around, but could only make out several halos of golden light. Candles? And one bigger one, a fireplace, maybe. He felt the warmth, smelled the fragrance. Yes, a fireplace. And he thought he was on a bed, but he couldn't be sure. "Where are we?"

"Damien's house . . . one of his houses, as he put it. We're safe here, Ramsey. Damien went to get rid of the car. When he comes back, I'm sending him for a doctor."

"A doctor can't help, Cuyler." He knew it, somewhere deep in his soul. Just the same way he knew her devastation. She sensed him slipping away, just as he did. And she was dying a little bit, right along with him.

He struggled to sit up, and she helped him. "I can't stand this, Ramsey. I can't stand losing you." She propped pillows at his back.

He caught her hands, brought them to his lips. "I've been a fool."

"You saved our lives, Ramsey. Even Damien knows what you did back there."

"A fool," he whispered. God, it was getting harder and harder to speak, to string words together. He had to focus every ounce of strength on saying what he had to say. "He's a decent man, Damien. I was wrong... about him. About... about everything."

"It doesn't matter now—"

"Yes. Yes, it does. I'm not..." He drew a painful breath, grated his teeth. "I'm not what you think I am, Cuyler. The insulin...all this time...they tricked me."

She sank onto the edge of the bed, running her hands through his hair. "Don't try to talk. Just rest—"

"I don't deserve...to be...to live. But I'm not ready to die, either."

She choked on a sob. Shaking all over, she lowered her head to his chest, clung to him.

"But I'll...make it up to you...to all of you."

She lifted her head and stared into his eyes. "What do you mean?"

"I want to live, Cuyler." He wanted to stop. He was panting, out of breath as if he'd just run a marathon, but he had to continue. "I want to be able...to love you...the way you deserve." The pain in his chest was unbearable. But the pain in his heart was worse. "I want it. I want you to do it to me, Cuyler. Right now."

Her brows drew together as she searched his face, desperation etched in her every feature. "Do... Ramsey, what are you saying? I can't transform you. The antigen—"

"I have it." He inhaled, but it was too shallow. His voice grew weaker with every word. "I have...all along. The insulin..." That was it. It was the end. He felt himself slipping steadily away from her. He tried to tighten his hold on her, but didn't have the strength. With supreme effort, he gasped, and in a harsh whisper, went on. "I love you, Cuyler..."

His eyes fell closed and the breath slowly escaped his lungs.

"Ramsey! Ramsey, no..."

But she knew the end was here. And she knew he'd been telling her something...something she didn't understand.

Go on, Cuyler. Damien's soft, deep voice floated across the boundaries of time and space. *He's one of us. Always has been. It's all in the files. They've masked it with some new drug or other. Told him it was insulin and that he was diabetic. They've brainwashed him through most of his life, and still he found his way to you. Go on, bring him over. If ever a man was worthy of the gift, it's him.*

Cuyler felt her eyes widen. She was shocked beyond belief, and half wondered if the voice in her mind might have been her own imagination. But if there was a chance...

She bent her head and kissed Ramsey's slack mouth. Then she bent lower, sliding her lips over his bristly jaw, to his throat. "Come back to me, love," she whispered, her lips moving over his salty skin.

When Ramsey opened his eyes a long while later, there were a hundred new and unbelievable sensations coursing through him. Things he'd never felt before, didn't understand, a sense of elation and strength and vitality he'd never had before.

But all of that paled beside the joy he felt at finding Cuyler cradling him in her arms. He looked up at her, saw the uncertainty in her huge onyx eyes as they searched his face.

"You did it, didn't you?" he asked her, and even his voice seemed different. Or maybe it was his hearing that had taken on a new intensity.

She nodded. "You said... I thought..." She bit her lip. "Don't hate me for it, Ramsey. It seemed to be what you wanted. If I misunderstood, then—"

"It's what I wanted."

"But—"

He lifted his head, silencing her by pressing his lips to hers. "I love you, Cuyler Jade. You know that, don't you?"

The worry fled her eyes and she smiled. "Of course I do. I knew it before you did. And it's a good thing."

"Why's that?"

She kissed his forehead, then his mouth. "Because, Ramsey, I love you, and I wouldn't settle for anything less in return. Especially since I have to put up with you for the rest of eternity.''

''Eternity with Tinkerbell,'' he said, grinning. He gathered her into his arms and held her close. ''I can't think of a sweeter fate.''

Dear Reader,

Silhouette Shadows is a special line, and this anthology is very exciting for me. Imagine, one book with stories by both Anne Stuart *and* Chelsea Quinn Yarbro! These ladies are two of my all-time favorites. I fell under the spell of Chelsea's Saint-Germain years ago, and began my love affair with Anne's work when I first read *Housebound.* So picture the expression on my face when I was asked to write a novella that would appear within the same covers as theirs! It was a cross between awe, exhilaration and paralyzing fear.

Never one to back away from a challenge, I set to work, heart in my throat, hoping I could come up with a story worthy of the two gems it would accompany.

As they have in the past, my vampire pals came to my rescue. The result is *Beyond Twilight,* or, as I fondly call it, *Wings in the Night, Three and a Half.*

Once mischievous Cuyler Jade began whispering her tale into my ears, the story poured through my fingertips and into my computer as naturally as blood through a jugular. (Forgive me, I couldn't resist.) When I finished, I felt as if I'd just increased my immortal family by two. I even got a chance to visit with a member I hadn't seen in a while.

Welcome to my nighttime world. The one that only exists…

Beyond Twilight…

Maggie Shayne

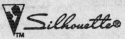

Become a Privileged Woman,
You'll be entitled to all these Free Benefits.
And Free Gifts, too.

To thank you for buying our books, we've designed an exclusive FREE program called *PAGES & PRIVILEGES™.* You can enroll with just one Proof of Purchase, and get the kind of luxuries that, until now, you could only read about.

BIG HOTEL DISCOUNTS

A privileged woman stays in the finest hotels. And so can you—at up to 60% off! Imagine standing in a hotel check-in line and watching as the guest in front of you pays $150 for the same room that's only costing you $60. Your *Pages & Privileges* discounts are good at Sheraton, Marriott, Best Western, Hyatt and thousands of other fine hotels all over the U.S., Canada and Europe.

FREE DISCOUNT TRAVEL SERVICE

A privileged woman is always jetting to romantic places.

When you fly, just make one phone call for the lowest published airfare at time of booking— or double the difference back!

PLUS—you'll get a $25 voucher to use the first time you book a flight AND 5% cash back on every ticket you buy thereafter through the travel service!